SHATTERING
GLASS

A Nasty Woman Press Anthology

Fiction and Nonfiction
by Bestselling Authors

Edited by Heather Graham

For information contact: Nasty Woman Press
Web: www.nastywomanpress.com
E-mail: info@nastywomanpress.com
ISBN: 978-1-7343879-2-6
First Edition: June 2020
10 9 8 7 6 5 4 3 2 1

To the memory of Bette Golden Lamb (1935–2019) and all the nasty women, past and present, who have led the way.

CONTENTS

CONTENTS

CONTENTS

Introduction

What you are holding in your hands—either as a physical book or on an e-reader—is an idea made real.

All art is, of course, an idea before it becomes art. But the art inside *Shattering Glass*—the first of what we hope will be many anthologies brought to readers by Nasty Woman Press—is part of an even larger idea that was born in the shock, horror, and grief of November 9th, 2016.

Surrounded by friends and colleagues palpably mourning for how America could have fallen so low, so quickly, in electing a venal, bullying, populist fascist, we feared the worst. Time, unfortunately, has proven that we were right in so fearing.

Meanwhile, however, paralysis was not an option. Autocracy is a monster, and it must be fought alongside its enablers: racism, misogyny, homophobia, transphobia, religious bigotry, ableism, and willful ignorance. All seven of these deadly sins have been and are being employed by those who seek power and fortune at the expense of human—and planetary—life.

Writers, as a rule, are solitary creatures—a demand of their profession. Marching, protesting, resisting oppression—these acts require working together, and are not easy for some. The best protest can often be one in which the protester protests simply by doing what she does best. And that, in essence, was the idea behind Nasty Woman Press.

What if writers—and readers and artists and editors and book designers—could form a resistance doing exactly what they normally do, but with a shared goal instead of a personal one? What if those of us who write could write with a greater purpose? What if our readers could participate in the Resistance through the sheer act of reading? What if we harnessed our creativity so that it became a synergy, created by and for one another, to give hope to a hope-starved nation and pragmatically help rights organizations that were under attack?

And so Nasty Woman Press was born. A 501(c)(4) nonprofit, we raise money for nonprofits on the front lines of attack. Any money raised beyond what we need to function—to keep publishing—is donated to one of these endangered organizations. Our plan is to publish anthologies of captivating fiction and thought-provoking nonfiction, each built around a general theme—the theme itself tying in to the nonprofit for which the book is raising money.

Shattering Glass is our first anthology. Our first theme is female empowerment, though you will find a wide swathe of works here, many of which touch on many other issues. The book is raising money for Planned Parenthood, which—along with the basic right of bodily autonomy for women—has been attacked over the years, but never as violently and brutishly as now. Both Planned Parenthood nationally and internationally—because autocracy and the concomitant dismantling of human rights is a global threat, just as it was in the 1930s—will receive profits from this book. And, I will add, the creation of Nasty Woman Press and *Shattering Glass* was entirely *pro bono*. We have been built on the generosity of donors who believe in our cause.

It is our hope that you will be inspired, consoled, nurtured, motivated and strengthened by *Shattering Glass*. We believe its impact will not only be physical in monies raised for Planned Parenthood, but spiritual and emotional, in the fact that readers—wherever they live—will know they are not alone in the battle for human rights, planetary survival and the documents and laws that protect the rights of the most vulnerable.

Thank you for reading this book and making an idea real and alive. Thank you for being a part of the Creative Resistance.

Kelli Stanley
Founder, Nasty Woman Press
February 10, 2020

On the Power of "Nasty Women"

Valerie Plame

There is a war on women in the United States of America. The most despicable example may be the latest round of abortion bans sweeping Republican-dominated statehouses, many penalizing women—whether they are minors, rape or incest victims—for the very act of being a victim. Not coincidentally, these laws also disproportionately impact women who are already the most marginalized: women living in poverty, women of color, trans women, and women in rural communities . . . women who may not be able to afford a doctor, and women who may not be part of the Republican "base."

The right to choose—a fundamental right to control our own bodies—was mandated by *Roe v. Wade* nearly fifty years ago. Yet under Trump and the party that supports him, it is under attack as never before, ultimately threatening to deprive all women of control over their bodies and lives.

Unfortunately, this attack is far from isolated. The Republican party has become a far-right, autocratic machine, weaponized against women in a variety of ways. Refusal to address the wage gap. Ambivalence towards the lack of affordable, quality childcare. Hostility towards the Equality Act to protect LGBTQ women from discrimination. Widespread opposition to renewing the Violence Against Women Act. And unyielding loyalty by those who know better to a president obsessed with calling strong, articulate women "nasty," a man who appointed an accused rapist to the Supreme Court and who himself is an admitted sexual predator who believes he has the God-given right to grab whatever woman he so chooses "by the pussy."

Make no mistake, the abortion bans and other medieval attempts to deprive half the population of human and civil rights are part of a deliberate, systematic effort. Right now, their most aggressive attacks are on a woman's right to choose. But they won't stop until they've dragged each and every one of us back to the Dark Ages where women were legally second-class citizens; their version of "Making America Great Again" is a world in which women weren't allowed to vote or own property, gay and transgender people were hidden from public record, jobs and housing advertisements warned "Christians Only Need Apply," and people of color were enslaved or lynched.

The truth is they are afraid of our power.

In 2003, when my covert CIA identity was revealed by senior officials in the Bush White House in retaliation for an op-ed written by my then-husband, Ambassador Joe Wilson, I was reluctantly thrust, kicking and screaming, into the public arena. We were relentlessly attacked by partisan forces who didn't take kindly to Joe pointing out that the invasion and conquest of Iraq was sold to the American public under false pretenses. Because I was still working for the CIA—although obviously no longer in a covert capacity—I was forbidden to speak out publicly. Joe and I were called liars, traitors, and a member of Congress called me a "glorified secretary." I guess because I was a girl?

It wasn't until I left the CIA that I was finally able to find my voice. It took some getting used to, given a career where discretion and blending into one's environment were paramount virtues. However, once I realized that my voice could shine a light on issues I cared passionately about—for example, the nuclear threat—I overcame my reluctance. Early on, that newfound public voice grew to include speaking loudly and fiercely about injustices against women. My reluctance is long gone, replaced by my determination to speak truth to power at every turn.

I am here to say that women's lives are NOT fair game. We must push back.

In this unprecedented war against two centuries of progress, presenting a united front is crucial. We must show that we are not backing down from the fight to not only protect but also expand on our hard-won progress.

We must fight and raise our voices loudly and clearly. We must run for office. We must fight to be industry leaders. Only once we are in the majority in these positions will we be able to protect the future for ourselves and our children.

In 2018, for the first time ever, one state—Nevada—finally elected a legislature whose majority is women. We need to see this change in every state, because that is how we protect women's rights as well as effect change across the board on all of the issues plaguing our nation. Protecting abortion rights, gun control, the climate crisis, healthcare reform—the Nevada legislature is making more progress on these issues in a few short months than their predecessors did in decades. As the saying goes, a woman's place is in the House . . . and the Senate.

In 2019, I decided to run for Congress to advance our achievements, expand our rights and opportunities, and make real change for the next generation of women and men. I will fight hard to win my race, but whether I do or not, I will never be covert about what I believe or reluctant to use my voice to speak truth to power in order to protect my country and its citizenry. Enough is enough.

Am I a "nasty woman"? Damn right I am, and proud of it. That means my voice and my actions are being heard, causing change, and displacing those who are so determined to try to push us back to a time when we had no power, no place, no voice. We have fought a long, hard battle to get where we are, and we will not backslide: We will prevail; we shall overcome.

The New Girl

Alexandra Sokoloff

So look, you don't need to know the name of our town.

All you need to know is that it's a football town.

There are thousands of them across the US, tens of thousands. More than you could possibly want to think.

Maybe there are good football teams out there. I wouldn't know.

Ours is one of those teams you read about. The ones that go to games and chant, "Build that wall!" or "Trump! Trump! Trump!" at teams that are less than 100 percent white. The ones that slam gay kids up against walls and taunt girls in the halls. And that's just the stuff they do in full view of faculty and administration.

So. You know.

I don't know why they call baseball the all-American sport. 'Cause from where I stand, as a national metaphor, it's football, all the way.

It's the team's pretty much stated mission to make everyone else's lives unbearable. They're really good at it. It doesn't take any particular skill to be an asshole, but these guys have turned it into a kind of art.

And maybe there's more to it than just assholery.

Like this. Go to any social media site and you'll see the guys on our football team posting stuff like:

What's the worst thing about gang rape?

Going last.

Their idea of a joke.

But is it?

You tell me.

'Cause there are rumors.

Things that again, teachers and admins and parents seem to be just oblivious to. And the coaches, well, they're just as bad.

The team rules the school. Nobody would dream of complaining. The whole town revolves around them, with the Boosters and the country club fundraisers and the two-time national championship.

Every player is assigned his own cheerleader, which in an actually enlightened country would be illegal, wouldn't you think? And the cheerleaders make actual baked goods for their players and decorate them and leave them in the guys' classes in these perfectly wrapped packages with balloons and streamers and stuff.

And if you're saying, "Hold on, this isn't 1950, we've moved past all that . . ."

You've never watched a televised NFL game, have you?

Fridays are the worst, because Fridays are Game Days. So there's the whole Game Day ritual. The *Go Wolfpack!* banners strung up in the halls, the baked goods, the cheerleaders decked out in micro skirts and halter tops, the semi-mandatory wearing of school colors.

And then last period of school, everyone has to leave class for the pep rally.

And really, shouldn't that be illegal, too? Forcing us to leave class to go cheer on guys who get drunk every weekend and throw up on other people's lawns and harass people who aren't them every chance they get?

And before you start jumping to conclusions, no, I'm not saying they do it to me.

I don't stick out. I'm not one of the popular crowd, but I'm not one of the fringe, either. I'm not that kind of Instagram gorgeous you have to be to get really noticed, and I'm not too heavy or too thin or awkward or—weird. I guess you could call me smart, but I don't broadcast it. I'm just normal enough to have that cloak of invisibility going for me, as far as the team is concerned.

The main thing is, I'm not a loner. Because those are the ones who really get the trouble. I'm a band kid, so I have other people who may not be BFFs, but it's a place I belong. And I have an actual BFF. I've known Suze since fourth grade. We've always been each other's safety nets.

Suze is just naturally more sunny than I am, and she honestly likes the games.

I always go mainly because I have to—being in band, that's just part of the deal, to play at the games. But Suze actually gets excited about them and dresses in school colors on Game Days and she'd sort of managed to coax me into doing all the stuff, and that made it bearable.

It's just that two weeks ago, Suze got sick.

It's weird, because I was the one who was sick first. Which was why I didn't go to this party that she'd been really hot on going to, our first big senior party that she managed to get us invited to even though we're just sophomores.

I was really out of it that night, fever and chills and my stomach turning over at even the thought of eating anything. Way too wretched to get out of bed, which when I think about it maybe was a tiny bit in my head, because I was pretty nervous about the party.

But I guess Suze went anyway.

I was in bed for the weekend and on Monday the bug was gone and when I went back to school, Suze wasn't there. I messaged her a couple of times between classes and she didn't answer. When she didn't show up the next day, I called her house on the actual landline.

Her mom said she'd come down with mono and she'd be out of school for a while. Weeks, maybe. She was so sick that she wasn't even allowed on social media. For a while, anyway.

Yeah, it was weird, but her mom's always been fussy and controlling that way, so I figured I'd give it a week to let her mom chill and I sent her a "get well" card by snail mail.

But almost immediately, without Suze around, things started to bug me that I'd never paid much attention to before. I was suddenly noticing much more of this stuff. Maybe it was that without Suze being so adorable and putting a positive spin on it all, it just seemed so unbearable.

And by "it," I mean the football team. And everything about it.

Just look at the whole setup. The meanest, dumbest, most useless guys in the school getting cheered on by magazine cover girls who are there basically to cook for them, flash boobs at them, and serve them.

And *they* get the scholarships. *They* go to the colleges that open up the whole world to them, where they join frats with nicknames like "Tit and Clit" and

"Sexual Assault Expected." After college their frat brothers give *them* the jobs. *They* run the corporations. *They* get elected to government office. Their friends appoint them judges. The meanest, dumbest, most useless guys in the country. Brain damage doesn't seem to be an impediment. My feeling is, how can you even tell? It obviously doesn't stop someone from becoming president.

So you look at all that and you don't have to be a genius to figure out why the world is like it is. War and global warming and the NRA and oil companies and Trump and Kavanagh and the whole stinking mess.

When everything in life starts out like that.

And here's a weird and alarming thing. Now that I was thinking things like that, the football guys started to actually notice me.

Especially Derek Brandt. You could call him the ringleader. Or you could call him the quarterback.

Derek was what passed for a brain on the team. And Lewis Bascombe was his enforcer. Derek could have beaten anyone up he felt like beating. But he didn't, because there was Lewis, a.k.a. "The Crusher," which pretty much tells you all you need to know.

And toward the end of that week without Suze, two things happened.

The first wasn't anything that didn't happen every day. It was before school, and Derek and Lewis and most of the other team guys were sitting outside in the Quad, the brick courtyard where in good weather everyone hangs out at lunch and between classes. There are these four square cement planters in the center of the Quad, and the team and the cheerleaders have had those planters staked out as their territory for as long as anyone can remember. No one else is allowed to sit there. The team parks itself on those seats, kind of like holding court in the round. The good thing is that because they're all crowded into the center of the Quad like that, you can go around the sides of the courtyard and avoid them.

But sometimes people forget or are just in a hurry or somehow attract the attention and step into team territory. And that day Sherry Trenton got too close.

I could see exactly what was happening. She had earbuds in and she must have been listening to music and some song she liked came on and she started unconsciously bopping along.

And because she wasn't paying attention, she committed the cardinal sin of stepping into the Quad. I've seen Derek and Lewis make freshmen who made the same mistake do sprints across the bricks until they vomited.

It wasn't just the stepping into the Quad, though. It was the bopping. Sherry was committing the even worse cardinal sin of feeling good in the team's presence. It was the thing that seemed to piss them off more than anything, the idea that anyone who wasn't them could be having a good time.

Did I mention that the team's nickname for Sherry is "Ten-Ton"? And that's all I need to say, right? We all know how this story goes.

And that's exactly how it went. Derek spotted Sherry doing her little head bop, and he nudged Lewis, and then all of the guys were calling, "Awesome moves, Ten-Ton." "Lookin' good, Ten-Ton." "Somebody call *America's Got Talent*."

Well, it's not like we get any better from the President of the United States.

And Sherry finally heard them through her earbuds and froze. Then she did the worst thing she could possibly do, which was to move faster. And she tripped. Fell flat on her stomach.

The team went crazy. Howling with laughter. Pointing, and miming, until everyone in the quad was looking.

"Whale on the beach!" "Ten Ton, meet gravity." "Just what the school needs—a trampoline."

It's not the kind of thing that anyone ever wants to get involved with because it just escalates.

But I was right there at the edge of the Quad. I saw the whole thing. And I guess it all showed on my face. The disgust. The loathing.

And Derek looked over at that exact moment and saw—me. The way I was looking at him.

I stared at Derek and he stared at me.

BOOM. Cloak of invisibility—gone.

It gave me such a twisty feeling in my stomach I had to duck into the restroom because I was afraid *I* would throw up.

I didn't.

But it was close.

And the second thing was, that day when I walked into third period physics, *she* was there.

A new girl.

This is hard to explain, but she was—different.

You couldn't help but notice her, and I wasn't sure why. She wasn't pretty, but she definitely wasn't plain. She was a bit boyish, but not really. Her hair was dark and longish, I think, and she had a dusting of freckles, I think. But mostly it was her eyes. They were big and dark and still. Amused and knowing and uncomfortably—intense. Focused. She just seemed to *know*.

Then the bell rang and Mr. Pring hustled in late, as usual, and started class.

Pring is one of the good guys. A little nutty, but brilliant. Enthusiastic as a little kid. He makes even impossible things seem worth learning. What he's doing in this school, I have no idea.

He was starting a new section in our "cosmic adventure." As he calls it. He's corny like that. He was talking about quantum theory, something about particles and waves and choice and observers and a cat in a box, and I was taking notes without really understanding it. I was too hung up on the whole Sherry Trenton incident. And the way Derek had stared at me.

Just at the end of class Pring looked over toward me and I kind of knew what he was going to say before he said it.

"Mason, you're out a lab partner at the moment, yes? Will you be a star and get the new girl your notes and get her up to speed?"

I stood and walked over toward the door. She met me there.

"Hey," I said.

"Hey," she responded. She had a low voice, kind of adult. Nothing girly about it at all. She was so—calm. It kind of freaked me out.

We walked out into the hall together. I lifted my class notebook and told her, "I can make a copy of my notes tonight and get it to you tomorrow."

I was just reaching into my backpack for my phone to get her info when the team came jostling around a corner, a whole wall of them in their athletic jackets that made them look twice as big.

And without really thinking about it I grabbed the new girl's arm and pulled her into a side hall to get her out of their path. I figured she didn't need to start her experience at a new school with that kind of attention. No one needs that on their first day.

She let me pull her, but when I stopped, out of the danger zone, she looked at me funny, or maybe just puzzled, and I said, "Trust me. You don't want to get in their way."

She glanced back toward the hall. "Why?"

"Well, the team. They can be pretty brutal."

She just looked at me. "Why doesn't somebody do something about them?"

She didn't exactly say "you," meaning "me." But it was clear that was what she meant. I could only stare at her, fairly stupefied. What the hell did she think I could do against the entire football team? And it wasn't just the football team. It was the school. It was the town. It was the world.

And there was just—me.

"It's a football town," I said, finally.

And the look she gave me was pure pity.

I WAS SO weirded out I forgot to ask for her accounts. At home that night I looked her up on Instagram. And then Snapchat and Twitter and Tumblr and Tik Tok. Even Facebook. Nothing. She either had a complete alias or she—I couldn't even imagine—wasn't *on* social media. At all.

I DON'T USUALLY remember my dreams. I thought for a long time I don't have them, but then I read somewhere that everyone dreams, every night. You have to, or you'd go crazy. It's just that most people don't remember dreaming.

I dreamed about her that night.

She was sitting in a room that looked like physics class, only it wasn't so distinct, and she had a chessboard in front of her, but instead of chess pieces there were these little moving figures on the board. Creatures, or maybe people, I couldn't tell.

And she didn't say anything, but she looked up at me with this tiny smile, like, "*Wanna play?*"

The very next day, it happened.

FIRST THERE WAS the social media thing. I gave her my notes in physics, and she thanked me and then I asked her, really casual, I thought: "What's your

Snapchat so we can message about the test?" Pring had announced one coming up next week.

"I'm not on it," she said. And before I could ask about other sites, she added, "Any of it."

I could only stare at her.

She shrugged. "More important things to do."

"But how do you . . ." I didn't even know how to finish the sentence. *How do you survive?* Was what I was thinking. But I knew that didn't make sense, really.

She was watching me—

No. She was *studying* me. "Does it make you feel good?" she asked.

Feel good? What did that have to do with anything?

But what came out of my mouth was: "Not really."

She shrugged. "So? Why give it energy?"

I didn't know what to do with that, so I said, "How are we supposed to get in touch for physics stuff, then?"

She sighed, rattled off a phone number. And then added, "Think before you use it."

Now what the hell was that supposed to mean?

Then Mr. Pring started class.

It was after physics that it happened, on the stairs between third and fourth periods. We all poured out of class and she was ahead of me, flowing with the crowd through the double doors into the stairwell. As I started the climb, she was headed up the stairs a little above me.

And a bunch of the football guys were coming down. Derek and Lewis right in front.

And they saw her. And they noticed her. It was all on their faces. A new girl. Fresh meat.

My heart plummeted.

She was heading straight for them, and I was holding my breath . . .

The new girl didn't even look at them. She wasn't pretending to ignore them like I do, which never really works. She didn't seem to see them at all.

Derek said something and the others started to laugh. Lewis louder than anyone.

Here it comes, I thought. And Lewis watched her pass and opened his mouth to say something, and you could just see how nasty it was going to be. Then before he could say a word, his foot missed a stair, somehow, and he sort of—lurched.

It's not like he fell or even stumbled. But I heard a snap.

Instead of the usual catcall or insult, what came out of his mouth was a strangled yelp. And then he was yelling, swearing. "My ankle. Shit. Fuck. MY ANKLE."

Two of the other guys leaped to hold him up, and he recovered immediately—typical Bascombe, he even raged at the two guys who were trying to help him. "Get off me, faggots! I'm fine!"

He wasn't fine.

I said I was in band, right? First clarinet. So I was out there on the field that night for the game, as usual.

Lewis couldn't play the game that night. It was so bad a break that everyone in band and everyone on the field and everyone in the bleachers was talking in whispers about it being the end of the season for him. Which was really bad news for us as a school. I mean, as a football school.

But you know? I wasn't feeling bad about it at all.

In fact I was feeling so good about it I actually had the nerve to do something I should have done a long, long time ago. When the team ran out on the field and everyone else took up instruments to play "The Star-Spangled Banner," I didn't play.

I took a knee instead.

People were so distracted by the Lewis Bascombe ankle thing that nobody seemed to notice. They probably thought I dropped my sheet music or was praying for the team, like some other people actually do at games. Seriously.

And it's not like anyone ever looks at the band, anyway.

Well, except for Derek Brandt. He noticed. And he knew for sure I wasn't praying for the team. He stood there in the lineup with his hand on his heart and stared across the field at me on my knee, with this look on his face like he couldn't believe what he was seeing.

Not good.

But he had other stuff to worry about just then. A whole lot of football stuff.

We lost the game. Lost doesn't even begin to describe it. It was a massacre.
I didn't feel bad about that, either.

PHYSICS WAS THE only class I had with the new girl. On Monday I waited in the hall until I saw her going in and then followed her in so I could get the seat behind her. I leaned forward and said really low, "I saw what happened."

"What happened?" she asked. All innocent.

"On the stairs. Lewis Bascombe broke his ankle when he said something to you."

She looked vaguely puzzled. "No one said anything to me."

"But he was about to."

I realized how silly that sounded even before she raised her eyebrows.

"Well, I didn't hear anything," she said. "Who is this guy, anyway?"

"Football team. Offensive tackle." As soon as I said it I wondered why I even knew that. Why did I pay any attention to any of them at all?

She gave me a tiny smile. "Not anymore," she said.

FROM THERE, THINGS only got weirder.

So I walked in to band practice and immediately what hit me was that on one wall was a mural with huge lettering: *Go Wolfpack!* in school colors. Wolfpack banners hung from doors, from the flagpole.

Now this is not new. They've always been there. But suddenly those banners just got to me.

We were starting practice for Homecoming. And as Mr. Aiello, the band teacher, was talking about the new pieces he wanted us to learn, I was getting more and more irritated and fidgety. It didn't help that I was on my period, but that wasn't all of it.

I didn't even realize I was doing it, but somehow I was standing, and everyone was looking at me. And I opened my mouth and I said, "No."

Mr. Aiello looked back at me in shock. "No?" he repeated.

"I'm not playing for Homecoming."

Now that I'd said it, it was easy to say what I said next. "I'm not going to play music for those creeps anymore."

At this point everyone was staring at me, mouths literally hanging open. I looked around the room. "Why should we?" I said. "We could be playing for ourselves. Anything we wanted to. Why should we do anything for them?"

Mr. Aiello was really flustered by now. "All right, Mason, just sit down and let's get back to—"

"No," I said again. "I'm not going to do it. I'm done."

And I took my case and my music and my backpack and I walked out. I even slammed the door behind me. Like I said, I was on my period.

I stood in the corridor, alone. I felt hot and flushed and disoriented and lost.

But I also felt—good.

WELL, I MISSED physics the next day because I got called into the VP's office. Which was a first for me, and Hadley obviously knew it, because he was being all stern and towering, but there was also something tentative about him.

I sat down in the chair (the electric chair, people call it) in front of his desk and looked across at him, with his Wolfpack banner hanging on the wall behind him and his Booster Club VIP membership plaques framed beside it.

He frowned and cleared his throat. "Apparently you disrupted band rehearsal and were extremely rude to Mr. Aiello."

I didn't say anything.

He sat back in his chair and steepled his hands. "This is your chance to explain what happened. I suggest you take it."

"I told him I wasn't going to play for Homecoming."

He frowned harder, obviously not knowing what to do with that. "Why is that?"

"I don't think that should be a requirement."

"Miss Mason. Let me explain something to you. You don't get to pick and choose, here—"

"Then I quit band. I want out. Put me in another class." I hadn't thought at all about what class, but I suddenly knew exactly what to say. I looked him straight in the face. "Spanish. I want to take Spanish. Everyone needs to know Spanish, right?"

Well, that got him. He jerked up like I'd just stabbed him with a cattle prod.

All the avuncular was gone. He pulled his hands apart and leaned forward with quiet menace. "Miss Mason, understand me. You have a good GPA. You're doing well in AP classes. But band is your only extracurricular activity. If you have any hope of getting into college, you'll reconsider this foolishness."

He took a breath. "Now. Go apologize to Mr. Aiello, and we can all move on—"

I looked straight over his head at his Wolfpack banner. "I'm not going to play for Homecoming. You can't make me. No one can."

I GOT DETENTION.

It could have been worse. He could've expelled me. I think he was just too thrown by the whole thing to come down hard. Or maybe he thought I was on my period. Which I was.

Anyway, I'd missed physics, which was a review for the test we had the next day, and at this point I realized I hadn't been paying much attention to the lectures because I was so . . . well, distracted I guess is the word.

I went to Pring's room before reporting to detention and he said the new girl was going to drop off the review notes at my house. Which was weird because I'd never told her where I lived.

I sat in detention with these waves of cramps and somehow made it through the hour and when I got home there was a sheet of paper under the doormat. Just one sheet.

I stooped and picked it up. And after the day I'd had I think you'll understand why I got so mad.

All there was on that page of "notes" was three words.

INTEND

FOCUS

RELEASE

Well, I couldn't message her, and I couldn't Snapchat her, and I was too mad to phone her, and I had cramps.

But that was only the beginning.

Because then my mom got home.

And of course the school had called and left a message about my insubordination and detention, and she hit the roof. "What were you thinking? You think you're going to get into college when you do something like this? What about scholarships? You think we're made of money?"

My dad got home in the middle of this and my mom got even madder because now she could be mad with someone to back her up. And my dad, good Wolfpack Booster that he is, was mad and appalled and confused at the same time. Why would I not want to play for Homecoming? What had gotten into me?

And I cried, and Mom cried, and she ordered me up to bed without dinner, as if I cared about dinner or anything else at that point.

I went upstairs and slammed the door. Because slamming the band room door had felt pretty good.

I dropped down on my bed and stared at the ceiling. I guess I could've studied, but there didn't seem to be any point. I was suddenly just exhausted and sick of the whole thing. So I fell asleep.

I DON'T REMEMBER what I dreamed, but I woke up with those words in my head.

INTEND. FOCUS. RELEASE.

I spent first period arranging my transfer into Spanish, and second period trying to figure out what the hell I was doing in Spanish class where everyone was already speaking the language. Then I went to physics in absolute dread and I was late because between classes I had to get to the bathroom and deal with the other period thing and I was seething when I got to class and the test had already started.

I felt sick. I felt furious. I had half a mind to just write her three words on the page and walk out.

INTEND. FOCUS. RELEASE.

Instead I grabbed the test page, and I shot a look made of daggers at the back of the new girl's head and I started the test.

I bet you can guess what comes next.

I aced it.

When I sat down I didn't know quantum physics from a hole in the ground. But I didn't have to get my paper back to know I'd gotten everything right. The answers just flowed out of me. And I understood what I was writing, even though I couldn't have told you one thing about it the night before.

I was so absorbed in writing I didn't hear the bell ring and Mr. Pring had to tell me to bring my paper up, and by the time I did that the new girl was already gone and I didn't have a chance to go after her and ask, "What the fuck??"

That afternoon, when I went to detention after school, Mr. Pring was standing outside the detention room, waiting for me, holding a couple of stapled pages in his hand.

He looked really concerned. "The front office said you had detention. And that you quit band. That's not like you, Mason. What happened?"

I shrugged. "Just got tired of it."

He looked like he was going to say something, but instead he passed me the papers he was holding.

It was my physics test. It had a huge red A on it, circled three times, and the words, *See me.*

I looked up from the page.

He was smiling. "That is the most thoughtful essay on quantum theory I've ever seen from a high school student. You should seriously consider a physics major in college."

I looked at him in complete disbelief. "College? You mean that place I'm not going to get to go because I won't play for Homecoming?"

I didn't say that aloud, of course.

But it was like he heard. He stopped smiling, and his voice got really serious. "It's not always going to be like this, you know."

Suddenly I was angry. What country was he living in? What school was he teaching in? All the teachers knew about the team. He was the adult, here. Why wasn't he doing anything about it?

And this wasn't just high school we were talking about. Guys like Lewis and Derek run this country, just like they run the school.

"Isn't it?" I said. I could hear how cold my voice was.

The look on Pring's face was so devastated, I felt bad. But it was true, wasn't it?

His voice got closed and guarded. "Anyway. It's something to think about."

Yeah. Right.

"I can't be late or I get another day," I said, and I opened the door and went in.

YOU CAN'T DO anything in detention but sit and think about your sins, so I couldn't help thinking about Mr. Pring. Which made me feel sad. But when I thought about the test, part of me couldn't help but feel good. I felt weightless. And something else. I felt power.

I felt almost like everything was going to be okay.

When I left detention, the halls were empty. I was headed for the front doors of the school when a door opened up ahead of me and I saw Derek and four other team guys walking out of the guys' bathroom. The last thing in the world I needed.

But they didn't notice me at first. And I could see something was off. For once they weren't talking. And there was just something about them that felt like even worse trouble than usual.

They were all breathing hard, like they'd just done laps. Their eyes were bright and unfocused at the same time and they were in this strange shoulder-to-shoulder clump.

Something about it made me:

a)   Pivot and make sure I was going the opposite direction while they moved down the hall in that weird solidarity formation. And then

b)   Turn back and look toward the restroom door.

After a minute, the door opened, and Brandon Tewkes walked out. Only it wasn't really walking so much as stumbling.

Brandon Tewkes is gay. He's not the only gay kid at the school, obviously. Ten percent of the population, right? Including, statistically, guys on the team, but no one ever talks about that.

Brandon was sobbing. He could barely stand upright. And he was soaking wet. His hair, his shirt, drips of water down his jeans. Big wet circles on his knees.

It didn't take quantum physics to work out what they'd just done to him.

He saw me and straightened, wiping his face.

We just stood there in the hall, looking at each other.

And then he said, "I hate them. I hate them so much."

THAT NIGHT I did remember what I dreamed.

I dreamed about the new girl. It was night, and she was standing in front of a big fire. Holding up Derek's severed head.

Yeah, you could say that freaked me out. Just a bit.

SHE WASN'T IN class on Friday. Of course, it was Game Day, so maybe she'd already decided she wasn't going to go along with all that rah-rah crap. I ditched the pep rally myself. I mean, I'd already taken my band stand, hah hah. I already had detention. I wasn't going to sit there and cheer.

But that night I went to the game.

That doesn't make a lot of sense, does it? After that whole week that I'd had. I was no longer obligated to perform for them. Why would I want to just go and watch?

Oh, did I say I went to the game?

What I mean is, I went to the football field. I sat in the Friday night crowd in the bleachers, by myself, silent, not moving, as the cheerleaders took everyone through the pregame chants and cheers. Cheers that got increasingly less cheery as kickoff time came and went. A half hour later even the cheerleaders weren't cheering anymore. We were all just sitting there, wondering.

And then the announcement came.

It was the weirdest thing. The whole arena went silent.

And then people started screaming.

The team bus had crashed. They didn't announce that at the game, but people were seeing it on their phones, on the news. Every station.

Because it wasn't just some little run-off-the-road accident. It was a real, skid off the bridge, fall to the bottom of the ravine, go up in fiery flames crash. A national news crash.

Half the team killed, the other half injured.

They say Derek Brandt was completely decapitated.

THE WHOLE TOWN was in . . . shock doesn't begin to cover it. It was like the Apocalypse. Everywhere you went people were sobbing. Flags all over town were at half mast, which I'm not sure is legal. School was canceled indefinitely while people scrambled to plan vigils for the hospitalized and funerals for the dead.

I don't remember much of the weekend. I didn't leave the house, though. Reporters roamed the streets. News stations had set up camp anywhere they could grab sound bites.

I was terrified about what I might say.

There was no school on Monday, or Tuesday. By then I was desperate to talk to her. And completely paralyzed at the same time.

But I had her phone number.

It took me hours to be able to pick up the phone. I was shaking and my mouth was so dry I wasn't sure I'd be able to talk. But all I got, all five times I tried, was that screechy three-ascending-tone recording: *You have reached this number in error. Please check the number and dial again.*

Eventually I left the house and went to the library, because I just couldn't stand being at home, what with my mom alternating talking on the phone to everyone in town and sobbing for hours on end, and my dad walking around like a zombie.

I figured at least I could start to get some grip on Spanish. And it would take my mind off the image of the new girl standing there, holding up Derek's head.

It worked for a while.

But I kept spacing out. Once I came to and had no idea how long I'd just been sitting there.

My notebook was open and I saw I'd written those three words.

INTEND. FOCUS. RELEASE.

And then I became aware of someone standing in front of my table.

"Well, what is it?" she asked, a little annoyed.

I stood up so fast I knocked my chair over. I didn't say hello. I didn't pretend there was any question about it. I just said it straight out. "How could you?"

"How could I?" she said, maddening as ever.

"The bus crash. I know you did it."

She looked at me wide-eyed. "Me? Why would I want to hurt those boys?"

It was that exaggerated innocence. Even calling them "boys" instead of "guys." I was so mad, or something, I had tears in my eyes. "They weren't *that* bad."

"If you say so."

That made me stop. But just for a second.

"No matter what, you can't . . . you can't just kill them."

"Kill them? *I* don't even know them."

But as she turned to walk away she said something else, with that enigmatic smile. "It's not like anyone's going to find a shirt soaked with brake fluid in my room. Or anything."

I COULDN'T STOP thinking about that.

I got home and the TV was still on. Still local news, still all tributes to the "town's fallen heroes." The parents hadn't even noticed I'd been gone. I just went upstairs to my room.

There were notebook pages on my bed. Physics notes.

I turned right around, bolted out the door, and tore down the stairs, shouting, "Mom!"

She was sitting in front of the TV with tears streaming down her face. I stood in front of her until she had to notice me. "Has someone been in my room? Someone from school?"

Her eyes were dull and bleary. Not just from crying—I strongly suspected Valium. But eventually something occurred to her, and she said, slurring a bit. "Your lab partner stopped by with your homework."

"You let her in my room?" I could hear how frantic my voice was.

She just looked up at me, dully. And then she turned her eyes back to the TV.

I TORE MY room apart, searching.

I finally found it stuffed at the back of a drawer.

A cute Old Navy T-shirt that wasn't mine. Soaked in some yellowy, oily, foul-smelling fluid.

I doubted it was the only piece of incriminating evidence she'd planted. The implication was clear. If I ratted her out, she could make it look like I did it. And who would suspect her? The new girl? Like she said, she didn't know them. Half the school had more of a motive than she did.

I didn't know who to tell.

And then I did.

THERE WAS A group memorial service. Not all of the parents agreed to participate, but it was such a close-knit team, and there were so many dead. Bottom line was, it was the obvious thing to do. It was in the big church in the cemetery in the country club part of town.

My parents went, of course, and I dressed up and went along, but when we got to the parking lot of the church I said I wanted to wait for my friends. They were too zoned out to care either way.

Reporters were dive-bombing everyone who got near the chapel so I stayed in the car watching out the window while these flocks of people, kids and teachers and half the town, filed up the front steps dressed in black and school colors.

I knew Mr. Pring would be late. He always was.

After everyone had gone inside and the doors were shut, I finally saw him park and get out of his car. I slipped out of our car to meet him.

Like all the other teachers I'd been seeing arrive that day, he looked ten years older. But when I said I really needed to talk to him, he made an obvious effort to pull himself together.

"Yes, Mason? How can I help?"

Like I said, he's one of the good ones.

I took a shaky breath and said, "I need to talk to you about the new girl."

I bet you can guess what happens next, right?

He looked at me with this curious, puzzled look on his face.

"What new girl?"

IT COULD HAVE been the Valium, but my mom didn't remember her, either. When I tried to talk to her, she thought I was asking her about Suze.

And when I called the school office, there was no record of her.

I guess it didn't help that I couldn't actually remember her name.

━━ ⋇ ━━

THAT NIGHT I had another dream.

I was standing in front of a window, and the new girl was looking out at me.

Only it wasn't a window. It was a mirror.

YOU GUYS DIDN'T expect us to take it forever, did you? Well, maybe you did. Maybe you just figured that after thousands of years of domination, there was no possible way for us to catch up or get free of you. That enough of the population was subjugated beyond redemption.

But inch by inch, we've crawled out of the mud to stand.

There was always going to be a tipping point.

It's here.

I am the new girl.

Welcome to the Sisterhood

Ellen Kirschman

Edwina thought the guys were gay, all flirty-eyed and nudgy. The secret touching. How their bodies slid together easily in the crowded bar. She said yes without a second thought when they offered to walk her to her car.

The whole evening had been an experiment, a baby step toward navigating the single life again. Three hours, four glasses of wine, and six beery men who didn't know enough to shower between work and play. Still the tipsy compliments and clumsy passes were reassuring, encouraging even. She wobbled a little on the way to her truck and dug in her oversized purse for her keys. It was an extravagant purchase and maybe a bit flashy for the understated look she was trying to achieve; pink leather, a bouquet of fake gems, and a long fringe.

The taller of the two was a good six foot three inches with the body of a weightlifter. He went first.

He slammed her face down on the front seat, tearing off her jeans, muffling her mouth with his fist. The smaller one, tiny actually, couldn't have weighed more than 120 pounds, went next for sloppy seconds.

The next morning she could barely remember driving home to her apartment, the pain was excruciating. She swung her legs over the side of her bed and pushed herself to her feet, reaching out with one hand to the bed table for support.

One step to the upholstered chair. Two steps to the chest of drawers. Two more to the handle on the bathroom door and then turning, sitting, doubled forward, bruises blooming on her thighs.

She thought about going to the doctor to make sure that nothing was damaged. But there would be questions. Mandatory reporting. And it wouldn't be any easier talking to her therapist. They'd been working together for so long Edwina could anticipate, word for word, his kind voice asking unkind questions. Didn't she know what she was doing? What was her part in the assault? What signs had she missed? She'd been pummeling herself with questions all night. No need to pay him to do the same.

Her reflection in the mirror was at once strange and familiar. Her skin smooth, her cheekbones prominent, no longer buried beneath the thirty pounds of extra weight she might have used to her advantage last night. It wasn't often she missed the bulk.

She dressed in a long skirt, a hip-length sweater, and hiking boots and drove out to the shrine she built for Edwin in a grassy meadow behind the ranch where they had both grown up.

It was a place of solitude. Of safety.

Two years ago, when it had become inevitable that what was going to happen would, in fact, happen, she'd winched out the large river rock where they used to sit dangling their feet in the water, and set it front of an abandoned rabbit warren. Later, when she told her therapist about it, he said she wasn't ready to let go of the past. It felt like an accusation. As though she was never supposed to look back. "Edwin is a legacy," he said. "Take what you need from him, leave the rest behind and move on."

Back then, she was in mourning. Unable and unwilling to march off into the future without acknowledging the loss of her past, as painful as her past had been. She felt unmoored, off balance. Bouts of grief kept her pinned to her bed for days.

Now she leaned against the warm rock, closed her eyes, and imagined herself as a massive thundercloud. Edwin would have known what to do about the men who had raped her. Edwin, who could bury a fence post with one swing, rope a calf, down a twelve-pack, and still walk a straight line. Edwin the target shooter, all that practice, those interminable sessions, just Edwin and father. Mother calling them in for dinner as it got darker and darker. Edwin, tears running down his face, forced to keep at it until he did it perfectly.

After Edwin departed—that was the word her parents preferred—her mother cried and her father tried harder than she might have expected to pretend it was okay with him. His feelings, as usual, were the deep heart of everything that mattered. Friends disappeared, but then, she reasoned, those kinds of friends weren't worth grieving over. Her parents were deeply hurt by their isolation, the sidelong looks of pity, the awkward encounters. Edwina spent as much time as possible trying to cheer them up, but the weight of their grief, half-hidden behind forced cheerfulness, felt like a prison. She was done hiding and it was time to step out into the world. Start over. Become whole.

Still, there were days when gathering different parts of herself into one coherent being felt like chasing chickens around the yard, each part squawking and running off in a different direction. It was hard to describe, even to her therapist.

Edwin was never like those men. Despite his pain, he never turned his private torment on anyone else, never disrespected women. All the macho talk, the bragging he did, was just to fit in. He would have stopped the rape, beaten the crap out of those two. Taken the sledgehammer from the back of the truck and smashed their skulls. Then he would have run off somewhere and cried his heart out.

Surgery offered hope, the promise of congruency, of feeling matched, inside and out, resting easy, safe and at home in the world. It was only post-surgery, after the initial euphoria wore off, that the different parts of herself began smashing together and splitting apart. The surgeon readjusted her hormones and suggested she go back to her therapist.

The rock was rougher to the touch now, the way her callused hands used to be. She inched it aside in tiny movements, the damaged, delicate parts of her body calling out in protest. She reached down and pulled out a black plastic sack filled with her old work clothes. The sight of them, earth-smelling and creased, made her sad. She stroked the soft plaid flannel shirt, smoothed her faded jeans with the flat of her hand, ran her fingers along the brim of her sweat-stained Stetson.

The shirt was baggy at the neck, and she had to punch three extra holes in her belt to keep the pants from falling over her hips. The socks bagged over her ankle bones and her boots felt loose. She pulled her hair into a ponytail, stuffed it under her hat, and went back for the revolver, the iconic Smith and Wesson model of "Dirty Harry" fame. The gun her father had bought her for her 16th birthday in a barely disguised effort to make her more of a man. She rolled the rock back in front of the den, drove to the bar, and waited.

The witnesses were all consistent in their descriptions, despite the fact that the parking lot was jammed with trucks and it was dark. The shooter was male, tall and thin, wearing a plaid shirt, jeans, and a Stetson hat, like every other man in town. There was no conversation between him and his targets, he just leveled his weapon and blasted them. By the time any potential witnesses dared raise their heads to look, the shooter had disappeared. One man saw him duck behind a building. Another watched him run across the road. Two more spotted him hiding in a truck. The cops agreed on one thing, witness testimony was useless. After they cordoned off the crime scene, they headed for the bar in search of more witnesses. They found four very drunk men and a dozen women patrons who were strangely unmoved by the murders in the parking lot. The gray-haired sergeant described the victims. One guy was big, body-builder big, and the other man, a shrimp.

"Pains in the arse," one woman said when the silence got uncomfortable, releasing a chorus of complaints. "Always looking down my shirt." "Leering, creepy." "Couldn't keep their hands to themselves." The list stretched on for so long the cop taking notes broke the point off his pencil and had to borrow one from the bartender.

Edwina pushed her way into the group of women waiting to be interviewed and laid her fringed pink bag on the counter with a clunk. Tried to catch her reflection in the mirror behind the bar. She liked the way the rhinestone barrette held her hair off her face. A little heavy on the eyeliner, but then the light in the men's room was bad.

"What you got in there, girl? Must weigh a ton." A woman with sad eyes pulled on the pink leather fringe. "Them dead guys hassle you too?" Edwina nodded. "Well then," the sad-eyed woman said, "Welcome to the sisterhood."

Birthright

James L'Etoile

A pregnant woman in prison experiences a special torment, a circle of hell deeper than Dante could imagine. In a place where physical weakness etched the line dividing predator from prey, Lydia Ramirez was on the losing end of the prison power struggle.

At six months pregnant, Lydia couldn't protect herself like she had when she was on the streets. Her round belly didn't intimidate La Mesa, the Los Angeles street gang that ran Barneburg Hall, her housing unit at Corona's California Institution for Women. With an ice pack on a swollen eye, she waited in the prison infirmary after another beating at the hands of the gang's enforcers. A nurse who looked close to retirement age checked over the red welts on Lydia's back, injuries that would blossom into blue and purple bruises before the end of the day.

"Tell custody what's going on and lock up," the nurse said.

"I'm no rat and you're not sending me to the hole over this." Lydia ran the palm of her hand over her belly.

"This keeps up, you'll lose your baby. It's your last trimester. I've seen what happens after the beatings. It's important to—"

"You know how things work in here. What it's like for me because my old man's a snitch . . ."

"But you have to think of the baby," the nurse said.

Lydia fell silent, and the nurse finished the exam with a quick ultrasound. The whoosh of the unborn child's heartbeat was steady and strong.

The prison nurse tossed her exam gloves into the trash. "Sergeant Conner is waiting to talk to you."

"Fuck the squad."

The squad was the prison's investigative unit charged with gathering evidence on crimes occurring on the inside. Crimes like assaulting a pregnant woman.

The nurse tucked a strand of salt-and-pepper hair behind her ear, shook her head grimly, and stepped into the hall. She nodded to someone outside. The sergeant entered the room, sat in the chair opposite the exam table, and glanced at Lydia's fresh injuries.

Lydia stared back at him. "Hope you got an earful 'cause that's all I gotta say."

"Miss Ramirez, this is the third time you've ended up in the infirmary. I don't buy the 'I tripped and fell' excuse anymore. Spill it."

"Snitching will just make it worse. In their eyes, I've got it coming after what my old man did."

Conner nodded. "Rolling over on the Eighteenth Street boys. I heard about that. He's in Corcoran, right?"

"Yeah, he went PC."

"Protective custody's not all that bad. You might consider the same thing. Get you out of here into a safe place for you and . . ." The sergeant nodded at her belly.

"Ain't nowhere safe." Lydia broke off eye contact and stared at the worn linoleum floor. "I told you, I'm no rat. I gotta go back and face these bitches. You don't."

The sergeant leaned forward. "What if you didn't have to? There's a program opening up for pregnant inmates at one of those private-run prisons up in the valley—away from Los Angeles and La Mesa."

"I've got eight months left to do. What happens when . . ."

"The way I hear it, you and your baby live together in the same place. Not like here, where we chain you to a hospital bed while you give birth, and then ship the baby off to foster care or some relative you haven't seen in five years. In this place, they have doctors on grounds and programs for you and the kid."

"My baby wouldn't have to go to a foster home like I did?"

"That's what they say. A guy from the program is here, want me to have him talk to you? Could be a win-win for both of us. Get you out of this place and I don't have to come chase you down after another beating."

Lydia nodded. She knew he was right, if Lydia stayed here, she and her baby wouldn't survive.

AFTER THE MIDDAY prison count, Thompson Scott presented himself as the caretaker of Willow Springs—a safe place for women and their children. Lydia and ten other pregnant inmates huddled together in the dining room listening to Scott talk about programs, daycare, and a nurturing prenatal environment. A video displayed brightly painted walls in a nursery, an outside garden area, and rooms with cribs next to the mother's beds. The images were enticing, and never once was the word *prison* used. While the video played, Scott, in his tailored navy blue suit, explained what Willow Springs would do for them with words like hope and opportunity.

She wanted hope. Hope was something that never spun Lydia's way on life's wheel of chance. One of her foster moms told her life is preordained and nothing could change your fate. "You are what you are and that's all you'll ever be." Where was the hope in that?

Once the man in the fancy suit finished talking about Willow Springs, he sat down with each woman, gathered a social history and identified family resources available to help her raise a child. Lydia couldn't answer most of his questions, because she had no one on the outside to lean on. A childhood marked with bouncing from one foster home to another before she ultimately ran off at sixteen didn't peg her as a potential success story. The fancy man wouldn't want to risk his program on someone like her. When she headed back to her dorm, Lydia felt small and insignificant, certain she wasn't going to be selected for Willow Springs.

An hour later, an officer came to Lydia's room with a ducat to Receiving and Release. "Pack your shit. You're moving."

"Where to?" Lydia figured it was another dorm move, so she was shocked when the officer said, "Willow Springs."

La Mesa members glared at her while she gathered her personal property. If the officer hadn't stuck around to watch her pack, she was certain she would've been jumped again by the vicious pack. The gang members followed her across the yard, boasting that they'd forced Lydia to run off and hide. They weren't wrong, she made the choice to protect her unborn child.

After a quick identification check, Lydia and four other inmates were handcuffed and chained, then crammed into a van for the four-hour drive to Willow Springs. The caged van stopped twice on the drive north because pregnant women pee—a lot. Their destination was a gray concrete prison building, encircled by coils of concertina wire. A sign announced the CORNERSTONE WILLOW SPRINGS WOMEN'S PRISON, THOMPSON SCOTT, WARDEN.

If the sign was accurate, when the van pulled through the double gate, Lydia and the others became the property of the Cornerstone Group, a private prison corporation. Gray-uniformed Cornerstone officers waited for the van, wearing belts with handcuffs, batons, and pepper spray. The private facility's uniforms were a different color than the state's, but they carried the same message: You're still in prison.

"New beginnings, my ass," the black woman shackled next to Lydia said.

"Same shit, different day," murmured another.

The intake process was the same as other lockups Lydia had seen. She was searched, photographed, fingerprinted, documents checked, and given a housing assignment—one of forty cells in something that, to Lydia's eye, looked like a concrete dungeon. She'd traded a four-woman dorm room at Corona for a concrete cell in a private prison.

The cell door slid shut. "What have I done?" she asked herself softly.

"Not what you expected, sweet pea?" The voice came from a pregnant woman resting on one of the two bunks. Stringy blonde hair hung down and partially covered a faded butterfly tattoo on the woman's neck.

The walls and the floor were the same shade of gray, and the lack of color was disorienting. The two bunks were separated by a stainless-steel toilet and sink combination unit bolted to the back wall.

"I'm Clem. Put your shit down over there and take a load off. They're gonna be coming around for orientation in a while. Let me guess—you signed on for the spa days and new beginnings bullshit?"

"Something like that. It looked so different . . ."

"Bait and switch. I came down from CCWF at Chowchilla. I'm what you might call a legacy, been through all this before."

"At Willow Springs? I thought it was new."

"Not this one. The Cornerstone cops run a couple of farms like this. I was in one near Stockton last time I got sent up."

Lydia put her boxes on the floor at the foot of her bunk and sank onto the mattress. She leaned against the wall and drew her knees up as far as she could.

"How come you called it a farm?"

"You'll find out soon enough."

The cell door slid open and a voice boomed over a loudspeaker, echoing off the concrete guts of the cellblock. "Ramirez and White, report to Medical."

Clem rolled off her bunk. "That's us, sweet pea. Time to go get weighed and measured."

Lydia followed Clem through the B-Pod day room, following the directions issued from a Cornerstone officer tucked behind a glass-fronted control booth. The officer hit switches closing their cell door and opening another door off the dayroom, signaling them onward.

The pair followed the signs down the main corridor to Medical and when they arrived, six other women were in line waiting for their exams. Each woman took a turn hovering over a huge digital scale and had her girth registered with a plastic tape. Lydia and Clem took their places in line and received a cursory once-over by the technician recording the weights and widths.

"You weren't kidding, were you?" Lydia said.

"They making sure we're fattening up."

From across the room, a uniformed officer called out. "You two, over here."

They joined a line with women Lydia recognized from Corona, and the group was led to a nearby classroom, where they found bare walls and a collection of uncomfortable chairs facing a television screen.

An officer waited for the group to settle down and sit, not a simple chore for pregnant women. He turned on the TV, and the Cornerstone Group logo bloomed to life, then Warden Scott appeared on the monitor. It was a less friendly version of the man Lydia met during the recruitment visit at Corona.

"You were selected for the Willow Springs program for two reasons. The first is you are pregnant, and the state is under federal mandate to improve medical care for inmates committed to prison. Willow Springs will provide you with all required care, so the state doesn't have to. The second reason for your selection is you are all complete social failures and cast-offs. You have nothing. You burned every bridge with family and friends and have no one to help you with the burden of your unborn child. Willow Springs is your only hope.

"There are three rules here at Willow Springs. Abide by them and you won't have any issues."

One of the women in the back yelled, "Fuck you. Send me back to Chowchilla!"

"He means it," Clem murmured.

"Quiet!" The officer in the back of the room took a menacing step forward.

The videotaped warden pointed to a chart on a wall. "The rules are simple. First, you will attend all classes and appointments. The second rule is that you will comply with all medical instructions issued for your care. Finally, all inmates are expected to follow staff directions at all times."

"It's a setup," Clem whispered.

"Violation of these rules will be handled swiftly. Offenders will be removed from the general population, their sentences will be extended, and they will forfeit all parental rights. Those who comply will have their sentences reduced and be released with sufficient funds to plan for a future with their child. The choice is yours." Scott disappeared, and the Cornerstone logo returned to the screen.

Lydia turned to Clem. "What the hell is this?"

"It's how they get you. It almost happened to me. Said I didn't follow directions—which was bullshit—and I got six months added to my bit. And they threatened to take my kid and put him in a foster home."

"They can do that?"

Clem nodded. "Guess who runs the foster home?"

Lydia shrugged.

"Fucking Cornerstone."

"You're shitting me."

"Unless we play by their rules, they'll take our babies."

"They can do that? Keep my baby?"

"That's what I mean about the farm. They want to steal babies to get more money from the state. Whatever they say to do—do it. I'm telling you, they'll look for any excuse to fuck you over."

Shit, shit, shit! Lydia would have been better off taking her chances with La Mesa. Here, she'd carry a healthy baby to term only to give it up to some fucking baby farm?

As the women filed from the classroom, an officer handed a schedule to each of them. Lydia glanced at hers and it was no list of parenting classes, prenatal nutrition workshops, or mommy-and-me yoga, only a work assignment.

"What'd you draw? I got maintenance," Clem said.

"Kitchen. Looks like I'm gonna be washing dishes."

"Remember what I said, do what they tell you," Clem said over her shoulder as she headed to her job.

Lydia found the prison kitchen down the main corridor, near the rear of the facility. She cracked the door and a free person—a prison worker not in uniform—glanced up.

"You Ramirez? You're late." The woman's tired eyes didn't hold anger; she was just trying to assert her position in the food chain. Her name tag identified her as Parker.

"I just got out of orientation. What do you need me to do?"

"Everything is prepared and prepackaged at another Cornerstone facility. When the trays come out of the oven, your job is to deliver them."

"Where do I go?"

"The first batch goes to Medical, the Nursery, and B-Pod."

"How many?"

"Five hundred trays."

"Five hundred?" Lydia's eyes widened at the number.

The timers went off, signaling the first rack was ready for delivery and Parker rolled the hot rack toward Lydia. "These need to be delivered while they are at temperature. If they get cold, we gotta toss them and start over. You gotta hustle. Got it?"

"Got it."

"Hit Medical first and work back this way. Deliver the trays and leave. When you're done, come back here for the next set from the oven.

"You'll go back and pick up the empties later. You know where to go?"

"Medical is up front, right?"

Parker nodded.

Lydia left the kitchen and pushed her cart to the locked Medical unit and punched the button on a speaker mounted beside the door. "Kitchen delivery."

The lock popped and the door slid back before Lydia had the last syllable out.

She shoved the heavy cart inside, and an officer in a control booth pointed down the unit hallway.

According to the instructions Parker had given her, there were four women who needed trays from her cart. The first six patient rooms were empty; the four women were in the last two rooms. Lydia pushed the cart to a room where she overheard people talking and paused.

A skinny male doctor in his mid-fifties was finishing up an exam with one of the women. He snapped off a pair of latex gloves and made notes in a medical file while he spoke with a young nurse.

"I'm getting pressure to induce labor on these four," the doctor said.

"They aren't due yet. Mendez is three weeks out." Her worry lines deepened.

If Lydia learned one thing in prison, it was that staff members talked too much, especially around inmates. Convict workers were often as invisible as the furniture.

The door popped open behind her and another set of footsteps approached. Warden Thompson Scott brushed past her and stormed up to the medical team.

"Why haven't they delivered yet?"

The doctor cleared his throat. "Sir, they aren't due for another few weeks, and there are no medical reasons why—"

"Get them induced. We need to start billing for those babies before the end of the shift. You understand me?"

"But, sir—"

"Every hour a bed goes empty in that nursery is coming out of your salary. Don't kid yourself—I can find another doctor running from a malpractice complaint if you don't have the stones to do your goddamn job."

Both medical people stiffened, then the doctor's thin shoulders slumped. "Yes, sir," he said.

Holy shit. Lydia wanted to back away before they noticed her. She stretched to set a tray on the table but misjudged the distance and the tray clattered to the floor. Shit!

She knelt to gather the spilled items back onto the tray. "I'm sorry. I'll go get a new one."

Warden Scott wheeled around, a look of contempt etched on his face.

Lydia's breath caught in her throat. Good. He hadn't noticed her listening earlier.

"Sorry, sir." Lydia rolled the cart out of Medical, down the corridor to the door marked NURSERY.

The trays were for the workers in the unit, not the nursing mothers, as Lydia anticipated. While three inmates grabbed their lunches off the rack, Lydia moved to a long window overlooking the nursery.

No brightly painted murals like in the video, just small metal cribs lining the walls, with another row down the center. Each crib held a child that couldn't have been over four months old. Everything was a fucking lie. The prison existed for one reason: to take money from the state by stealing the babies of female prisoners, just like Clem said.

"How many are there?" Lydia asked.

A big woman responded around a mouthful of chicken and rice. "We got twenty-four now."

A baby began to cry, and the scream was transmitted through a speaker above the window.

"Which one is it?" a brown-skinned woman asked Lydia.

She didn't know how to respond. She saw only the baby, red-faced and writhing.

"The number. What's the number on the crib?"

Lydia spotted the metal tag with the number etched in white on a black background. "Seventeen?"

"Dammit," the big woman said. "I'm eatin' and that little shit can wait. He gotta learn that somehow."

"Is he yours?" Lydia asked.

"Don't tie me down like that. Mine's out in foster care."

"Who do these belong to?"

"Their moms got rolled up."

"Back to prison? What did they do?

"Hell if I know. They here one day and then they gone. Not back to Corona, though."

"I hear they got run off to another Cornerstone joint," the brown-skinned woman said.

"What's gonna happen to them?" Lydia asked, pointing to the cribs.

"Ain't up to us. We feed 'em and what Cornerstone does with 'em after that is on them. But new ones come in every day."

A slender black woman pushed her tray away. "They get moved to group homes, after they been here a while, I guess."

Lydia took the trays and shoved them back into the rack.

The remaining lunches were destined for B-Pod, the unit where Lydia and Clem lived. The eighty-seat dining room was full, and she was greeted with a mix of sarcastic cheers and nasty tempers when she rolled in.

A uniformed officer, a short red-haired man with a scar on his lip, inspected the rack. His name, Hyatt, was displayed on his uniform.

"You're late, Ramirez. I'm writing you up."

"A beef for a few minutes late?"

He jabbed a thermometer into a lump of packaged food on one of the trays. Hyatt pulled it out and read the display. "It's cold. Take it back."

"Oh, bitch, come on," the closest inmate said. An angry murmur started throughout the dining room.

Lydia put a hand on one of the trays. "It feels warm to me."

Officer Hyatt closed within inches of Lydia. She smelled the cigarette smoke on his breath. "It's below the required temp. You trying to make these women and their children sick?"

"No."

"Hey, we getting lunch or not?"

"Take these back and double-time it, Ramirez. Get me the replacements so I can feed this crowd."

Lydia jogged the cart back to the kitchen and was back to the dining room with reheated meals in ten minutes. The women were louder when she returned.

Officer Hyatt glared at her. "You put everyone off schedule for the afternoon."

"I didn't mean to—"

"Lock it up. You're confined to quarters. Leave your shit here. I'll have someone who wants to work take over your job."

Lydia retreated to her cell, back aching, and collapsed on the bunk. That red-haired bastard was fucking with her. She filed Hyatt's name away on the mental list of staff to avoid. There were always a few hardasses in any joint. She'd always been able to tell right away who they were, but this place was cruelly different.

An hour later, Clem joined her in the cell and perched on the edge of her bed. She looked worn and a little flushed.

"You okay?" Lydia asked.

"Yeah, just a long day."

"It wasn't for me. I think I got fired."

"Not a good start, Ramirez." Clem took off her shoes and rubbed her swollen feet.

"That officer, Hyatt, gave me shit for being late."

A slip of paper slid under the door. Lydia bent to retrieve it and saw her name typed on the document.

"Son of a bitch! The asshole wrote me up for disobeying orders, delaying count, and destruction of state property!"

Clem shook her head. "They're after you."

Lydia refused dinner and stayed in her cell for the rest of the day. She couldn't sleep. She'd been issued rules violations at Corona but they'd been deserved—she'd pushed the rules too far and always accepted the consequences. She'd been a few minutes late pushing a cart and they were going to take fucking time from her for that?

She tried closing her eyes again, replaying the scene from earlier, remembering the nursery that felt more like a processing plant. Then her eyes opened wide, and she sat up against the wall, breathing hard.

They wanted her kid. They'd add to her sentence. Just like the warden said in the infirmary—keep the beds filled. Lydia and her unborn child had just become part of the padded billing for the Cornerstone accountants.

She'd be one of those women, induced into labor for a baby that may never make it out alive. Or maybe, if she was lucky, she'd be allowed to have the baby, only to have it ripped away and stuck in that concrete bunker called a nursery. She remembered Hyatt's eyes on her and that stale cigarette breath. Maybe they'd even get her pregnant again . . .

After a restless night, Lydia was anxious to get out of her cell and go to work, but the unit officer stopped her before she left the dayroom. "Ramirez, you gotta go see the lieutenant for a disciplinary hearing."

Fuck. That didn't take long.

The lieutenant's office was near the central control room for the facility. Lydia sat in the hallway waiting her turn in the box.

A woman shoved the door open and stormed out of the office. Red-faced and holding back tears, she muttered, "Assholes."

"Ramirez!" A voice called from inside.

Lydia stood and noticed a monitor in the control room. It displayed a view of a sally port, different from the main entrance the van had used when she first arrived. This small gate was isolated. Cornerstone officers took four babies from the back of the prison and loaded them into a van. Lydia squinted and made out part of the sign on the vehicle's door as it closed.

CORNERSTONE CHILD SERVICES.

"Ramirez!"

Lydia turned into the office, where a man in a Cornerstone gray uniform with lieutenant's bars waited behind a desk. He was white, about fifty, with close-cropped gray hair and deep lines down the sides of his mouth.

She forced a slight smile, which evaporated when she saw Hyatt standing in the room.

"Gonna keep us waiting again?" Hyatt said.

The lieutenant pointed to a chair. "Sit. Ramirez, you've been charged with three separate violations of institutional rules. You received your copy of the allegations?"

"Yes, I have. I—"

"Let's get on with this."

"The first charge is destruction of state property. How do you plead?"

"I didn't destroy anything," she said.

"Officer Hyatt? Care to clarify?"

Hyatt tucked his thumbs into his utility belt and rocked back on his heels. "The food cart was delivered late and was under temperature. The meals had to be replaced and that caused additional cost to the facility."

"I didn't destroy anything."

"Were you late delivering food to B-Pod?"

Lydia glared back at Hyatt's shit-eating grin. "I was a few minutes late."

The lieutenant never looked up from the desk. "By your own admission, you caused an additional expense. I find you guilty."

"But—"

"The second charge is delaying count. How do you plead?"

"What count? There was no count." She felt the back of her neck burn.

The lieutenant sighed and looked over at Hyatt.

"Her delay pushed back the afternoon schedules and impacted the afternoon count because the meal took longer than it should've."

The lieutenant wrote something down. "Guilty. Next charge is disobeying orders. Let me guess, you're pleading not guilty here, too?" He didn't bother to wait for Lydia's response. "Hyatt reports he had to ask you repeatedly to take the cart back to the kitchen, and that you became agitated and upset, refusing his orders."

"That's bullshit!"

"See what I mean, LT? She goes off at the slightest thing," Hyatt said.

She'd stepped right into their trap and knew what was coming next.

"I'm concerned about your mental health, particularly your propensity for anger and disrespect toward authority," the lieutenant said. "That behavior will prove detrimental to the upbringing of your child. I'm scheduling you for a mental health evaluation to determine your fitness to retain custody upon birth. As to these rules violations, we're taking thirty days of credit for each violation, for a total of ninety days. That is all."

Lydia strode out of the office, and like the woman before her, she muttered, "Assholes." What the hell could she do? She was powerless in prison. It wasn't even a state joint or a county lockup, but a private-run baby farm disguised as a fucking prison. Clem was right, Cornerstone was going to take her baby.

Lydia's stomach twisted when the control-room monitor showed a woman being loaded into an ambulance from the back entrance. The skinny doctor she'd seen in the medical unit was holding a stethoscope to the woman's abdomen. Grim faces all around, including Warden Scott, who pounded a fist against the side of the ambulance. He was red-faced when the emergency vehicle pulled away.

Lydia rubbed her belly as a plan came to her. It was risky, but the possibility of having her child stripped from her outweighed anything else.

Lydia reported to the kitchen and started loading carts for the next meal delivery. While the trays heated, she downed three cups of thick prison coffee, the caffeine jolting her system.

She grabbed a cup of red punch, mixed it with coffee, and tucked it into the cart among the trays. Her delivery this time was B-Pod only.

When Lydia rolled the cart into the unit, Hyatt glanced at his watch. She wasn't late, so he couldn't jam her for that. The bastard looked disappointed. She took a tray from the cart, locked eyes with Hyatt, and held the tray out in front of her. Then she let it fall, food and drinks splattering over the floor.

"Clean that up, bitch!"

"You clean it up."

"What did you say?" He closed on her.

"I said you clean it up, needle dick."

Hyatt shoved her. Lydia pivoted and fell into her cart, toppling the entire thing to the floor.

Women started shouting in the small dayroom, the noise deafening as it bounced off the concrete. The officer up in the control booth hit an alarm and the shrill bleat added to the cacophony.

Hyatt grabbed Lydia from behind and rolled her over. He rocked back when he saw the dark red stain down her legs.

"What did you do to her?" an inmate shouted.

"Her water broke."

"The baby!" said another.

"He killed her baby!"

The women surrounded Hyatt. The control booth officer called Medical and ordered the prisoners to lockup.

The women shouted at Hyatt, ignoring the PA system blaring at them to stand down. The control-booth officer stuck a pepperball gun through the gun port and popped off a single round, striking one of the women in the back. The capsule exploded in a white mist. The closest women gagged, wheezed, and stumbled back. Lydia writhed on the floor, holding her abdomen, the red stain spreading.

Hyatt knelt beside her, his forehead sweaty. "I'm sorry. I didn't mean to . . ."

Lydia groaned when medical staff lifted her to a gurney. She spotted a trampled empty cup on the floor—one that once held a mix of red punch and coffee.

In the infirmary, when the doctor started an exam, Lydia screamed. "My baby! What's happening?"

Warden Scott rushed in, pulling at his tie and speaking fast.

"Was there a fucking riot? What the hell's going on?"

"Hyatt shoved her," an officer said.

"Dammit. The child?"

Lydia doubled up and whimpered, hoping the caffeine, fear and adrenalin would keep her vitals elevated. She couldn't let that skinny doctor check her too closely and discover the coffee and red punch stain.

"It hurts . . . it hurts. My baby," she moaned. "What have you done to my baby?"

"Get her to the hospital," Scott said.

"I can take care of—" the doctor said.

"Like you did the last one? Get her out now. We can't afford to lose another one. Billing's down already from the last fuckup."

Within five minutes, Lydia went into an ambulance at the rear sally port. Another ten minutes and she was in the Santa Romita Hospital emergency room, the only medical facility within fifty miles.

A young female doctor stepped to the gurney as it rolled into the room. She quickly checked Lydia and noticed the bruises on her side and back.

"What happened?"

The escort officer was busy leering at a nurse in the next room. This was Lydia's chance.

"A guard pushed me. I'm not safe there and neither is my child, I don't know what to do. Please, don't make me go back." She had to trust someone and the doctor with kind eyes was her last resort.

The doctor met her gaze, then finished her exam and made notes in a file. "Officer, tell your supervisor I'm admitting Miss Ramirez for observation."

The officer took out his phone and stepped into the hall.

"Thank you," Lydia whispered.

"You aren't the first woman with problems at Willow Springs. A woman came in earlier with a stillborn—they tried to induce labor too early. You and your baby have rights—human rights."

Lydia was assigned a room where another pregnant woman occupied the far bed. The officer handcuffed Lydia's left arm to the bedrail and retreated to a chair in the hall.

"Rough day?" The woman was blonde, in her mid-thirties, and smiled at Lydia. "I'm Teresa."

"I'm Lydia." She sighed, the tension starting to unknot her body, and rubbed her hand over her swollen abdomen. "And yeah, it's been a rough one."

"I work in Sacramento, but I was here at the district office when this little guy had other ideas, so here I am." Teresa patted her belly. "What about you, what brings you to our little hospital? I know most of the people in town, but don't remember meeting you before."

Over the next four hours, Lydia explained to Teresa what had happened to her, and how the private prison was adding time to women's sentences and making them stay until they filled the company's foster care beds with stolen children.

Lydia cried, as the reality of what she was facing hit her. "I can't go back there. I know I have to do my time, but not there."

Teresa was sitting up in bed, looking at her thoughtfully. "What if you didn't have to?"

JUGGLING A THICK binder under one arm and a baby girl on her hip, Lydia hurried past a television news crew setting up on the state capitol steps. In the nine months since she'd bluffed her way out of Willow Springs, she'd served her remaining time in a county facility, one that actually provided services for pregnant and parenting women. It was a tough challenge, but one that Lydia needed to do to break the cycle of foster home placements and sentences to state-run institutions. She'd found a cleaning job and shared an apartment with another mother from the program. They supported one another and shared childcare responsibilities.

A week after she'd finished her jail time, state investigators tracked her down and she figured they were out to punish her for the deception at Willow Springs. Lydia steeled herself for the worst and told them everything she knew about the private prison, Thompson Scott, and the corruption inside. Snitching on people who wanted to steal her baby and that of every other woman in prison wasn't snitching at all. It was justice.

She was certain no one believed the story of a brown-skinned ex-con until a man in a suit handed her a subpoena to appear in front of the State Senate Committee on Government Operations. The subpoena made her stomach turn to ice. One name on the witness list made her want to disappear—Thompson Scott. She'd have to face the warden again.

The committee room was an old-fashioned affair, a dais where the senators would look down on her and the others. She'd had her fill of courtrooms. Would this be another example of the powerful blaming the weak, of not-so-subtle remarks about her community, her heritage, her background? She felt even weaker when Thompson Scott strode into the room with his Cornerstone entourage. Entitlement and privilege seemed to form a protective shield around the gathering of older white men. Even the media in the room seemed enraptured with the private prison executives, snapping photos of that bastard Scott, all smiles while glad-handing his Cornerstone cronies.

Lydia held her baby tight, as if to reclaim her all over again.

A rap from a gavel at the dais drew everyone's attention. A blonde woman placed the gavel next to the nameplate saying STATE SENATOR TERESA LONG. The same woman Lydia had confided in that night at the hospital. Three other senators took their places on the dais.

"This committee is now in session."

Thompson Scott and the Cornerstone CEO sat at the witness table, ready to defend their private prison's corporate reputation.

Senator Long looked down at them. "Let's cut to the chase, shall we? The committee has received evidence that the Willow Springs Women's Prison has engaged in illegal and immoral practices. Had I not been home in my Central Valley district while the senate was on recess, I may have never heard about children being ripped away, stolen from their birth mothers, and placed in Cornerstone foster care facilities—facilities which exist to collect and profit from the children born in the private prisons you operate. As a new mother myself, I find this utterly reprehensible."

"I'd like to respond, Madam Chairman," said the red-faced Cornerstone CEO, a shortish burly man in a blue suit.

Senator Long's voice was ice. "It's Chairwoman, and you'll have your opportunity." The senator opened a thick file in front of her.

"These are rules violation report forms written at Willow Springs in the past six months. Based on these, I'd guess you were running something like Pelican Bay out there, with incredibly violent and unruly inmates. Then I dove into the violations themselves. They are all, without exception, superficial and petty." She sifted through the reports. "Disrespect, disobedience, refusing to follow orders—not only petty infractions, but based on testimony, even these citations were trumped up to justify extended sentences."

"There's more to it than that. These inmates—" Warden Scott's voice was higher than Lydia remembered.

"Is that right? More to it? When you calculate all the time you added to the sentences of these women, based on these reports alone, it comes out to five-plus years of additional confinement. Time that you billed the state for. So, tell me, Warden Scott, how much income did all these reports generate for Cornerstone?"

"They broke the rules and must be held accountable."

"Who holds you accountable?"

Scott shrank back into his chair and looked to the CEO, who remained silent and subtly moved his chair, distancing himself from Scott.

"Your scheme of puffed-up rules violations cost the state over eight hundred thousand dollars."

The warden rallied. "If the beds are full, then we bill the state accordingly."

"Because these mothers aren't getting out of prison on time, their children require housing, too, right?"

"We can't just turn them loose on the street."

"Here is an invoice for an additional seven hundred fifty thousand dollars for in-facility childcare. Oh, and another for one point one million for Cornerstone Child Services." She looked over the top of her glasses at Scott. "Care to explain what that entails?"

He cleared his throat. "A community-based shelter where the children of these unfit mothers are housed."

"Who makes that determination? Who deems them unfit?"

Scott started to regain his composure. "We are in the best position to make that call. These women are a burden on society. They've burnt every bridge, used up family resources until they have nothing left. They've been in and out of foster homes, jails, and prisons all their lives. They'll drag their children into criminality, drug use, and dependence on social services. What kind of life—what kind of birthright is that?"

"Birthright?" The senator's voice rose, and she seemed to grow taller. "What kind of birthright is handed down to the children in the Cornerstone foster care facility? I'd like to ask a woman who survived Willow Springs to come forward. Miss Ramirez, if you please." Teresa gestured to a seat alongside Scott.

Lydia sat next to Scott, who twitched uncomfortably in his chair.

Senator Long's eyes softened when she saw Lydia.

"Miss Ramirez, please tell us your experience at Willow Springs."

Lydia adjusted her daughter's pink blanket and placed the baby in her lap. She recounted her short incarceration at the Cornerstone facility in detail, to a silent committee and equally quiet Cornerstone CEO. If the executive claimed ignorance of Scott's self-dealing before, he couldn't now.

"The place was nothing like what we were told. There were no parenting classes, prenatal care, or programs to help us. Part of what Warden Scott says is true. We are the products of our past. But that doesn't mean we don't want to break free from it. It's even more important now with our children in our lives. We owe it to them. Their birthright is to have a better life than their mothers."

The click of camera shutters and flashes startled Lydia, but over the course of the next hour, she told every detail she'd witnessed at Willow Springs—the abuse, inducing pregnancy, and the underlying plan to take babies from their mothers. Scott grew increasingly more agitated when the cameras turned on him.

"I'd like a moment to respond," Warden Scott said. "This woman is nothing but—"

"I've heard enough," the senator countered. After a brief, hushed conversation between the committee members, Senator Long said, "It is this committee's decision to withdraw all state funding from Cornerstone operations and require that all Cornerstone facilities housing state inmates be closed within thirty days."

"Senator!"

"Further, I'm referring this matter to the state attorney general for possible criminal prosecution."

"Senator, this is ridiculous! You're going to close the prison based on the ravings of a worthless piece of—"

"Watch yourself, Warden Scott. You treated the Willow Springs facility as a farm to nurture future crops of inmates that would fill Cornerstone facilities for years to come. Private prisons like yours are why the state should never contract out its legal and moral responsibilities to those committed to its care. This hearing is adjourned." Senator Long banged her gavel. The stunned Cornerstone executives filed out of the hearing room, Scott trailing.

Senator Long looked down at Lydia. "I'm glad my baby decided to come early and we met that night in the hospital. Because of you, we've ended a corrupt private prison. You've saved countless women from going through the torment you experienced. Because of you, there is hope."

Lydia looked down at her baby girl and looked at the perfect little face. It was only appropriate that she had named her little girl Hope.

Women Writing
(After the Penmanship Prize)

A Conversation with
Cara Black and Hallie Ephron

When we cast about for our favorite nasty women from history or literature, both of us came up with women artists from eras dominated by men. Their works are featured in the world's great art museums; each of them, for better and for worse, was defined by her own #MeToo moment.

Cara chose the late nineteenth century French sculptor Camille Claudel. The great sculptor Auguste Rodin was her mentor, and her surviving works rival his genius for realistically depicting the human form imbued with passion and emotion. She's best remembered for *Maturity* (now in the Musée d'Orsay in Paris), which depicts three figures: an aging Rodin, his older longtime mistress, and the young Camille, who was also his mistress. Camille sculpts herself on her knees, naked, beseeching Rodin to choose her even as he pulls away, in the embrace of his older lover. Rodin cut off his contact with her upon seeing the work, which revealed Camille's pain and her brokenness. After that, she suffered a breakdown and though she continued to sculpt, she would destroy her own work. Finally, her brother committed her to a mental asylum, where she lived out the last thirty years of her life.

Hallie chose Artemisia Gentileschi, a seventeenth-century Baroque painter who followed the style invented by Caravaggio, using light and shadow to create dramatic tableaus. She was the daughter of a popular painter who recognized her genius and encouraged her. The tutor her father brought into his workshop to work with her when she was seventeen raped her, then convinced her that he would marry her. He reneged on his promise, and her father sued the tutor. At the trial, Artemisia had to prove that *she'd* been an innocent virgin when she was raped.

Today she's best known for her depictions of Biblical women overpowering violent men. In *Judith Slaying Holofernes,* which now hangs in Italy's Uffizi Gallery in Florence, we watch as Judith wields a scimitar and beheads the fierce army general. It's easy to imagine that through this mature painting, Artemisia was wreaking her own form of vengeance.

As we talked about these two great artists, one who was broken and the other who went on to thrive, we dug into our own personal histories, looking for the people in our own lives who broke with custom and affected us directly, showing us how to find our own way as writers.

CARA: In my all-girl elementary school, prizes were awarded for penmanship, behavior (yes, really), and writing essays. Only once, in fourth grade, did I win a prize—the book *Rascal* by Sterling North. I loved this book about a boy and the raccoon he rescues, his acceptance into a family, a lovely coming-of-age story that's universal. Yet part of me wondered why it couldn't have been about a girl who found the raccoon. Still, I treasure this book and read it to my son.

Before college, I travelled for several years, working my way through Europe, India, and Asia. My grandfather encouraged me on my return to 'write down your travels, what you saw and felt,' but I said who'd be interested? He said he would.

I never forgot what my grandfather said. Along the way I read and was bowled over by *The Lover,* by Marguerite Duras, a coming-of-age story set in French Colonial Indochina about forbidden love. Maybe that explains why years later, when an illness intervened, I realized that maybe I had experiences to write about and I'd better get in my two centimes before I couldn't.

Paris was where I'd felt the urge to write, where I'd heard incredible stories that I wanted to explore. So what better beautiful, complex, and sometimes infuriating place to start.

Hallie, you come from a writing family, I'd love to have been at your dinner table. You had your own family and career before you began writing, what prompted you?

HALLIE: Ah, the dinner table. My parents were screenwriters and my three sisters would all become prolific, bestselling authors, so you can imagine the Darwinian struggle to make oneself heard at the Ephron dinner table. Occasionally, at the end of a meal, my mother would recite poetry. Edwin Arlington Robinson's "Miniver Cheevy" (". . . child of scorn") was a favorite. So was Edna St. Vincent Millay's "First Fig" ("My candle burns at both ends . . .") My mother was also brilliant at giving us books that featured strong girl characters (Dorothy Gale, Anne Shirley, Jo March, Eloise, Madeline).

For my sixteenth birthday, my mother gave me a copy of Virginia Woolf's *A Room of One's Own*. I gave it a try but failed to make my way through its dense prose (where was the story?) Perhaps it's just as well, because I wasn't ready to hear its message. I didn't pick it up again until decades later, when I listened to an audiobook of the essay while driving to work at Digital Equipment Corporation, where I was writing computer training manuals and toying with writing a book. I remember being gobsmacked by these words:

> Suppose, for instance, that men were only represented in literature
> as the lovers of women, and were never the friends of men, soldiers,
> thinkers, dreamers; how few parts in the plays of Shakespeare could be
> allotted to them; how literature would suffer!

Later, Virginia Woolf makes it absolutely clear what she's getting at:

> And since a novel has this correspondence to real life, its values are to
> some extent those of real life. But it is obvious that the values of women
> differ very often from the values which have been made by the other
> sex; naturally this is so. Yet is it the masculine values that prevail. Speaking crudely, football and sport are "important"; the worship of fashion,

the buying of clothes "trivial." And these values are inevitably transferred from life to fiction. **This is an important book, the critic assumes,
because it deals with war. This is an insignificant book because it deals
with the feelings of women in a drawing-room.**

This was one of the excuses I'd given myself for putting off, and putting off,
and putting off writing while all of my sisters had long ago launched their literary
careers. The core question that stymied me: what had I experienced that was worthy of writing about? I'd been a sister. A wife. A mother. A teacher. A corporate
trainer. What could I write about, and who'd care? That's why I wrote my first
novels with a writing partner. A man.

Cara, how did you end up writing mysteries and finding Aimée Leduc? Did
you have to get over "she's only a woman?" And I'm dying to know which award
you won in elementary school? (I won one for penmanship.)

CARA: Hallie, it certainly wasn't an award for proper behavior! Funny, mine was
for penmanship, too. No wonder we get along.

You would think being in an all-girls school empowers females, and in a way
I'm sure it does, but writing, for me, seemed a high hurdle. The voice I always
heard was the mother in this quote from the French novelist and playwright,
Marguerite Duras, in *The Lover*:

> I want to write. I've already told my mother: That's what I want to
> do—write. No answer the first time. Then she asks, Write what? I say,
> Books, novels. [. . .] She's against it, it's not worthy, it's not real work, it's
> nonsense. Later she said, A childish idea.

It wasn't until I revisited Paris in 1984, on a break from teaching preschool
in Head Start, and stayed with a Parisian friend that I experienced the city in
another way. Paris was so full of history, you couldn't get away from it, not that
you'd want to. Left Bank to the Right Bank, all the quartiers breathed their own
unique ambiance. And stories.

Seeing the city with my friend who grew up there, hearing her anecdotes about a place, discussion with her local cheesemonger over the 'right' cheese for after dinner—the French always have cheese after dessert. I thought it only went in sandwiches—who knew? Staying with her and hearing that Simone de Beauvoir had written in the café around the corner during the war—it had heating—the one we passed all the time.

One day she took me to the Marais—not as gentrified as today—and shared the story of her mother, who'd lived there as a young girl. Her mother was fourteen, wore a yellow star, and came back to the family apartment after school in 1942. Her family were gone. She waited for them to return, hidden and fed by the concierge, and survived the German Occupation. Her family never came back. We stood on that narrow street in the Marais, looking at her mother's former apartment building, and I tried to imagine being fourteen years old, hiding, losing my family. Horrific. I'd grown up so differently; food on my plate, a family, not threatened by an occupier. It lodged in my heart.

Ten years later, my husband, young son, and I were in Paris and that story came back to me, not that I'd ever forgotten it, but in a new way. I was a mother now, what would I have done if I'd been a mother in 1942 with a young child to protect, to feed, what would I have done for us to survive? Probably anything. What if what I did to survive came back to bite me fifty years later—it was in 1994 fifty years after the war. There was a story I wanted to tell, was passionate about—women and what they do to survive and what comes back to haunt them.

Hallie, since you wrote several books with your writing partner, a man, what sparked you to break away? To write on your own?

HALLIE EPHRON: The eight years that I spent writing with a partner was far from wasted. I learned a lot about human psychology from my learned collaborator. He let me do all of the writing. And along the way, I discovered my sweet spot: suspense with a healthy dose of setting. Guns and car chases, not so much. After co-authoring five mystery novels I had the confidence to fly solo, but I wasn't sure what to write about.

It was at about that time that I read *The Stone Diaries*, Carol Shields's Pulitzer Prize–winning novel. Written in diary format, it tells the life story (birth to death) of Daisy Stone Goodwill. Daisy is a wife, a mother, and a widow. Full stop. An ordinary woman, she witnesses her own birth, her own death, and what happens in between. The book's tour-de-force opening, which describes Daisy's mother's death while giving birth to Daisy, seared itself into my brain. When the novel came out, Mrs. Shields explained to a *New York Times* reporter why she wrote it: "None of the novels I read seemed to have anything to do with my life. So that was the kind of novel I tried to write—the novel I couldn't find."

I found it additionally encouraging that Carol Shields was forty years old when she published her first novel. *Stone Diaries* was her eighth, and she was nearly sixty when it came out. And though I would never in a million years try to write a literary novel, her book demonstrated that feminine domesticity was interesting, in and of itself, and could be written about in a compelling way. I only had to take a slight detour to find my way from writing a traditional mystery to the stand-alone suspense novels that I now write, grounded in women's experiences.

Cara, while domesticity lit the way for me, it sounds as if history has been much more your guiding light. And yet one of my favorite things about Aimee is her fashion sense. Her makeup. Her femininity. And, in one of my favorite plot twists, she has a child.

CARA BLACK: Hallie, I love that quote of Carol Shields's, "write . . . the novel I couldn't find." So true in my case, too. Many of the books I'd read about Paris were the beret-and-baguette stereotype. Where was the off-the-beaten track Paris I'd come to know, the narrow passages, the thirteenth century building that housed a pho noodle shop, the plaques to Resistance leaders, all those layers of history, and ten times more interesting.

We know it's all about putting obstacles in our protagonists' path for them to overcome, making it hard for the characters and forcing them to show their mettle—what better difficulty to give a not very domesticated woman like Aimée—who doesn't cook, burns water and believes bistros were invented for a reason—than to become a mother! It's a challenge for her—and me. My editor encouraged me to give this fashion-forward young woman the ultimate challenge: care for baby. Yet she still must run a detective agency and wears heels.

Hallie, I'll never forget taking a walk in your lovely neighborhood in Milton, where you pointed out the birds and as we were casually passing a neighbor's house, you were saying, "There was an estate sale there once and I wondered what would happen if someone went inside the house and never came out." Talk about domestic suspense—and twisted—but I love how your mind works. How the most 'normal' in the everyday can springboard a story. That's almost the most terrifying, don't you find?

HALLIE EPHRON: You've put your finger on it, Cara. Both of us are trying to write stories that make the reader think, "Yikes, that could happen to me." And thank goodness we're living at a time when we don't have to rely on men to define what that might look like.

Thoughts and Prayers

Joe Clifford

When Nadine's father called that morning, insisting she bring her mother to the memorial service, her initial reaction was to say no. Nadine had plenty of time to pick up her mom—the ceremony at Litchfolk High School wasn't slated to kick off till later that morning, and given her mother's Alzheimer's, which wasn't getting better, Nadine *wanted* to spend more time together. It was the way he demanded, imposed himself on her, the underlying tension that had been building since Peter's death. Nadine had questions—why couldn't *he* bring her mom? He was still planning on attending the ceremony, wasn't he? Before she could ask him any anything, he ended the call. That was her father, able to divorce himself from the unpleasant, always dictating and demanding. Nadine thought of calling back but knew one of the caretakers would answer the phone, and her father would suddenly be indisposed.

Driving along Interstate 84, a cool November rain starting to fall, Nadine reminded herself that her father had lost someone, too. Peter was his only grandson, his only grandchild. The tragedy should've brought them closer. And her dad had tried, in his own way. Following the spring shooting, when she was still in shock, he'd said all the right things, attempted to comfort her, to make her feel safe again like when she was a little girl and never worried about being harmed because Barry Gilmore, big man that he was, would never let anything bad happen to her or her mom.

Nadine darted between cars, navigating the morning rush, switching lanes a little too fast, feeling the power of the motor with each acceleration. She tried to stave off her anger. Her father's defense of the NRA didn't put that gun in some lunatic's hand. Her father wasn't the reason her only child was dead. That was also part of the problem—a preventable tragedy. So many ideologies to target, so few people to actually hold accountable. Lax laws, loopholes, political pandering. Free hands could throw stones all day long and never hit the target.

No one was qualified to shoulder all the responsibility. Not even the kid with the gun, the kid with the "history of mental illness," Derek Coates, a name Nadine hadn't heard until the morning she learned Peter was dead, one of three victims shot in the school cafeteria on the last day of school. No, she didn't feel sorry for Derek Coates, the murderer who took justice out of the equation when he turned the gun on himself. Clearly the boy was disturbed. Why hadn't anyone noticed? Why hadn't someone identified the problem, isolated it, removed it?

Nadine watched the rain fall in shimmering sheets on the asphalt, stewing over how long it had taken for a public acknowledgment in the form of a ceremony. It couldn't take place during the summer when school wasn't in session, and then school officials decreed the new year shouldn't kick off on such a somber, dour note. Or maybe there were bigger forces at play, certain politicians who wanted to wait closer to election time.

Nadine had waited six long months. Six months with no acceptance, no processing, no reconciliation. Not with the loss. Not with her dad. Not with watching her mother slowly slip away.

The logical part of Nadine knew her dad wasn't responsible for Peter's death any more than he was for her mother's escalating dementia. Ruth was getting old, sick, her mind dying before her body. But Barry was still the same steadfast, stubborn man he'd always been, and Nadine resented her father's beliefs. If this weren't Peter, if it was some other faceless kid, at some other nameless school, her father would've lectured about personal freedoms, the sovereignty of the many outweighing the discomfort of the few, the sanctity of the Second Amendment.

As Nadine pulled off the West Hartford exit, she noticed a homeless woman at the intersection of Park Street and Prospect Avenue, standing on the corner, head tilted back, bellowing at the sky.

The traffic didn't slow. Nor did Nadine, forced to keep up with the flow of cars and trucks, buses and bundled-up bicyclists. She clutched the steering wheel tighter. Nadine wanted to believe she might have stopped to help the woman.

Maybe offered her the half of the banana nut muffin sitting in her center console. Nadine didn't give away money, it was too hard to come by, but in that moment, witnessing the soundless scream outside her windshield, lost in the churnings of engines and grinding of gears, she needed to believe that today of all days something might've been different.

As Nadine turned onto West Park, she could still see the woman in her rearview mirror, perched beside her cart, baying into the void.

Nadine pulled past the gates into her parents' long driveway. She steeled her nerves, ready to confront her father. He was avoiding the ceremony, which was bad enough, but she at least expected him to be home—he owned the company, so he could call the shots. When Gracie opened the door, the caretaker's placid face should've been a relief. But it wasn't.

"Where's my father?"

Gracie stammered. "He said to tell you he's sorry, but he had to go into the office."

"Today? Of all days? Sorry doesn't really cut it, does it?" Nadine pushed past the caretaker. "What was the urgency? Why was he calling me at dawn then? If he wasn't planning on coming to his own grandson's—"

"It's because of last night. Your father thinks you being here, taking your mom, will somehow make what happened last night disappear."

"What happened last night?"

Nadine could see a couple of other women working in the background, one gathering soiled laundry and another in a blue uniform who was measuring medication.

"Your mother wandered out of the house in the middle of the night."

"Dear God—" Nadine stopped. *With all these people here?* "How?"

"It was during the shift change." Gracie followed Nadine's gaze down the hall. The young woman with the medication was administering the morning dose to the frail, tiny woman who was her mother.

Had her mom always been that little? Nadine remembered laughing with her, the ice cream cookie sandwiches, the picnics in Elizabeth Park among the roses . . . how her mom had shaken her head over her husband's growing trophy room of pistols and assault rifles.

Nadine remembered that the more the collection grew, the less her parents seemed to communicate. Her mom hated those goddamn things as much as Nadine did. Maybe a bigger, stronger woman would've stood up to her father, told him to get them out of the house, but Nadine didn't really believe that. Her mother had done the best she could, she wasn't responsible for her husband's beliefs—and no one could tell Barry Gilmore what to do. But sometimes the animosity would surface, shame over her mother's inability to have a voice. And a part of her hated Barry for that too.

"The police found her by the Shell Station off Prospect," Gracie said.

Nadine knew the section of town. It was not a good section for a woman to be in, especially someone her mother's age.

"Your father wants to pretend nothing is wrong," Gracie said. "That we can ignore it and she won't get worse. But your mother needs to be somewhere with round-the-clock care. Your mother is sick. I am here, every day, I see it. She is not getting better."

"I know."

"She needs to go to a residential facility. A place with locks on the doors. Your father thinks if he hires enough workers, we can keep her safe here. But the center sends college kids, students. They are not equipped to care for someone like your mother."

Nadine didn't want to be a part of this conversation. Like everyone, except her father apparently, Nadine knew what these episodes were: the degeneration that comes with old age and is infinitely worsened with Alzheimer's, a withering of the mind that does not magically get better with wishful thinking. It was a reminder that soon Nadine would lose her mother too. She was almost gone now.

The young woman in the blue health worker's uniform, whom Nadine had never seen before, was helping her mother put on a winter coat. "Please," Nadine replied to Gracie, exasperation sharpening her voice. *Please, only one tragedy at a time.* "I will deal with it. Promise. I will talk to him."

"Talking won't help. She needs a facility."

"And we will place her in one. Okay? Right now I've got to take her to the ceremony. Then I'll talk to my father and the three of us can come up with a better solution, all right? Today I don't have the capacity—I just don't." Nadine fought back the tears threatening to choke her. Gracie took her hand, squeezing it softly.

"I'm so sorry, Nadine."

THE CEREMONY WAS what the media liked to call "tasteful." The school principal and Peter's favorite art teacher eulogized her son. The priest who delivered the blessing spoke at length about God's grace and mercy, and how that mercy revealed itself in the fact that one of the students had survived. No blame was assigned, no responsibility taken.

As if the Litchfolk High shooting had simply been the byproduct of misfortune and not due to a gun placed in the wrong hands. Each time an administrator, some stuffed suit from the Board of Education, took the microphone, Nadine would glance at her mother, whose gaze landed unfocused in space, eyes vacant, uncomprehending. In that instant, Nadine didn't lament the loss of her mother's cognitive function; she envied it. How lovely it would be to be able to tune out the pain.

Nadine always knew that the ceremony wouldn't grant her the closure she craved. She wouldn't have bothered to participate at all if not for the opportunity to talk to the senator. To get the one-on-one time that until now she'd been denied.

Today the senator would get his picture taken with the grieving mothers and families, offering words of consolation; it was his chance to look like a decent human being.

With shootings like this a weekly—if not daily—national occurrence, the Litchfolk murders had stayed on top of the news cycle for only a matter of hours. Now it had been relegated to the trash heap of ancient history, another mass shooting to show pity over for a day or two before the next one took its place. But Senator Todd was locked in a real barnburner, a neck-to-neck bid for reelection, so he was using her son's death as a talking point to distance himself from his opponent.

At the conclusion of the ceremony, the senator took the stage.

This was Nadine's moment.

"It's important in times like this," the senator said into the microphone, "to allow the grieving process to play out." He paused to sip his water. "People with agendas will try to politicize this tragedy. Right now my thoughts and prayers are with the victims and the victims' families—"

Nadine rose from her seat. "What does your office plan to do to stop this from happening again?"

All eyes turned to her, the crowd surprised, shocked, puzzled, a murmur rising. The senator's handlers whispered to each other and started to move quickly down the aisle. Senator Todd waved them off.

Nadine's voice got louder. "My son Peter died that day. That's why I'm here. Why are you here, Senator?"

The aides tensed and turned to the senator, awaiting instruction. Senator Todd wasn't going to have a grieving mother escorted from a memorial for her dead son, not with all these cameras pointed at him.

"Mrs. Gilmore—" he said with mournful theatricality.

Nadine interrupted him before he could deliver another platitude. "No mother should have to bury her child."

Todd descended the podium and walked to her, sorrow painted on his face, a calculated mix of empathy and distance. "I'm sorry for your loss," he said, hand cupped over hers, as he readied for his close-up.

Nadine was ready for hers, too.

"I don't care about condolences, Senator, or what you say in front of the cameras to save your job. I've got one simple question: what are you going to do to prevent another mother from losing her child? How do you plan to stop the easy access to assault weapons and semi-automatics—"

"Please, Mrs. Gilmore," Senator Todd said. "Since 1994, the Public Safety and Recreation Act, which my office—"

"I don't care about your watered-down laws that do nothing or your campaign!" Her eyes bore into him. "I don't care about the 'rights' of gun owners. How about my 'right' as a mother? How will you stop boys like my son from dying senselessly?"

"I can assure you, Mrs. . . . Ms. Gilmore . . . that my office is doing everything within its power—"

"Stop!" The word came out as both a shriek and an order, its accusation aimed at every member of the senator's party, all complicit through inaction, each guilty of murder. "You all go round and around spouting the same crap, every month—every week—every goddamn day this happens! I don't care what name you give your so-called public safety bills, the ones the NRA pays you to pass that do nothing, absolutely nothing, to keep people safe from gun violence—you and every politician like you put these guns on our streets, in our churches, in our classrooms!"

"Ms. Gilmore," the senator said. "We *will* find a solution. But measures and laws . . . it is important that . . . we have to remember that prohibition does not work." Before she could respond, the senator's voice rose and swelled, his "patriotic" message carrying over the crowd. "The Second Amendment is one of the governing principles enacted by our forefathers. We cannot throw out the baby with the bathwater. But I, for one, thank you for raising these important concerns—"

"I don't want your sound bites! I want my son back! Your cowardice helped kill him!" Her voice wavered but found itself again. "Do you have children?"

"Yes, I have a son. I can only imagine—" The senator tried to maintain his smile, as his eyes darted in a panic to his aides, who closed in around her like a curtain.

"But you don't have to, do you? Imagine. You don't have to wonder how you would feel if it was *your* child! Gunmen don't mow down fancy private schools, do they? Oh, I did my research, Senator Todd. Chote Academy. On the hill. No, it's only us, down here! We are the ones who suffer and die because you and your fucking bosses at the NRA are slaughtering us!"

Nadine screamed these last words, but by now staffers and security had moved in, pushing, pulling, like a mass of solid flesh, literally lifting her up and extracting her from the scrum. The reporters, sensing a lead, bellowed questions and tried to follow, only to be cut off and redirected, easily distracted with more empty promises.

Nadine and her mother were escorted off grounds.

On the way to drop off her mom, Nadine again took the Park Street exit. So many thoughts whirling through her brain, so many emotions—fury, remorse, the ache to pay back some of the hurt. She looked over at her mom, gazing vacantly out the window, and remembered the homeless woman she'd seen earlier. Passing the Shell Station, she felt for her purse, but the woman was gone.

Sitting in the driveway, waiting for Gracie to come outside, Nadine felt a sudden, relentless urge for a cigarette. She hadn't smoked in twenty years. Not even the occasional girls' night out when she'd had one too many. She didn't smoke when she heard about the shooting or when she got the call and her worst fears were confirmed that Peter had been one of the victims. She didn't smoke when Kevin, her husband and the only man she'd ever slept with, left over the summer, when the grieving was at its worst, because seeing their son in each other's face proved too much for their marriage to handle.

Right now, the temptation for a smoke was unbearable, and she wished Gracie would hurry the fuck up because as soon as her mother was inside, she was going to the Shell Station and pick up a pack of Camel filters. The realization that she didn't have a clue what cigarettes cost these days made her blurt out a laugh. Her voice sounded alien.

"What's wrong, honey?" her mother said.

The sound of her mom's voice—still kind, still full of motherly concern—shocked Nadine. Her mom had witnessed Nadine's outburst at the school, but she'd said nothing. Not when they were being ushered away by the senator's security service. Not on the entire ride back home. Now she was acting as if Nadine were just a small girl with a skinned knee, in need of consoling.

"I guess I just miss Peter, Mom."

"I know, honey."

Gracie descended the stairs. Nadine climbed out of the car to meet her. As Gracie led her mom inside, Nadine thought her mother said something but when she turned around, the old woman was shuffling inside, back turned, silent once more.

THE PHONE RINGING at nine a.m. woke Nadine. It wasn't often she slept in, but she'd emailed her boss last night that she wasn't feeling well and would be taking a personal day. She was still on the couch, TV on, sound off, where she'd fallen asleep after four glasses of wine.

As soon as she heard her father's voice, she knew it was bad news.

"Your mother is missing."

"What do you—where is she?"

"We don't know. I take it you haven't spoken with her since yesterday?"

"No. Not since I dropped her off."

"I'm sorry I couldn't make the ceremony—"

"Dad," Nadine said, firmly. "What happened to Mom? You're scaring me. Where is she?"

"I told you. I don't know. I woke up this morning, and . . ." The pause was long and pained.

"And what?"

"I don't want you to worry."

"Dad!"

"One of the cars is gone."

"Mom doesn't drive. She hasn't driven in fifteen years!"

"I know!" She heard her father collect himself. "That's not all."

"What's not all?"

"I don't want you to panic—"

"Tell me!"

"One of the gun cabinets. It's open. A gun is missing."

"Are you saying someone broke in?" Surely her mom wouldn't touch a gun. "Have you called the police?"

"I was about to."

"Hang up," Nadine said. "Call the police and then call me back." She searched the couch and end tables for her car keys. "I'm going to drive over—"

The image on the television stopped Nadine cold. She looked for the remote to turn up the sound, but the banner running underneath told her all she needed to know.

Active Shooter at Chote Prep School.

"Dad," Nadine said. "Turn on the TV."

Lifetime Appointment

Josh Stallings

By the ballot or the Bible or the bullet, change is gonna come. Take away the ballot and corrupt God's word with misogynist pastors, the only choice left is the bullet.

Sashay Freedom (2001–2024)

Alabama is no place to run to. Freedom is always North. Wildness is West. Intellectual pursuit is East. Angel knew this was bullshit regionalism. But fuck it, she needed some guiding principles if she was to survive the shifting landscape that was modern America. So she went as far north as she could. Didn't stop until she pushed up against the Canadian border. Or as close to it as she could before the barb wire and trenches held her back. From a perch two hundred feet up an ancient Douglas fir she could just see the demilitarized zone. A short three years ago all you needed to cross into Canada was a passport and a desire for poutine. Then the trade wars went hot.

On the southern border, the U.S. built the wall to keep out brown people, or that was what the propaganda said. When a Congresswoman spoke against it, Forty-Five, the President for Life tweeted, "Don't like the Wall? Go home, you anti-American bitch. Bet you love getting raped by MS13 GANGSTERS."

When they built the wall on the Canadian border, it was not to protect our nation from our overly polite northern cousins. No. It was built to keep the citizenry from escaping the theocratic death squads. Theocratic is a misnomer.

They started with a pretense to evangelical leanings, but a couple of years in they dropped the whole right-to-life angle and went pure strongarm removal of all civil rights.

Pussy hats. Million Woman March. #MeToo. Blue Wave. It all felt powerful at the time. Now it seemed quaint and dangerously naïve. The AG dropping a warrant for Mueller's arrest was a not-too-subtle hint of where this roller coaster was heading. To be fair, most intellectuals had read or seen Margaret Atwood's *The Handmaid's Tale* and thus were expecting a much more overt takeover.

That wasn't how it played out.

No cool costumes or flashy set-pieces.

America was lost one degree at a time. The frogs in the pot didn't notice when the Feds went after the press. They bitched to their compatriots on social media, but not much more. When the Feds went after brown people—nothing new there—the frogs chanted and wrung their hands. When the Feds created laws that made it dangerous to be female or, worse, to be sexually fluid, the frogs tried civil disobedience. Sit-ins and lockdowns. They failed to see that civil wars are never fought with civility. While they planned and talked and caucused, their once-great country boiled the skin off those frogs.

WHEN ANGEL RAN out of road, she parked her ass on the northern-most bar stool she could find and hoped for freedom by osmosis or proximity. Barring that, she was looking for a soft place to pull the covers over her head and prayed to live undiscovered.

Chandler's Last Stand served a strange mixture of homemade whiskey, craft beers, and walls overflowing with banned books. The bartender was a blacklisted writer who'd traded his keyboard for a speed rail. He was furry and soft, in a mountain-man-with-a-pancake-addiction kinda way. "What you want, sugar lips?" he asked Angel.

"Not to be called sugar lips."

"Fair enough. Ma'am, that better?"

"It's a start. A dark ale would be a good next move."

"Don't have a dark ale. Got Mailer's Malaise, Kerouac's Dream, and Hemingway's Headache on tap."

"Anything with a little less testosterone?"

"I have a few bottles of Plath's Pussy in the back room. Smooth as silk with a hint of a bitter aftertaste. Don't know why it didn't sell."

"Can't imagine." Angel looked around the barroom. It was stocked with a couple of real lumberjacks, some bikers, a mountain man or two. Most bearded, old and missing body parts. Fingers from saws, legs from high-speed motorcycle get-offs. One rather piratical-looking guy had a black leather patch over one eye and a mirrored monocle over the other. "Seems like a way woke crowd."

"Don't judge a book by its . . ." The bartender tried to finish but couldn't. "Oh hell, you're correct. Sad-sack bunch of old-school dudes. They are exactly what they seem to be."

"Refreshing." Angel said. "Out in California, they dress metro, speak feminist, drink daiquiris, and keep their Gucci loafers planted on a gal's neck as hard as anywhere else. Hashtag me too, no shit. Remember that one? Bunch of Hollywood assholes looking shocked and praying they didn't get called out next. Not one of them a good enough actor to make us believe they hadn't known that crap was going on from day one. The only reason D. W. Griffith and the Lumière brothers weren't indicted is because all their victims are dead."

"Angry much?"

"A bit."

"Me too." The bartender lowered his voice, "Ebooks killed the libraries. All they had to do then was shut down the internet. Bam, no more books." He popped the cap off a sweating beer bottle. "Glass?"

"Never." Angel took a deep swallow. It was piney with a hint of wildflowers. It reminded her of a spring day in the Ozarks on a family vacation. Of the smell of dew on a meadow. Of when she had hope.

"Like it?" The bartender asked.

"It'll do to wash away the dust." Better not show too much enthusiasm until she knew what was what and who was who. Let them know what you like and what you don't, and you were just a step away from giving them the tools needed to lock you down. She'd headed north for freedom, not a shiny new pair of shackles.

DETECTIVE WINSLOW SMELLED like a Fed. Clean. He obviously had access to a shower and deodorant. His beard and hair lacked grease. His vintage Sanders T-shirt had holes but zero stains. He was tall and thin, workout thin, not hunger thin. When he chose to sit next to Angel, she swallowed her fear and commanded her sweat glands to shut down production. They didn't listen.

"You okay?" Winslow asked.

"I'm fine, like sparkling wine." She spoke to her own image in the back-bar mirror.

"It has got to be forty-five degrees in here and you're perspiring?"

"I guess I run hot." She dropped it plain, an explanation, not a flirty come-on.

"Must be it. Can I buy you a drink?"

Angel held up her half-full bottle, shaking her head.

Winslow nodded thoughtfully. Stepping off his stool, he made to go, then sat back down.

"Forget something?" she asked.

Winslow caught the furry bartender's eye and motioning to Angel's drink, he held up two fingers. He smiled at her but said nothing until the bottles arrived and he tasted his. "Um, that's rather nice, what is it?"

"Local microbrew," the bartender said, "Called 'Plath's Pussy.'" Winslow neither spit it out nor smirked. He took another sip and nodded his pleasure to the bartender who ambled away.

"Weird name, good beer." Lifting his bottle, he nodded to Angel. She didn't seem to notice his presence. "Did I do something to piss you off?"

"Well . . ." Keeping her gaze forward, she moved her feet so that the barstool seat swung her around until she was staring at him. "Why do you think foisting an unwanted drink on me buys you the right to have me speak to or even acknowledge you?"

"Whoa up. 'Foist'? I was just looking for some casual conversation."

"No, you weren't." Angel felt before she saw the other men in the room tense that she had stepped over the line. No one wanted some loudmouth woman bringing Federal attention to their tiny corner of the world. "Sorry." She forced an easy smile. "My ex left me with an empty bank account and a bad taste for handsome men."

"Handsome?"

She looked him over, then nodded. "Not bad, for a city boy." Angel knew the dance. If she wanted to survive the night, she needed to play coy. Convince Winslow there wasn't a place on Earth she'd rather be than at this bar with him. He was smart though, so she also needed to make him work for her attention.

She was tired of this shit.

She wanted to spit in his face.

Tell him "*Hell yes, I am who you think I am. I did what you think I did.*"

Talk him into her truck. Slip her blade between his ribs and bury it in his heart.

"One more?" Winslow clinked his bottle neck against her empty.

"You attempting to get me drunk?"

"Maybe." The bastard had a disarming smile.

"Good luck with that."

"Really?" Winslow cocked his eyebrow. He ordered two Crumley's Candy-Canes.

Angel dropped a shot of the high-octane peppermint-flavored moonshine. It hit hard. The room blurred for a moment. Golden rule Numero Uno, never get drunk with a man who has the power to have you locked up for the rest of your natural life. The room was getting slippery.

AS A LITTLE GIRL, Angel woke every morning to her momma singing from the Doris Day songbook. The woman had boundless optimism. "The sun is smiling and the birds are all chirping for you, Darleen," her momma would say.

Darleen.

Angel hadn't been called that in forever.

Dar had been her preferred alias.

She was not quite sixteen when the country went to hell.

After the last 'liberal' Supreme Court judge had been forcibly retired, Forty-Five and his crew of old men went at reinterpreting the U.S. Constitution. Roe v. Wade, gone. Women's right to vote, gone. Nonwhite men got three-fifths of a vote, lucky them. 13th Amendment hadn't been repealed yet. All rubber-stamped by the Supreme Court. Nine men in black robes. All members of the woman-haters club. All riding hard on lifetime appointments.

Angel didn't think that was fair . . . because, well, it wasn't. Nothing was.

"WHAT'S THA . . . ?" Detective Winslow asked.

"It's Stringer's Stinger." The bartender set down the cloudy amber drink. "A shot of cheap Scotch floating on a glass of cheaper malt liquor."

"Sounds wonder . . . something . . ."

"It's not. Trick to this drink is lowered expectations."

"Okay, then." Winslow took a healthy pull. To his credit he didn't spit it out. "Want one?" He asked Angel.

"That'd be a hard pass."

"I'd like to make a hard pass at you." Winslow was drunk or playing drunk. Without asking or making any comment, the bartender had switched Angel's beer to Frey's Fake-Out, a nonalcoholic brew. Any slurring on her part was pure theater.

"I'm hungry. You hungry?" Winslow struggled to focus on a chalkboard menu. "You want a BLT? I want a BLT."

"No. I heard they feed cops to the hogs up here." She watched Winslow for a reaction, got none, so she asked the bartender, "That true?"

"Hell, no. Ours are some discerning little piggies."

"Don't eat their own kind?"

"Something like that." The bartender feared upsetting the Fed. "Kidding, just kidding. Two BLTs?"

"Why . . . not." If Winslow registered the threat, he didn't show it. He gazed at Angel, long and deeply.

"What? I have a booger in my nose?"

"No." He touched her nose gently. "You remind me of something . . . one."

Bile backed into Angel's mouth. She stuffed it and the panic down, best she could.

LIFETIME APPOINTMENT. Only one way to remove them.

The first Supreme Court justice was that beer-loving frat boy. He died when his morning jog was cut short by a crossbow bolt.

Second slipped off a subway platform and into an oncoming train.

Third got on the wrong elevator and grabbed the ass of the wrong woman. Darleen pulled up her clear plastic raincoat and slit his throat. She dipped a finger in his blood and wrote—*The angel of death is coming*—on the elevator door.

Members of the underground stopped calling the young revolutionary Dar and started calling her Angel.

"YOU . . . YOU EVER been to D.C.?" Winslow drunkenly closed one eye, squinting the other.

"No. Born and raised in Utah." It was one of the few states she had never been to.

"Big sky country, huh?"

"Montana."

"Whaaat?"

"Montana is big sky country. *Industry* is Utah's motto." She had no idea how she knew that.

"You sure you haven't been to D.C.?" If he wasn't drunk, he could have been an Academy Award–caliber actor, had the Academy still existed. It was shut down the day after Steven Seagal became the Commissar of Filmic Art.

"What makes you so sure I've been in D.C.?"

ANGEL OF DEATH IS COMING—Copycat pink graffiti started appearing all over the capital. Soon it bled across the nation, the message sprayed from coast to coast.

Angel used a car bomb to atomize the pubic-hair-loving fourth Supreme Court judge.

Martial law kept judges Number Five through Nine safe.

National Guardsmen and Secret Service agents on every corner in D.C. convinced Angel it was time to take a permanent road trip north.

The Angel of Death was no longer a woman. She became an icon, a symbol for an idea. A command. A freedom to do what must be done. The mayor of Bakersfield, California, was found trampled to a bloody paste at his slaughterhouse. Written across the side of the abattoir in pink letters ten feet tall was *ANGEL OF DEATH IS HERE.*

It wasn't the only movement. Some cells wrote pamphlets calling for the resumption of elections. Some decried violence as a tool. Some led sit-ins. And some took heads and put them on spikes. Angel felt zero guilt about her part in raising the game to a new bloody level. Feminine warriors, be it the Viking shieldmaidens or the Amazonian archers, had been demoted by history from flesh and blood heroes into fantasies and myths. Angel did her small bit to reclaim the battlefield as one more place women could choose to inhabit.

"SOMETHING IN YOUR eyes, it's . . . it is . . . familiar."

"Okay, sailor. Let's get you to your car." Angel had Winslow's arm over her shoulder. At last call, the bar emptied out in seconds. No man there wanted to be a witness to what the Fed or the hard woman might do to each other. The parking lot was empty save for a Ford Explorer and Angel's battered pickup. Leaning the Fed against his car, she searched his jacket pockets for keys.

"Whoa, I ain't that kinda guy." He tried to laugh but it came out creepy.

"Bet you are." She pushed his key fob and the locks popped open. Depositing him in the passenger seat, she secured his seatbelt and got behind the wheel.

"Where you taking me?"

"My place."

"Nice . . . Where is it?" He asked.

"Not far." Angel turned down a gravel fire road. She stopped on a sandstone bank, overlooking a fast-moving river. The moon cast ominous shadows.

Winslow sat up, sobering too quickly. "What the hell? Where are we?"

"Um." Angel looked out the windshield, "It looks like the end of the road."

Winslow grabbed at his pocket, searching for a pistol that wasn't there.

It was in Angel's palm. "This? Oops." She flipped her hand and the gun went out the window, disappearing into the dark.

Winslow struggled to free his seatbelt, but the clasp had been jammed. "You are the Angel of Death, right?" He relaxed into the inevitable.

"Yes. But you knew that when you walked into the bar."

"No, actually, I didn't."

"Then why'd you follow me in there?"

"Didn't. I was thirsty." He motioned with his thumb. The back of the Explorer was full of camping and fly-fishing gear. "I'm on vacation."

"Then, I guess . . ." Angel looked Winslow over and shrugged. "I'm sorry for what comes next."

Look at the Water, How It Sparkles in the Sun

Seanan McGuire

The swamp doesn't look anything like I expected. Here, no puppeteer has ever set a felt frog on a sunlit log, banjo on its bended knee. Even if someone wanted to try, they'd find themselves facing a severe lack of sunlight, of dry ground, of photogenic butterflies flitting around against a perfect background of weeping willows and Spanish moss.

This swamp is a living, rotting, vibrant thing. The air is fetid, rich with the smell of a thousand kinds of decay . . . but it's also sweet, and as I inhale again and again, I smell distant flowers and good things growing green, their roots reaching deep into the murky water, deep below the matted beds of lilies and creepers. This place is real, and alive, and unforgiving, and here I am, alone, because this is how it has to happen. Over and over again, this is how it has to happen.

They dressed me before they put me in the back of the car, blindfold over my eyes and rope around my wrists, and drove me to the killing ground, pretty painted sacrifice, latest in a long, long line. I didn't fight, not when they took me, and not when they pulled the blindfold from my eyes and left me standing at the edge of the swamp. I've been bound for this since childhood, and I know my part in the production. Go willingly, without complaint, and my family gets compensated beyond their wildest dreams. They get full stomachs and soft beds and roofs that don't leak and cars that don't break down, and they get them for three generations, paid out of the bottomless coffers of the people who understand how the world really works.

There's no such thing as old money or new money. There's just blood money, and the only question is who had to bleed to get it on the ground. Old money has the knives, and new money has the veins, right up by the surface of the skin, where they're easy to find and always, always available for the right price.

My mother asked for my permission to send me here when I was eight years old: middle child of five; "gifted" by the standards of a school system that knew it would never be able to do right by me; and a nerdy little freak by the standards of the other children in our neighborhood, the ones who looked at my outstretched hands and open mouth and didn't see anything but someone weaker than themselves. It was kill or be killed, and not one of us looked like we were going to get out completely innocent. That's not the way the story goes.

"Baby girl," she said, sitting me down on our threadbare couch and folding her hands between her knees, looking at me like I was an adult, like I was someone with the right to have opinions about the world, "I want to know . . . what do you want to be when you grow up?"

"I want to get a good job so I can buy you a nice house and you can be happy, Mama," I replied, and I meant every word, because I was a good girl who loved her mother—I love her still—and because I'd heard her crying at night, the bills spread out in front of her and the future stretching outward like a life sentence, one that didn't come with time off for good behavior.

She laughed, and the laughter turned into a sob before she could catch herself, and she asked, "If I told you that you could make everything good for this family forever, if you'd just agree to take a little walk one day, what would you say?"

I said yes, of course. What little girl wouldn't?

I said yes again when she asked me again at sixteen, when I was angry at the world and crackling with hormones and hatred, when I could barely tell up from down but I could tell that the kids with money were going to get a thousand second chances while I'd be lucky to get one. She told me more about the walk that time, more about what I'd be expected to do and whether she'd ever see me again. I said yes anyway, over and over until she got the hell out of my room and left me to my beautiful, brilliant, curated misery. No one had ever felt anything as intensely as I did, and knowing that I was going to be the sacrificial maiden who solved my family's problems was, well . . .

I guess some people would have felt a little hard-done by that. I guess I probably should have felt hard-done by that. I tried, a few times, and I failed, every time, because everything about it suited my view of the world. I was too smart and too poor and too plain and too trapped, and here was this fairy tale waiting to swoop in and sweep me away. I was going to be a part of a story so much bigger than myself. I was going to fix everything, and all I had to do was take a walk.

The third time she asked me, I was twenty-four, and there were two men with her, one of them I recognized from television, a famous chef who'd come from nothing, just like me, whose sister had died in a flash flood when he was sixteen. He'd dedicated his first cookbook to her, named his first restaurant after her, and there were shadows in his eyes. He looked at me like he was sorry, and I guess that's when I understood this wasn't a fairy tale. This was real life, and whatever I said, the consequences of it were going to exist, no matter how much I might come to regret them later.

Well, I thought, at least there was no way I'd regret them for very long. So I offered those men my hands, and I smiled at them like I was Miss American Human Sacrifice, and I said yes, I said yes, I gave consent every way I could think of, and we all knew that consent under duress didn't count for anything, that none of this would stand up in a court of law, and we all knew that there was no court of law for things like I was committing to do. It didn't matter. It didn't matter at eight, or at sixteen, or at twenty-four, and now I'm thirty-two years old and standing at the edge of a swamp that doesn't look like any swamp I've ever seen before. It looks old. It looks primal.

It looks hungry.

"Leave your shoes at the waterline," they instructed, and so I do, stepping out of them and into the soft mud at the swamp's edge. It squishes between my toes, trying to suck me down. Little creatures are kicked up by the displacement of their murky home, things that dart faster than my eyes can follow, things that writhe and squirm and swim around my ankles. I feel a few of them settle against my skin. Leeches, probably, unable to believe their good fortune.

I worry my wrists together until I work them free of the rope that holds them.

It isn't hard; the men tied me with no expectation that I'd try to escape. I want to lean down and scrape the leeches off. I don't. For one thing, I'm not sure whether it's allowed. For another . . .

The whole point of this is sending me into the swamp to die. My body will be fertilizer for all these wonderful, terrible things, my bones will rest in the muck alongside all the sacrifices who came before me. Maybe someone will find them in a thousand years and write me off as some careless camper who wandered too far from the road, but the swamp will know the truth, and so will I, on whatever spiritual plane is set aside for willing sacrifices. Why shouldn't the leeches have a good meal before I go into the ground? Let them drink their fill. It won't change my ending.

I begin to wade deeper. The water is cold, and my feet quickly kick up so much muck that I can't see the bottom anymore, even before I reach the first patch of water weeds. They give way to cattails, until it feels like I'm wading through solid ground, like I'm already a ghost.

I leave my robe in the cattails. It flaps in the breeze, diaphanous and thin, and I have one less thing to hold me down. This, too, was in the instructions: I'm supposed to shed my clothing as I go, until I'm naked when I reach the heart of the swamp. I'm just glad I won't be anywhere near the road when I get down to my underthings. The last thing I need is to have my sacrifice interrupted by some dude who thinks he can get a date by pulling the naked lady out of the reeds.

The green surrounds me. I don't even notice the smell anymore. It's every-where, so it's nowhere, like water to a fish or air to a bird. This is my home. This is where I've always been going. For thirty-two years I've struggled and saved and supported my mother and my siblings and waited for the day the men would come to carry me away, and now here I am, and here's the swamp, and everything is good, and green, and the water is warm, and I'm still walking.

The water is filled with silt and tangled roots; I don't see the rock I step on, but I feel it, the way it slices through the skin and parts the flesh of my left foot. I yelp in pain and surprise, nearly falling forward into the water, and for some fucked-up reason, the first thing I think is that this is completely unsanitary: I'm going to get an infection.

My second thought is that infections aren't my problem anymore. And now

I'm crying, and bleeding, and standing in the middle of the swamp with leeches on my feet and who knows what else coming in for a taste, and this isn't a fairy tale, this isn't a dream, this isn't something beautiful, this isn't what I wanted, this isn't what I wanted at all—

And the water in front of me begins to roil, like something is being pulled up from the bottom, displacing everything in its way. It almost seems like it's boiling, but there's no heat, no sound, only the water, rising and rising, until something is rising through it, shoulders, broader than mine, covered in shimmering scales in a hundred shades of green, mint and olive and almost-ivory and almost-onyx, and I can't name them all, and—

And then it's standing, the creature is standing, *he's* standing, broad, pale scales on the front of him and dark, ridged scales on the back, hairless head and fishlike mouth and nictating membranes sliding across his eyes every time he blinks, webbed hands with wicked claws and no nose, no ears, bipedal, yes, but not human, never in a million years human, and they never told me there was going to be a monster here, this isn't what I expected—

"Um," I say. My voice is small and shrill and far away. "I've seen *The Shape of Water*. I'm not going to have sex with you, even if that's supposed to be part of the sacrifice. I mean, I'm sort of gay? And also they told me what I was supposed to do, and nowhere on the list was 'let a really impressive fish guy put his reproductive organs against yours.' Sorry. But no. You're going to need a different plan."

He blinks, first one set of eyelids and then the other, and his shoulders shake, and I realize, with slow dismay, that he's laughing at me. This impossible nightmare creature from the not-actually-a-lagoon is *laughing* at me. I pull off my sodden shirt and fling it at him. It hits him in the middle of the chest with a wet *splat* that only makes him laugh harder.

"Hey! This could have been a weird sex thing!" My head feels light, like the air has changed qualities while I was yelling at the living special effect. I guess this sacrifice is really happening. Once you meet your first monster, denial gets a lot harder. "Don't you laugh at me! I could totally have been chosen as the sacrifice for a weird sex thing!"

The monster—my monster—stops laughing and spreads his hands in what I take as an apology. He doesn't look like a special effect, not really. He's too solid for that, too organic, too *messy*. Some of his scales overlap, like ingrown toenails happening all over the body. Some of them are missing. When he bares his teeth at me, there are gaps, places where the thinner teeth have snapped off and broken. He looks like a living thing, like an aberration of science, like the sort of creature that people might decide desired human sacrifices.

But the money is real. I know the money is real. They showed me the first check before they put me in the car, they pressed it into my mother's hands and told her that the compact was sealed. She's never going to want for anything ever again. She's going to be fed and cared for and comfortable until the day she dies, and the same goes for my siblings, and this is all I've ever lived for. I suppose I should be angry about that. I should feel like I've been used, like I've been exploited, like I somehow deserved better, but honestly, all I have is relief. This wasn't a joke. I haven't spent my life waiting for a punchline. I said I'd be their sacrifice, and by God, I'm going to be.

"Okay," I say, and spread my arms. "Take me."

The monster blinks again and makes a querulous noise.

"I'm your sacrifice. Take me. Just, you know, make it quick if you can." I've always known there could be pain. I'm ready for it. If I can minimize it, though, why shouldn't I at least try?

The monster shakes his head and turns away from me, wading deeper into the swamp. I don't know what to do with that. I was chosen, as a child, to be a human sacrifice; I was driven here, as an adult, in a car with no license plates, and left by the side of a swamp with no identification to help whoever finds me get my body home. I'm a girl, half-naked, in a swamp, and now there's a monster, and this should all be so *easy*, this should be *simple*, but he's walking away from me, and this isn't simple at all.

"Hey! Don't walk away while I'm talking to you!" I stumble after him, the water weeds and cattails catching at my legs. My skirt snags on something sturdier, a sunken log or other obstacle, and so I rip it off, wading in the monster's wake wearing nothing but my bra and panties. I should feel exposed, I guess, but everything is veiled beneath my irritation. This was a story, dammit. Stories are supposed to make *sense*.

I barely notice the pain in my foot, I'm so focused on my pursuit of the monster who refuses to kill me. The water deepens reaching my waist, and then the bottom of my ribcage. It starts soaking into my bra, so I peel the bra off and throw it away. It lands in an open patch of water and sinks out of sight, one more piece of my old life stripped away.

The swamp seems to go on forever. It is eternity in murk and moss and unforgiving green, grabbing my ankles, still fighting to keep me where I am. But the monster is ahead of me, and I'm going to see this to the end. The swamp doesn't seem to be fighting him at all. He moves easily, unflinchingly, and it's all I can do to keep him in sight.

When I realize that the water has reached my shoulders, it's too late. It was too late when I stepped off the bank, when the leech settled against my ankle, but up until now, I could at least pretend I could change my mind, that I could turn around and go, if that was what I really wanted. It doesn't matter that I would never in a million years have done it. The fantasy has been enough to get me here, and now it's gone, and this is real, I am a real woman following a real monster into a real swamp. He's not going to turn into a handsome prince. He's not going to smile and say that I've passed his inscrutable test, I get to go home with the money and the peace of mind and never come back here again.

I'm going to die.

Somehow, that's reassuring; if I'm going to die, I can at least do it gracefully. I never thought of this as suicide. It's always been sacrifice, all the way back to the day when my mother asked me how much I was willing to do for my family. It's always been a destination, and now I'm almost there, and it's enough that I came of my own free will, it's enough that I knew what I was doing.

The monster's head vanishes beneath the water. I take a deep breath and duck under, eyes open, following him.

The muck burns my eyes for a moment, and then the burning passes, and between one blink and the next, the water seems to clear, becoming almost crystalline. The monster is ahead of me, swimming smoothly, his legs together and his arms flat by his sides. He swims like an alligator, like something born to this environment. I feel thick and clumsy as I flail to follow, until I find my rhythm, until I press my legs together and kick and kick and slide through the water like a knife, so smooth, so easy.

He swims, and I follow, and my lungs don't ache, and maybe I'm already dead; maybe the afterlife that follows a sacrifice is chasing a monster into the dark forever and ever, until the end of time. I don't mind as much as I always thought I would. The water is cool, and comforting, and safe. I'm safe here.

Then hands reach up from the muck beneath me and drag me down.

I kick, I thrash, I lose the last of the air from my lungs and take a great breath of swamp water. I don't drown. I don't drown, and the reality of that is enough to stun me to a stop. The hands keep pulling, until I'm passing through the muck, until the water is gone, until I tumble into a muddy hole in the ground. The walls are slick. The floor is the same. Everywhere around me there are bodies, bodies like my monster, tangled together like a nest of eels.

"Welcome," says one, extending a webbed hand toward my face in greeting. "Welcome, welcome, welcome."

I shouldn't be able to see her. There's no light here, beneath the ground.

I should be frightened.

I'm not.

"Where am I?" I ask, and my voice is wrong, too thin and too high and too filled with hissing. I look at my own hand. The webbing between my fingers is bright and new, the color of fresh limes. The shreds of my panties cling to my hips, ripped by my sharp-edged scales.

"Where the sacrifices go," she says, and that makes sense, and it makes no sense at all.

"Why . . . ?"

"We come here when the time is right, and we wait for the one who goes to the water. We help them here, and then we scatter to all the waters of the world." She cups my face, smiling. "You're going to make a difference somewhere. You're going to guard, and you're going to protect, and you're going to see the world made better."

"How is this a sacrifice?"

"Humans killed us once, and now we take their children." She drops her hand away. "We make them over in the image of the protectors once lost. You'll be happy here, if you allow yourself to be. You'll be happy, in the water."

What she's saying should sound impossible, but it sounds so reasonable, so right, that I nod, and close my eyes, and let the bodies of the sacrifices before me fold around me, pulling me deeper into the mud, deeper into the home I have been heading for since I was a little girl.

I hope my mother feels like she got enough when she sold me.

I hope the swamp that calls me will be kind.

An Interview with Beloved Bestselling Author Anne Lamott

Jacqueline Winspear
January 2019

J: When did you know you wanted to be a writer? Was it something you just assumed from an early age, or was there a definite decision and declaration at some point?

A: I always kind-of-sort-of knew. My parents were atheists but we devoutedly worshipped the written word. We went to the library every Thursday night as a family and stocked up spiritually for a week, and I really wanted to be one of these worshipped storytellers when I grew up. Plus, I seemed to have some sort of gift for it, for telling the stories of my family and comrades—starting in schoolyards. I was always the kid who could help explain to other kids what we had all just seen, or gone through together, and what to make of it. I always wrote. At 18, after a year of college on the East Coast, I announced I was dropping out after my sophomore year to pursue a career as a writer, so that was that. (Making a living at it was another story . . . .)

J: What is your routine when you write?

A: My dad was a writer, and taught me that writing was about habit, not inspiration. So when I am writing, I sit down at the exact same time every morning, as early as possible. I am *much* smarter in the early morning, before the world and Internet get their mitts on me. I use bribes and threats to get myself to write one passage, badly—*Scribble Scribble,* as Nora Ephron wrote. Then I will often go back and write a slightly less awful draft of that passage, and then if there is time, lurch forward into one more passage or section. The best bribe is that if I write the passage, or for an hour or whatever, I get to stop and watch MSNBC for 15 minutes (with a cup of tea, or the random Fun-Size Snickers bar). The threat involves me making my sternest face, and getting out my imaginary Christopher Robin pop-gun, holding it to my head, and saying, "We *are* going to write this scene today."

J: You've written fiction, nonfiction, memoir, and essays . . . do you consciously tailor the type of writing to the subject or does it emerge organically?

A: Not really. I notice what I am obsessed with, and what the people I am close to are obsessed with, and I start wanting to address that for us all. For instance, I started *Stitches* the day after the massacre of children at Sandy Hook, because we were all in the deepest stunned grief that could ever be. People experience this horror after they have lost a wife, a child, their health, their livelihood, and I wanted to see if I could help with a short book on where we even *begin* the healing. I get these ideas for a piece or a collection seemingly out of the blue, like a tug on the sleeve of my soul's shirt, because I need to immerse myself in that subject—mercy, or hope, or writing. I always told my writing students to write what they would like to come upon, and this guides me, too.

J: You've often been called "The People's Author" . . . what does that mean to you, and how has it impacted what and how you write?

A: It's so sweet! Maybe it's because I am such a Nana to my audience. I want people to know that we are all pretty much the same inside. We all know from loneliness and despair and the fear that we are frauds, and when I share my details of those very human experiences, it gives people a lift, that they are not uniquely screwed up and doomed. We're all in the same boat! Let's stick together!

J: You've stated, "Books are medicine" . . . right now, in the era of Trump, what kind of medicine would you prescribe?

A: Truth and compassion, self-forgiveness and great art, precious community, attitudes of mercy and gratitude (and of *course* pets) are the medicine that will save us. This has been true since humankind has been here, and I believe, always will be.

J: You've written at length about mental illness and the effect it has on a family. There are those who are of the opinion that this country—if not the entire world—is in the throes of a mental breakdown at the present time. What do you think we can do to help this extended family?

A: See above—that's the medicine. The Persian mystic Rumi said that through love, all pain will turn to medicine.

J: Your passion for your faith and your ability to write so eloquently from a place of deep belief have been balm for thousands of readers around the world. For the reader, there is a sense of feeling safe the moment the book is opened and your words begin to weave a warm cloak of connection around the shoulders. Can you tell us what it means to be a follower of Jesus and a feminist—especially given that God has been masculine for about 2000 years, and prior to that point the feminine was worshipped in cultures around the world for 20,000 years? (Personally, I don't think the two are mutually exclusive. I'm pretty sure Jesus was a feminist!)

A: Well, I would need to write a whole book about this—and have dealt with it extensively in every spiritual book I've written, so I'll just add that Jesus surrounded himself with women. His best friend was a woman. In the Jesus stories where he is radicalized in his thinking, it is almost always in the company of women—think of the desperate Samaritan woman with her Mother Strength, who stands up to him—she persisted! And he sees that his ministry of Love is to *all* people. I found actual Salvation with a capital S in the women's movement when I was 16. That is when I was Reborn. Then I converted to Christianity when I was 31. And the message of both paths is pretty much the same: I am loved and chosen, safe in my previous communities, here on earth to be who I was born to be—not in man's image, but in the image of the Divinity, which equally includes Mother Mary, Quan Yin, and of course, Bette Midler.

J: Your most recent book, *Almost Everything*, is so deeply honest about our current "predicament" and yet as you write, it is as if the sun is breaking through the clouds. I love the image of stockpiling antibiotics while waiting for paperwhites to blossom, which is a perfect metaphor for the book. What can your readers look forward to next, Anne? I know they're waiting anxiously!

A: Oh my God, I don't have a *clue*. I live by the slogan that more will be revealed. I am taking notes about life, and love and especially our collective societal uprising against Trump. But also the Rising Up inside each of us, which getting a bit older facilitates. I will have to get back to you on this.

J: And finally—your favorite "nasty women?"

A: Pippi Longstocking, Gertrude Stein, and Jo March.

Down Girl

Rachel Howzell Hall

1

THIS ANIMAL SHELTER in Los Angeles exists on a dead-end street alongside lifeless houses and dying trees. Someone painted our building turquoise, usually a cheerful color. Summer resorts. Seaside villas. I used to think of those things anytime I saw turquoise. Not anymore. There's nothing cheerful or relaxing at a shelter. Especially on a Monday, two hours before noon. The worst time for a mutt.

Lady sits up in her cage for me like she does every morning. I scratch her ears, give her a treat. Back on my first day here, Alvin—a kindly, slow-thinking black man who never frowned despite having worked *here* for fifteen years—used to say, "Mackenzie, don't ever get attached to these animals. You'll go crazy if you do."

The bell over the entrance dings. The dogs bark. Freedom for one of them.

Seth and Aurora have visited three times before to adopt—they've left empty-handed each time. They are young and white. Porkpie hat, distressed jeans, and Elvis Costello glasses for him; sundress, red lips, and pale skin for her, do-gooder perfect with their hipster accessories and Feel the Bern vibe. Ignoring Lady the mutt altogether, they head over to Tucker, a German shepherd: the dog that represents The Establishment and fascism. Aren't hipsters supposed to like dogs that are outside the mainstream? Aren't they supposed to embrace the quirk? #Diversity?

"What about him?" Seth peers at the dog's identification card. "Honey, his name's Tucker."

Aurora points at my chest. "Ooh. I *adore* your shirt."

"Thanks." I gaze at my shirt's block letters. DOG LIVES MATTER.

I don't like these people. Aurora and Seth look like they were born in Iowa, then relocated to "Cali" and bought their Angeleno cred on Etsy. I'm white but I'm not *this* kind of white. I wouldn't let them have Lady now even if they wanted to be her forever family. They are collectors with enough good shit in their lives—a convertible 1975 Dart, heirloom brooches, and straw purses.

Aurora peers at me. "You look *so* familiar."

She says this every visit.

And I say (again), "I've heard that before." Jennifer Aniston drawn by Picasso. Left eye a little higher than the right. Nose not broken but still zigzaggy down its ridge. A cheap jigsaw puzzle of a face with pieces that technically fit but somehow . . . *don't*. Yes, I've heard that before, and I hate hearing it from *this* woman, and now the roots of my not-Rachel hair prickle and I want to pull out every limp strand and . . .

Yes. I'd rather Lady die.

2

MY DRIVE HOME takes over an hour. Sixty minutes of watching zombies in their cars pick their noses and talk on cell phones. None of them have any idea, nor do they care about Lady's final hours alive.

Me? I'm woke. Being "woke" is adopting the mutt. Moving into an urban neighborhood and sharing all that you know with people who never met a white person. Being "woke" isn't a costume like Seth's dorky hat or Aurora's sundress. Being woke is like . . . pouring oil into your mouth, then setting your face on fire every day. The pain is unbearable but beautiful.

By the time I pull into our garage, the sun is sitting directly above our house in the Hollywood Hills. Our new Mexican gardeners are trimming the rosebushes that take up our sidewalk. The sun carves a trail across the sky. Music drifts from one of the houses, and heat waves shimmer above the parched chaparral.

All sound drops into the high grass like a set of keys, never to be seen again. If I look at it too long, the brush will combust and burn us all down. And so I look. But nothing happens. Nothing ever happens. So much brush—you can leave all kinds of shit in the chaparral. And anything you leave, the mountain lions gladly take.

My mother, Judith, sits at her desk in her bright, cluttered scrapbooking room. Dressed in a pink SCRAPBOOKING IS CHEAPER THAN THERAPY hoodie and a bedazzled trucker hat over her platinum blonde bob, she looks like she's sitting on top of a Rose Parade float. A lit Virginia Slim lives between her sticky, manicured fingers.

At twenty-two, she married shaggy-haired, blue-eyed Carter Fordham, an up-and-coming film director with family money to burn. Tobacco. Literally money to burn. Daddy directed blockbuster movies in the seventies and early eighties and made enough money to buy this house in the hills, with an editing room in the basement and Mom's scrapbooking room that overlooks the canyon, a room filled with sparkly bullshit and a mini-crystal chandelier to light it all up.

Mom peers at me over the tops of her glasses. "How was the pound today?"

"Shelter. Awful like always." I linger at the room's threshold, avoiding bric-a-brac and googly eyes that always stick to my sneakers.

Aunt Trudy marches down the hallway with a 7 Up can in one hand and a plate of cheese in the other. She's not my biological aunt—she's black—just my mother's best friend. "How was the pound?"

"Shelter."

"Don't care. Just being polite."

Mom says, "Denver's coming to do your makeup tonight."

Excitement skitters in my belly. Aunt Trudy's daughter is Naomi Campbell tall, as colorful as RuPaul, and smells like cinnamon. It's obvious from her Instagram that I'm her only white friend.

Not that race matters.

I don't see color.

I see *humans*.

3

TONIGHT, WE ARE attending a fundraising gala to honor rich Hollywood types who have done the absolute minimum to protect the First Amendment.

The blue lace dress I'm wearing matches my mood: dark, itchy. It's a little after five as fog crawls over the hills. The sound of rushing blood fills my ears, and there's so much pressure in my head that I can barely hear. I want to cry but I can't, so instead I glare out the living room window at the city that sucks.

Denver isn't here.

"Mac," Aunt Trudy says now, "you gon' be okay?"

"Oh, Mackie." Mom click-clacks over to me in silver kitten-heels and a span-gled blue-and-pink cocktail dress. "Mackie, don't worry. I'll do your makeup." She reaches to touch my face.

My scalp tightens as I dodge my mother's pasty, anemic hand.

Aunt Trudy trundles over to me and squeezes my wrist. "Don't worry, honey. *I'll* do your makeup." Then she smiles, and her strong and perfect white teeth glow against her dark skin.

4

THE BALLROOM OF the Beverly Wilshire Hotel sucks the energy I've been hoarding since Aunt Trudy finished my makeup. I now look like Red-Carpet Jennifer Aniston—my blue eyes are sapphires lined with onyx fairy dust and shadowed in the softest dove gray. My lips are pink surprises: shimmery, ladylike. Thanks to my fairy godmother, tonight I am perfect.

Laughter from Table 7 pulls my attention away from my plate of lemon chicken. The guests there are smiling and hopping in their chairs. Eyes half closed, their hands wave. It's like they're at a different party. And then I notice: They're all black.

I look around the ballroom. With just a few exceptions, the blacks are all sitting at Tables 7, 12, and 32. They are Ferraris and Bentleys, while at my table, number 9, we are Chevrolets and Subarus. They are Coltrane and Davis, and we are Lawrence Welk and Kenny G.

If I stay in my seat, I'll scream and cry. And if I scream and cry, Mom will chop off my head in her scrapbooking room high above the city. Then she'll stick golden bows and silk flowers into my still-drying blood.

I mouth *bathroom* to my mother, then retreat to the near-empty lobby. I find a cocktail table that looks out at the hotel's porte cochére. My eyes burn, and I lift my hand to rub them but stop. Foundation, powder, eyeliner, eyeshadow, mascara—all of it's on my face. I can feel the liquid eyeliner melting, having its Cinderella moment and transforming back into caulk.

I mutter, "Shit, shit, shit."

That's when it happens. That's when my life changes.

That's when *she* asks, "Are you okay?"

5

THE HUSKY VOICE belongs to a black woman seated at another cocktail table. She has a sweet smile and a profile like a gazelle's. She tucks a long braid, an escapee from the braided bun atop her head, behind her ear. "Didn't mean to scare you," she says.

"It's okay."

"You look done."

"Done with . . . ?"

"This event. You look like you're ready to go home."

"Oh." I blush. "I *am*."

She stands from the table. "I'm Eleanor, but friends call me Elle."

I also stand. "I'm Mackenzie, but friends call me . . ." *Strange. Crazy. They don't call me.* "They call me Mac."

"Nice to meet you, Mackenzie. Hey, want a drink? My treat." She holds up two drink tickets. "Since we're sitting here."

"Uhh . . . I'm . . ."

"You're what—Twelve-step? Atkins? Jehovah's Witness?"

"Drink. Yes."

Eleanor finds a bartender at a setup near the ballroom's main entryway.

"Your makeup game is on point," Eleanor says, squinting at me. "You're good with a brush. I can't contour at all."

I touch my cheek. "Thank you. You look great, too. Your skin . . . it's so perfect."

Eleanor sips from her glass of red wine. "It's hard finding the best shades for my tone. Some foundations make my skin look ashy."

Ashy?

"And don't get me started with the cosmetics industry. 'Nude,' my ass. Only you guys get to be nude."

We talk about Hollywood and writing, and I tell her that I know Ted, the agent she's trying to woo. She tells me about a talk at the DGA tomorrow night and asks if I want to join her. Yes, I do! Then we skim over Daddy's unsolved murder—my witnessing it, the books about it, the ridiculous documentaries that accuse my mother, me, the Night Stalker, and the Zodiac of being suspects.

Eleanor gasps. "That's awful. You were just a kid, but people thought . . . ?"

My eyes burn with tears. "I loved him and . . . It's still hard to talk about."

Eleanor says, "I'm sorry," then plucks her phone from her handbag. "I'm supposed to meet friends—shit, my battery's dead. You mind getting an Uber for me on your phone? I'll give you cash."

"Sure." I fumble through my purse, reaching past tubs of Ambien and Valium, and the Swiss Army knife that belonged to Daddy. "Here you go." I hand her my iPhone.

Eleanor's finger swipes from screen to screen. "You don't have the app?"

"You can download it. I should probably have it anyway." I don't need a ride service. I drive to the shelter, to the supermarket near my house, and then back home again.

"You'll have to put in your credit card info." She watches as I type in the required fields. Smiles once I hand her back the phone. Eleanor types. "So you said you know that agent? The one reading my pages?"

"Uh-huh. Ted and my father went to film school together."

She hands me the device and two twenty-dollar bills. "I really appreciate it."

I wave away the money. "No, that's okay."

She holds out the cash. "Please take it. I'm not a deadbeat. My car's in the shop so I've been relying on Uber and the kindness of friends. And now I'm using their phones. I know—I suck. Anyway, a car's three minutes away."

I take the money.

"What are you doing now?"

I nod toward the ballroom. "Going back in there, I guess."

She puts her hand on my wrist. "Wanna go dancing instead?"

6

A PINK NEON tongue flicks at me from the top of The Lick Sunset Strip. A mob of young blacks dressed in platform heels and suit pants are milling in the parking lot. It's a different crowd from the one Elle and I just left behind in Beverly Hills.

Inside, Elle waves to a couple sitting in a booth on the other side of the balcony. "There they are!" She takes my hand and leads the way.

"Finally!" A black woman with an auburn Afro slides out of the booth and hugs Elle.

Elle touches my shoulder. "Mackenzie, these are my friends Cecile and Scott."

Cecile and Scott and almost everyone I see sport piercings on eyelids, nostrils, and cheeks. I try not to stare but I can't help it.

A brown-skinned waitress with Pocahontas braids places two champagne flutes before Elle and me, then pours from a bottle of champagne.

Elle lifts her glass. "To old friends and new."

Five minutes later, I'm also bopping in my seat to the beat. I'm cold, so Elle hands me her jacket. Then she tells a great story about the fundraiser in Beverly Hills honoring Burt Saberly.

"Music producer Burt?" Cecile rolls her eyes. "That nigga's a straight sellout."

Scott snorts. "I didn't realize that brotha *was* a nigga, he's so white."

My face burns, and I gaze into my glass.

Cecile laughs. "We're making you uncomfortable using that word?" Three pairs of dark eyes land on me.

My shoulder lifts in a noncommittal shrug. "I don't wanna . . . I just . . ."

"You wanna know why we still say it?" Cecile asks, eyebrow cocked.

"I mean . . ." My nose hurts as though someone has already punched me in the face. "It *is* an offensive word, isn't it? That's what I've been told."

Three pairs of eyes glaze, and then three pairs of lips smile. They've practiced making this synchronized reaction.

"I got a question," Scott asks me. "Since you're here representin'. Why do y'all like runny eggs?"

I laugh. "Runny eggs? You mean, sunny-side up?"

"Yeah."

"Is there any other way to eat them?"

"Scramble that shit *hard*," Cecile says. "And then put some cheese on it."

I grimace. "Can I ask *you* guys a question? Well-done meat, butterflied? Why?"

Cecile and Elle burst into laughter.

"Easy," Scott says. "Cuz niggas like some burnt-ass meat."

My eyebrows scrunch. That word again.

Eleanor squeezes my wrist. "Don't worry, Mackenzie. We're just having fun."

I run my trembling hand through my hair. "I just don't want you guys to think that I'm okay with the N-word. I know: It's an unfair burden, but you have to be the first to stop—"

"Can we not do this in the middle of the fucking Lick tonight?" Scott asks.

Eleanor touches my wrist again. "It's like . . . you know how *you* can call your mother a bitch—"

"I'd never call my mother a bitch."

"Whatever. It's like *you* can use that word to talk about your mom, but *I* can't. It's a privilege. Understand?"

I squint at her. "But *bitch* doesn't have the same negative historical baggage as the N-word. It's a derogatory—"

"We *know*," the trio says.

Eleanor nods. "We're fully aware of the origin story."

"But you still say it."

"Yes."

"Because?"

"Oh, for fuck's sake, really?" Cecile throws up her hands. "Who wants to dance?" She scoots, pushing Scott out of the booth. Pulls down her tiny skirt that looks horrid on her wide hips and ass. Then she grabs Scott's hand and pulls him to the dance floor.

Eleanor and I stay in the booth. Tears burn my eyes. "To be honest: It's also wrong to keep blaming us for something that happened a million years ago. My people weren't slaveholders."

"Your dad's family owned a tobacco plantation."

"Farm."

"*Faaarrrmmm.*" Eleanor chuckles.

"That's what it was. There were chickens, pigs . . . farm things."

"Okay. Sure." She looks at her phone, which should be dead.

Hot tears slip down my cheek. "Didn't mean to ruin your night."

Eleanor keeps her eyes on the phone. "You didn't ruin it."

And I didn't. Five minutes later, we're dancing and laughing. It's all good.

Since she lives on the other side of town with Scott and Cecile, Eleanor tells me to get an Uber home.

I do—a car is three minutes away. "I had fun," I tell her.

Elle says, "Yeah, me, too," then climbs into the back of Scott's Lexus.

At five in the morning, my phone vibrates. *Hey, Mac. It's Eleanor. Here are the details re Ava DuVernay talk. I'll get there around 7:30. Thanks in advance for talking to Ted on my behalf!*

7

AT BREAKFAST, I tell Mom about my fantastic night on the town with Elle.

Our Mexican housekeeper, Abigail, sets a plate of bacon and eggs before me.

"*Gracias*, Abby." Mom returns to gawking at me.

"Why do you look so shocked?" I ask.

"Do I? I'm not trying to be harsh, but sweetie . . . Why would someone like *her* want to hang out with *you*? People are users, that's why. They know we have wealth—"

"Not anymore—"

"You know what I mean. We're still doing better than most. And what we have plenty of are connections to the industry." Mom picks up her fork. "This Eleanor is being nice so that you'll introduce her to Uncle Ted."

Fuck Mom. She has no clue. And I want to see my friend before tonight. If I return her jacket now, I can take her to lunch.

Elle teaches composition at West Los Angeles College. The campus is in Culver City, twenty miles east of my house. The information kiosk guy directs me to a glass building across from a childcare center.

I run since her class ends in ten minutes, then slow as I near the classroom door.

"So what is the relationship between the two paragraphs I just read?"

Elle's voice.

I wait outside for class to end, and soon, she strolls out of the building. She's wearing yellow, a great color on her. Another black woman walks beside her. Short, round, weird twists in her hair like little worms. Medusa.

I follow them, mixing in with a group of girls.

Eleanor and Medusa laugh, chat, lean in close to talk.

Something in me snags like spurs on wool. I hate this Medusa bitch.

The two stop at a coffee cart.

I leave the gaggle of girls and rush over. "Hey, Elle. I brought this since I was in the area . . ." I hold up her jacket.

Both women aren't shocked to see me. "It took you long enough," Medusa says.

"Excuse me?"

Eleanor smiles. "We saw you a long time ago."

Medusa winks at Eleanor. "You got a Single White Female."

I blink. "What's that supposed to mean?"

"It's a movie, Mackenzie." Eleanor sounds tired. "Why are you—?"

"Or maybe *Fatal Attraction*," Medusa says, chuckling.

"Fuck you," I snap. I'd seen *that* movie, and I'd never put an innocent rabbit in a boiling pot of water.

Eleanor takes the jacket. "Thanks for bringing this. I'll talk to you later, okay?"

Back in the Benz, I cry. What Mom said—it's true, isn't it? My stomach cramps as I watch Eleanor and Medusa fix their drinks at the coffee cart. I grab my phone from the passenger seat and send a text. *Hey! Are we meeting inside or outside the DGA? Forgot to ask.*

Over at the cart, Eleanor picks up her phone, reads my text, then places the phone back on the cart.

She isn't texting me back. Why isn't she texting me back?

8

I FOLLOW HER all afternoon. Back to her classroom, down to the rideshare pickup area not far from where I've parked. She climbs into a red Prius that drops her at the mall.

I park in a handicap space and run inside.

She's about to enter Nordstrom Rack.

I need to look as though I'm also shopping, so I buy a shitty scrunchie at a lousy boutique and slink back to Nordstrom Rack. What's the point of this? All I want is to be—

Seen.

She's standing at the purse racks and looks up as I walk past the store window. At first, her eyes flick back to the bag in her hand, but then those eyes lift and grow big.

My eyes also grow big. Not from shock—I knew Eleanor went in—but because I'm caught.

Eleanor smiles and her mouth forms to say, "Hey." She points toward the door.

I head to the entrance.

She stands there, weekender in hand. "Twice in one day, huh? I'm sorry about earlier. Vanessa can be brutal. Why are you here?"

"Shopping therapy. A lot's going on right now, and since I was over here . . ." I try to smile, then point to the bag. "Nice."

She holds it up. "I don't know . . . . It's cute, but not as big as I'd like."

"Yeah, so I texted you."

Eleanor looks inside the bag. "Yeah? When?"

"Earlier today. About the screening."

"I haven't checked my phone."

Liar.

"Yeah." I fake interest in a pink tote. "So, tonight—"

"I can't make it." She gives me a sad face. "Sorry."

I feel those spurs again. My vision wavers and nausea washes over me.

"Yeah," Eleanor says. "Cecile, the friend you met last night? She has a place up in Big Bear, and we're going to drive up."

"*Tonight?*" My voice breaks at the perfect time.

"Last minute, I know."

A teardrop slips down my cheeks. "I'm sorry. I was just looking forward to . . ."

"Oh, I feel awful."

I fake a sniffle and squeeze out another teardrop. "A lot's going on right now. My mom—" *Is on her way to Vegas.* "—is dying and I've been taking care of her and her friend Trudy was coming over tonight to watch her so that I could catch a breath."

Eleanor's eyes soften. "Oh, no."

"Guess I'm gonna have a lot of time to catch my breath this time next week. That's when her oncologist thinks . . ."

Eleanor glances at her watch. "Wanna have an early dinner? There's an Olive Garden . . ."

I would rather eat salt straight from the tub.

"Yum," I say. "I *love* Olive Garden. Their breadsticks are—"

"Da bomb," Elle says.

We giggle.

The bag will do. Two hundred dollars and ten minutes later, Elle and I are sitting at a table in the near-empty Italian restaurant. A bottle of the house red sits near our hands.

"Your car's fixed?" I asked.

"Nope." She sips from her wineglass.

"You rented?"

"A friend dropped me. I'll just call an Uber to get home."

"No. I'll drop you."

"It's okay—"

"It's no problem. Unless you live, like, in Uzbekistan."

"Ha. Just Baldwin Hills."

"Where's that?"

"Three miles east of here. Never heard of it?"

"No."

"A lot of white folks haven't. It's predominantly black. Actually, it's one of the wealthiest black areas in America."

"Why is that so important?"

Elle tears a breadstick in half. "Why is *what* important?"

"That you distinguish that it's a black neighborhood? Why the separation?"

"Because it would be nothing to tout if we didn't put a signifier on it." She winks.

"I guess I just don't see color."

Elle stops chewing. She wipes her fingers on a napkin, then stands. "I need to use the restroom. A lot of coffee today." She leaves her phone and purse on the seat. Friends do that, trust each other with their possessions.

I don't want this to end. I want to learn more about black neighborhoods and makeup and words like *ashy* and *da bomb*. I want to hang out. I want to drink more wine.

How can I get her to stay? I've used the dying-mother card already.

And then it comes to me.

9

BY THE TIME the check comes, Eleanor is yawning. "I am wiped *out*," she says, reaching for her wallet.

I swipe at her hand. "My treat. You got last night, remember?"

She yawns again. "I need a nap—I guess all these carbs and wine made me sleepy."

"Glad I'm driving you home."

My bag is an atom lighter—Ambien was liberated into Elle's wine during her bathroom trip. She drained the rest of her glass when she returned.

She trudges beside me now, glassy-eyed, as we pass the Dairy Queen.

We reach my car in the parking lot.

Eleanor plops into the passenger seat.

"So where am I heading?" I ask.

"2-8-0-6 . . ." Elle's head drops back against the seat.

"Elle? You okay?" I stare at the pulse in the scoop in her neck. I touch it. So soft. I dip my hand into Elle's handbag to find her wallet.

Driver's license. A smiling, pretty Elle with her long hair. Last name Curtis, 280671 Hillcrest Drive. Fifty-six dollars in cash. Twelve-step card. Elle's a drunk.

She's snoring now.

Alive.

I exhale. I didn't use too many this time.

I bend toward her and whisper, "You can stay with me if you'd like."

If she—no, *when* she wakes, will she know that she's been drugged? Will she call the police? She shouldn't have left her wine like that.

The thrumming in my head is louder than Elle's snoring.

I'll explain if she accuses me, acts like I've done something wrong.

She shouldn't have left her wine like that.

10

AS ELLE SLEEPS, I place her brown thumb onto the iPhone's home button. Immediately, the phone screen brightens.

Text messages from Cecile.

What time am I getting u?

Eleanor's eyelids are fluttering. She's gonna wake up soon. My fingers fly across the phone's keyboard.

Ran into a friend and having a drink. Will call you when I get home.

The drive home takes forty minutes. Mom is on her way to Vegas with Aunt Trudy.

I pull into the garage and bustle to the passenger side. I lift Eleanor. She's light but dense, all muscle. I can't carry her down to the basement.

The garage is crammed with boxes, Mom's aging Bentley, and the wheelchair from *Doctor Dollar, Baby*, one of Daddy's films. In that movie, this gold-plated beast belonged to a crippled pimp.

I ease Eleanor into the chair and roll her down to our basement—no stairs, but an Art Deco ramp with walls lined with posters from Daddy's movies. I dump her onto the floor.

Sasha nips at her braids. Malia smells her feet, then growls.

Goosebumps tickle my skin. This plush basement is meant to be cold; Daddy kept his editing equipment here. Mom said he kept it cold so he could see his actresses' nipples.

I leave my sleeping bestie and hurry to the kitchen with Sasha and Malia yapping at my heels.

What if Elle demands to go?

She can't run if she's too sleepy to run.

I grab my bag from the living room floor and pluck out the tub of Ambien. *5 mg. Place tablet under the tongue. Total dose should not exceed 10 mg.*

I crushed two Ambien into Elle's wine back at the Olive Garden. And now, I dump another two tablets into a glass of water and mix it with a straw.

In the fridge, Abigail has left Tupperware marked with sticky notes. Enchiladas, Wednesday. Pozole, Thursday. Tamales, Friday.

I make a ham sandwich and add chips to the plate. I carry the meal on a tray down to the basement. From my back pocket, Elle's phone buzzes with texts from Vanessa and some guy named Drew who "wants dat ass."

"How does it feel now?" I ask the phone screen. "To be ignored cuz she's with her *other* friend?"

"Mackenzie?"

11

THE VOICE—FEMALE, Spanish accent—comes from behind me.

Abigail stands in the doorway. She gapes at Eleanor on the floor.

I force a smile, as though being down here with a sleeping woman is a normal thing. "*Hola*, Abby. *Como estás?*"

"Everything okay?" Her gaze stays on Eleanor.

"Oh, yeah. My friend—we went to dinner earlier. She had a little too much to drink so I bought her here to sleep it off. I didn't want her to get pulled over. You know how police have been treating minorities lately. They'd end up killing her. So . . ." I shrug. "Thank you for the meals. You can go now."

Abigail finally looks at me. The fear in her eyes grows like wildfire. "You call me if you need anything."

She's always there for our family. Always there for me. So faithful. So loyal.

The maid backs away from the door and hustles up the ramp.

Abigail will never betray me. But then, with all this, "*Sí se puede*" shit—it's a good thing, 'yes, we can,' empowerment—the Mexican maid may feel a little *too* empowered. See something, say something.

But nothing's happened, nothing's wrong here. My friend, she's just passed out on the couch from drinking . . .

12

"WHAT . . . WHERE . . . ?"

This time, the voice comes down from the carpet.

Eleanor's eyes, still hooded from the sedative, are open. "What happened?"

I stoop beside her. "You had too much to drink. And when we got to my car, you passed out. I tried to wake you but . . ."

Eleanor's eyes dart this way and that, trying to remember. "But I only had one drink, a glass of red . . ."

"And then another glass of red and then another glass. You kept talking about Drew, but it didn't make sense. So I paid our bill and got you out of there."

Eleanor frowns. "Why didn't you drive me home?"

"I have no idea where you live."

"Why didn't you look at my driver's license?"

"I thought of that but peeking in your bag just felt skeevy to me."

"And bringing me here, wherever this is, didn't feel skeevy?" Razor blades line her words.

"I did what was the best at the time," I say, words hard now. "First of all, I wasn't the one who got drunk and passed out. Second, I could've left you there but—"

Eleanor closes her bloodshot eyes. "Okay, okay, I'm sorry. Crap."

I glare at her. This is what I get, trying to help people.

Eleanor spots the tumbler of water on the coffee table and reaches for it. She also grabs her purse from the foot of the couch and paws through it. "Where's my phone?"

"It's not in there?" I lean forward, pretend to be confused.

"No. Shit. Can you call it?" She shoves her hands between the couch cushions.

"Sure." I won't because what if she wants it to call Cecile or Vanessa or Drew? "My phone's dead, though. Give it fifteen minutes?"

Finally, she sticks the straw in her mouth. Sucks until half of the water is gone. "You think I left it at the Olive Garden?"

"No idea. I didn't see you drop anything, but I was more concerned about you making it to the car." I nod back to the coffee table. "I made you a sandwich."

Eleanor grabs half the sandwich. "Where are we?" She glances around as she chews.

"My parents' place up in San Bernardino."

Eleanor stops in mid-chew. "*What?*"

"You kept saying you needed to go to Big Bear, you had to reach Big Bear, that someone needed you in Big Bear. We have a place in Big Bear, and I wanted you to be here for your trip, so . . . I made the drive. Figured you could go to the store and get supplies and clothes."

Eleanor gapes at me. "You're fucking kidding me."

My smile falters. "Huh?"

"You drove me . . . ?" She slumps some. Her eyelids flutter, and she slowly clambers onto the couch. "Take me."

"Sure. Where am I taking you?"

She cocks her head. "I don't know the address. I need to call."

"Okay," I chirp, standing now. "I can see if my phone is charged enough. You keep resting. I'll close the door—we have a Doberman and he's not used to having visitors. Okay?"

Eleanor lays back on the couch. "'kay."

I pad out of the room, planning to lock the door. But I stop.

The lock keeps people from *entering* but does jack-shit for people *exiting*.

"Fuck. Stupid." I slap myself in the face.

This isn't a problem *now* since Eleanor will be sleep in four minutes.

But I can't keep her sedated forever. Right?

13

I'VE THOUGHT ABOUT it now.

Abigail must go. She'll tattle on me. She's not loyal. She's a bad girl.

I texted her. *Hola, Abby! My friend is allergic to wheat and dairy. And the food you prepared is nothing but. I know you just left but could you come back and whip something up?*

Ellipses. Abby's responding. *The pozole should be fine. I cook for you tomorrow.*

Eleanor won't be here tomorrow. And honestly? The pozole does not taste good. Just being honest. See you soon.

No longer asking. *Telling*. Abigail is *the help*. She *has* no say.

I pluck Eleanor's phone from my back pocket. Three texts since the last time I looked.

Cecile: *A drink? REALLY?? Not cool.*

Cecile: *I hope this isn't becoming a regular thing.*

I'm pissed on behalf of my friend and send a text. *Stop scolding me. I'm not a child.*

These text messages are now bouncing off cell phone towers across Hollywood Hills to whatever aspirational ghetto Cecile now resides in.

I power down Eleanor's phone. Later, I'll have to dump it somewhere.

My phone vibrates—a picture. Mom and Aunt Trudy in pink feather boas in front of Celine Dion's poster.

Headlamps from a car illuminate the living room.

Abigail's back.

I grab the Taser we keep on the fireplace mantel and sit on the couch.

This won't take long.

14

ABIGAIL HAS NO skills other than cleaning, cooking, gardening, sewing, some electrical work, and changing the cars' oil. She was referred to my family by the studio executive who employs Abigail's sister. Daddy gave Abigail a job as our maid.

If it hadn't been for my family, Abigail would be dead in the Sonoran Desert or drowned in the Rio Bravo or making cocaine bundles or whatever. When she first came to America, we gave her shelter in the room by the basement, food left over from cooking for my family, nice mops, and the harshest, most effective cleaning stuff so she doesn't have to scrub hard. Then we employed her cousin Rafael to garden and her younger brother Esteban as a handyman. They didn't even have green cards or visas, but Daddy still gave them work. So, in many ways, Abigail owes me.

"I can make *asada*," Abigail says. "Or fry chicken without flour."

My hands are sweating—the Taser is slippery. "You make good fried chicken."

I slink next to our maid, then hit the zapper. Electricity shoots out from the device and hits her in the back. She jerks and shimmies, crumples to the tile. She jerks some more, then stops moving.

I stare at the maid's wrinkled, peaceful face. Her mouth is open, and gold molars twinkle in the kitchen light.

"Abigail?" I nudge her with my foot.

The maid's glazed eyes stay fixed. The scoop in her neck, where her pulse lives is still. Where her pulse *lived*.

"You owed me." And as I roll the gold wheelchair into the kitchen, I regret that she had witnessed Elle in the basement.

But I couldn't trust her.

I roll her to the patio door.

What now?

I glace around the kitchen.

The best place to stow a body—the hillside near our house—has already been taken. Esteban is there . . . *Or is it Rafael . . . ?* I cannot keep track. My eyes roam the backyard and stop at our raised deck.

There.

15

THE COOL NIGHT air kisses my skin as I push the wheelchair onto the deck. The deck's panels resemble stained wood but they're plastic and they unsnap. Five unsnapped planks later, the empty Jacuzzi reveals itself.

What if she starts to stink?

Well, the canyon already stinks of dead coyotes, the remains of whatever the coyote ate, skunks, the gardener . . .

What's one more rotting thing?

Okay. I'll drive Abigail to the other side of the canyon. I'll take all identifying items from her, maybe file down her fingerprints and dump her. Just another illegal.

"Is that woman dead?"

I whirl around.

Eleanor stands in the patio door, eyes fixed on the wheelchair.

My pulse bursts like a dam. I take a step toward her to close the gap.

"What's going on here?" Eleanor is saying. "I need to know what—"

I thrust the Taser out for the second time tonight.

16

I DON'T OWN HANDCUFFS.

If I were at USC County Hospital, there'd be thousands of those plastic restraints around. They were everywhere—in pans, on counters, in chairs. At County Hospital, those restraints are like peppermints in jars.

Unlike Abigail's, the scoop between Eleanor's clavicles beats. Slowly, yes, but still there. When I tucked Abigail into the trunk of her car, I didn't feel any pulse.

I search through the paper and plastic bags beneath the sink. Dishwashing detergent, steel wool pads, toilet bowl cleaner . . .

How much shit do you need to clean one little house?

Eleanor is still knocked out on the threshold between the patio and kitchen. Malia and Sasha sniff her hair and feet, tug at her braids.

I pull open drawers and cabinet doors.

Bungee cord. It will have to do until I can get rope. I can't leave Eleanor alone, though. I wrap her hands with the cord. Ease off her tennis shoes and pause to look at her toenails. Painted bluish-green, the color of mermaids.

My own toenails are chipped and painted the color of traffic cones. I like Eleanor's color better.

The knots I make with the bungee cord are janky—I'm no Boy Scout. Eleanor will be so confused, though, and untying knots will be her last thought.

She twists as I hurry to finish the third knot. But I can't finish—an explosive stream of pink and beige stuff, ham and breadsticks, erupts from her mouth.

I hop back as vomit splatters the floor and cabinets.

The sound—that splatter, that *grrr* from her belly and throat . . .

And the stink—stomach acids, half-digested food . . .

I cover my mouth as bile burns the back of my throat. I close my eyes as Eleanor slips in the mess, tries to gain leverage with bound hands but just slips and slides. And now her hands, face and chin are covered in vomit.

"Help me," she croaks. "Why are you doing this?"

I keep my hand clamped over my mouth and my eyes squeezed shut.

Why did she have to leave the room?

Why did she have to vomit?

Why is she weeping?

What the fuck is wrong with her?

"Help me," Eleanor says again, softer this time. "Please?"

Please?

The black woman keeps saying that word. She says 'please' as soft as a slug, then shouts it, demanding, as though she's owed help.

And then, she says nothing.

I peek out from behind my hands.

She's staring at me. Vomit is drying on her cheeks and around her lips. Her big eyes are wet and pleading.

"That's better," I say. "I can't think with all that going on."

Eleanor's nostrils flare but she simply nods.

I shake my head. "You're a mess. You need to get cleaned up."

I certainly won't let her use one of the three house showers. There's Abigail's bathroom but it's cramped and not that well-lit and . . .

I hook my hands beneath Eleanor's armpits and pull her back out to the patio. I grab the water hose coiled near the potted ferns.

While I spray her with the hose, Eleanor holds my gaze. She doesn't look away.

I look up at the sky. "I can kill you, you know. I've done it before. I can lock you under the deck, in the Jacuzzi, let you starve to death. You'd die alone. Anything to say?"

A teardrop tumbles down her cheek. "Thank you for keeping me . . . safe. You're a good friend . . . Mac."

"Then why didn't you text me back yesterday? Why did you cancel on me?"

A second tear falls. "Yesterday . . . ? It's Wednesday?"

"Answer my question."

"I didn't see your text."

"And now, you're gonna *lie* to me? I watched you at the coffee cart, right after I texted you. You picked up the phone. I saw you."

Her eyes widen and I can see her breath move up and down more quickly. "I'm sorry. We'll go to another event, okay?"

I spray her again.

17

ELEANOR'S NIPPLES ARE coffee-colored. Darker than her dark skin. Moles speckle her shoulders and the center of her breast bone. And her butt. No. She has an *ass*, the kind I've seen in rap videos.

She turns away from me. "May I have clothes, please?" She drops the wet towel to the deck.

I toss her boxers and a Taylor Swift shirt.

She pulls the shirt over her head. A braid drops onto the deck.

I recoil. "Why did your braid do that?"

"Because my real hair is growing—"

"None of this is your real hair?"

She plucks the braid from the ground. "Indian hair braided in."

I shudder—this is the most repulsive thing I've witnessed all day.

Down in the basement, I tell her to lay on the carpet, hands behind her back. She pauses.

I aim the Taser at her belly. "Down, girl."

She obeys.

"Good girl."

"When will I get to go home?"

"When you're better." I grab the ends of the bungee cord and pull. "How's that?"

"Too tight. My fingers are tingling."

"Good."

"I feel better."

"Not enough to travel."

"I can make it down the mountain."

I start to say, "Hill," but remember that I'd told her that we were high in the San Bernardino Mountains. "No. All that twisting road down the highway, you'd vomit again."

"Give me something to settle my stomach, then."

So bossy. No 'please.' No 'thank you.' No wonder black men date white women.

"If I give you something, will you shut up?"

"Yes."

I lead her back into the kitchen. I order my friend to sit against the trash compactor (can it squash big, bulky items?), then I grab one of Mom's cans of 7 Up from the fridge. I select a plastic tumbler from the cabinet. After pouring soda into the cup, I turn away from my guest and dump two Valium into the soda. It fizzes and dissolves. I turn around—Eleanor's staring at me.

"What did you put in it?" she asks.

"Nothing." I stand over her. "Here."

She reaches for the glass, but swings her feet, crashing into me.

The cup flies out of my hand as I topple to the ground.

Eleanor digs into my pockets. Her phone! She's seen her phone!

I twist away from her.

She tries to swing her legs again, but I roll away. I yank the Taser from my front pocket and aim it at her.

She screams, "No, please don't!"

I grin.

Her eyes bug as one million volts berserk through her body. She thwaps against the floor like a . . . a . . . *catfish.*

18

I CROSS THE threshold of Kitty's Secrets, and step into a land of leather corsets and fruit-flavored condoms. A chubby man wearing a Smashing Pumpkins T-shirt sits behind the register. He holds a battered D.H. Lawrence paperback in one hand and a sweating Popeye's cup in the other.

"Handcuffs?" I ask.

"Aisle 6," he says, then goes back to Lady Chatterley.

The good cuffs cost almost $100. I grab them as this slutty white girl wearing a romper winks at me. "Showing him who's boss, huh?"

"Yeah."

"You should buy a whip. They like that." She beckons me, and I follow her down Aisle 3. Rows of whips, riding crops, and ball gags. "Now, if you're just starting out, just experimenting? I suggest . . ." Her pink-shellacked fingernails stop at a black leather switch. "Not too intimidating. Just a pat here and there for punctuation. Make him your slave, you know?" She hands me the switch. "See? Lighter than it looks."

A minute later, I stride out of Kitty's Secrets with a switch, handcuffs, and a ball gag.

Eleanor talks too much.

19

ELEANOR HASN'T LEFT the basement or the couch. Although she is breathing, she hasn't opened her eyes.

I lock one cuff around her right wrist and the other cuff to the leg of the coffee table. I sit in the armchair with the switch in my hand, with the ball gag on my lap.

Malia and Sasha are sleeping in the corner of the room.

What if Cecile calls the cops? What if Eleanor doesn't wake up? What if she's reported missing?

So?

Adults can disappear if they want.

That's what my defense attorney argued that last time.

Do I want to chance it, though?

"Be right back," I whisper to my sleeping friend.

Yes, I will drive the maid up the hill, leave her in the car, and hike back down.

I turn on the lights in every room, ensuring that the neighbors see that the house looks inhabited. I pull on Nikes, the kind that don't have reflective tape, and then I grab Abigail's purse and keys from the breakfast counter.

In the garage, I aim the remote at Abigail's Toyota. The lights blink. I open the trunk.

A bag of lemons. Mom's dry-cleaning . . .

No body.

No maid.

Abigail's gone.

Shit.

20

STAY CALM.

I push aside the dry-cleaning and the bag of fruit just to make sure the tiny woman didn't roll or whatever during the death process.

No Abigail.

I notice something at the back of the trunk: a green button the size of a can's bottom. Black letters say, PUSH IN CASE OF EMERGENCY.

That sneaky bitch.

I slam down the trunk door. I look under the car, in the box of old Christmas decorations, inside the full-size freezer. No Abigail. I take a 9-iron from Daddy's old golf set and slam it into the windshield of the Mexican woman's car.

A scream catches me in mid-swing. Hysterical shrieks that can be heard all the way in the garage.

Still holding the golf club, I dash through the living room and down to the basement toward those high-pitched, bloodcurdling screams.

Elle is twisting against the handcuffs as though she's on fire.

"What's wrong?" I ask.

Her face is covered in sweat. Her (my) shirt is sweat drenched and clings to her skin.

"Eleanor," I shout. "Shut up or—"

She keeps screaming.

I pull the Taser from my pocket and hit the button. The sizzle of electricity cuts above her cries. "You want this again?"

Eleanor's thrashing slows as sobs rack her body.

"Calm down."

"I want—" *Sob.* "I wanna—" *Hiccup.* "Go ho-ho-home."

She looks a mess, all that snot and those swollen eyelids. No longer the noble queen. Just another black girl with raggedy braids.

"Be quiet," I say, "and I'll let you *live.*"

Not 'go.' Not this time.

And Eleanor notices, too. Her swollen eyes take me in, and her mouth hangs open. There it is. Submission. Finally.

Elle sighs, hiccups, eyes on the carpet.

"I made dinner. Pozole. Your screaming took me away from preparing that for you." When she doesn't respond, I frown. "Aren't you gonna say—?"

"Thank you," she rasps.

I run back to the kitchen, grab the pozole from the fridge. Zap it in the microwave, then hurry back to the basement. "You look too sad to be having homemade pozole brought to you."

"This is my last meal," Elle says. "You just said that I'm gonna die."

"I said no such thing." I kneel in front of her with the container in one hand and a spoon in the other. "You're my friend, Elle." I feed her like she's a baby or an invalid. In-VAL-id. "I didn't want to do any of this. It just happened so quickly before I had time to think." I squint at her. "You haven't said it yet."

"Haven't said *what*?"

" 'If you let me go, I won't say anything to anyone.' People usually say that."

"Which people?"

I scoop up some veggies and hold out the spoon. "The people on TV and in the movies. My other friend said it, too."

"Other . . . friend?"

"Gloria."

"What happened to Gloria?"

"You should eat," I nod at the spoon. "This shit's nasty when it's cold."

"What happened to Gloria?" Elle asks again, firmer.

I can't stay and talk like she wants me to. I still need to find Abigail—

The doorbell rings.

21

I POINT TO Eleanor. "You say a word and you die. Understand?"

Eyes hard, she nods.

I shuffle out of the basement and shout, "Coming!" as I run to the door. I glance at my reflection in the foyer window—my hair is all over my head. There's a scratch on my cheek. How did that . . . ? Can't do anything about it now.

I take a deep breath, then pull open the door.

A cop fills the doorway. He's holding Sasha. What the *fuck*?

"You found my dog!" I reach for the pooch. "So glad she has her tags."

"Is everything okay, Miss?" The silver badge on his shirt pocket says BERING-ER. He has iceberg-blue eyes and a chiseled face.

"Now it is." I nuzzle my puppy. "I was cleaning up, and I opened the door and this pretty girl got out. Thanks so much for bringing her home." I start to close the door, but Officer Beringer stops the motion with his large hand.

"I got a call," he says, "that someone needs help?"

"Not at this house."

He holds up one of Eleanor's braids. "The dog had this in her mouth."

My bowels loosen and I almost shit myself.

"It obviously doesn't belong to you," he says. "May I look around?"

"They bring home all kinds of random . . . No one's here except me."

"Yeah?" He twirls the braid. "May I have a look?"

I step aside, then drop the dog.

Sasha yelps, then darts to the kitchen.

The cop's flashlight beam plays against the Pollocks and the Ruschas in the living room and dining room.

"Who was this caller?" I follow him, fingering the Taser shoved into my jeans pocket.

"A woman is missing." He toes the still-wet spots on the kitchen floor. "She has that 'Find my Friends' app on her phone. And for some reason . . ." He plucks another braid from beneath the fridge. "Wow. Someone's coming undone."

I stare at the braid. "They're old and they come off when they're old."

"Your friend?"

I nod. "She's black. She was here earlier but she left a while ago."

"What is 'a while ago'?" His eyes scan the breakfast counter.

"Around six. She said she was driving to Big Bear to meet a friend or something."

He wanders to the powder room. Peeks under the bed in my room, then Mom's room. His police radio crackles as he makes his way back to the foyer. He bends his head to the shoulder radio and presses a button. "No one's here. Disregard." To me, he says, "If you hear from your friend, ask her to check in with her family as soon as possible."

After he leaves, I storm into Daddy's room with Eleanor's phone clutched in my hand. "Why didn't you tell me?"

Eleanor doesn't speak.

I discover FIND FRIENDS on her phone and disable it. Then, I delete FIND MY IPHONE. Back in the living room, I turn the phone on and shove it down into the couch cushions.

Officer Beringer is still sitting in his patrol car. He rolls down the passenger window as I approach.

"Hi. Me again," I say. "Maybe she left her phone here. Try calling her number."

He follows me back into the house, then pulls out his own phone. He taps something, then says into the phone, "Tell Cecile to try calling again."

That bitch.

The phone's vibrations push against the couch cushions.

"Wait," he says to the person on the other end. "I hear something." He turns toward the couch, steps closer, listens . . . Then, he slips his hand into the cushion and plucks out the phone. "Found it." He listens . . . shakes his head. "But she's not here . . . I looked . . ." He gazes at me. "She says she left for Big Bear around six . . . Okay." He ends the call.

I clutch my neck. "Is everything okay? Should I be worried?"

He slips his phone into his shirt pocket. "A friend says she's been acting strange. Been drinking a lot lately, and she hasn't spoken to her since yesterday. We'll find her, though."

"Should I keep her phone? In case she realizes she's forgotten it and drives back?"

He shakes his head. "I'll make sure her friend gets it."

"*I'm* her friend, too."

He says, "Okay," but doesn't hand me the phone.

Twenty minutes—that's how long I stand in the foyer after Officer Beringer leaves. I stand as still as a speck of dust. Just to be sure that he's gone. Then, I turn off all the lights in the house.

22

MALIA'S BARKS PULL me back to the present. Sasha, another braid in her mouth, watches her sister bark at the front door, barking as though someone is standing there.

I look out the peephole.

No one is there.

I open the door.

The night's cool air drifts past me like a ghost.

Malia and Sasha scoot past me, and run into the night.

I shout, "Get back here, you fuckers." I whistle for the dogs, but those bitches don't return. "Let the hawks get you then." I slam the door, then pat my pockets.

The Taser.

I don't have the Taser.

Am I losing my mind?

"Again?" That makes me chuckle.

"This is serious," I say.

First the maid, and now . . .

I run back to the basement.

Eleanor is finishing the pozole.

I look under the coffee table.

She pauses between bites of soup. "What's wrong?"

"Stand up."

"I'm eating."

"Stand. Up." My face feels lava-hot and by the way Eleanor's face twists, I must look awful.

"I can't stand," she says. "I'm handcuffed to the fucking leg of the table."

"Then, scooch over."

She does.

Nothing but grains of rice and chunks of cooked carrots.

I swipe at the litter. "You're making a mess." I shove her.

The bowl of soup topples from her lap to the floor.

"See what you did?" I slap Eleanor across the face as a sob erupts from my own body.

She keeps eyes closed and her face turned. No whimpers break from her lips.

I slap her again.

Not a sound.

Eleanor's mouth is a tight line. Her eyes are squeezed shut.

Another hit, this time with my closed fist on that bitch's ear.

Nothing.

In tears, I cry out, "Why are you making me do this to you?" Another hit. Another 'why?'

Through it all, Eleanor sits, eyes closed, even as welts and bruises form around her face.

My arms grow tired from all the beating, all the crying, all the anxiety of the last two days. I collapse atop Eleanor in a heap of sobs. I just wanted a friend. I just wanted to share my life with someone who needed me, who needed to be rescued, who needed to see that there was a better life, a better way.

Eleanor's body isn't soft or welcoming. It's rigid. Muscular. Manly.

I don't want to be like her. What was I thinking? She's so stubborn, too stupid to live . . . Untrainable. Elle isn't like Lady at all.

And what do you do to dogs that no one wants?

I sit up and whisper, "Put her to sleep." I whisper that again into Eleanor's manly shoulder. My head is pounding. My sinuses are clogged. My mind twists and crinkles. "Put her down."

Eleanor still hasn't moved out of her clenched state.

I stand over her. "You're no good for any other owner. I'm sorry." I trudge out of the basement, not seeing the fallen braids or the Pollocks or anything. In the garage, I find the shovel hidden behind the Christmas ornaments. It's heavy but not as heavy as the last time . . .

The Jacuzzi will have to do.

23

AND IF THEY find Eleanor here, so what? They won't send me to jail. Just back to the county hospital or some other psychiatric facility. I'll get meds, nice meals, my own room with a television and jigsaw puzzles of waterfalls.

With tears in my eyes, I stomp back to the basement.

Lady had been my friend, the only one who'd loved me for me. She'd never taken advantage of my wealth or my . . . *vulnerabilities*. She yapped happily every time I approached her cage. Not Eleanor. She's still clenched in her brown ball, still wearing my clothes, still eating my food, still sitting on my carpet. Is anything *hers*? Has she earned any of this? Take, take, take. Free stuff. They all want free stuff.

Well, my benevolence is over.

"You wanna say anything before you go?" I stand over her, shovel held across my stomach.

"No."

"You made me do this. We were friends. We were close and you . . . You disappoint me. You're no different from the rest of them."

No response from her.

My anger twists through me like it twisted that night with Daddy, and I grip the shovel handle tighter. Lift it over my head.

Eleanor sticks out her hand—the hand now holding the Taser. *My* Taser.

Electricity travels up my arms, my shoulders and . . . and I want to scream, 'Stop!' but the words won't fall from my tongue.

Eleanor's mouth lifts into a smile. She's enjoying this. Depraved bitch.

Finally, thankfully, I collapse to the carpet. The shovel gets there first, and the pointy end jabs into my forehead. Blood flows into my left eye and I try to move my legs. But I can't move my legs.

A tug. Someone is tugging at me.

Abigail is standing over me.

I smile at the old woman and try to say, "Abby," but my tongue still refuses to work.

"Found it." Abigail holds up the key to the handcuffs.

I blink.

Abigail is gone.

I crane my head to look to my left.

The maid is freeing Eleanor from the handcuffs.

Eleanor's gaze is trained on me. That triumphant smirk, the haughty, uppity eyes . . .

Still untrainable. Still unlovable.

Eleanor holds out the Taser again.

Another zap of electricity sends me squirming across the carpet. My teeth click against each other until they crack. My shorts feel wet and the smell of urine fills my nostrils. Daddy smelled the same way on the night that I . . .

Eleanor's standing over me now, Taser poised, my phone to her thick lips.

A woman's voice says, "9-1-1, what's your emergency?"

Eleanor says, "I want to report a kidnapping . . . Mine."

After

PATROL OFFICER DELVECCHIO, tasked with sealing off the scene with yellow tape, glares at the black girl sitting in the ambulance. Standing at the end of the block, he sees that she looks okay. An ambulance has already taken the Mexican grandma to the hospital. Either woman will say anything to avoid jail or being sent back to Mexico.

The frail white woman is barely clinging to life. Her face is a bloody mess, and . . . . Wow. She looks like his favorite actress on *Friends*. The one who played Rachel.

"I hope they fuckin' fry these bitches," he mutters to his partner, Abrams.

"You see what they did to her?" Abrams's eyes flick from Eleanor Curtis to Mackenzie Fordham. "It's fucked up what they did to that little white girl."

"They're animals. Fucking animals."

A Little off the Top

Angel Luis Colón

His name was like a curse on the appointment book: *Carlos Z.—2:45 PM* in thick red ink.

Paula read it three times in a row, willing the words to change to a different name. Maybe the receptionist misheard. Maybe it was a holdover from last month and the appointment was never confirmed.

"Is this asshole really coming in today?" Paula asked out loud.

Rosie, the desk girl, adjusted her seat and grimaced. "Sorry. He called yesterday. Light month means we had the room for him. Even with me lying about the time."

Light month. That was putting it nicely. In ten years of working at the salon, Paula had never seen a drought of customers quite like this. It was the height of the summer, the perfect time for people to come pouring in for haircuts and dye-jobs . . . but nothing. Money was tight for everyone, but money was extra tight for beauticians since they depended on folk with cash to burn. Extra cash meant bigger tips and more opportunities to upsell a client on fancy shampoo or conditioner.

Paula made a shit commission for services rendered. She depended on the extras to pay tuition for her kid's school and to keep herself looking like a professional. Nobody was going to trust a frumpy woman to tell them how to style their hair or do their makeup.

The dry spells meant desperation, which meant catering to the more annoying regulars among her customers. If it were busier, she could have Rosie call

Carlos and reschedule a few times. 'No hard feelings, things are crazy, so sorry this keeps happening,' but that wasn't possible.

Paula went to the bathroom and caught a glimpse of what she was wearing in the mirror. She was decked out. Tight blouse, tight jeans. Mile-high heels. Of all the days, she thought, to dress like this, it had to be when this asshole was penciled in.

It wasn't that Carlos was outright mean—no, he was something else.

He was a lawyer in the city, a real power player. Drove a fancy new Jaguar and wore crisp, tailored suits that were probably worth more than Paula's furniture. Beyond the façade, Carlos was, simply put, an asshole. He leered at the younger girls in the salon. Acted as if he was too good for the music, the smells, or some of the chattier clientele. He also had the most miserable habit on planet Earth when it came to Paula: He graded her haircuts.

Every single time he judged her. When Carlos crashed to sleep throughout the haircut, or when Paula slipped the cape from around his neck—it was time for the assessment, despite her cleaning the back of his neck with her expensive horse-hair brush.

Carlos would lean forward and cock his head to the side. He'd scan his struggling hairline and then glance at Paula's reflection as she struggled to angle a hand mirror to give the perfect view of the back of Carlos's head. The bastard would lick his lips, lean back, make a big show of cleaning any errant hair from his dress shirt, and say, "This was okay. You get a 'B' today, Paula," or "Not your best effort, a 'D'."

The grade corresponded with the amount Carlos would tip. A 'B' normally meant ten or twenty bucks. Anything less was worth five bucks if Paula caught Carlos on a nice day. It was a demeaning system, and Paula wished she knew the logic behind it. Carlos never made a single advance on her; he never implied in conversation that he wanted anything more than the relationship between hairdresser and customer. There was a glimmer in his eye whenever he provided the grade too, as if the pressure and demeaning nature of his little game was the highlight of his day. The more she flinched at his behavior, the more it egged him on. The suffering got him off, Paula reasoned; he wasn't there for the haircut, but for the power trip.

Still, he was a customer, no matter how much he was hated.

And it wasn't that Paula ate the humiliation on purpose. She tried to keep Carlos from coming—aiming to get an 'F' or purposely taking a day off when he would schedule ahead of time. She referred other hairdressers to him and even argued with him once to dredge up the whole 'I need to speak to your manager' situation. Nothing worked. The bastard was focused on making her suffer through his haircuts, as if he had a vendetta against her from a past life.

There wasn't any other work, Paula thought. It was vacation season, so walk-in clients were going to be rare and fought over by the other girls in the salon. She was trapped in the corner. She needed something to go home with, something to buy dinner with. Twenty bucks could go a long way to making her night a better one, but Carlos's strange rules were going to be in the way. Paula poured some extra coffee, double-checked her makeup, and decided this motherfucker was going to get the best damn haircut of his life.

CARLOS SHOWED UP a half hour late, interrupting Paula's lunch, because of course he would. He parked his Jaguar in a spot reserved for the disabled and nearly skipped to the door, walking in as if he were the king of strip-mall hair salons.

"It's okay, finish up," Carlos said as he sat across from her with a tight smile.

Paula ate her lunch with haste. Carlos watched the whole time, his eyes darting from her paper plate to her sandwich. He didn't speak but gave the impression he was at the edge of starting a sentence. It made Paula nervous, and she leaned forward between bites to cover her mouth with a napkin while she chewed. She felt pressured to finish quickly and nearly choked a few times. She cleared her throat instead of coughing to avoid any extra attention. Paula wished the salon was busy. At least then the sound of hair dryers and voices would drown everything out.

"You ready?" Carlos stood as Paula shoved the last of her sandwich into her mouth.

Paula motioned to the shampooing station behind Carlos and spoke with her mouth full. She took a sip of soda and tried to avoid eye contact with Carlos as he grimaced.

"I'm doing well, and you?" he said sarcastically as he walked over to get his hair shampooed. "New girl?" he asked, motioning with his head to the girl waiting by the sink.

Santina, the shampoo girl, had been with the salon for a year and a half. She was nearly ready to start cutting hair. She always washed Carlos. He never tipped her well and he never remembered her face.

Paula wondered what it was about the man that made him so cruel towards everyone in the salon. Did he feel a sense of superiority? Was he attracted to someone there and acted out because of his insecurity? Maybe he had an ex that was a beautician, and this was how he got his petty, coward's revenge . . .

None of that mattered, though. She hated him. She hated him with every ounce of her soul. Hated him in ways only lovers hated each other. Her hands trembled. Paula rubbed the flesh between her thumb and pointer finger on each hand—she had read this was supposed to help relax people in a pinch—and stood up. She quickly prepared her station, laying out each of her scissors, her hair clipper attachments, and checking the large blue vial of Barbicide for one of her combs.

Paula pointed at a comb. "Can I borrow this?" she asked another beautician, Gracie, who was busy reading an issue of *Cosmopolitan*.

"Sure. Just put it back in the jar when you're done with him." That last word had a little stank on it.

Paula slipped on a pair of surgical gloves—another Carlos-only perk—and stood at her station waiting. Carlos sat in the shampoo chair with his head back and a smirk on his face. He stared up at the ceiling, unblinking, as Santina worked. She tried small talk, but Carlos didn't respond. It was a strange game of chess, but nobody else knew the rules.

Shampoo finished, Carlos stood up and dried his head with a white towel. He handed the towel to Paula as he sauntered around to the front of her barber's chair and sat down slowly. "Can you use the coloring cape this time? The other ones are too tight around the neck," he said.

"Uh, sure." Paula walked over to the last chair in her row and grabbed the cape he mentioned. She wrapped it around his front and clasped it closed around his neck. "Trim or cut?"

"How long has it been since I was here?" Carlos asked.

Paula smiled. "I can't remember. Looks like you've had maybe a month of growth."

"Then if it's a month, what do you think I need?"

"Trim it is."

Paula quickly pulled a pair of her cutting scissors from her smock and quickly opened and closed them. She retrieved a comb from her front pocket, placed its teeth right where Carlos' hairline met his forehead, and dragged the comb back through his wet hair.

Paula twisted her wrist towards her gently and stopped the comb, uneven strands of thick, black hair fanning out from between the comb's teeth. She traced the scissor blades across the comb and quickly snipped the hair even. She repeated the motion, traveling across the hairline and then further back, tackling Carlos' hair as if it was a grid. Even strokes; comb back, snip, comb back. Paula measured the hair length against the comb, she fell into trance; desperate to avoid Carlos stare through the mirror in front of them.

"How's life been?" Carlos asked.

"Good," Paula half-sang the word and trailed off.

"You sure?"

Paula nodded and continued cutting Carlos's hair. She walked around the chair, giving it a wider berth than she would for another customer, and grabbed a small pair of hair clippers. She plugged the clippers into an outlet at her station and turned them on. The sound of the tiny motor satisfied her.

"Look down," Paula said as she quickly combed the hair at the nape of Carlos's neck and used the clippers to even the hairline. An anger swelled in the pit of her stomach and seemed to send flames up her chest and through her arms. She wondered what it would be like if she drove the clippers harder against the skin. Wondered how much pressure it would take to break through and take a chunk of flesh away.

"You look tired." Carlos voice was sharp—a hint of sarcasm always treading the surface of his words.

It drove her fucking crazy.

Paula wondered if she was overreacting. She wondered if this attitude towards

Carlos was more about her own issues than his. Still, the little comments. The rude way he seemed to assume the room belonged to him. How could it not drive anyone over the edge?

He acted like he owned the place, like he was better than anyone in here, but needed them to look his part. He needed women like Paula to put his hair—what was left of it—together. He needed them to guarantee that he didn't look like a maniac. No, Carlos was a man who believed the maniacs sat at the other side of the courtroom. Maniacs lived behind bars, not behind the wheel of a luxury sedan.

Paula took a deep breath.

"You done back there?"

She realized the clippers were still on but there was nothing left for her to straighten.

"Sorry," Paula said, "Daydreaming."

"Not the best path to an A grade, is it?"

She laughed. It was the only response she could muster without violence. "You're never wrong."

Carlos furrowed his brow. "Not sure how funny that really is."

Paula turned to Santina and smiled. "Raise the volume of this song. Love it."

"I'm speaking to you, though," Carlos leaned to the side and eyed Santina lustily. "Let's not be rude."

The anger made Paula almost giddy. She gently pushed Carlos' head back into position. "Don't ruin the mood. This is a beauty parlor, not a courtroom."

"Are you drunk?" Carlos scowled and tried to turn.

"Stop it and keep your head steady. I need to cut behind your ears." Paula pushed his head again.

Santina turned the music up.

Carlos cursed in Spanish. He again tried to turn around. He of course did this right as Paula went in to get a bushy tuft of hair between the top of his ear and his scalp.

Hairdresser scissors were sharp—they had to be. Hair wasn't easy to cut, and it wore down blades efficiently. But Paula prided herself on always maintaining incredibly sharp scissors. She reasoned that the damn things cost over $300, so it was worth keeping them in as near mint condition as possible. Her coworkers called her "the Samurai" because she paid so much attention to those scissors.

Those scissors sank into the skin like a diver breaking into water.

From Paula's view, they must have sunk in to the hilt, but she yanked her hand back as soon as the blades found a target. The room felt like it emptied of air and sound. The drone of the radio became indecipherable and as realization dawned on Paula's face, it also dawned on Carlos, as he watched her realize what had happened at the same time as he experienced what had to be an intense and sudden burst of pain at the top of his ear and scalp.

Carlos was up on his feet and Paula recoiled. He held a hand to his ear and didn't turn. He stared at her through the mirror, his mouth agape and his breathing getting deeper and deeper. "Did . . . did you fucking stab me?"

Paula looked from the back of Carlos' head to his face in the mirror. She licked her lips with a dry tongue. "I . . . slipped." She turned to Santina to ask her to cut the radio but found the entire staff staring back at her.

The desk girl, Rosie, was the first to move. She grabbed a pile of black towels from the rack above the sinks. Carlos's wound, as if responding to the sudden shift in the air, immediately unleashed an ungodly amount of blood.

He finally turned around, blood already coating his fingers. The steady stream met the collar of his cape and dripped right past, the cape doing nothing to keep his clothes safe.

"You fucking cunt," Carlos hissed.

The other women in the salon sounded off at the word, murmurs and harmonies of "Calm down" and "Don't say that," with the chorus of angry voices only worsening the situation.

Paula felt trapped between Carlos and her coworkers. Rosie tried to jump in and give Carlos a towel, but he shoved her away, his free hand rising with the index finger pointed directly at Paula.

"You're going to live on the fucking street when I'm finished with you. All of you. I'm suing the owners, the managers, and your disgusting ass into the fucking ground."

His lips curled. "Maybe I'll adopt your fucking bastard kid too. He could probably stand to be brought up away from all these street spics."

Paula blinked. The anger was replaced with a sudden calm she hadn't felt in years. His words were hollow, and she realized for the first time just how small a man he was, how he stood nearly a head shorter than her and how his shoulders were so narrow.

She took note of his sunken chest, the little pot belly he cinched his belt buckle two holes too far to hide from the world.

She noticed the way the pleat of his pants was crooked—he didn't know how to iron them and was too cheap to have them pressed at a dry cleaner.

Carlos was a nobody, and all it took for Paula to realize that was blood.

The cops came promptly. There was yelling. Carlos screamed at each staff member in turn, the loss of blood doing little to deflate him. Paula sat at a shampoo sink, leaned back, and wished for the upholstery to swallow her up. The cops approached her last after walking Carlos outside to collect his details and for an EMT to get him to a hospital. She watched him screaming in the back of an ambulance, swinging his arms like a madman towards the beauty parlor.

That she wasn't in handcuffs probably drove him insane, and that gave Paula a little bit of relief. She still couldn't track what it was about Carlos that set her on edge, but none of her assumptions felt very wrong. She'd made a mistake, and his reaction was to create an entire circus around it.

There would be no more walk-in business that day. Everyone would go home with light or empty pockets and sure, she had something to do with it, but what if the man had merely withheld his goddamn tip? What if he had just left? Everyone would be working. Everyone would be making their living.

The anger rose back up like morning sickness, inevitable and unstoppable. That hate for him gestating and growing ever larger.

Rosie wandered over and sat in the chair next to Paula's. "I called Julius."

Julius, the salon owner. He and Carlos got along. "Am I fired?" Paula asked.

"Hell, no. We all told the cops he wigged the fuck out for nothing. You did nothing wrong but slip. Told Julius the same thing. He asked if you were holding up or if you needed the rest of the day off."

"What did you tell him?"

Rosie smiled. "Told him you needed the rest of the day."

Paula leaned over and held her head in her hands. "Thank you, hun. Maybe I need to take a walk or whatever. Truth is, I can't tell if it was a mistake or not. He gets me so riled up." She realized her hands were shaking. "What if I—"

"*No te preocupes*," Rosie said as she wrapped her hands around Paula's. "There's nothing to worry about. We got your back. Nobody liked him here. Know how many times that piece of shit coincidentally showed up on my block before I had my man scare him off? He's trash, honey, pure trash."

They sat quietly as order returned to the beauty salon. Carlos left in his flashy Jaguar and soon two of three police cruisers that had responded left as well. The last pair of cops had a chat with the EMT team before the ambulance left, then came into the salon to check in on everyone. The cops ignored Paula for the most part as Rosie ran interference, assuring them everyone was fine.

"Mater of fact, she's going to take the rest of the day off, right, Paula?"

Paula was lost, staring out the window. She perked up two beats after her name registered.

"Oh? Um, yeah. Yeah," she answered. It felt like the day after an all-nighter, as if she had dreamt her way into the salon.

IT FELT THE same when she left. Walking to the bus stop. Climbing onto the bus and finding a seat in the back. Everything was in a haze. Paula realized she had her bag two stops before her own but couldn't remember when she grabbed it on her way out. Did Rosie tell her to take it? She checked the time. It wasn't even time to pick her little boy, Brendan, up from school. Maybe she could ask her father to borrow the car and surprise him. They could go to the toy store. Go out for ice cream—anything to shove the wheels back into place.

Paula did exactly that. She picked up her eight-year-old from school. She drove and sang songs at the top of her lungs with him until they were hoarse enough for triple scoop cones. Brendan told her terrible knock-knock jokes and she laughed sincerely. It was a good late afternoon that made the hours before easily fade away. There was guilt about tomorrow, though. Guilt about what she'd done and what the consequences would be. Would she be out of a job once Julius had time to think things over? She hurt a *lawyer*, for Christ's sake, of course he was going to sue her into oblivion.

"Thanks, Ma," Brendan smiled at her as he licked his ice cream cone, careful not to topple one of the scoops to the ground. He moved closer to her on the bench they were sitting on despite the weather being a little crisp for eating ice cream outdoors.

Paula smiled. "You're welcome, *mijo*." She combed her fingers through his head and stared at the passing traffic.

A black Jaguar slowly rolled past. The windows were tinted. Paula couldn't remember if Carlos's windows were tinted or not. She struggled to pull something from her memory—anything—but couldn't find the image. The car slowly veered towards the curb a few hundred feet away and double-parked. It sat there, the driver not exiting, and idled for a few minutes.

Paula pulled her hand from her son's head and dipped it into her purse. She fingered her cutting scissors and kept her hand there as she watched the car.

"You okay, Ma?"

Paula watched the car and nodded. "Everything is fine, sweetie. It's fine."

The car's lights shut off and the driver's side door opened.

Paula inhaled and pulled the scissors out of her bag.

Living Alone

Eric Beetner

The doorbell chimed a fifth time, then a sixth and seventh rapid-fire. Martha looked up from her crossword, banged down her pencil, and let out a dramatic sigh for no one to hear. She stood from the kitchen table and padded for the door in bare feet. She didn't bother to tie her robe around her. She was hot and when the temperature went above her age of eighty-two, she didn't give a good goddamn anymore. Not that she did much when the temperatures were lower. Right then the house was hotter than the outside and the window-mounted air conditioner wheezed worse than her husband had before he succumbed to the emphysema.

She jerked the door open, the breeze from the swinging door fanning her robe open, and barked, "Well, you got my attention, now what do you want?"

The young man standing there looked stricken at the threadbare bra and gym shorts on the woman in front of him and all the exposed flesh in between. The kangaroo tattoo on Martha's hip peek-a-booed out from her waistband.

The young man gathered himself. "Where's Gavin at?"

"He ain't here. He's gone, like your manners."

She eyeballed him as hard as he avoided looking at her body. Baggy pants drooped off his hips, T-shirt with a photo of Al Pacino as *Scarface* on it, baseball cap with the sticker still on it. Might as well be a Halloween costume for GENERIC THUG. She scoffed at him.

The young man tried to look beyond her into the house. "Bullshit, man. This his address."

"He was staying here for a while, but I kicked him out for being rude and insubordinate. I can tell you're one of his friends."

The kid waved her away. "Friends? Dude owes me money, yo."

Martha's robe stayed parted in the front like a curtain about to open a show. The man before her was maybe twenty. His tattoos on one arm outnumbered the ones on her whole body. Her three she'd gotten to commemorate important things like her trip to Australia, the flower in honor of her late husband, and her last day of work at the DMV.

She kept one hand on the door, ready to slam at any moment.

"You best take that up with him. As for me, I don't owe you a damn thing."

She began to shut the door in his face. He pushed forward and put a foot in the way.

"I know he's here, man."

The young man pushed the door open, moving Martha aside. She moved willingly, not looking to get into a shoving match she knew she'd lose. She had other ways of dealing with him.

"Yo, Gavin. It's Mario, man! Better have my shit."

"Son, this isn't your house. You can't just barge in and—"

As she spoke, Martha reached out a hand and put it on Mario's arm. He jerked away.

"Yo, get off me, you nasty bitch. Go watch your stories while I find my boy and leave me alone."

"What did you call me?"

He moved deeper into the house. "Yo, Gavin!"

Mario began pushing open doors. First the sewing room piled high with fabric and patterns that would never get used. Then to Martha's room, with the queen bed and Willard's clothes still hanging in the closet.

"Young man . . ."

At the end of the hall he pushed open what used to be Gavin's room. She hadn't cleaned it out since she'd kicked her grandson out three months earlier. Why bother? All he left in there was a stained futon, a few pairs of soiled Jockey shorts, an empty terrarium for the iguana she made him get rid of, and a box of old high school wrestling trophies.

"A-ha!" Mario said. "I knew he was here."

Martha let the young man search the room. She went to the kitchen, her robe catching wind as she walked and flapping open like butterfly wings.

By the time she got back down the hall, Mario was exiting the room.

"Yo, where the fuck Gavin at?"

"Didn't we have this conversation?"

"He owes me a thousand bucks."

"That's your problem, not mine. Now I'll ask you to go."

"I ain't leaving without my money."

"Young man—"

"Why don't you pay me, nasty bitch. Yeah, you got, like, social security and shit."

Martha tightened her grip on the frying pan. "I really wish you wouldn't use that language."

Proud as a peacock, Mario waved an arm like he owned the place.

"You don't like my fuckin' language, then fuckin' pay me, bitch."

The flat cast iron caught him across the temple with a hollow-sounding thunk. His head caromed off the door jamb, and Mario went down.

Swinging the pan brought Martha's temperature up even higher. Her swelling anger didn't help. She shed the robe entirely, leaving it in a pile at her feet that mirrored Mario.

He bled from his nose and a gash in his scalp. His eyes were unfocused and swirled in their sockets, trying to find something to lock on to.

She bent down, the waistband of her shorts slipping to reveal a piece of her tattoo she was most proud of: a replica of the sign she used at the DMV counter for twenty-two years which read ON BREAK—BACK IN.

But where her real sign said FIFTEEN, her tattoo said NEVER. She was quite proud of her little tweak for the occasion of her retirement.

SHE LIFTED MARIO'S right ankle in her hand and started to drag. It took all of her body weight to get him moving. With a white-knuckled grip on his ankle, she tilted her body and let the inertia work for her as she slid him across the carpet. Sweat beaded on her forehead, and that made her even more angry at the young man. She got him down the hall with only minor grunts of complaint from him. She worried she might have hit him too hard. The nosebleed probably wasn't a good sign. But he was the one who barged in. Home invasion. Breaking and entering. Any of these are reason enough to defend your own home.

As she pulled him, the hooded sweatshirt he wore—how in this heat?—rode up his torso. It exposed a gun tucked in the loose waistband of his pants. He'd been more dangerous than she thought. Would it have stopped her? Doubtful.

When she got him from the hall back to the living room, another young man was on the porch peering through the door.

"Mario? Yo, man, where you at?"

"Oh, good," Martha said. She dropped his leg, panting a little. "You can take him the rest of the way."

The new man stared at Mario, furrow-browed and looking for who may have done this to him. Looking for Gavin.

"The fuck . . . ?"

"He broke in. And before you ask, Gavin ain't here."

"Is he dead?"

The man looked up, and the sight of Mario's bleeding skull took a sharp left turn to the vision of the half-naked grandma in front of him. She could see the gears grinding in his brain.

"He's not dead, dummy. He's gonna have a headache for a few days."

The new man reached under a baggy T-shirt and drew his own waistband gun.

"That Gavin's a fuckin' dead man."

He moved past Martha and toward the hall. She was offended that he didn't think a woman of her age would be capable of laying out his buddy. Martha wiped the palm of her hand across the sweat on her forehead and pushed back some strands of silver hair.

"I told you, Gavin isn't here."

But the man wasn't listening. With a deep sigh, Martha bent down and drew Mario's gun from his waistband and followed down the hall. With her robe shed, the tattoo on her right bicep was exposed. A single red rose. Her most recent. The same kind of rose Willard gave her every Valentine's Day and birthday. The one she got to remember him. To remember the good times, not the last day when she held the pillow over his face to stop his breathing, which had become nothing more than a choked wheeze. She'd agreed to it after weeks of his begging and gasping for air. She kissed him once and then covered his face.

Her grip on the gun was weak after dragging the young punk through her house, but she tightened her fist around it and slid her finger onto the trigger before she continued down the hall to where the second young man was searching for Gavin in vain.

BONNIE KNOCKED TWICE but knew better than to wait for her mother to come to the door. She pushed it open and called out.

"Mom, it's me."

She found Martha in the kitchen sitting in only her bra and gym shorts.

"Oh, for heaven's sake, Mom. What are you doing?"

"Sitting in my own house trying to stay cool. What's it to you?"

"Well, I guess whatever works for you."

Bonnie set down a plastic bag from the pharmacy and started to unpack it.

"I got you your Lipitor and some more of those butterscotch candies you like. I brought you another stick of deodorant, but from the smell of things you either ran out a while ago or still haven't opened the last one I got you."

"It's hot and I'm sweaty. Besides, who the hell am I trying to smell like a goddamn rose garden for?"

"How about for me?"

"Set it over there." She pointed to the counter. Martha hadn't gotten up. A glass of iced tea sat sweating on the table in front of her.

"I got you some more trash bags and some sponges for the dishes."

Bonnie moved to put the things away for her mother.

Martha scooted her chrome-legged chair out to block Bonnie's path.

"I can do it."

"Well, Jesus Christ, Mom, I was just trying to help."

"I can help myself. And maybe you need *my* help if you're going around taking the Lord's name in vain like that."

"Mom, you act like you ain't got the foulest mouth in this whole county."

"When you get to be my age and you bury a husband and you live long enough to see the government go to shit and put a goddamn racist game show host in the White House, then you can say anything you damn well please."

Martha's eyes darted quickly over Bonnie's shoulder. Trouble.

Bonnie balled up the plastic bag in her fist. "That iced tea looks good."

"More in the fridge."

As Bonnie turned her back to Martha, she spun in her chair. She'd been right on her quick glance. A thin line of blood seeped from under the pantry door. Martha stood and swiped the kitchen towel hanging from the oven door handle. She didn't have time to do anything with it before Bonnie turned around again with a pitcher in her hand.

"Clean glasses in the dishwasher," Martha said.

Bonnie set the pitcher on the counter and bent over to look in the dishwasher. Martha flung the towel toward the pantry door. It landed and skidded near the seeping blood. Martha scooted the chair closer and nudged the towel with her toe until it started soaking up the mess.

Bonnie straightened, holding a glass up to the light.

"Mom, these are *not* clean. Is your dishwasher broken?"

"I must not have run it. Get one out of the cabinet."

As Bonnie reached up for her glass, she said, "I didn't just come to bring you your Lipitor. I have some news."

"Oh?"

Bonnie turned to her mother. "You don't have to keep Gavin's room anymore. He got sent up to prison."

"I wasn't keeping his room. I just haven't cleaned it out yet."

Bonnie's shoulders sank. "Is that all you got to say when I tell you my only son is going to prison?"

"Maybe if I was even a bit surprised, I'd have a bigger reaction."

Bonnie hung her head. "Oh, Mama. I just can't believe it, but I can believe it, you know what I mean?"

Martha let out a long breath and tried to soften her tone to let her daughter know she felt bad for her, even if she didn't feel sorry for Gavin at all. "For how long?"

"Two to three years."

"That ain't bad."

"Well, it ain't *good* either."

"Maybe because *he* ain't much good."

"Mama . . ."

Bonnie put a hand to her mouth, trying to stop herself from crying. Martha stepped over to her.

"I'm sorry. Now don't cry." She held her daughter, turning her away from the pantry and the dish towel soaking in red. "He'll be out before you know it."

"I don't know where I went wrong."

"You know what I got to say to that."

"I know, I know, I never should've married Angus. He's long gone. Won't even know his only boy is in jail."

"You really think that human crap doesn't have a dozen bastard children all up and down the Mississippi?"

Bonnie broke the hug, wiped away the tears.

"I guess maybe not." Without filling her glass, she set the wrinkled plastic bag on the counter.

"I should go," Bonnie said. "Gavin said the only thing he'd like you to save is his terrarium. He wants to get another iguana when he gets out. He said it will be good responsibility to look after a pet."

"Fine. I can keep it in the garage."

"You doing okay, though, Mom? Everything all right?"

"Doing fine. You know me."

"I sure do."

Bonnie went to put away her glass.

"I can do that," Martha said.

"No, it's okay. I might as well help you clean up a bit."

"Really, Bonnie, I got it."

Bonnie ignored her mother, putting the pitcher of tea back in the fridge.

"You know I don't like you being here all alone, Mom."

"I can handle myself."

Bonnie put two dirty glasses from the sink into the dishwasher.

"Look at this place, Mom." She put the lid on the butter dish, shooing a fly away before he became trapped inside. "You know you can move in with me."

"I'm doing just fine and so are you. We're tough ladies, you and me. We don't need anyone else."

"You sure, Mom? Look at this."

Bonnie lifted the iron frying pan off the stove.

"This has got crud all over it. Sauce or something? What is that?"

Bonnie looked at her fingers, the red smear there.

"Didn't you say you were leaving?"

Bonnie set the pan down with a crack.

"Sorry, Mom. Just trying to help."

Bonnie reached for a dishtowel to wipe her fingers. The oven door handle was empty.

"You don't even have towels to wash up with."

Martha turned on the faucet in the sink and waved a hand at it. Bonnie rinsed the blood off her hand then dried it on her pants.

"I'll see you soon, Mom."

"I'll be here. I'm not going anywhere."

Martha heard the door close behind Bonnie. She went to the pantry door and lifted the towel off the floor. It dripped red. She dropped it in the sink. There will be more clean up ahead if those bodies are leaking that bad, she knew. But there would be time for that. Bonnie had brought her meds so Martha knew she wouldn't see her daughter for another week. Plenty of time for a little housekeeping. Next time Bonnie stopped by she'd be amazed at how clean the place was, so long as it got a little cooler so Martha could do the work. She was sweating just thinking about moving those two punks.

DOWN THE HALL and past her room she walked into Gavin's old room.

"Boy thinks I'm some kind of senile old idiot," she muttered to herself.

She went to the terrarium. She dug her hands in, pushing aside the sand and the half log that had acted as the iguana's shelter. She pushed her hand to the bottom glass. Shaking the sand off, she lifted the bundle out. She brushed away months-old iguana poop from the stack of bills. A thousand dollars.

Only thing I should keep, huh?, she thought. *He's just lucky I didn't already toss the damn thing. Guess I'm lucky too.*

It wasn't a huge windfall, but it would buy her some more dishtowels. And a few boards to cover the well in the backyard like she'd been meaning to do.

Right after a few things went in it.

Signs

Jess Lourey

Whenever things get really bad in my life—*really* bad—I receive a sign that lets me know I'm not alone.

The first time I remember this happening was in 2001. My then-husband and I had gotten into a fight. He walked out and didn't return. When I woke up the next morning, my wedding ring had somehow slipped off my pregnancy-swollen finger, and a page from a photograph album was lying on the floor of our bedroom. It held a card someone had sent my husband years earlier. The card read, "please remember the good times."

I didn't yet know that my husband had driven to an old house and committed suicide immediately after our fight.

The next message came twelve years later. I'd finally worked up the courage to enter a serious relationship, my first since Jay's suicide. Steve and I had been together four years when I found out he was cheating, courting a woman half his age, promising her he'd leave me if she would take him (she didn't; at twenty, she had fantastic instincts).

My world grew dark and lonely after Steve and I broke up. It stayed that way until one early morning, pre-sunrise. I was walking my dog. Ahead, I spotted a glowing circle on the ground, a child's flashlight left on even though the city had been asleep for hours. I picked up the lantern and brought it home.

My personal darkness began receding that day.

Three years later, I was forced back into a job that strangled me. I'd had a year off to write full time, gotten a taste of the creative, passion-filled life, but I couldn't make a financial go of it, not as a single mom. I mourned on my walk to work my first day back, kicking my feet. One punt unearthed a small glass globe, a marble-sized Earth. I lifted it up to the sun.

I held the whole world in my hand.

All three of these messages were hopeful, empowering. *Remember the good times. Find the light. Know your worth.* Then came the fall of 2016. I was walking my dog again, deep in my head, imagining a bright future. We were about to have our first female president of the United States.

Something caught my eye just ahead, something bright embedded in the dirt.

I reached for it.

It was a tiny helmet.

THE TWO YEARS after the election leveled me. Racism, sexism, heterosexism, and ableism were winning on the world stage, and (unsurprisingly) they were terrible sports about it. Fear and Fox News were in charge, and they gloated at our pain.

The political and the personal merged when I finally screwed up the courage to confront my mom, dad, and sister about our toxic family secrets—alcoholism, drugs, sexual abuse, protecting my father from the consequences of his behaviors. I'd been pushing off that meeting for years, but then the unaddressed behaviors and pain began showing up in the next generation, as they always do (we deal with our problems, or our problems deal with us). I had to speak up.

"Nobody has done anything unforgivable," I said, my voice shaking as I spoke the words I'd rehearsed a hundred times on the drive over, "and we've all played our part, but it's time to come clean because these secrets are hurting the people we love."

They couldn't hear it.

Not only have I not seen the three of them since, but when I reach out to my mom every few months asking her to visit a counselor with me, she attacks, constructing elaborate lies to make sense of why she feels betrayed. The simple answer—because I told—demands too much accountability from her, so this woman who was my biggest champion, who until that family meeting I had spoken to every week for 46 years, my *mother*, calls me evil in very personal ways, each with enough fleck of truth that I can't function for days after.

My family destruction didn't happen in a vacuum. The 2016 United States election was a mammoth hairy hand ripping the blanket off the world's ugliness, forcing us all to either claim our stories and march toward the light or double down in our darkness. And so it is that one of my closest friends (and one of the world's best moms) finds herself fighting for parenting rights in a system that doesn't recognize nonbiological lesbian mothers; my husband is confronting his own false family narrative as his father was discovered, alive but weak, on the floor of his hoarding home; so many of my friends are sharing their stories of being sexually assaulted that it seems as though there isn't one of us who escaped.

The news shows us all writhing in this painful reality that we think cannot possibly get worse.

And then it does.

THE LATEST SIGN reached me the month before the midterms. It was the first message I'd received since the tiny helmet.

I found myself in San Francisco teaching an editing workshop held the day the nation discovered that Brett Kavanaugh was being confirmed as Supreme Court justice, despite (or possibly because of?) credible accusations of sexual assault leveled against him, despite lying under oath, and despite throwing a pitch-perfect white male Republican entitlement tantrum during his job interview for *one of nine people in the nation who should never, under any circumstances, throw a pitch-perfect, politically-motivated, white male tantrum.*

My hopelessness couldn't even.

At the end of this depressing day, I saw a woman lean over to one of the workshop organizers. She asked if she could make an announcement. The organizer nodded. That woman, Dr. Ellen Kirschman, stood, turned to the room of fifty, and said, her voice shaking, "I stand with Dr. Blasey Ford. I haven't told anyone but my husband this, but five decades ago, I was raped by two men. My story will be published on the *Psychology Today* blog, and I'd be honored if you'd read it and share it."

Then she fell back into her seat.

Some other announcements were made, I'm not sure what. The workshop ended. We all rushed toward Ellen, hugged her. But then something happened, something I still cannot fully explain. Ellen's integrity and her story had unleashed something. We began to talk—*really* talk, in a vulnerable, sacred way—to cry, to laugh too loud, to take jubilant photos together. Looking back, I believe we were holding an impromptu funeral for the stories and shame we'd been carrying that *had never been ours.* If that funeral had a banner, it would be Fuck That Shit, Finally and Forever.

In that space, as we handed our shame back to its true owners (*here, I think you dropped this*) and claimed our own stories in its stead, we grew dangerous and grand.

In this safe and kickass circle of women and community, I realized I was holding the next sign, the first since the helmet, gifted to me by a friend earlier in the workshop.

"I found this on a walk," she'd said, sliding it over. "I was going to keep it because it reminded me of my mom, but something told me I needed to give it to you."

It was a miniature of the Eiffel Tower.

The tower built to celebrate the centennial of the French Revolution.

I was familiar with the history. Leading up to the revolution, the government was being mismanaged by its unqualified leaders, the environment was so ill-used that crops were failing, the Catholic church was abusing its power. The working class was paying an unfair burden in body, thought, and money, while the very wealthy paid little. Women were treated as passive citizens, entirely dependent on the whims of men.

Then people began to come together in the cafés, kitchens, and corners, sharing their stories. From this community rose a revolution.

It's a good sign.

The Elephant in the Room

Wendy Corsi Staub

Sofía Belinda trudges with the others toward the wall, her exhaustion-seared shoulders hunched in an unseasonable chill.

She'd stayed awake in front of the television until well past two—long enough to see that the last few swing states had gone red. Curtailing the acceptance speech with a click of the remote, she'd gone to bed.

Bobby was already there. "He won?"

"*Sí.*"

"Don't be afraid. It'll be okay."

Sofía Belinda said nothing. She knew Bobby hadn't voted for him; hadn't voted at all. His mother had.

"Mom's Catholic, babe. You know she has to go with the pro-life candidate."

Sofía Belinda, too, had been Catholic, before . . .

Before.

Ordinarily, the half-mile journey from the bus stop is brisk and social. Today, a funereal pall trails the black-uniformed group beneath an incongruous sunlit cobalt sky. Ahead, wrought iron gates open and a gleaming white Lexus SUV glides between pillars marked by gilded *Bougainvillea Knolls* placards. The eponymous vines scaling the wall's perimeter have withered in an early overnight frost. A grounds crew is already on the scene, hacking the dying purple blooms, carting them away.

Inside the guardhouse, the uniformed officer scarcely looks up from his newspaper as he waves the group past. They scatter at the crossroads, and Sofía Belinda drags along the winding maze of five-thousand-square-foot brick colonials.

Ordinarily, Wednesdays are good days. The *Señor* golfs and the *Señora* does volunteer work and their daughter is in school. Sofía Belinda has the house all to herself. No one criticizes her dusting and vacuuming patterns or questions the ingredients as she preps a suitably bland dinner for the *Señora* to "cook"—put the chicken into the oven and take it out again, toss the salad, nuke the rice.

On Wednesdays, she can even use the microwave to heat her own lunch without overhearing a meant-to-be-overheard "*What* is that godawful smell?" and she can eat it on the sunny poolside patio, though she wouldn't dare dip a toe in the sparkling aqua water on the hottest Texas day. Not there, surrounded by security cameras and neighbors in duplicate brick colonials surveying the landscape for suspicious activity: toe-dipping housekeepers and—in the wake of a neighboring development's recent home invasion—rapists and thieves.

Checking her watch as she reaches the house, Sofía Belinda is surprised, and relieved, to find that she's a few minutes early.

A lithe, porcelain-skinned redhead throws open the back door. Her taupe-chalked lids glitter in the sun. "You're late."

"But . . . it's not yet eight o'clock."

"It's almost five after."

She looks at her watch. The hour hand is nearly at the eight, the minute hand is just past the ten, and the second hand is . . . stalled.

"Is it broken?"

"No. I just forgot to wind it."

"Wind it! Are you serious?" *Señora* shakes her head. "You really need to get yourself a decent watch."

Sofía Belinda stares down at the Timex. Bobby gave it to her, wrapped like a birthday present in plain white paper, embellished with a loopy satin bow. Red. Ileana's favorite color.

She'd have turned ten years old on that September day. Bobby had known that, though of course he hadn't known her daughter. Hadn't even known about her, or Rafael, until he and Sofía Belinda had been together more than a year.

Now it's been two.

He's a good man, Bobby. Kind. Hardworking. Patient.

He'd offered his pocketknife to cut the red ribbon, but she'd worked the knot until it unfurled, and she'd cried when she'd seen the beautiful watch. He'd found it at a flea market, but it looks almost new, just a few nicks on the face and an enlarged pockmark along the red leather band where a larger wrist had worn it.

Every morning, she takes pleasure in winding it and strapping it on, admiring its sophisticated flash on her wrist. And every morning, she tucks the red satin ribbon into her pocket—a reminder of a little girl with a glossy black mane of hair like her mama's. A reminder of promises Sofía Belinda had made and hadn't been able to keep.

"*En los Estados Unidos, te ponemos cintas en tu pelo,*" she'd whispered into the smothering darkness, stroking her daughter's head as people and sirens howled in the street.

In the United States, we'll tie ribbons in your hair . . .

Sofía Belinda crosses the threshold into a mudroom that has never seen a lick of mud. *Señora* locks the door after her, sealing them into hushed sterility, and resets the alarm. She's been jittery ever since that home invasion. The perpetrators haven't been caught.

Changing the master bedroom sheets, Sofía Belinda once found a pistol under *Señor's* pillow—licensed and legal, he'd assured her. "And they'd better not come knocking trying to take it away. It's my right to protect my family."

Sofía Belinda had said nothing. She'd never told him or *Señora* about Ileana and Rafael. Perhaps if they'd asked . . .

But why would they ask?

She hangs her drawstring lunch bag on a wall hook with her sweater. Her first day here, five years ago, she'd stashed her plastic container of pork carnitas, rice, and beans in the family's Sub-Zero refrigerator. *Señora* later complained that her Greek yogurt tasted of garlic.

In the kitchen, with its all-white custom cabinetry, granite counters, and tile floor, *Señora* indicates an orange-labeled green bottle beyond the wine refrigerator's glass face. "Open that after you make the orange juice. We'll have mimosas to celebrate. We'll use the Baccarat toasting flutes."

Sofía Belinda doesn't ask what they're celebrating.

She squeezes oranges into the etched glass pitcher, same as every morning.

Then she sets the polished mahogany dining room table with a linen cloth and four bone-china place settings, silver flatware, and crystal flutes.

When she hears a sudden *bang*, she jumps, pressing her hand to her racing heart. Just a door slamming upstairs.

"*¡Querido Díos!*" her mother-in-law would cry out on the other side of the thin bedroom wall whenever shots peppered the night. She'd offer frantic prayers for Rafael, whose work carried him into violent streets after dark, and for the souls of his two younger brothers, massacred in a cartel ambush at a friend's *quinceañera*.

"*¿Mamá, Mamá—dónde está papa?*"

"*No tengas miedo. Estará bien,*" Sofía Belinda had assured her little girl in the darkness.

Don't be afraid. It'll be okay . . .

"*What* is *this?*" *Señora* calls from the dining room.

Sofía Belinda finds her standing beside the table, now dressed in a white cashmere sweater and trim black slacks, glaring at the glassware.

"I thought you wanted—"

"The *toasting* flutes. The engraved Baccarat ones from our wedding. These are Waterford! And why are there *four*? We're drinking *champagne*. You know Lauren isn't old enough to drink *champagne*."

"*Perdón.*"

"In English, please."

"I'm sorry." She replaces the offending glasses with three flutes engraved *October 26, 1991* and one juice glass.

"No, only two," *Señora* tells her. "Hailey is catching a flight home this morning."

Hailey is *Señora's* twenty-year-old niece, who came from New York to stay with their daughter while they spent last week in Paris for their twenty-fifth anniversary. They'd bought the tickets before *Señor* got laid off from his job last spring.

"I thought Miss Hailey was staying until Saturday," Sofía Belinda says.

"Nope. Changed my mind last night, Sophie B."

She looks up to see Hailey, auburn curls tousled, wearing the boots and jacket she'd had on when she'd arrived.

"The car will be here in a few minutes. My bag's by the door, and I just said goodbye to Lauren."

Her aunt purses her lips. "I'm afraid she's going to be disappointed that you can't go to her soccer game as you promised."

"Yeah, well . . . I'm afraid of what might happen if I stay."

I'm afraid . . .

Afraid . . .

Sofía Belinda tries not to clink the fourth place setting as she puts it back into the china cabinet, remembering Hailey's first day here. The *Señor* and *Señora* had watched Fox News downstairs as Sofía Belinda helped their niece settle into the guest room.

"This election is a shit show," Hailey had said, stashing a stack of yoga pants and a baggie of weed in a drawer. "I would've gone back to Pennsylvania to vote for Bernie if he were running. That's where I'm registered. I went to Bucknell last year, but I'm taking a gap semester. I might switch my major to environmental studies. What's happening to this planet is so scary, you know? So who did you vote for, Sophie B?"

"I can't vote here. I'm . . . Mexican."

"Last year, my roommate went to Cancún on spring break. She said the beaches there are amazing. And the margaritas. How come you left?"

Sofía Belinda had searched for the right words and settled on one. "Asylum."

"*¿Mamá, Mamá—dónde está Abuelo?*" Ileana had asked in the night that last year, when the murderous cartels had tightened their stranglehold with abductions and extortion.

"*No tengas miedo. Estará bien.*"

Don't be afraid. It'll be okay . . .

Outside, a car honks.

"Time to go." Hailey gives her aunt a stiff hug, and then embraces Sofía Belinda. "Goodbye, Sophie B. You're the bravest woman I've ever met. Stay strong."

She watches through the tall, arched window as the girl climbs into a sleek black car and disappears.

Señor whistles down the stairs, clean-shaven and dressed in a golf shirt and khakis. Most mornings, he carries his laptop, fretting about his investment portfolio and finding a new job before the family runs out of money.

Sofía Belinda and Rafael had spent all their savings on his father's ransom. Ileana's beloved *Abuelo* had been released. Someday, they promised each other, they would rebuild their escape fund, and Ileana would wear red ribbons in her hair. Someday . . .

Señora is back, accompanied by a ten-year-old girl who resembles her blond daddy and is spoiled rotten like her mama. They sit down at the table, the three of them, a picture-perfect family.

"I'm going to be deported," Sofía Belinda had told Bobby this morning.

"Not if I marry you. I love you. I can support us both. We'll have children . . ."

She'd shaken her head and turned away. She has—*had*—a child; was—*is*—married.

"We're ready for our mimosas," *Señora* tells her.

Sofía Belinda goes to the kitchen and tears the foil top from the champagne. She wraps a clean white towel around the cork, pulls, and winces when it *pops*. She stares at the bottleneck, wisping mist like a smoking gun barrel.

When Ileana was taken, they had no money for ransom. Rafael tried to bargain with the cartel's gang enforcers, and then he, too, vanished.

"Sofía Belinda? What are you doing in there? Where's the champagne?"

"*Perdón.*"

"In English, please."

"I'm sorry." She pours amber bubbles into the Baccarat flutes, tops them with orange juice, and turns away.

"Sofía Belinda! Come back. I almost forgot. This is for you." *Señora* hands her a gold watch. "You can have it."

Sofía Belinda looks at it. "*Gracias,*" she says softly.

"In English, please."

She turns and walks silently away.

Behind her, she hears the *Señor* ask, "You're giving her a Gucci watch?"

"I never wear it. It's too gaudy."

"She didn't even say thank you," Lauren says. "That's bad manners, isn't it, Mommy?"

"Yes, sweetheart, but she doesn't know any better."

In the kitchen, Sofía Belinda sets the gold watch on the counter, takes off the Timex and stares at its motionless hands.

Six years have passed since Ileana's body was found in a shallow grave out in the desert. Rafael's was not. His parents believed he was still alive, that one day, he would come home. They refused to flee for the border with Sofía Belinda, so she promised to write with her new address in America, just in case . . .

She'd kept that promise. Every Christmas, she sends a letter to Mexico, and last year, she got one in return. Things are better there now, Rafael's father reported. Rafael's mother is still waiting for her lost son to come home, still praying, still frightened.

Isn't everyone? Afraid for their children's safety, for strangers' unborn babies, for their financial future and the planet's . . .

Afraid of dying, afraid of living, of loving . . .

No tengas miedo . . .

Sofía Belinda gently winds the Timex, rotating the tiny knob between her thumb and forefinger. The second hand begins to jump along, time moving forward again.

She fastens the red leather strap onto her wrist, walks to the back door, and throws it open. Fresh air, sunlight, a bleating alarm.

"What are you doing?" *Señora* cries out in the dining room.

"It's time to go."

"But where are you going?"

She ignores the question, walking out of the house, down the driveway, down the lane, headlong into a strong, chilly wind. She thinks of her sweater on the hook with the drawstring bag; imagines her forgotten lunch ripening as the day goes on, and she smiles.

At the crossroads, she turns toward the gate. The wind is behind her now, whipping long dark hair around her face, blinding her. She pauses, gathering the long strands into a ponytail with her left hand, reaching into her pocket with the right.

The red ribbon flutters like a streamer. She ties it around her hair and she can see again.

Estará bien.

Sofía Belinda walks through the gate, and past the white stone wall, and she doesn't look back.

A Test for Juniper Green

Danny Gardner

Juniper Green was a nice young woman. Kind to a fault. Eager to assist. Unless it was Wednesday. Step to her wrong in the middle of the week and you'd get a piece of her mind. Or five to the face. Wednesdays were when she steered her used and battered Honda Civic from West Oakland to U.C. Berkeley for her weekly meeting with Professor Keating, her Master's thesis advisor.

The arrogant prick didn't care she had no other business on campus that day or that the commute was excruciating. Since rebuffing his sexual advances back when she was his Public Policy student, Keating made his respect for her a moving target. She decided it was better to play the game and let him hear himself talk for an hour per week, rather than be sabotaged. Juniper wanted to do things the right way, and though that didn't necessarily mean taking other people's shit, or having sex with them, she bit her lip and thought of the long con, just like her daddy Mac G taught her. Be it a dig on her blackness here, or a suggestive rub of her shoulders there, it would all be worth it, as long as she secured what no other member of her family had, which was a future away from crime.

She parked on the street and hustled to the Sather Gate entrance. Her intention was to make a beeline toward the Faculty Club, except the spontaneous eruption of a Black Lives Matter protest completely cut off access. She clutched her computer bag, blitzed toward the far end of campus, and finally arrived to see Keating rising from his seat.

"Professor," Juniper said, as she caught her breath. He didn't look at her face but instead checked his watch.

"You're late," he said.

"BLM had the Sather Gate blocked."

Keating retook his seat and stretched out his hand. Juniper reached into her computer bag and then handed him the printed abstract of her thesis. He put on his glasses and read the first page.

"The Flint, Michigan, Water Crisis."

"It amounts to public policy that punishes citizens for being poor and black."

"Took a pass on the protest?"

"Not my style."

"With your temperament?"

"Race isn't a temperament."

Keating read on. His only tell was an occasional shake of his head.

"The police kill us one at a time," Juniper said. "Michigan is killing an entire community."

"They'll survive Flint," Keating said. "You don't survive a fight with the police."

"Sure, you do."

Keating looked up at Juniper, then back at the abstract.

"And how is your father?"

"Good. He gets out of San Quentin in two weeks."

"Oh?"

Keating adjusted his glasses.

"I'm really excited to show him our campus."

He swallowed and lingered on the page.

"Even from prison, he's interested in my education. And they say black fathers aren't—"

Keating looked up.

"I'll email my notes."

Juniper nodded, turned, and walked out of the Faculty Club with a smirk.

FROM THE CAR, Juniper called her tutoring family and offered them an extra hour, which they gladly accepted. She parked downhill on the steep incline leading up to the large house. She struggled to police up her laptop bag and workbooks when her phone rang with the familiar number of her older brother,

Robert. He left Juniper in Oakland to traipse off to Chicago and foolishly follow in their father's criminal footsteps.

"Hey, Junie."

"Hey, Bobby, I can't talk right now. What do you need?"

"Why you figure I always need someth—"

"It's Wednesday."

"And you tutor the white kid up in . . . whatzzat?"

"Glenview."

"I was gonna say Glenview."

Robert's insensitivity never hurt Juniper more than when he feigned concern for her hustle.

"I said I'm busy."

"Too busy for—"

"Come with it, already, Bobby."

Juniper looked up the hillside stairs to see her student, and her parents, waiting for her on the front steps. Her student smiled. The parents didn't.

"You spoke with the old man?"

"Not this week."

"What the fuck, Junie?"

"I can't do everything and keep money on his calling card on too, Bobby. Now look, I gotta go."

"Wait."

"What?"

She stepped out the car, kicked the door with her foot, then kicked it again to make sure it remained closed. She waved up the hill, but no one waved back, save the pretty blonde teenager. She walked up the stairs to the front door. The adults walked away. Her student remained, smiling.

"Bobby!"

"Look, if you speak to dad, ask him if he knows someone from his old neighborhood named Fluke."

"What's that about?"

"I've been workin' with this dude who took me to meet him. He says they were real tight, but I dunno."

"I don't think you want to be involved with anyone dad knew from that life, Bobby."

"Just ask him, okay?"

"Fine. Fluke. Got it. Now I have to go. I love you. I'm sorr—"

Three sharp beeps from the mobile network were her only reply. She wondered why she felt cold. Her student opened the door, hugged her, and took her things. Her sense of dread would have to wait until tutoring was done.

JUNIPER OPENED THE front door of the tiny West Oakland two-bedroom to see Aunt Carolyn seated on her corduroy couch. She smoked a cigarette while staring daggers at her. Juniper also noticed the half-full tumbler in front of her on the glass-and-chrome coffee table. It wasn't her water glass.

"Hi, Aunt Carolyn."

"What's wrong with your phone?"

Carolyn dumped her ashes. Juniper watched and wondered why sad middle-aged women always smoked and drank alone while wearing robes.

"Nothing. Why?"

"Collect call from that no-account daddy of yours came in here an hour ago."

Juniper checked her phone and saw no missed calls from San Quentin State Prison.

"And, of course, you didn't accept the charges."

Carolyn snorted into her vodka.

"It could have been an emergency, Aunt Carolyn."

Carolyn pointed the two fingers in which she held her Kool Menthol 100 at Juniper.

"I didn't like that nigga when my sister met him and ain't nuthin' happenin' in San Quentin that's gonna make me like him when he gets out."

Juniper left the room and marched down the hall to her bedroom before she said something she'd regret. Her mother was Aunt Carolyn's younger sister, Debbie, who left Oaktown to run off with the Chicago outlaw who fathered her and her brother. An ovarian cancer diagnosis later, Aunt Carolyn becomes the guardian of her sister's kids after their father survived a police shootout in a drug bust gone wrong, copped a plea, and wound up transferred out of Illinois.

Carolyn took no rent from her niece, so Juniper felt paying the cable television bill—atop enduring the occasional rant of drunken grief—was a small price to pay for proximity to MacArthur Green, the infamous Mac G, her father, hero, and burden.

She closed her door, took out her computer, and laid it on her bed. She wanted to work, but the anxiety of the missed call was too great a distraction. Juniper grabbed her mobile and rang Robert instead. If nothing else, she could at least ease the guilt of their earlier interaction. After four rings, she ended the call and dialed again. After three more rings, the line was answered, but by someone other than Robert.

"Who dis?" went the giggly lady voice on the other end. Juniper assumed it was some thot playin' games. She could hear loud rap beats in the background.

"Lemme speak to Bobby."

The beats stopped.

"Fuck you doin'?" a man's voice from within the room said. A voice that wasn't Robert's.

"Phone was ringin'," the lady said.

"Bitch, don't be on the phone up in here when we layin' down bars."

"Then turn the ringer off, nigga!"

Three sharp beeps. Juniper's cold feeling returned.

THE NEXT MORNING, Juniper cut class and drove 580 West, over the San Francisco Bay, to San Quentin. As she watched the sun dance atop the water, she reflected on the family folk tales of the Green men, uncompromising toughs since they first stepped upon Chicago asphalt back in the 1920s. She grew up so proud of the stories of fisticuffs, knifings, shootouts, robberies, and burglaries. She thought it honorable to be a black gangster in the white man's America. Once she reached puberty, bearing the misfortune of gender, Juniper learned all that kept her safe from the outlaws she worshiped was their fear of her father, a nastier outlaw. Otherwise, she would be subject to the same pressure felt by so many vulnerable black women squeezed between the misogyny of the white and the black, until they wound up compliant, or crushed.

In the Visitors vestibule, she was waved through the metal detector by a lady guard she recognized. It was well-known that Juniper was a black woman in college, which, in that place, was like wearing a halo. She was given only a cursory search before being sent upon her way. MacArthur Green may have flourished in rehabilitation, and informed on the cartel that set him up, but he was still a convicted felon with a shootout involving undercover DEA officers on his record, thus he was permanently under administrative segregation. In exchange for his confidential testimony, he was allowed to serve his sentence away from Chicago. He appealed to his woman's sister to take in Juniper and Robert, and arrangements were made for him to live out his sentence in San Quentin, far from anyone who would want to kill him, and close enough to his kids to maintain the illusion of fatherhood.

Juniper waited patiently on the other side of the glass partition. Soon, Mac G, in handcuffs, was led in by a guard. Mac's limp in his bad leg was worse, as it was a cold spring morning and a good bit of the federal government's lead was still lodged close to the bone. His broad shoulders lumbered from stiffness. The big, bad man was getting old.

The security guard nudged Mac into his seat, nodded in Juniper's direction, and then stepped backward to the wall behind him. Mac picked up the black phone receiver at the same time Juniper grabbed hers.

"Tried to call you."

"Aunt Carolyn said. Sorry she was rude."

"She's got the right," Mac said, and he touched the glass partition with his large hands. Juniper reached back and placed her fingers on the glass in front of his.

"Sorry I haven't been able to put money on your card, or commissary."

"I'll be out soon. You heard from your brother?"

"He called, but I couldn't talk. I tried him back, but someone else answered his phone."

"Is that right?"

"Yeah. Some chick. Must've been a Fluke."

The tension in Mac G's jaw was the tell. Robert was in trouble involving an old associate of Juniper's father. Mac looked past Juniper as if she was no longer there. His eyes were blank. That's how they seemed when he stared into the violent immediate future.

"Once I'm out of here, I'll see about it."

It was all in his voice. *I'll see about it.* It may as well have been a forever goodbye. Had Mac G not been in San Quentin, Juniper wouldn't have attended Berkeley, which she hated. Had he been present, she wouldn't have been afraid for her brother, who was far too stupid to be afraid for himself. The picture she kept in her mind that made all the bullshit worthwhile was her father finally in her life. No way he was going to Chicago to fuck that up for her. Not even to save Robert's dumb ass.

"No."

"What?"

Even behind the glass, with a guard, Juniper was afraid of him.

"I said, I'll take care of it."

"What you gonna do is go back to school."

Juniper looked, not into the face of her incarcerated patriarch, but at the thick annealed glass and polycarbonate barrier. She realized her fears of him were like all things between them; a construct of her own wants and needs.

"What you gonna do is go back to your cell and wait two weeks for me to come back and get you," she said. "I got it."

"Juniper . . ."

"I'm the one out here, dad. I'm always the one."

"Ju-Ju," Mac said.

Juniper stood and waved.

"Done already?" the guard said.

"Not y—"

"Done," Juniper said. She put her fist on the glass. Mac was shocked at her audacity. He slowly rose from his seat and pressed his fist into the image of hers. He almost appeared heartbroken as he turned from her and walked toward the guard.

Once he was out of sight, Juniper cried.

※

SHE USED HER student credit card with the horrible interest rate to purchase round-trip airfare to Chicago Midway Airport. She packed lightly and walked to the nearby BART station. On the train, she pulled out her phone and opened the app that locates registered devices via GPS. Robert was a fuckup, with a credit rating to match, so, as with most things, it fell on Juniper to secure for him a mobile phone. After he lost the first two, she signed off on the third with the caveat he enabled location services permanently. Were another phone to go missing, he'd be finding it. Now she'd be able to find him, or at least his last known whereabouts.

Her options were limited. Robert was a low-rent criminal, so she couldn't go to the police. She had no backup, as her life was rooted in the Bay Area. It was likely Fluke was one of many who lost big in Mac's deal with the Feds, so reasoning with him on Bobby's behalf wasn't going to work. Everything stunk from the start.

After a turbulent flight, Juniper rented a car and drove to the last address Bobby's phone was active: 7701 S. Halsted Street, on the edge of the most dangerous neighborhood in Chicago three years running. It was the home of Maxwell Restaurant, a place that served area fast-food staples. Robert was allergic to hard work, so either it was the wrong place or a front. She went inside. It was empty save for the cashier and cook behind a thick bulletproof acrylic wall. She could hear the hard bump of bass coming from somewhere inside.

"We just opened so you g'on have to wait," said the cashier, a disinterested teenage black girl who should have been in school. "And we ain't got no Italian beefs."

"Actually, I'm lookin' for Bobby."

"Who?" the girl said, loudly, through the air holes in the security glass.

"Lil Mac," Juniper said. She hid her disgust at identifying her brother with the nickname he created to trade on their father's reputation. The cook, an older black man, round in the middle, who wore a stocking cap, approached the glass.

"You want the studio?" he said, and Juniper remembered the starting and stopping of rap beats back when she called Robert's phone.

"Yeah," she said. "Where it at?"

"G'on back outside," the cook said. "Walk around the corner and it's off the alley."

Juniper thanked the man, walked out, turned right, and ventured toward the alley. Two luxury cars were parked outside the back of the restaurant. A painted wooden sign on the wall read Ill Drill, the words outlined in the shape of the state of Illinois. A big black man dressed in a Chicago Bulls snapback cap, black Ben Davis jacket, and jeans that were far too skinny stood in front of a door. Juniper put a switch of her ass in her gait and approached.

"This the studio?" she asked.

"You dressed kind of weak, ain'tcha? We don't need any bitches on YouTube lookin' like schoolteachers."

"I just came from work. I need to change," Juniper said.

"Bathroom is around the corner."

He waved her inside, Juniper approached the door and then turned back around.

"Ay, Fluke been here?"

"He in there," said the big man. "What you want him fo'?"

"My daddy said to tell him hey."

The big man turned his back on Juniper as she ventured further. The hallway was dimly lit with red lights. Street posters for rap shows and photos of the famous and infamous hung on either wall. Her hunch was confirmed.

Ill Drill was a recording studio built within a vacant space next to the restaurant. That's where the action was. She pushed past a black curtain at the end of the hall and stepped inside the lounge, where two young women smoked weed with a gang-gang soldier and nodded along to the music. Just then, the door to the control room opened and a young woman dressed in jeans, boots, and a short red leather jacket entered the room, her tight braids tucked underneath a black LA Dodgers snapback. She walked and spoke like a woman who endured bad men.

"Ay, Tuffy," one of the girls said.

"Where Rel at?" the hard woman said.

"Ain't nobody seen Rel today," replied one of the young women, and Juniper immediately recognized the voice as the girl who answered Robert's phone.

"Fuck you is?" The hard woman glared at Juniper.

"I saw him this mornin'."

"Again, who are you?"

"Ju-Ju," Juniper said. "Me and Rel hook up sometimes."

"The fuck y'all do!" said the other young woman, and she hopped up from her seat.

"Dash wit' all that noise," Tuffy said. "Hit his phone fuh me."

Juniper pulled out her phone, looked at it, and then shrugged her shoulders.

"No signal," she said, stalling.

"That's 'cuz the ceiling is concrete. Come on in the control room."

The hard woman led her through the control room door. Juniper looked at the locator app. She was within fifty feet of Robert's phone, but there was no sign of him. She looked up and saw a nerdy young man, also in Chicago Bulls cap, seated at a computer workstation. Behind him stood a man who could have been around her father's age. He was grayed with more salt than pepper, wore wire-rimmed glasses, a white tunic shirt, and bore a deep scar the length of the right side of his face.

"You straight?" Tuffy was impatient.

"I think so."

Juniper's hands shook as she stared at the display of her phone.

"Here, lemme see." The boss girl reached for Juniper's phone. She nervously stepped back a foot.

"I'm good."

Juniper switched apps and dialed a number. She heard the faint sound of a ring tone in what must have been another room. Everyone else heard it as well.

"Where's Robert?"

"What?"

"Lil Mac," Juniper said. "Where the fuck is my brother?"

The middle-aged man, who was most obviously Fluke, turned around and looked at Juniper.

"Handle that," he said.

Tuffy grabbed Juniper's hand and, with the other hand, punched her hard in the face. Juniper attempted to break away, but the man-girl was upon her. Soon

Juniper was on her back. She kicked upward, which lifted her opponent off her, but as she scrambled to her feet, Tuffy yanked her hair back and grabbed her around the neck. Juniper looked up through the control room window to see more people in the lounge, all getting high and drinking from the same bottle of Crown Royal.

The big man who guarded the door barreled into the room, and they all went down like bowling pins. Tuffy fumbled underneath her jacket for a pistol with the arm she wasn't choking Juniper with. On the opposite side of the glass, the big man was rising to his feet. Juniper bucked wildly. She threw her head back, smashing Tuffy's nose. She then stumbled forward into a counter where an out-dated mixing console was installed. That's where she learned the three things that are in abundance in any gangster's recording studio were girls, weed, and guns. At her fingertips was the Chicago gangster's weapon of choice: a Nina with the 30. She panic-grabbed the 9mm, turned, and let off a spray of bullets that knocked Tuffy four feet backward. She collapsed into a heap on the floor. Fluke dashed through a side door into a corridor. The poor nerdy sound engineer was underneath the workstation covering his face. When the big man breached the control room door, Juniper shot wildly, and he fell backward, his blood and brain matter all over the glass. The hangers-on dispersed, all except for two, who were now reaching for their own guns. Juniper exhausted the last of the bullets in the clip on shattering the glass. Without really thinking, she ran through the door Fluke escaped through, into the corridor, and didn't watch the rest of the half-gangsters in the lounge bolt in terror.

At the end of the corridor was a stairwell that led to the storage cellar of the entire building. The utility light was on.

"Bobby!"

"Junie?"

Juniper ran down the stairs and into several boxes of restaurant supplies, fenced goods, and other contraband. She looked around.

"Bobby!"

"In here!"

Juniper followed the sound of her brother's voice to a small bathroom on the far end of the cellar. She opened the door to find him beaten and bloodied, though alive. His wrists were cable-tied tightly to the drain.

"I'll find something."

Juniper ran out the bathroom, back out into the cellar, and over to a utility cabinet on the opposite wall. As she rummaged through the top drawer, she heard footsteps behind her.

"How's ya daddy?"

Startled, Juniper turned around and was staring up at Fluke, who was bleeding from the left side of his abdomen, where one of her wild shots caught him. He held a white shop cloth to the wound.

"Hear he's gettin' out soon."

"Who'd you hear that from?"

"Friends in high places."

"My father didn't snitch on you. Only the cartel."

"Snitchin' is snitchin', L'il Ju-Ju."

Fluke coughed, wobbled, and then looked over at the bathroom.

"Guess you tryin' to take yo' brother home. He sure can take a beatin'. Ain't give up nuthin'."

"That's because he doesn't know anything," said Juniper. "We haven't seen my father in years."

"You see him every other week," Fluke said. "Told ya. Friends in high places."

Fluke raised a revolver to waist level. Juniper swallowed hard.

"You made quite a mess up there. Seem like the Green family always fuckin' my shit up."

Juniper and Fluke stared at one another. Fluke teetered on his feet a bit, then nodded over to the utility cabinet.

"Wire cutters are in the second drawer."

Fluke backed up two steps, turned around and angled toward the stairwell.

"Let yo daddy know Fluke say whaddup."

Juniper watched until Fluke was out of sight, then found the wire cutters and freed Robert from the bathroom sink. He was so roughed up he couldn't move by himself.

"You were right, Junie," Robert said. He winced through the pain of bruised ribs. "You're right, about everything."

Bobby squeezed tears through his two swollen black eyes. Juniper knelt down to her older brother who just couldn't figure out what to do with himself and kissed him on the forehead, likely the only place his body didn't hurt.

"It's okay, Bobby," she said. "Let's go home."

ALONGSIDE ROBERT, JUNIPER Green leaned against her Honda Civic as they waited for the gate to San Quentin State Prison to open. Juniper wore a sundress and put a flower in her hair. Robert cleaned up as well, though his eyes were still blackened. Aunt Carolyn was so horrified at the sight of him, she softened to the idea of Mac G staying with them in West Oakland, at least until he could get on his feet. Juniper knew enough of fate not to allow herself to feel optimistic, but at least she would have both Green family men right where she wanted them, if only for a time.

A loud buzzer sounded, and the giant steel door began to rise. As soon as they could see MacArthur Green's feet, Robert began to cry, beating Juniper to it.

A stiff wind blew across the San Francisco Bay and it chilled her bare shoulders. The ordeal in Chicago was not yet behind them, but perhaps a better future was in front of them if the three faced forward together. Fluke was still out there, along with who knows how many enemies Mac G made. It didn't matter. She had killed. She'd kill again. It'd be easier the next time.

It's always easy for a Green.

No Body

Clea Simon

Before she even woke, she knew her body was gone. It had been a struggle, losing it. She had felt pressure. Straining and then a searing heat. That pain—raw and sharp—was what brought her back, floated her to the surface. But it was not herself, not her body she felt. This was above her. Against her. Yes, inside her. This was not her—not her body. Her body was gone.

The first thing she saw, on opening her eyes, was his face. Contorted and straining, it no longer looked handsome. His cheeks flushed red. His sweat dripped onto her from that dimpled chin. From the cheekbones she'd once thought so distinguished, so refined. The tendons of his neck stood out as if he were in pain. But it was her pain, wasn't it? The shock and tearing that woke her. That recurred with each thrust. She opened her mouth to cry out, and his hand clamped over it. She had no voice, not anymore. Better to have no body, then, if this is what it brought.

In the days that followed, she shrank in on herself. If she could have, she would have disappeared, big as she was, the better to avoid the stares. The words, just loud enough for her to hear: "Easy." "Slut." The laughter was the worst, the joke she never got.

Most days, she could avoid them all, waiting until late to leave the library, the lab. Until late to come home, as if that dorm room, that bed, still offered some semblance of safety.

Once she nearly ran into him, on his way out. She ducked behind the door just in time. He glanced her way, but she doubted he could see her, crouching in the shadow. He looked different, she thought. Hungry, those hollows under his cheekbones giving him a ravenous look, like a beast. No wonder he had hurt her, so angled and sharp. She couldn't understand why she ever thought he was handsome, although she could still remember how she had flushed when he had come by. A campus star so far out of her league. When he had invited her—the chubby girl—to taste a batch of the cocktails he had mixed up special, just to share. Now he looked feral, as if he were about to bolt and disappear.

If only she could do that. If only. She even approached him once. Wanting to understand, but as she drew near, she realized he was not alone. He was never alone, and the laughter stopped her, as cruel and sharp as pain. "She's nobody," she heard him say, to the others who gathered around him. "Nobody at all."

If only. As the weeks passed, she thought she would disappear. But her body, inconvenient and stubborn, kept intruding. Her abdomen, already soft, asserted itself, pushing against the waistband of her jeans. Her breasts ached, with a dull heat like the bruising. Like the twisting. When she least expected it, she caught sight of herself in windows. In the doors that closed, cutting the laughter off. Her eyes, large and dark. Her outline blurred.

Then one morning she felt sick and raced from her room to the common dorm bath. Although she hadn't eaten—couldn't eat much, not anymore—she heaved, her too-big, too-soft body spasming in pain. And when it was over, she remained, kneeling. She longed to lay her head down on the cool tiles, but she forced herself to stand. And there it was. A real mirror, on the bathroom wall. Despite everything, she had grown bigger. She stared, gauging the difference. Contemplating just how else she had changed.

Then, just like that, the world exploded. Before she could make up her mind, the glass shattered with an explosive crash. She stepped back, stunned. Only then did she hear the harsh laughter behind her.

"So ugly the mirror couldn't take it." She knew that voice. "Bad luck, you nobody. Better clean that up."

She didn't turn. Better not to see. Instead, she fetched the dustpan and brush and spent the next hour on her knees, taking care to track down every splinter. She jumped as she heard the door open again, not daring to look up. To her surprise, it was the wall-eyed girl from down the hall—the one nobody spoke to.

She knelt and held out a paper bag and together they swept the shards into the bag for safety, along with the rock that lay among them, mute.

That night was hard, her body betraying her once again. It wasn't the tears. She had learned to be silent as they fell, but her voice choked up on the lie. As she told her mother that all was fine. That she needed the money for books.

"Are you okay, honey?" Her mother's voice a reminder of tenderness lost. "Are you sure you don't want to come home this weekend?"

A few days later, when the care package arrived, she cried. Her mother couldn't know the cause. Couldn't know how serendipitous her timing was. The procedure required fasting for twelve hours, but the brownies would be a sweet thing—a touch of comfort—for after.

But she had grown careless. Used to being invisible—the nobody—now that she had nothing he wanted. And the still-fresh baked goods must have given her away. She opened the box after signing for it in the mailroom. Lifted the top to reveal the cracked brown crust, the chocolate cake beneath, and he was there, reaching for the tray before she could even cry out.

She watched as he grabbed a handful of the brownies, crushing them between his fingers. Even when he shoved them into his mouth, she didn't dare move, transfixed as he chewed, open mouthed, as pieces of the sodden, broken cake fell to the floor.

It was the wall-eyed girl, the one from down the hall, who knocked softly, hours later. She had a package of Duncan Hines brownie mix, and in the small hours of the morning, the two stirred and baked, working in the dorm kitchen. They kept the room dark, their voices soft.

Although the two were nearly silent, the aroma betrayed them. The door slammed open, and she saw his face, shiny and red. "What's this?" His voice was slurred. They had come back from drinking, the lot of them. Without waiting for an answer, he grabbed the pan. "Don't you get it? You're nobody." He turned to his buddy. "Fatso thinks she can have sweets."

His follower must have drunk more. He only stared, speechless. His mouth hung open, a thread of saliva spooling out, making him look helpless, like an oversized baby.

She seemed to see something in that face. Something softer or more human.

"Wait—" She reached out, but the follower pushed back, and she stumbled against the wall.

"Come on," his leader muttered, as the wall-eyed girl cowered, waiting her turn. "These bitches are nasty."

She wasn't invisible. Far from it. The next morning, she seemed clumsier than usual. Although the wall-eyed girl was at her side, guiding her, she collided with a protester. "Baby killer!" the woman yelled, spraying saliva. "You'll burn in hell!"

Her friend pulled at her arm, as if to rush her past the angry line, but she paused. Neither woman spoke, but as they stood there, looking into each other's faces, the protesters took heart.

"Don't do it! Don't stop a beating heart!" A girl of about twelve shouted, her voice shrill. A light flashed. "I've got your picture. We know who you are!" A man, this time. But the light served to waken her from her reverie, and they rushed into the clinic.

Afterward, she cried. Made a fuss, she heard one of the clinic workers say. They were all overworked, and the attendant didn't mean to be cruel. Still, the way she carried on caused concern. They checked her blood pressure and heart rate more often than was usual. Her bleeding wasn't excessive, nor did she report her pain level as more than the expected "four." But with needing time and heat and water, she didn't leave until the clinic was ready to close for the night, and only then because the staffers told her they couldn't accommodate her. That they could arrange transportation to a hospital, if that was what she really wanted.

The ambulance was waiting when they got back to the dorm. The spinning light coloring the wide eyes red. Mouths opened as they brought the first stretcher out, the murmurs growing louder as the vehicle sped away.

"His face," she heard someone whisper. "Did you see it?" She had. Blood darkened his clenched teeth. Trickled down the side of his face, contorted in agony as they carried him out. No longer handsome, his cheeks went from red to white in that light. The tendons of his neck standing out, sharp like knives. Poison, someone said. Something he ate, she heard. He and his friend both.

She had a moment of panic, as she went back to her room, leaning on the arm of her wall-eyed friend. Would the protesters at the clinic remember her? Remember the fat, unwashed woman who stumbled into them and drew their ire? Would the nurses at the clinic recall how she cried and wouldn't leave, all that day? When the surgeons found the glass shards in his belly, blood and mucus obscuring their mirrored surfaces, would the police make the connection? Would anyone wonder at a tray of brownies, half-eaten but still fresh?

As the days progressed, she would start at nothing, jumping at the slightest noise. She slept badly and healed slowly. But as the days turned into weeks, she began to feel better. The pain was gone, and she began to bathe again. To eat healthily and to venture forth, tentative but further each day. Waiting for the call to halt—the command—that never came. There was no reason to stop her, after all. She had nothing. She was nobody . . . and she was free.

Suspended in Time

Kaira Rouda

Remember the feeling, the day after the 2016 presidential election? Sorry to bring it up. I know it's a hopeless, helpless place. But then we marched. We activated. We resisted.

And some of us talked our spouses into running for Congress.

As I write this piece I'm in about the same helpless place right now, with a bit more hope sprinkled in, and here's why: After nearly twenty months on the campaign trail, a new poll shows my husband's race tied with Putin's favorite congressman, a man who has represented this district for 30 years and has only passed three pieces of legislation, the last one 14 years ago. He's a climate change denier who appeared on a television show and agreed with a supposed program in Israel to arm school children to combat school gun violence. He hasn't had a town hall for as long as anyone around here can remember, and he's using his daughter's illness to claim he'll support covering pre-existing conditions even though he's voted against healthcare legislation at least 14 times.

These are just some of the facts I can rattle off. There are many more. But I'm not the one on the speaking, talking, house party–attending, debating, handshaking, photo-taking, town hall–hosting circuit. I'm not the one running for office. I'm the spouse. The support person. I smile. I clap. I nod. I agree with everything my husband is doing, and what he represents. He's an authentically great guy. We've built a life together, these past thirty years. We've raised four kids together, and built a large, successful company together as a team. We created charities together. Homes together. Lives together. And we're a good balance for each other. I guess you could call it equals, if such a thing exists in the ebb and flow of life.

Whatever it is, we are a good team. And we still are, behind the scenes, in this most important election of our lifetime.

The difference is, in this team effort, when the lights go on, or the crowd stills with anticipation, I'm just smiling. Silent and clapping. As a feminist and activist, I'll admit it's a role that took a while to get comfortable in.

A few days ago I was doing my job at a rally. I'd become squished against a wall in one of our field offices due to an amazing overflow crowd who had appeared from across the state to canvass for Harley's campaign. The room was excited and burst into cheers of "Harley," "Harley," "Harley," as he walked to the front. During his rally speech, Harley, as always, acknowledges the family.

"My wife of almost thirty years, Kaira, is here." He couldn't see me, so I popped my hand in the air and waved. A woman leaning against the wall in front of me turned her body in my direction.

"Nobody has heard from you, have they?" she said. "No interviews?"

"Well, no, this isn't my campaign. It's his." I answered. "I'm just here to support him."

As a side note, please know every spouse of a politician who I know has an identity of his or her own. They do have their own lives. I promise. They are just suspended in time during the political season, which for a new-to-politics candidate is a long time, I hear.

The woman in front of me turns all the way around now and I notice her notepad, iPhone perched and likely recording. At this stage in the campaign we've been warned anyone can be a tracker. (These are aggressive, paparazzi-like folks who appear out of nowhere with a camera in hand and attempt to capture the worst about a candidate. I could write a whole column about these folks. But I digress.)

"So what do you do?" she asked.

It was an amazingly simple question, but one that momentarily gripped me with panic. Was I allowed to mention myself, outside of this political circus we'd found ourselves in? Harley's race had become one of the most high-profile congressional battles in the country. Any misstep by me would be a disaster. What do I do?

A simple question had restarted time and lifted the veil surrounding me.

"I'm a writer," I said with pride. My husband and I have both launched what I term our second acts: Politics for him, writing for me. I know it sounds corny, but I am living my dream of becoming a novelist. Just to be clear, this piece is the only thing I've managed to write lately. My head is too filled with anxiety, uncertainty, and all of the things I know, and think, and worry about. Things like death threats on the dark web, what all this means if he actually pulls this off, about the Southern Poverty Law Center's hate crimes map with too many red dots in our district.

"That's interesting. What do you write? I'm with the *LA Times*," she said. "Robin Abcarian."

Just then I notice the campaign's communications manager watching me talking to a reporter. He began swimming against the current through the hundreds of assembled volunteers trying to reach us. His panic was warranted, I suppose. But really, I'm a lifelong Democrat, an activist, a former reporter and columnist myself, and the first one who told my husband he should do this, he could do this. He must. I could be on message, or I suppose, I could ruin everything. I am, at least for the past 20 months on the campaign trail, in a supporting role: clapping, smiling wife.

I take a deep breath. "I write novels. My latest is *Best Day Ever.* Thank you for asking me." I smiled as I felt the veil lift, the reality that she was seeing me for me. She began to launch into a series of new questions but Jack, our campaign communications director, had reached our side.

"Harley's ready for you," he noted with a tense smile.

The reporter and I parted ways. The veil returned, and I clapped as my husband finished his speech.

Robin mentioned our encounter in her piece for the *LA Times:* "In deepest red Orange County, a blue flame is sparking in a district that has long supported Rep. Rohrabacher ..."

The question is, as it has been for almost two years, whether that spark will turn into a blue wave. We will find out on Election Day.

It happened again yesterday, by the way. I was seen. A woman burst through the crowd and came right up to me and said, "I heard you speak at Sisters in Crime. I loved your talk. I loved your novel. I can't wait for the next one."

She reminded me I'm here, too. It's me. As the woman who encouraged my husband to attend the Women's March, who pushed him into this political circus because I know he's the right man for the job. I'm all in on this campaign, of course, because for the last thirty years, it has been team Harley and Kaira. In two days, life will reset. Until then I'll enjoy my new role as head number-one fan and supporter. I feel blessed by the incredible new friends I've made through this campaign. Together we have made a real difference in Orange County, I can feel it. We all can.

No matter what happens in two days, I've learned a lot about the campaign trail. I've seen the hope and courage in the faces of the volunteers at rallies. I now know first-hand the reality of dark money, trackers, political attack ads, the lack of recourse for outright lies, the things you cannot say even when you really want to say them. I've learned to harden myself to the attacks, to smile and carry on in the face of lies. In the end, this is all about much more than me, or my family. I do believe, as Harley states over and over again at each rally, our democracy is at risk. That's why my family has made this commitment. We believe that we *are* the people, just like you are the people, who must stand up, all of us, and do our part. Because this is what democracy looks like.

Even if it's just smiling and clapping, each of us participating in his or her own way, it's all-important right now.

Update!

Since I wrote this piece, Harley has won the election and will represent the 48th district of California in the next congress. When I look back at what I wrote before the election, I find myself wondering about this new, new role I'll be stepping into. I'll try to uphold my end of the bargain, the expectations placed upon the spouse. I'm honored to serve and looking forward to the two years ahead of us. Whatever unfolds, I know this election, this Blue Wave-filled House of Representatives, will make change for the better. I know this because it's already begun.

Hysterical

Kelli Stanley

Even the seats in first class aren't what they used to be, he thought, pushing his head backward against the thin cushion. Nothing's the way it used to be.

He glanced toward the woman hesitating in the aisle, then leaned in a little for a closer look.

Probably early forties and still very attractive—she'd taken good care of herself. Not one of those fat, suburban women who ate constantly, huge wobbling butts in polyester pants, or, even worse, the scrawny-necked middle-aged academic types bleating about the dangers of cosmetics. Good God, the only danger was to the public when they flopped around, sagging breasts and wrinkled skin and underarm hair, screaming hysterically about one thing or another.

He smiled as she opened the overhead compartment and pushed in a small piece of blue luggage. No, this one looked like she'd had some Botox here, a pull there—and her arms and breasts were still firm enough to be distracting, especially through the gauzy overwrap and the hot pink T-shirt that set off some nice, tanned décolletage.

He suddenly felt like having a beer. This was going to be a good flight.

She dropped her eyes and met his. He smiled with his teeth. "Need any help?"

"No, thanks. I'm okay." Her voice was pleasant, with just a hint, possibly, of helplessness, which made the whole package that much more attractive. Yes, this was going to be a good flight . . .

She settled into the aisle seat next to him, placing her large purse—a Tommy

Hilfiger, he noted with approval—under the seat in front after removing an iPad and her mobile phone. She noticed him watching her and smiled apologetically.

"Too much technology, isn't it? Tablet for business, phone for the kids. Even on a short flight, I try to keep tabs on them—not that they need me anymore, of course, but you know how mothers are."

He nodded indulgently. "Of course. Once that instinct kicks in, there's no going back."

And all for the better, he thought. He didn't agree with the men who thought desirability ended at nineteen. Once a woman's body had been through the sanctity of childbearing, it gained a certain pliability that compensated for the lack of tightness. In fact, some of the best nights he'd ever enjoyed had been with mothers—especially married ones. He grinned to himself rather boyishly, reflecting on that profane acronym "MILF." And here, on this little regional jet, he found himself sitting next to one.

The flight attendant, another blonde on the older side, approached with a tray. "We're serving cheese and rosemary crackers with wine—unless you'd like something else to drink."

"Beer, please," he said. "Got any microbrews?"

"Let's see . . . we have Fat Tire, Lagunitas, Blue Point, Sam Adams—"

"I'll take a Sam Adams." Sam Adams. Brought back the memories, and maybe he'd even make a few more on this trip . . .

"And for you, ma'am?" The flight attendant bent toward his companion, smiling broadly, and for a moment he wondered if they knew each other. Or if they were, God forbid, lesbians? He gave himself an internal slap on the head and looked out the window while the attractive blonde gave her order.

He was being stupid. His imagination was getting the better of him—especially after all the utter crap he'd been through recently. All those frustrated, dried-up shrews protesting, protesting . . . it was enough to drive any man to the brink. He needed a vacation, and the time off would settle things—his practice would calm down, and his friends in Washington would see that the protestors were dealt with.

He turned back toward the blonde, following the lines of her T-shirt and skinny jeans with admiration. She and the stewardess were still smiling and chatting, typically oblivious. At least neither one had recognized him, not that he'd been on TV so very much, but that latest case did get quite a bit of Fox News coverage. Fame could be inconvenient sometimes.

The stewardess finally left, threading her way through the hordes of economy class filing through, carrying backpacks and roller boards and everything but goats and chickens. Really, the airline should clamp down on the freeloaders, always abusing the system. He leaned in toward the woman.

"It's always a wait, but at least we got our orders in."

"Yes, and these little snack packs look interesting." She pointed at the small white plate sitting on her pulled-down tray. "Should go well with the Chardonnay."

He stretched out a hand, grinning. "My name's Troy. Troy Cavendish."

She smiled and clasped his hand. "Nice to meet you, Mr. Cavendish. I'm Dinah Spivic."

The stewardess appeared again, and they busied themselves with the wine and beer, no sign of anything odd passing between the women. He sipped the Samuel Adams and shook his head. Overactive imagination, Troy, my boy. Overactive. Put it to good use and imagine them naked.

The endless stream of economy travelers was slowing down—the Embraer could only hold so many. He lowered his voice to a conspiratorial whisper.

"How's the food?"

"Not bad. How's your beer?"

He grinned. "Not as good as I remember from grad school."

She laughed. Better and better.

"I'd better text my daughter and then shut off everything . . . we should be taking off in a few minutes."

"Of course."

He stretched a little and looked around the first-class cabin while she swiped open the iPhone. All the seats were full, and the funny thing was that the passengers were all women. Only six seats in all, of course, two rows of two on the right, two rows of one on the left, but still kind of strange. He was the only man in first class.

Dinah switched her phone to airplane mode and stowed it and her iPad in the flap of the seat in front of her. She buckled herself in, asking him brightly, "So is this a business trip or pleasure?"

"Pleasure. Two weeks of fishing."

"Saginaw Bay or somewhere else?"

He raised his eyebrows. "You know the sport?"

She smiled. "Just a little. My husband used to fish."

Used to? He glanced down at her left hand—no ring. That meant either divorced or widowed. Probably divorced. Not as much of a challenge, but he'd had enough challenges lately.

He smiled back. "As a matter of fact, I'll be in Saginaw for a week before driving up to Hubbard Lake. I've got a cabin up there."

She looked suitably impressed. "How nice! I'm sure it helps with stress. So what do you do—are you in business?"

Crackle and feedback from the audio system drowned him out. The blond stewardess was making the typical announcement about safety doors and placards. Dinah actually seemed to be paying attention. He liked that.

Smiling to himself, he glanced out the window at the tarmac.

His eyes widened and he caught his breath.

No—no, damn it, couldn't be . . .

His hand clenched the armrest, head snapping toward the aisle, no, can't be her, can't be her, then back again to the window, refusing to believe she was . . .

Gone.

She—it—whatever it was—gone.

Nothing there.

He wiped the tiny window with his sleeve, peering through it. Jesus Christ, Troy . . . better make that beer a Scotch—

"Sir, please fasten your seatbelt. We are preparing for take-off."

The stewardess again.

"Yeah, fine—can you get me a Scotch and soda?"

"As soon as we are in the air, sir."

He grunted, unnerved. Dinah looked at him with curiosity. "Are you all right, Mr. Cavendish?"

Her voice and the glimpse of those tanned breasts straining against the

T-shirt helped clear his head. What the hell—he obviously needed this break more than he'd suspected.

"I'm—I'm perfectly fine. Just thought I saw someone I knew on the tarmac for a second . . . silly of me. And please—call me Troy."

Her laugh was tinkly, very feminine. "Oh, I've done that. A few times. Thought I saw someone or something, at the window or on the street or when we were out driving. No one else ever sees it, of course . . . my husband used to get so mad about it. He never believed me. Always accused me of being a hysterical female."

Husband in past tense again. The flight was only a little over an hour—not much time to set things up, but once he had the Scotch . . .

He swallowed the rest of the beer, eyes on Dinah. "That was unchivalrous. Women should always be believed . . . even when they're wrong." He chased it with a grin and noted the flush of color that rose to her face.

Rumble and roar filled the small jet, pushing them both back against the seats as the engines revved and the plane built up speed on the runway.

He gave in to the force, closing his eyes and smiling to himself over a vision of taking off Dinah's T-shirt at the cabin on Hubbard Lake.

The plane lifted, angle steep, and he kept his eyes closed for a few more minutes as it curved around Chicago, heading for Michigan.

He opened his eyes, surprised, when he felt her hand patting his.

"She should bring you your Scotch any second now."

"I hope so. Would you like more wine?"

She shook her head. "I don't think so. It's such a short flight."

He nodded, then hesitated. Not much time, after all, better get on with it.

"I noticed you, uh, referred to your husband in the past tense. I hope I'm not getting too personal, but—are you divorced?"

Her blue eyes opened wide. She was interested. She was definitely interested.

"Yes, as a matter of fact . . . and you?"

"Two years ago, last week." He laughed. "Not that I'm counting."

The stewardess showed up with some Scotch and soda in a plastic cup. "Johnnie Walker is all we have on board. I hope that'll do."

He smiled at her. "That'll be just fine."

Dinah asked: "Can we access Wi-Fi now?"

The blonde nodded. "Just log in to the app. And let me know if I can get you two another snack plate or anything else. More wine?"

"Well . . . all right. Another Chardonnay?"

Dinah leaned against him a little, as if in confidence. "I really shouldn't. I have no head for alcohol."

He sipped the Scotch and grinned. "Don't worry. I'll watch out for you."

One of the women across the aisle—this one young, with short pink hair and a pierced nose, the kind he'd seen enough of for one lifetime—got up to use the restroom near the cockpit. He wondered how someone like that could get the money to fly first class but dismissed the thought almost immediately. Things were not what they used to be.

Dinah smiled and asked him, again, what he did.

"I'm a psychiatrist," he said.

Not a lie, but not the whole truth. Just enough to get her in that cabin . . .

"Really? That must be such a stressful job! So important, too, what with all the troubles these days."

The way she said "troubles" suggested she understood things, that here was a woman with whom he shared more than a first-class seat and a physical attraction. He looked at her with renewed appreciation . . . clearly, Dinah was on the right wavelength.

She continued, thoughtfully, as she drained her plastic wine glass: "My husband wanted me to see one, you know, but it's so difficult to find the right person."

He shrugged modestly. "I do what I can to help people."

She leaned over a little closer, breasts against his arm. The wine must be working, and she wasn't on the second glass yet.

"I think it's very noble. I'd trust you."

He placed his hand over hers on the armrest. "Thank you, Dinah. I feel like . . . oh, I don't know. I feel like this was my lucky day, meeting you on this flight."

She smiled again. "I think I'll use the ladies' room. Be right back."

She got up a little clumsily, standing near the hatch to let the flight attendant pass her. They shared a few words, Dinah pointing back to her seat.

The stewardess approached with the wine. "Your seat companion said to leave this on her tray."

He nodded. "I'll take care of it."

The clock was ticking and he wanted to get on with things, but Dinah, like all women, was taking her time. He drummed his fingers on the open tray and scanned the passengers again. Across the aisle, the one with the pierced nose and a black woman with those hair row things. In front of him, a grandmother in her sixties and another woman in her forties—the kind you'd never look at twice.

He smiled contentedly to himself. Yessir, Troy, you were a lucky man today. Dinah is practically in the bag—

He looked out the window again and stopped breathing.

By the engine—35,000 feet up—staring right at him—no, no, goddamn it, it was impossible, impossible, she was dead and buried and it was over, all over, and he'd won, they'd won, they'd silenced her once and for all, with his help, with his indispensable help, and there was no goddamn way she was crouched on the wing of a plane flying over 400 miles an hour—

Troy jumped up and pushed the button for the stewardess.

The blonde came over smiling, just as Dinah opened the restroom door. "More Scotch?"

He was having a hard time getting the words out. "I—I saw—look out this window. You see anything weird? Anything that shouldn't be there?"

The other passengers were turning around to stare at him, and he lowered his voice with difficulty.

"I saw something. Something out there."

Dinah was looking at him, her pretty face framed with concern. The stewardess frowned.

"I can assure you, sir—this flight is on-time, on-schedule, and everything is proceeding to plan. The weather is clear, and there've been no indications of large flocks of birds or anything else on the Doppler. What do you think you saw?"

He looked from one woman to the other and licked his lips. His breath was coming out in jerks.

"I—nothing. I think I'm just—I'm all right, I'm all right. Maybe some water—no more Scotch."

"I can ask the co-pilot or pilot to come talk to you. Would that make you feel better?"

The expression of maternal pity was more than he could bear. "No, I'm—I'm sure I probably just, uh, just fell asleep and—and had a dream. No need to bother the pilots."

"No bother. I'll see who's available."

She left, murmuring a few words to Dinah, who picked up her wine glass and sat down next to him, fastening her seat belt.

"Are you sure you're okay, Troy? What did you think you saw? Nothing—well, nothing like a bomb, right? I mean, after 9-11, I never wanted to fly again . . ."

He shook his head. "Forget about it. I'm just—just overtired. Had some—uh, some important cases, high-pressure, high-stakes. I'm fine."

She reached over and squeezed his hand. "I know what it's like not to be believed. If you saw something, you can tell me."

Maybe it was the shakeup he'd had or the wine glass in her hand, maybe the thought of those breasts in his, or maybe the feeling that this woman was the kind he knew was out there but rarely met, the kind who was just happy being a woman, being a mother, not asking for anything beyond maybe a little indulgence once in a while, some special piece of jewelry, an occasional vacation together, some sympathetic murmurs when she got emotional over a soap opera or scary movie . . . a woman, a real woman, a woman who appreciated, above all, traditional values.

He shook his head. "Strange. I—I feel almost as though I've known you for a lifetime, Dinah, and yet we've just met. Perhaps this was God's way of telling me I needed some rest, and in His infinite kindness, He sent me you."

Her hand flew to her chest. "That is one of the nicest things anyone has ever said to me."

He swallowed, blinking his eyes. What the hell was wrong with him? Move it, Troy! He picked up her other hand and raised it to his lips.

"I meant it. I don't know what your plans are—"

"Sir, here's the co-pilot for you."

Startled, he dropped Dinah's hand and looked up.

Another woman. Jesus, what was this—bring your daughter on a flight day?

She was small, dark, about fifty. Nothing he'd take home, and not exactly what he felt comfortable with in the cockpit.

"You had a question about the plane, sir?" she asked.

His tone was more short-tempered than intended. "I'm fine. I wish you'd all—I just fell asleep, for God's sake. No questions, nothing's wrong."

"Sir, if you think you saw something—"

"I told you, I fell asleep! I'm fine!"

All the women in first class were looking at him again. He hadn't realized he'd stood up and raised his voice.

The co-pilot's response was measured. "Very well, sir. But why don't you shut the window shade so as not to agitate yourself or the other passengers if it happens again. We are only about thirty minutes from landing. We're starting our descent now."

She stepped away just as the seatbelt light came back on. Dinah turned toward him, voice full of care.

"Troy—let me email my daughter. My only plans are to spend time with her—she's a first year at Central. I think . . . I think I'd like to keep seeing you."

He watched her open the phone and text something with one finger, breath in, breath out, and he inhaled too, in-out, in-out, feeling so much better. That tanned, firm skin would be under his fingers soon enough, soft, compliant, but, if he was any judge of women, not too compliant. She'd make noises about it being too soon, too quick, but ultimately, they'd both get what they wanted.

Maybe some things were still what they used to be.

His mouth was still dry, and he swallowed again. Tired, that's all he was. Tired. The recent publicity had been gratifying in many ways but was still exhausting. No wonder he'd suffered a little slip. And then there were those others—like that nose-ring girl, he imagined—who'd made him a target. A colleague had sent him the—what did they call them? Memes?—circulating on social media. Ultimately, though, he'd won. They'd won. And they'd keep on winning.

He took another deep breath and smiled. Who cares if he'd had a momentary lapse? It didn't matter, and nobody would ever know, anyway. Nobody that counted. Plus, it helped him get this one on the hook. Clean air, blue sky, green lake and a soft piece of ass . . .

Turning to lower the shade, he glanced out the window.

Je-sus . . .

Troy started whimpering.

Face stoic and clenched against the wind, finger jutting out like an accusation, there she was, the woman he'd said was unfit, the woman whose political career he'd ended, just like Tom Eagleton, old playbook working well in a brave new era, and now—now somehow she was on the fucking plane at fucking 20,000 feet up or however much they were and she had been on the tarmac, he had seen her, goddamnit, she was there, taunting him and stalking him, stalking him for fuck's sake, but she was dead, goddamn it, dead and fucking buried . . .

He pushed past Dinah and plunged into the aisle, wide-eyed. The women all stared at him.

He ran past them toward the economy seats, people murmuring. Someone whipped out a cell phone.

He shoved himself in between a large woman on the aisle and an older man in sweatpants. They were saying something, saying something loudly, but he had to look out the window, get a better look at the wing, after all, he'd only caught a glimpse from the second row, had to make sure . . .

The co-pilot was walking toward him, and a thin white guy in slacks and a burly black man with an Afro stood up and wrestled him to the floor.

THERE WERE VOICES. He opened his eyes. Was the plane on the ground?

Two women in pilot uniforms stood by the hatch, talking to some men in white. Two female pilots? Was this some sort of joke, a prank? He struggled against the handcuffs and managed to prop himself up.

The women in first class were lined up, apparently waiting for something. Next were the two men he vaguely remembered tackling him. Tackling him? Then he saw Dinah.

Dinah. Thank God.

She walked toward him, carrying the little blue bag he remembered her stowing away. She lowered herself into the nearest seat and looked down at him, a gentle smile on her face.

Her voice was as soft as her hand . . . as soft as those breasts that were almost within his reach . . .

"Troy. There are some doctors waiting to see you. They say—they say you had a hallucinatory fit. You were—well, I hate to say it—you were hysterical. Shout-ing about a woman on the wing of the plane."

He shook his head, trying to clear it, but it was heavy, fuzzy, and the weight of the plane, the weight of the earth, was too much and all on top of him. He felt depressed, hopeless. Why? There was nothing wrong. He'd seen her—he'd seen . . . He shook his head again. His voice was thick and slurry.

"I don't know what's wrong. I did—I did see something. Her."

Dinah smiled, a different kind of smile than he'd seen before. She nodded.

"The Supreme Court Justice you called a liar on television, in front of your pals in Congress, labeling her a criminal and calmly stating that she ought to be 'locked up' for perverting justice and morality, if not for psychological infirmity. The Justice whose testimony you pooh-poohed, laughing off the thirteen accu-sations of rape against the man who did, in fact, rape her. The Justice who was then murdered, shot in the back by one of your leader's slavering cult followers shouting, 'Lock her up' and 'Baby Killer.' The Justice who could have prevent-ed . . . well, we won't go into that."

There seemed to be two Dinahs now, which meant four breasts, so that was okay. But she—she was different. Didn't make sense.

Things weren't how they should be.

"Don't you believe me? I saw her! I did!"

The Dinahs nodded. "I believe you. I believe you, Troy, just like you believed the woman you testified against. Just like you believed Casey Martin."

Casey Martin? Rang a bell, ding dong, ding dong, but he couldn't answer it, no he couldn't . . .

There were even more Dinahs now, and they were all leaning over him.

"Casey Martin was my sister, Troy. You pretended not to believe her when she said she'd been raped. Back before you were testifying for Congress and were just testifying for rapists. Back before you and your friends made sure that they were one and the same thing. You swore that she was psychologically incompetent. That she was a liar. Just like you have with so many other women . . . women who had mothers, sisters, grandmothers and daughters. Women who had husbands and brothers and fathers, too."

She looked up and nodded her head at one of the women from first class, who nodded in triplicate to the nine pilots and co-pilots standing guard at the hatch.

"Casey killed herself, Troy. Because no one believed her. Because you said she was just a hysterical woman."

The Dinahs opened up the blue box, holding something in a bag, and whispered in his ear. His eyes were large and swimming, and his cheeks felt wet.

"When they take you off the plane, they will find flakka in your system and in your beer and Scotch. Flakka in your pocket. My niece does go to Central, Troy—Central Medical."

The Dinahs looked back toward the six young women with pink hair and nose rings.

"You'll be arrested and kicked out of the medical profession. You've got a state license to practice in Illinois and Washington, D.C., and we're back in Illinois, Troy, true-blue Illinois. Seems you caused a hazardous situation, so we turned around and landed at O'Hare because Saginaw didn't have the security we needed. And since this isn't the District of Columbia, nobody's flashing a badge of immunity and escorting you to safety."

The Dinahs bent even closer, voices a chorus of whispers.

"Your political allies will ostracize you. Your church will disown you. And even if they don't . . . it won't matter. It's over. Your brain chemistry's been changed, Troy, and you may find yourself experiencing hallucinations from time to time. But here's one thing to make you feel better, something you never did for Casey, even though you knew she was telling the truth: You weren't imagining things, Troy. You really did see something out there. And she's going to chase you for the rest of your miserable life."

That's when Troy Cavendish started screaming.

To the best of anyone's knowledge, he's never stopped.

Tiger Daughter

S. J. Rozan

Chapter One

González felt like shit.

His skull pounded with sickening thuds. Opening his eyes, he saw only darkness. He shivered on sweat-soaked sheets. Not his. A hotel. Some *puta* from the bar had brought him here. Goddamn her! *Una china*, he thought, but he couldn't really remember. Whoever she was, she wasn't worth this. He coughed and tasted thick, sweet smoke.

"Awaken."

A low, harsh voice issued the order; or maybe it was his own, trying to will himself out of this nightmare.

"González. Awaken."

Who was speaking?

"Look at me!"

González squinted. He saw no one. His stomach turned over. He tasted his own bile, and the painful thumping in his head got louder.

But no, not just in his head. With a shudder of bewilderment and fear, he recognized the rhythm: this was not only his own blood pounding. Somewhere, somewhere close, the *batá* drums called to each other, *iya* and *itotele* and *okonkolu*, speaking timeless secrets in the ancient, wordless tongue.

A burst of white light blinded González. He whimpered. When he could see again, a figure stood before him. It spoke, and it smiled. "González, you are a fortunate man."

González's blood froze.

The figure wore flowing robes of green, gold, and blue. Below a half-mask with cowrie-shell eyes, its face and its hands gleamed a ghostly white, like polished bone. For a moment it stood motionless. Then it howled.

González's heart hammered madly as the figure erupted. To the music of the drums, it leapt and stomped and shook. The beads on its wrapped headdress whipped the air. The mask made it resemble Elegguá, but this was not Elegguá. These were not Elegguá's colors. And Elegguá was not known to hold a short, curved knife in his right hand.

That it was an *orisha*, though, was certain. The drums and the smoke and the fear told him that.

An *orisha*, a spirit, with a knife, appearing to González. Telling him he was fortunate in tones that said otherwise.

Leaping high, it let out a scream and suddenly stopped still. The drums fell into terrifying silence.

The *orisha* fixed its cowrie-shell eyes on González. "I wanted to come collect you." It leaned forward. "I said, this man has no *ashé*. He has squandered his life force and worse, he steals it from others. Let me take him. But Olorún chastised me." The *orisha* bowed its head. "He said, no man is without *ashé*. González has done much evil. Still he may yet save himself. You will give him the chance."

González wanted to answer, at least to bow his head at the mention of Olorún. But he couldn't speak, could barely move, was able only to follow the *orisha* with his eyes as it drew closer.

"González, what you have done in your life no sacrifice of chickens or goats— not even your own blood—can wash away. But because it is the will of Olorún, I have come to tell you what you must do now." The *orisha's* black lips in its bone-white face curved into a terrible smile. "The beautiful woman who lives with you. Clara. Barely more than a girl. You seduced her with power and with the things she lacked,and chained her to you with violence and fear. Now she has borne you a son. Clara wants to leave you, González. You know that. For the sake of her child she wants to escape your wickedness and your world. But you beat her, you torment her, you threaten the child. Do you think Olorún doesn't see?"

"That will be your sacrifice, González. You will let them go. Clara will take the child and leave you. You will not look for them, not try to see them, ever again."

The beat of the drums began once more. The *orisha* threw its arms wide, raised its face to the ceiling in the swirling smoke. González could not take his eyes from the knife. Cowrie-shell eyes glittering, the *orisha* brought the blade's tip to González's chest. González felt himself constrict in fear. The knife touched the skin over his heart.

"No," González heard himself whisper. "Please. *Por favor.*"

The *orisha* threw back its head with a cackle as horrible as its smile. It slid the knife into its leather belt.

"No, González. Not this night. But you must swear it."

González couldn't speak.

"Swear it!" the *orisha* thundered, over the hurtling drums. "You will permit Clara and the child to leave you. Make a vow!"

"I swear." González could only whisper.

"Again. Louder."

"I swear it," González said. It wasn't louder, but he could do no more.

The *orisha* lifted González's sweating left hand. Onto his finger it slid a ring, beaded in the same colors the *orisha* wore.

"You will never remove this, González. When you see it, you will remember your vow. And you will remember me. This is the chance Olorún said I must give you. There will not be another."

Again, a violent white flash. Then González was alone, in darkness and silence. Once more he whimpered. He felt himself falling into oblivion and did not fight against it.

Chapter Two

Still grinning, Lily Lee slung her duffel bag onto the kitchen counter. She'd changed and washed up in the hotel bathroom, to minimize subway stares. She'd gotten them anyway, for the grin she'd made no effort to hide, and for the smell that clung to her, to the bag, and to the gear inside.

Not much you could do about incense smoke that strong. Maybe she should've left the white greasepaint and black lipstick on and really spiced up people's mornings.

She gulped down a glass of water. Afro-Caribbean dance was hot work, especially in all that smoke. Maybe the hotel would charge González extra for cleaning. Fantastic.

She drank another glassful. If she were sensible, she'd sleep now. If she were sensible, though, she wouldn't do this for a living. And she couldn't sleep yet. When the inevitable crash came, she'd be wiped, but that was hours away.

No, after a shower she'd get some powerful caffeine—her drug of choice, though she'd tried others—and deal with the gear. The cloth for the headdress and robes would get cleaned and stored in the other apartment, alias the prop closet. The unused flash-bangs and the knife, too. The papier-mâché mask, smelly and wet with sweat, could go. If she ever had to scare the crap out of a *santerista* again, she'd make a new one. She'd needed a mask, for sure: What *santerista*, even one as dumb, drunk, and drugged as González, would fall for an Asian-eyed *orisha*? Though next time she'd use something easier to see through than goddamn sliced-up cowrie shells.

Lily crossed the room and threw open the window. The breeze off the Hudson brought birdsong and traffic whoosh. Her skin tingled. Adrenaline still bathed every nerve, every cell. She was invincible. She could defeat armies.

She was ready to take on anyone.

Dangerous Deductions

Maria Alexander

Daddy *says* we're going to see *Star Wars*.

So Benny and I scramble into the back seat of Daddy's Pinto, knees digging into the sharp cracks in the vinyl upholstery, and Daddy slams the door shut. He then slides behind the wheel. "Put your goddamn seatbelts on!" His sweaty face turns to watch Benny as she struggles to clip the heavy buckle over her tiny legs.

"Do it like this, dummy," I say, tightening the belt. Benny is short for Benita. She's five years old. I'm nine, so I have to show her how to do everything.

Daddy fumbles with something in the glove compartment and then starts the car, lurching backward with a roar.

I'm so excited! Since I first heard that deep voice say, "A long time ago, in a galaxy far, far away . . ." I couldn't wait to see this movie. When the commercial first came on, Daddy was at the dining room table, sighing "Christ" over and over as he scribbled on his legal pad. It was "audit" time. My daddy is a tax investigator for the Franchise Tax Board, but he seems to get investigated more than anybody else for some reason.

Anyway, I yelled, "Daddy Daddy Daddy I gotta see this moooviiieee! There's a guy in a black helmet, and people swinging over stuff, and spaceships . . ."

"Oh, for Chrissake. Will you shut up if I take you?"

Benny and I nodded.

And today we're finally going. But the thing with Daddy is that he doesn't always go where he says we're going. And he can't leave us alone.

The car races down Balboa Boulevard. Daddy drives much faster when

Mommy isn't here. Mommy works at Sav-On Drugs. She wears a white dress and helps people find things and scoops ice cream. That's where she is today.

"Where do my babies wanna eat?"

Benny bounces in her seat. "Taco Bell! Taco Bell!"

"But Daddy," I say, "We just ate breakfast."

"Well, you don't wanna get hungry during the movie, do ya?"

"No."

"Then Taco Bell it is!"

Benny may be stupid, but we agree on one thing: Taco Bell bean burritos with extra onions and taco sauce are really yummy.

Daddy buys a big pile of squishy burritos. We swivel in the iron chairs at the Formica tables as we eat. The sky is hazy like the toilet bowl after Daddy has flushed. And the air stinks like robot farts. After two bites of her burrito, Benny announces she isn't hungry.

Daddy smokes and doesn't eat anything. "For later, then." He puts the remaining burritos in the bag.

Slurping down the last of my Coke, I hold the warm bag as he drives. The Pinto makes its way onto the 101. "Daddy, where are we going?"

"Settle down," he growls, turning off the freeway onto a maze of streets. "I got something to do before we go to the theater." He eyes me in the rearview mirror. "And if you don't behave, Three, we're not gonna see *Star Wars*. Got that?"

My name is Theresa, but everyone calls me Three. I was almost born on the Number Three line to Lenox station in Brooklyn. Mommy says her water broke as she was hanging onto the strap. Fluid gushed from her panties, splashing over the gummy floor and onto everybody's shoes. The man next to her yelled, "Jesus Christ, lady! What're you, a fuckin' fire hose?"

We're not allowed to say "fuck." Daddy gets *really* upset . . . like, so upset that he makes the Hulk look like Mr. Rogers. So I don't repeat that part of the story. But that's okay. I like it when Mommy does.

We moved to Los Angeles seven years ago. It's the only place I remember.

Soon the diners and bars give way to steep streets and thick weepy trees. Towering houses with wide windows are shoved back from the road, some hidden by bushes and metal gates topped with lions. We drive really slow through the sleepy neighborhood. Everyone is probably still watching cartoons. The Pinto stops before a tall hedge next to a house that must be owned by Thurston Howell the Third. I imagine it has butlers, and the furniture is like what's in *The Jetsons*, but I can't see inside. The windows are choked with thick drapes.

Daddy's eyes flicker in the rearview mirror. "You two, get down!" His hairy hand swipes back at Benny's head. "Get out of the seat belt and slide down behind the front seats. NOW!"

I pop the seat belt and drop down behind the passenger seat. Benny does likewise. The cooling burrito bag sits at eye level. Daddy grabs something from the glove compartment and gets out of the car, shutting the door carefully.

Benny's head pokes up. "Get down, dummy!" I pull her below the window. Resigned, Benny fingers her Mary Janes, unbuckling the shoes. Soon, her shoes are off and she plays with her toes through her pink tights.

Like a turtle, I crane my head carefully to see out the window. A dog barks in the distance. Daddy digs for several minutes through a garbage can on the far side of Thurston Howell's house. He pulls out some papers and smiles.

And then something bad happens. A man appears through the white wooden side gate and points a gun at Daddy's head. A cold feeling shoots down my throat and into my tummy.

The man says something to Daddy I can't hear. Daddy drops the papers and puts his hands in the air. With his gun, the man prods Daddy through the gate and they disappear behind the house.

Great. Now we'll *never* see *Star Wars*.

I sink below the window. Still scared, but mostly mad.

"What's Daddy doing?" Benny grabs her feet. "I don't like the car. It smells like gazoleen."

I shimmy over the seat and shove open the door on Benny's side. "Put on your shoes! We've gotta get Daddy."

The morning air from the shady street cools my cheeks as I step out onto the asphalt, Benny landing with a *slap* behind me. I peek around the car at the place where Daddy had been standing. The lawn smell tickles my nose. I motion to Benny. She scurries with me along the hedge up to the house. We then sneak past the front door and into the bushes that sprout under the first-story windows by the gate. Someone rattles a chain as they exit the gate with what sounds like a dog. We press against the house.

"Goooood booooby," a strange man says.

Footsteps retreat through the gate and a door slams in the distance. The dog barks twice and growls. I inch toward it, my sneakers grinding into the pebbles and dirt. We've got to get past. Maybe he's actually a nice doggy, like the little dachshund named Dynamite that lives in the apartment downstairs. Dynamite can be really mean, but he loves treats.

I get an idea. "Benny, go get the burritos. But be quiet and super-quick like Road Runner, okay?"

She dashes across the lawn, making soft car noises. Although she wavers with confusion after she retrieves the bag, I signal to her and she returns to my hiding place. I open the bag and unwrap one of the burritos. The dog barks louder. I step out of the bushes and find a massive, snarling Doberman tethered to a post at the backyard gate. Straining against his chain, he curls back his lips to reveal razor-sharp teeth as he growls.

"Benny . . . *you* give doggy the burrito."

Benny cries. "Nooooooo-ho-hooooo!"

"Shhhhh! You want to see *Star Wars*, don't you?"

She nods, sobbing.

"Okay, then."

Benny shuffles toward the dog, holding the limp burrito out in front of her like an offering to a volcano god. The dog barks furiously, about to sink his slob-bery teeth into her throat. She drops the burrito at the dog's feet and shuffles backward. The dog sniffs the burrito and to my surprise gobbles it up, its tongue scraping the cement to savor every doughy bit. The dog then cocks its head at us, whining.

I peel open another wrapper and pass the burrito to Benny. The dog gobbles up that one, too.

I hand Benny the bag. "Don't give him another whole burrito. Feed him little pieces until I get back, okay?"

Standing on my toes, I unlatch the gate and let myself into the backyard as the dog happily licks Benny's fingers and hands. Behind the big white house there's an open garage packed with cars, a swimming pool, and a much smaller house that leaks rock music.

I dart across the yard and peer through the shutters of the small house.

Daddy sits in a chair, slumped forward, with three men around a low table, dealing cards. Two people are kissing on a couch in the background as the radio plays.

I wish I could knock on someone's door and ask them to call the police but Daddy hates cops. I have no idea how I'm going to save him, but I need to get inside.

Sneaking around the back of the little house, I find an open window. My fingers pry into the gaps where the window screen is bent and I wrench it out. I then climb into a steamy bathroom with heaps of clothes and towels. Someone moans behind the curtain of the running shower. Startled, I hurry into the hallway past a kitchen. White painting masks and lots of strange equipment are spread over a table surrounded by chairs.

"BULLSHIT!"

In the front room, a large man points to Daddy. He reminds me of Grizzly Adams. He's bald on top but his long blonde hair drifts over his mountainous shoulders.

"Just be cool, man," says a skinny guy with a heavy mustache and sunglasses. Mr. Cool wears an orange-and-brown mottled disco shirt with a wide-open collar revealing a hairless chest. "Jazz'll be here any minute."

Grizzly Adams paces. "And how are we going to explain this? What the fuck were you thinking?" He grimaces at the man who pointed the gun at Daddy's head.

Mr. Gun wears a brown suit and smokes a lumpy cigarette with a funny smell. I'm pretty sure it's marijuana. Mommy says only bad people smoke marijuana. He blows smoke in the air and sits back, knees spread. "What was I supposed to do? He got some incriminating shit. What would Jazz say if he landed in prison because of this garbage thief? You and me? It would be worse than unemployment. It would be unen-life-ment."

"You could have unen-lifed *him*!"

Mr. Gun shakes his head. "Killing isn't my thing. You dig? Relax. It's just a complication."

"Jazz is gonna shit when he sees this *complication*." Grizzly Adams notices something across the room. "Hey! Get a room. This isn't a fucking porno!" Grizzly Adams then leans over, picks up a straw and sniffs a line of white powder up off a piece of paper on the table.

"I'm cuttin' you off, man," Mr. Gun says. "You're paranoid."

"Go ahead and cut me off, you lazy cunt. I'm the only one awake and ready to work when Jazz gets back."

And so they argue. Black hair falling in his bruised eyes, bloody lips cracked, hands tied behind his back with a telephone cord, Daddy stirs. His eyes land on me and widen, his head wagging in slow motion.

Suddenly, Grizzly Adams, Mr. Cool and Mr. Gun stop arguing. They're all staring at me, too.

I turn to run back into the bathroom, but two naked people are kissing on the plush bath rug, blocking my escape route. While my teachers say I'm too smart for my own good, I should have had a plan, like Fred on *Scooby-Doo*. Heck, even "danger-prone" Daphne has a plan sometimes. But I don't. So, I walk timidly into the front room.

Mr. Gun's mouth drops open. "The fuck?"

"Let my Daddy go," I say. "We're going to miss the movie."

Daddy hangs his head. "Shit," he whispers.

Grizzly Adams whines. "*Now* what are we going to do? It's a motherfucking kid! *His* motherfucking kid!"

I scan the room. An older man makes out on the couch with a young redhead, his hand under her dress between her legs. I feel embarrassed watching them. Distracted, the woman pushes him away. "Al, look! It's a little girl! She's so cute!"

The room doesn't have much furniture. A television sits silently in the corner. The radio plays on a short bookshelf on the wall closest to the hallway. Empty pizza boxes and fast food trash are stacked in the corners. The table is strewn with playing cards, ashtrays, beer cans, coffee mugs, and a mirror with two rows of white dust, as well as two guns; one looks kinda like Daddy's gun. I know the white dust is a drug and that the weird stink in the little house is pot.

"Hey, Daddy! They have a gun just like yours!"

It then occurs to me it *is* Daddy's gun. These bad guys have it *and* Daddy.

"Magic Carpet Ride" comes on the radio. Benny and I love dancing in our underwear to this song. But instead of dancing, I dive onto the table for Daddy's gun. Mr. Cool staggers to his feet. Mr. Gun catches Mr. Cool's lumpy cigarette. The redhead leaps off the couch and screams. The table crashes beneath me and everything hits the floor.

Grizzly Adams yanks me off the collapsed table. His thick arm clamps me at the waist to his bulging belly. "Gotcha, ya little shit."

Daddy glowers. "You hurt her and I'll kill you."

Everybody laughs.

Sleepy eyes. Runny noses. No one here is even really awake except Grizzly Adams. If only Daddy could break out of his bonds. Like the Hulk . . .

"You better let us go," I say. "Because WE'RE GOING TO MISS THAT FUCKING MOVIE."

Daddy explodes: "*What did I say about using that word, Three?*"

"FUCK FUCK FUCK FUCK FUCK!" I yell before Grizzly Adams clamps his hand over my mouth.

Daddy quakes, face and arms bulging with the rage. He all but turns green. His chair rocks as he rips away the phone cords. But just as Daddy breaks free, Grizzly Adams pulls a gun from his pants and points it at him.

"Siddown!"

Something scratches at the door. And then whines.

The door flies open and the big doggie bounds into the guesthouse with Benny riding his back like Paul Revere. The Doberman barfs Taco Bell burrito everywhere. People yell, dodging dog puke as it flies around, slipping in it as they try to get a hold of the dog, Benny, and the guns.

I kick Grizzly Adams in the knee. He drops me and the gun, clutching his chest, knees buckling. "I'm having a heart attack. Call the hospital! CALL THE FUCKING HOSPITAL."

Daddy punches Mr. Gun and grabs two of the guns from where they fell on the floor. He then points them at the startled crowd. Everyone immediately quiets down. "Three, get the other gun."

I pick it up carefully. Mommy said I shouldn't handle Daddy's guns, but I guess this is what Daddy would call "an exception."

"Come on, girls," he says, backing out. "Let's split."

THE PINTO ROARS back up the 101, three guns in the front seat, me and Benny in the back. Daddy coughs, hugging his ribs. He winces at every turn of the wheel. Benny picks dog hairs off of her pink tights. I eventually break the silence. "Daddy, are we going to see *Star Wars?*"

"After you both disobeyed me? No way, Three. You're not going to any damn movie. Ever."

I cross my arms and glare at him in the rearview mirror. "If you don't take us to see *Star Wars* right now, *we're* telling Mommy what happened."

Benny nods. "Yeah. Telling Mommy."

So, that's how we end up seeing *Star Wars*. It's the best thing I've ever seen in my life. I love the aliens and the music, but I especially love Darth Vader.

He kinda reminds me of someone. I'm not quite sure who.

Coffee Conversation with
Rhys Bowen and Jacqueline Winspear

November 2018

JACKIE: Rhys, I love our chats over coffee, so for this one we're going to have to pretend we're talking over lattes at Rulli's in Larkspur (California). We'll probably end up finishing the conversation there, if I know us! But something I'd like to know—you have a massive body of work behind you, beloved by readers, from children's fiction to mystery and everything in between—what has inspired your storytelling? Where do your ideas come from?

RHYS: I think I became a storyteller because as a child I had to invent my own pretend worlds. I grew up isolated from other children, first with my grandmother and great aunt and after that in a big house in the country in Kent (England). One of the many things we have in common! As a young child I invented pretend friends called the Gott family. There were four sisters: Gorna, Leur, Goo Goo, and Perambulator Gott. They had to come everywhere with us. Obviously, they were my desire for friends to play with.

As I got older I would pretend to be someone else: Patsy of the Circus, Fairy Marigold, a girl sleuth like George in the *Famous Five* series . . . always in a different reality from my own. As a teenager I wanted to be a movie star and I started writing scripts for me to star in. All very dramatic and tragic! So you can see that storytelling has always come naturally to me.

You also grew up in rural Kent, didn't you? Was yours a solitary childhood with plenty of opportunity for imagination?

JACKIE: Yes, I grew up in the heart of the Weald of Kent; we were surrounded by fields, woods, and farmland. My brother was born when I was four, so he was still a baby by the time I started school, and school was two miles away. I lived in my world of stories and even then felt very much allied with the natural world, and a sort of imaginary terrain of woodland creatures and otherworldly beings. It's a wonder I don't write fantasy, really! My mother was a wonderful storyteller, but many of her stories were about the war, so I had a very, very close sense of what it meant to be at war, even from an early age. Even when I went to school, living outside the town meant that I didn't see my friends much over the weekend. School holidays were spent on the local farms where my mother worked, and where I also worked over the summer holidays as soon as I was old enough. I loved books about girls having adventures. I wanted so much to be a pupil at Enid Blyton's *Malory Towers* (Blyton based it upon Benenden School, which was close to our home), or to have the life of Jill with her horses in Ruby Ferguson's books. I tried to get some of my friends at school to start our own version of the *Famous Five*, but no one else wanted to be a sleuth or have those kinds of adventures, whereas I loved a good mystery, even then! I think the last "boarding school" book I read was *The Trouble With Angels*, by Jane Trahey, when I was eleven. I still love that book!

How about you, Rhys—what were your favorite childhood stories?

RHYS: When I was young, I loved Enid Blyton's *The Adventures of the Wishing-Chair*. I really wanted a chair that flew and took me to magical places. Unfortunately, none of the chairs in our house developed wings. Around ten I moved on to *The Famous Five*, like you. They were so exciting: to be part of a group of children who went camping on their own, cooked sausages over a fire, and solved mysteries was my absolute fantasy. And I also loved all the boarding school books: the *Chalet School*, *Malory Towers*, although looking back on them they were full of snobbery and prejudice.

The book that really opened my eyes and really changed my world was *The Lord of the Rings*. I read it at about 16 and it showed me for the first time the scope of fiction, how someone could create a fictional world and actually take me there. I can't tell you how many times I've read it since then, even though I almost know it by heart.

I think a good thing about our childhoods was that we had freedom and time. I used to go off on my bike and be gone all day. Nobody asked me where I was going. And I had time to just think, swinging on the swing in our orchard. I feel sorry for today's overscheduled children. How do their imaginations ever develop?

So now I'm curious, Jackie: Did you want to be a writer when you were growing up?

JACKIE: Rhys, I think you and I mirror each other in our reading habits as children and young adults. Just the mention of *The Lord of the Rings* brings back so many memories—starting my A levels at a boys' school (I know—there's a story) and almost everyone clutching a copy of the book, as it had become almost a cult favorite. But about being a writer—ah yes, I remember the very day I decided I wanted to be a writer, and it's a bit of a tale. By the time I was five, it was clear that something was not quite right with my eyes, and finally it was discovered that I had a lazy eye. In fact, two lazy eyes, and to correct the problem, surgery would be necessary. However, in the year prior to surgery, I had to go to the hospital ophthalmology department to see the "orthoptist" every two weeks— they're like physiotherapists for eyes!

It was an exhausting appointment filled with exercises designed to prepare my eyes for the best outcome in surgery and to give the surgeon an idea about the extent to which my eye muscles had to be cut. Ugh! The journey to the hospital by bus was arduous, but on the way home I would not allow myself to doze off until after we'd passed the house next to the bus stop in Pembury. I always sat upstairs on the double-decker bus, as it was the only way to see over the tall hedge into the Edwardian villa with two big bay windows either side of the front door. From there I could see straight into this one room that fascinated me: there was a desk in the window with a black typewriter on top and usually a sheaf of papers alongside. Sometimes a book would be open to one side, or a teacup placed on the pile of books at the corner of the desk. A cardigan over the chair suggested the owner of the house had just left the room and the room was lined with books. So many books! In winter a fire burned in the grate beyond.

I remember making my mother come up to the top of the bus because I wanted to know who might own that house. Mum hated heights, so would rarely come up the stairs. "Who do you think lives there?" I asked. She looked down into the room while passengers below clambered onto the bus. "Oh, that looks like a writer's room," she said. So I made my declaration at the age of five: "I'm going to be a writer when I grow up."

Over the next year I tried to recreate that room in the bedroom I shared with my brother. Our local shopkeeper gave me an old ledger-type desk, and the elderly lady along the road asked me if I wanted a desk lamp. It was so ancient, I almost electrocuted myself when I plugged it in. I lobbied for a "Petite" typewriter until my mother used her Kensitas cigarette coupons to get one for me, and I began to write every single day. I was a terrible typist, but I sat at my desk and I wrote. Mind you, I didn't become a professional writer until my mid-thirties, but I got there in the end! And I still have the black typewriter I bought years later.

Rhys—now you—what was the catalyst for you becoming a writer?

RHYS: I knew I would be a writer in my teens. First it was poetry, inspired by Gerard Manley Hopkins, but then dark and brooding short stories in the manner of the post-war German novels I was reading. Ingeborg Bachman, etc. I had a short story broadcast on the BBC when I was sixteen. That was pretty special. But I still wanted to be an actress. I went to drama school, and that was when I realized that I could feel all these characters inside me, but somehow I just wasn't good enough to bring them to life. So I did as my parents wanted and went to university. While I was there, I wrote a couple of angst-filled novels that one writes at 19. And after uni I went into BRC drama on the production side, becoming a studio manager. I found myself thinking, as I worked on a play, "If I'd written this I would have ended it differently." I went home and wrote my own play, and with the bravado of a twenty-two-year-old I went down the hall to the head of drama and said, "I've written this play." A few days later he called me into his office and said, 'Yes, we like this. We're going to produce it."

I've actually never looked back since then. I've been a working, published writer pretty much all my life. But it took a while before I realized that writing was going to be my career, not a sideline to my career.

What led to Maisie Dobbs, Jackie? Was she someone who formed slowly over years or did she present herself to you fully formed and full of life?

JACKIE: Maisie Dobbs came to me fully formed, and while I was stuck in traffic on my way to work! I was literally daydreaming at a stoplight on Second Street in San Rafael (CA)—the one alongside the oil change place. It was raining and all I could see ahead of me were red stoplights and red taillights. Ugh! But I am a bit of a daydreamer, and I was in a sort of early morning zone—and at once Maisie Dobbs walked into my life. It was like watching a movie in my mind's eye, and so vivid.

I saw a woman in the garb of the mid-1920s emerge from Warren Street tube station. I knew it was Warren Street, because I used to work in Fitzroy Square, except that in my mind-movie the escalator was old and wooden, and there was a turnstile and not a machine to take my ticket. The woman walked outside, stopped to talk to the newspaper vendor, who thought she was "stuck up," and then she walked down the street, took an envelope with two keys from her black document case, opened the door, and went up the dingy staircase to another door, where she entered a small office that she had just rented. I basically saw the entire first chapter in my mind's eye, but then I heard all this honking behind me and realized the lights had changed, probably several times, and traffic had moved along. I heard a man yell, "It ain't getting any greener, lady!"

By the time I arrived at work, which was south of San Francisco, I had that whole story in my head, and I could not wait to get home to start writing—my first fiction since schooldays. I have since described the experience as one of "artistic grace." I was given a gift, in a way. But I also don't think those moments happen in a vacuum, because since childhood I had been interested in what happens to people impacted by war after the war is done. I was curious about the Great War, about the way people's lives were changed, and as I grew older that childhood curiosity became a more adult interest and inquiry. I was so interested in the lives of the women of the era, roughly from just before the Great War began in 1914, until the end of rationing, post-Second World War in the

mid-1950s. I am particularly interested in that amazing First World War generation of women in Britain, the first generation of women to go to war in modern
times in very significant numbers.

Now we're getting down to the subject we both love, Rhys, the generations
of women represented by our grandmothers and mothers; the generations of
women who demonstrated such grit, such bravery and resilience—I bet a certain
someone would call them "nasty women" today—and we know they had a few
equally demeaning names thrown at them in their day. Let's start talking about
those strong women! Shall we start with Molly Murphy? What was your inspiration for the character, and what did you want to bring to her story?

RHYS: My inspiration for Molly Murphy came after I had written a few Con-
stable Evans books. I liked him, but he was beginning to annoy me because he
was always so polite. When his superiors were rude to him, he just slunk away.
I wanted to write about someone who was not always so polite. A gutsy, feisty
female with a strong sense of justice . . . . Someone a lot more like me, I have
to admit. I spent a lot of time in school standing outside the principal's office
because I had spoken up in class. Usually it was to defend a schoolmate who was
unjustly picked on by a teacher.

I was wondering where to set my feisty female sleuth when I went to Ellis
Island. I was quite unprepared for the emotional overload I felt there and knew
I had to write about it. So, Molly became an Irish immigrant who had to flee for
her life and makes it as far as Ellis Island, where she is implicated in a murder.
I knew she'd be brave but not always wise, but I had no idea when I started this
series that she'd become a champion of women's rights. As I researched the time
period, it became clear to me that women did not have the vote. In New York a
married woman was essentially the property of her husband. When she married,
all her assets became his. If she left the marriage, the children remained his. He
could beat her if he wished with a stick no bigger than his thumb (the rule of
thumb, folks). He could commit her to an insane asylum with just the signature
of himself and one doctor.

Of course, Molly seethes at the injustice of this and with her friends becomes involved in the suffrage movement. I have now heard that these books have made it to the curriculum of women's studies courses! Molly would have been proud!

Jackie, when I think of Maisie, she has had the benefit, if you could call it that, of serving in a war, which had the byproduct of helping the women's cause. Do you think her life would have been very different if the war had not happened?

JACKIE: Good question. Had the Great War not happened, doubtless some aspects of Maisie Dobbs's life would have been different, but I believe she would still have been an independent woman. The fact is that the "New Woman" was emerging a good two decades before the war—in fact, while I was doing some research at the Women's Library in London, I came across an article in a women's journal published in early 1912 in which the question was posed: Is this the end of marriage? It seemed so many women were turning their backs on marriage, the statistics were becoming worrisome to those in power. And in the United States, politicians were very fearful indeed that the American suffragettes would become as strong and aggressive as their "sisters" in Britain. The truth is that the suffrage movement in the UK saw the war as an opportunity, and there was collusion with Lloyd George: Suffragette leaders made a pact to support the war because they could see that women would have to move into men's jobs to release men for the battlefield. Giving (some) women the vote in 1918 was a sort of "Thank you, ladies!" for the war effort. In the UK, as we know, the wartime contribution by women was considerable, because not one field of endeavor was left untouched by a woman's hand.

I too had that deep emotional response when I first went to Ellis Island. I took the first ferry of the day, so when I got there it was all but deserted. I could feel the emotion just seeping from the walls, as if it had leached from the souls of the thousands who had passed through there.

Rhys, I'm curious, is there a part of women's history that you'd like to explore in your writing?

RHYS: I am actually exploring a time close to your heart in my next book, *The Victory Garden*. It is set in World War I and is about women who join the Women's Land Army, i.e., the land girls. I don't think it is widely known that the

Women's Land Army was formed in the first war, toward the end when Britain was facing the prospect of starvation, because of German U-boats and because men were not returning home to work in the fields. It was a huge step for most women—wearing bloomers, cutting their hair, living away from home. It showed them they were capable of so much more than they believed. I asked myself what happens in a village when the men don't come home. Who becomes the blacksmith, who runs the pub, who is the carter, etc. Women have to step into roles they would never have believed possible. And in doing so, they achieve new confidence and self-worth, also a great camaraderie with fellow women.

Jackie, I think we should each single out a "nasty woman" from our own lives. The one that comes to mind for me was my great-aunt Sarah. Her father became very sick and couldn't work when she was fourteen, so she was forced to leave school, which she loved, and become a maid in the house of a *nouveau riche* butcher. She had to get up at five to light the fires, carry hot water for baths, and do all kinds of drudgery but she never lost her self-respect. Her last name was Spinks. When the daughter of the house said, "I shall call you Spinks," she replied, "In that case I shall call you Wadsworth."

The girl looked shocked. "But they do it in all the big houses," she said.

"Then let's wait until I get to a big house," my aunt replied and walked away. Later she became a schoolteacher and a passionate reader. She could recite Shakespeare by heart. She was going blind when I met her and she was my constant companion as I grew up.

And for me the absolute example of a nasty woman was Mother Theresa. When she was told that things couldn't be done, she just calmly went on assuming that they would be done . . . and they were!

JACKIE: As you know, Rhys, the women of World War I have been of interest to me since childhood. In our street there were several women of a certain age who were "Miss" — women who had never married due to the losses of marriageable-age men during the Great War. One of the great tragedies of that generation of women was that they did not have children, so they brought children into their lives—hence so many of those teachers who were "Miss This" or "Miss That." As a small child, I was often invited to tea with one of the "spinsters" of a certain age who lived on our street. My mother realized that the last intimate relationship those women had with children was probably their own Edwardian childhood, so I always wore my best dress and was reminded to mind my manners—I was only about four at the time. What I remember most about each visit is looking at the sepia photograph on the mantelpiece of a young man lost to war and being intrigued by the image. The women of World War I became my heroines. As I mentioned earlier, during the Great War there was not a field of endeavor left untouched by a woman's hand. They not only worked in direct war-related fields, but they worked the land, they drove trains and buses, plus they mended the trains and buses. They buried the dead and delivered the milk and the post, and the first women police auxiliaries pounded the beat. They were absolutely extraordinary in the way they moved into public life as never before, working in highly visible fields. The British Secret Service was built on the hard work of women—over 50,000 working in intelligence in World War I, from covert operations to code breaking, right down to the Girl Guides who ran messages across London. The Boy Scouts were given the job initially, but they made a bit of a mess of it and would go off to play football or something, so the job went to the girls, who were lauded for the way they did their duty.

My personal "nasty woman" has to be my mother. She won a scholarship to a very prestigious private girl's school at age 12—one of only two scholarships awarded each year—and her parents would not let her go, for two reasons. One was that an older sister had won a previous year's scholarship and had larked around too much rather than study—and after they'd shelled out a fortune for the uniform (my grandparents had ten children, so none of this was easy). The second was because the teacher knew her daughter was the first reserve and persuaded my parents that it would not be fair to their other children if my mother took up the scholarship. My mother began work in a laundry at the age of fourteen. But the women in my family are known to be rather single-minded. By the time my mother retired at the age of sixty, she was a very senior civil servant working in the Home Office Prisons' Department. She was offered two plum jobs as "recognition" in the final years of her service, and both she turned down. If she'd accepted the first, she would have become the first woman administrator of Britain's most notorious high security prison, but when she visited she thought it was creepy. The second was as a special Home Office representative attached to the Prime Minister's office—it was a job that would have demanded a lot of international travel with the PM's entourage. I was stunned when she turned it down and when I asked why, she replied, "I just don't want to spend that much time away from your dad—not at this time in my life." Exercising choice is part of being a nasty woman, even if it will be a few years before your twenty-eight-year-old daughter completely understands your decision.

Finally, my favourite nasty woman of history is probably Gertrude Bell. Had the Allied leaders took note of her reports and her knowledge during the Paris Peace Conference in 1919, it is arguable that we would not have half the trouble in the Middle East—especially Iraq—that we have today.

Well, Rhys, this has been another of our wonderful conversations! See you for coffee at Rulli's again soon!

Raven and the Cave Girl:

An "A/K/A Jayne" story

Dana Cameron

I couldn't move my arms or legs. As I tried to suppress the panic that threatened to overwhelm me, I realized I couldn't see a damn thing, save for the blinking of what looked like a hard drive in front of me. That blinking light, along with the notion that someone had spent a leisurely hour bashing my head with a cement block, and the fact that my mouth tasted like the floor of a Fort Lauderdale motel room after spring break, confirmed that I was conscious. I missed the comfort of insensibility, but I was, quite frankly, surprised to find myself alive.

A blinding white light suddenly forced my eyes shut and introduced a new bolt of agony. After a moment, I heard a familiar voice, and when I could open my eyes again, I could see my murdered colleague speaking on the now-lit computer screen.

"If you're watching this, you probably know my name is Marcus Stapleton. Or maybe you can't tell; I'm not looking my best." He was in obvious pain—the dark skin of his face was a mass of cuts and bruises, one eye was swollen and almost closed, with blood still flowing freely from a wound somewhere on his grizzled scalp. That gallows humor was the hallmark of our trade, especially when we know death is at hand.

"The person who will . . . who has killed me is Nicole Bradley. I'm recording this because she's said that if I tell the truth, she'll leave my wife and daughter alive, and that's all I want, now. That's the best I can do."

His voice broke, and I felt sorry for him. Attachments complicate things, which is why I went a long way to avoid them, even within the Department.

He mastered his emotions. "She's going to kill me because I'm one of three people about to dissolve the Department. The reason for that is simple: our budget. We got too big, and we got noticed by the bean counters in Ops Oversight. Thing is, we can't have our people running around, not with the information they have. Not with their . . . skills. We had orders. This is the best way for us to get those orders accomplished."

We had orders. I, too, had done terrible things in the name of obeying orders, but the murder of fifty brave and loyal people who'd done nothing but their jobs? After faithfully serving their country? How could Stapleton? How could . . . ?

A pause, then, "I'm sorry, Bethany. I love you and Ellie more than I imagined poss—"

The screen went dead. End of message. Presumably followed shortly by the gunshots that had entered the back of his head and ended his life.

The only thing I remembered was that we'd found Stapleton's body about twenty-five days ago. Nothing much had been done to conceal the murder because he was meant to be found.

Then the rest came back to me: I'd been sent to kill the woman who murdered him, Nicole Bradley, the one I called Raven. Once that memory clicked on, everything else came back to me with terrible speed and detail: the grim meeting with my boss, Mr. Heath, and his news of Stapleton's murder and the traitor in our midst. The weeks of trailing the traitor, and my work in setting up how I'd remove her with the least possible commotion and notice. My choice of location for the job, an alley that suited my needs perfectly. Then pain, confusion, and darkness as things went horribly awry.

I took inventory: According to my circadian clock and my bladder, I'd only been out an hour or two. My arms were secured to the steel arms of an office chair with duct tape. I could move my feet a little; because I'm so short, a band of tape pulled them almost, but not quite, to the legs that extended from the central base of the chair. And even though Raven had taken the extra precaution of taping my thighs to the seat, I could use that to my advantage. I could feel my arms and legs now, and the nail on my right forefinger was busted, damn it all, but at least she hadn't pulled it clean off.

My attitude did a miraculous reverse into hopeful, because that broken nail I mentioned? It was a ceramic press-on that a friend of mine made for me, with an edge like a knife. I really had to be careful after I put it on because it was thin and strong and sharp as hell. I could just reach the duct tape securing my legs and, very carefully, began sawing at it. It was hard work, but it was a start. If I could move one limb just a little faster, at some point, I might be able to save myself. I realized that if Raven had wanted me dead, I'd be dead already.

After a few more desperate minutes—saw, flex leg muscles, work against the tape, saw—my finger ached, and I was starting to get sloppy, nicking myself through my dark leggings. I hoped the blood wouldn't show. And I needed, with a passion that burned almost as bright as my will to survive, to learn how she'd discovered that I was stalking her.

I called her Raven, back in training, because she'd roomed with a friend of mine, and she always was tap, tap, tapping away at her keyboard. It was freaky, like the bird in that poem. The nickname annoyed her, which was fine because she bugged the hell out of me. She might as well have been a head floating in a jar for the way she disdained physical violence back then. For me, the equation was simple: some asshole needs killing, you kill them. You do the job, you know it's done.

She called me "Cave Girl," because she thought my approach was crude and barbaric. I argued that it was direct, and when I said so, she called me a "fucking australopithecine," which I knew wasn't a compliment but had to look up. She always argued there was a better, more efficient, and stealthier way to go. It figured that she came from the NSA's "Tailored Access Operations." Fucking hackers weird me out, but I knew she had a point, and after a while, arguing with her was more a habit than anything, just something for us both to blow off steam.

As if my thoughts had summoned her, I heard the lock turn and Raven was there. She must have known how long I'd be out, based on the tranquilizer, and when I'd come to and be able to take in the video. She's like that: all math, and unlike me, Raven loves working at a distance.

But she wasn't working at a distance this time. Hmmm . . .

She turned on the overhead light abruptly, making me squint.

"You came here to kill me," she said. Her voice was quiet, almost a whisper—it always had been. We were alike in that, and in a lot of other ways as well: Both of us were small, strong, with unassuming looks, neither noticeably attractive nor repellent. Forgettable was an asset for us. Her skin and hair reflected a distant West African ancestry, while—for now—my look suggested Irish or Anglo heritage. I was strawberry blonde today.

She continued. "You're still alive because I'm not the one you need to kill."

I swallowed. "That's a novel approach. Prove it."

I was still grappling with the disturbing idea that Raven had somehow figured out that I'd been on her trail. No one I killed had ever realized I was on to them—no, combat doesn't count—much less captured me. Especially not a geek like Raven.

"That alley was perfect," she said, taking me back to the stalk and prompting me to follow her logic. "I'd get back from my cover job, park, and go in the townhouse from the rear, same as I had every other time you'd followed me. It didn't matter what route I took; I'd end up there four nights out of seven. Those are good odds."

"There were no windows, only the entrances from the streets and a door," I said slowly, revisiting the scene carefully. "The trash cans and recycling bins along one side made a nice bit of cover."

I glanced at her abruptly, as it dawned on me. "Too perfect."

Nothing but the ghost of a grin. "You looked down," she said.

"A rat. I had to make sure it wouldn't give me away. There was something wrong with the car, but then . . ."

"Then I shot you with the tranquilizer."

Finally, I understood. "The rear window of the SUV was rolled down. That's what was wrong. That's how you could shoot me so accurately."

She sighed. "I was trying to guide you in to do this stuff by hacking your systems, but you're so far off the grid I had to come out into RL and shoot your ass with a trank . . ."

"Okay, you have my attention. How did you—oh. You knew Heath would send me after you. I'm his best."

A slight shrug.

"Why keep me alive?"

"I need you. You need me."

When I said nothing, she continued. "I'm not the traitor. Heath is."

A raised eyebrow told her how thin I found that lie.

"You saw the video."

"Pretty damning stuff. Why'd you make it?"

"Because Stapleton was telling the truth. And I needed to have that much to prove it to you."

I shook my head. I flexed my thigh and felt the tape give. I had to be careful now. "Tell me how Heath is the traitor? What exactly has he done?" I kept my tone bored, like there was nothing she could say that would convince me. "Make it ten words or less."

"I can do it in three words: Clarke. Reid. Albano."

My thoughts crashed to a halt, and my chest tightened. I was so amazed that my fingernail blade slipped and jabbed me deep in the thigh. Two of those names, she might barely have a reason to know: My last job, I'd been sent to remove Clarke but realized that the man I had in my sights was really a former colleague gone bad named Reid. Trying to untangle that mess led me to root out a traitor, and at one point, I'd been forced to consider that my boss, Mr. Heath, might be it. By the end of it, I'd taken out everyone involved, including two Mob gangs, and cleared Heath.

But that third name . . .

The third should have been buried deep, with my old identity, out in the middle of the Nevada desert. No one, not even within the Department, should have known it. Could have known it.

But I'm as much of a professional as she is: My voice was even. "Uh huh. Tell me more."

"The Clarke-Reid job got very messy. Very public. It wasn't just bad intel being fed to you by our informer. The whole thing was orchestrated by Heath."

I felt a pang of fear but shoved it aside. "Nope. I found all the connections that proved it *wasn't* him."

"You proved nothing. That job should have left you dead and out of the way;

there were too many ways for you to die, but you evaded them all. So you, without knowing, were worked into Heath's plan. He made you his very own one-woman human resources department, sent to let me and the rest of the Department go." She frowned in disdain at the euphemism. "To 'right-size' us."

"Bullshit." But something about her tone, so sure, so steady, made me wonder . . . and it made that pang grow into a sick feeling deep in my gut. Paying attention to my gut had gotten me out of a lot of bad situations, and so far, I was beginning to believe this was the worst yet.

"What happened was that you figured out the traitor wasn't Reid, which was always a possibility, but you also figured out how Heath had set it up in the first place, without knowing it was him. And then you dismantled that as well." Raven gave a harsh, ironic laugh. "No one figured you'd take out the fake Reid, the real Reid, the leak, *and* two OC crews. It was, as Heath told you, several stratospheres above your pay grade."

My mind reeled. Only Mr. Heath and I had been in the room when he'd used those exact words. She had real information she couldn't have gotten from anyone but him.

"You know he almost killed you that day, in his office. Stapleton told me Heath couldn't believe that you'd done all that, seen all the connections, and missed that he was behind it. He couldn't believe you'd been that blind."

"Loyal is the word I'd use," I said, my throat dry. But I knew the truth; I'd felt it that day in the tension between us and had attributed it to my admitting to Heath that I'd had cause to suspect him.

I had to fight to keep from vomiting; there was still too much I didn't know. I also kept wriggling at the tape on my right wrist, which was getting looser. "So, why didn't he?"

"Simple math; he figured your loyalty to him was such that he could use you, his best operative, to take out the staff he needed to vanish, no questions asked."

The idea of such treachery—against me, against the Department itself—almost unhinged me. "So he sent me after you . . . ?" I was buying more time to collect myself and work on my bonds.

"To finish the housecleaning he needed. You would have done it brilliantly, and he would have had you in his office, given you a pat on the back and that dribble of bourbon you insist is a celebration." Something about her demeanor changed slightly, indicating a sadness I'm not sure she knew she felt. "And then he would have shot you, too."

The words hit me like a brick in the face, a knee to the stomach. The problem was, although I could see she wasn't telling me the whole truth, the rest of it was so . . . logical. Irrefutable. I just couldn't see my way around her story, so for the moment, I had to believe her. Why would she want to take down the Department? None of us would have lasted through our training if we hadn't had utter faith in the organization and its mission: to do the impossible, in secret, in service to the nation.

But believing her meant that my world had come apart at the seams. And of all the times I'd been faced with the end of my world, or the end of my life, I probably would not survive this one. Odds were very much against it. And that pissed me off.

Dying . . . dying was nothing. Betrayal was the thing that left me unmoored, left me falling into the abyss and removed my guiding stars from their black night sky. It was the faithlessness toward me and my colleagues by a brother-in-arms. Worse, a mentor. Every time I thought about her claims that we'd been badly manipulated, I could feel the roughness of rope tightening around my throat as someone kicked the metaphysical stool out from under me.

I found myself breathing as if I'd run a mile; I felt a hand on my shoulder and flinched. I hadn't seen her cross the room. I never lost that kind of control; ordinarily I would have been well aware of my surroundings. Flinching was for amateurs.

The look of sympathy and recognition on her face was unfeigned. "I felt the same. Not about Heath, but Stapleton and . . . others. They build a family around you, then use it against you, and even then you can forgive them. I could see them using me, but in a way, it was what I was signing up for. I knew I'd be yanked around; it happens, in service. But this . . ." She shrugged, helplessly. "I can't even begin to describe it."

I couldn't make myself say the word either. *Unforgivable.* More than that, either we'd die, we'd live, but there was no realistic response to this perfidy. That gnawed at me: I wanted to hurt the bastards, but I couldn't count on living, much less taking a strip off them.

Here next words shocked me even more. "I'm going to cut you free now."

"Why?" I needed a few more seconds to focus. It was time to go.

"I told you. I need you to help me save the rest of the Department. They don't deserve this, and neither do we."

She knelt by my right leg and snipped away the tape around my ankle. She sat back just a little, frowning at the way I'd pulled and stretched the tape there.

I pulled my leg free and kicked her onto her back. The next part was gonna hurt: I pulled the chair as close to her as fast as I could and shoved my weight over onto my knees. I landed with my left knee, and the chair on her stomach, knocking the wind out of her. As she was gasping, straining to get a lungful of air, I swung my freed right leg out and over her body, which brought me right next to the blade she'd used to cut me loose. I grabbed that with my right hand, and reversing the blade, began to cut at the tape still on my right wrist. My action was awkward, but the tape came off quickly, with my full weight pulling tight against it. When Raven finally caught a full, hitching breath, I punched her in the head, which bought me enough time to cut the rest of me free. I kicked the damned chair away and gave myself a solid minute of swearing to walk off the blow to my knees and the pain in my thigh where I'd cut myself.

She came to and woozily tried to crawl away. I threw myself at her, scrambled on top of her. After I got into the mount, I held her own knife to her throat.

"One more time. Why do you need me alive?"

"Jesus, you fucking Neanderthal," she gasped. "I was telling you. I almost didn't get Stapleton. See?"

She tugged at her shirt, so I could see an ugly and hastily stitched wound. "When I learned how fast this was happening, I realized I couldn't do this at a distance, and I had to get personal—that should tell you just how desperate I am. Stapleton, he almost took my head off with a vase. And of the three of them, at the top, I judged he would be the easiest to take down. He was, but I barely made it. And when I figured that Heath would sic you on me, and I knew I had to take you out of the equation. I need help if I'm going to get O'Malley and Heath. You're the only one I believe can do it." Her voice was full of resignation. "All I'm trying to do is save the lives of the other operatives. If I was lying, why wouldn't I kill you? Why wouldn't I just vanish? Think about it. I need you to help me save the rest of them."

"Okay," I said, thinking hard.

"I wanted to do it with the minimum of bloodshed—I don't kill for fun—but that meant three lives instead of one. That's why I needed to convince you, and that's why I need you on my side."

"Why don't they just dissolve the Department and launch the Taps protocol to scatter us, like they always warned us could happen?"

"For all the reasons Stapleton said. Did you really think that if they'd shut down the Department they'd let us live?"

My shoulders slumped when I realized the answer. "I always thought I'd die in the traces."

"Yeah, me, too."

"They'll never believe us," I said, finally. "Even if we take out O'Malley and Heath, the rest will just assume *we're* the assholes who sold out."

"Yes, so . . . ?"

I got what her plan was, now. "So *we* have to launch Taps. Make it look like them, so the others don't come after us, because they'll think we scattered like they did when they got the call."

Raven seemed surprised that I figured it out so fast. Well, fuck her anyway.

She nodded. "That way we can also vanish. No one will know we're behind it."

"So what do we need to do this?" I didn't see holding Heath at knifepoint and getting him to do what we wanted. In fact, I had no idea how we'd get to Heath at all. I shook myself, trying to focus.

"The whole point of the Taps protocol was that it was meant to be the last resort. So it was important that the power to use it rested only with the three at the top. Stapleton held the key—an authentication code generator on his phone that changed minute to minute—and I have that. O'Malley has the list of operatives. And Heath has the command order to make them all work. But I already have the command, from my time working on Taps."

I shook my head. "Bullshit. That program's been around since before we were recruited."

"But they needed a patch for it, and they hired me to do that."

"They will have cut off your access since then." I didn't know much more than a bit of programming and a few basic hacks, but that was just common sense.

She cocked her head, a barely concealed and condescending smile flickering across her lips. "My dear, sweet summer child. The point of a hacker is not to get in *once*. It's to get in undetected and then leave a way to get in again any time you want. That's what I've got."

"How about the list?"

"Not so easy. It's in the office, on an offline system. The administrator—you know, Rodriguez?—has access to the list—you may imagine that our ranks change in number frequently—and she gives it to O'Malley every day. Rodriguez will give it to me, once O'Malley's out of the way, and if I can assure her that you're on board and that you're going to help us."

"Why's that?"

"Because Rodriguez is the one who told me about the plan. She doesn't know what they intend for her, and she doesn't like it. If you're on board, she'll believe we can pull this off."

I began to wonder about Rodriguez's role in all this.

"We wait until this evening, when O'Malley leaves work. O'Malley is no fool; she varies her routes every day, just like all of us. But my analysis shows there's a better-than-even chance she'll visit a certain coffee shop today."

I shrugged. It was a better estimate than I could provide at the moment.

AT THE COFFEE shop, we picked out the outside table we'd both choose, assuming that would be O'Malley's choice, too. Her usual MO was to go through the drive-through and then park and drink her coffee outside. We moved to another picnic table slightly farther away and into the cover of some bushes, so we had a clear vantage of the whole place. Raven was waiting in the car to give chase if necessary; I was ready to take care of O'Malley.

"Something's wrong," Raven said, her voice low and inside my head, thanks to the earpiece. "She's parked. She went into the store."

"Shit," I muttered to myself. "Can you see her?"

"Yeah, she's coming back out. If she gets into her car, get back here and we'll try to get her at home."

"I was hoping to avoid that. Too many unknowns, too many potential ties to us."

"Yeah, me, too. Hang on—she's going around back."

"I got it."

O'Malley sauntered, looking as normal as anyone, glanced around, was not interested in me, my knapsack, or my stack of books. She sat at her table. I wasn't completely behind her, but enough that I could move stealthily out of my chair, and toward her a few steps before she noticed.

She glanced toward me as I approached, of course, but then, almost providentially, her phone rang. Her eyes flicked away again, just long enough for me to—

I heard a squawk in my earpiece. "Jesus, it's Hsu, he's made me. I'm going after him!"

He must have been going to meet O'Malley.

I cursed and dropped my bag. I put one hand on O'Malley's shoulder, and as she looked up, there was an instant of confusion, of panic, and finally, recognition of . . . something. It sure wasn't me, because I looked even less like me than I usually do. While she was processing the thought that someone trying to get her attention, I slammed the knife up and angled between her ribs, once, twice. The blade was long and thin, and while it would have snapped if I'd been even a little off my target, it was barely visible from any other direction. Anyone walking by might have thought I was pounding her on the back, either in greeting or trying to help her from choking. The blade—how I loved that perfect steel!—sliced open her lung like a scalpel gliding through silk.

A sick sucking noise, a couple of gasps, and it was over. I felt that band that had been closing around my chest loosen, the one that had been there since I regained consciousness. The sick feeling in my stomach eased. I propped her up on my books so it looked like she was working. One down.

I turned and ran to the front, only to see Hsu stagger to his car, clutching his belly. He pulled out of the parking lot with a squeal, and I could see Raven struggling to decide whether to try for a shot at the tires.

"Drive," I yelled, diving into the car.

She pulled back, but we were blocked by another car, some civilian asshole. By the time we pulled onto the street, we couldn't find Hsu.

"Shit," I said. "He's gonna go straight to Heath!"

"No, wait," Raven said as she tried another loop in an attempt to find his car. "Scenario one: He dies before he gets anywhere or can talk to anyone. Good for us, nothing to do."

"Okay, scenario two," I said. "He comes back for us, checks our known haunts. Can't do anything about that yet but make sure we're ready for him."

"Scenario three: He knew from O'Malley that the Department was being culled. He assumes he's next because he thinks Heath always meant to take her out. He scrams. Good for us, but less certain."

"Right. Scenario four: He runs and tells someone. Who would that be? Friends, colleagues, family?"

I didn't like the way her eyes unfocused as she concentrated on the problem, but her driving was perfect, just under the speed limit, obeying the rules of the road while executing the last spiral. "No one. I mean, it would have been O'Malley, but now, he has to assume she's dead."

Raven glanced over at me. "Part of why we were hired is that we all tend to be loners. Mostly orphans, too."

I shrugged, looking away. "It's easier, without entanglements."

She frowned and shook her head. "Yes, but . . . you know 'entanglements' means 'culture,' or 'society,' right? It's how we all get along?"

And now I had to accept the fact that shared commitment and loyalty didn't ensure anything, either. I rolled my eyes. "Fine. But we have to hit Heath ASAP."

Raven shook her head again. "The first stop is to meet Rodriguez. She can give us the list of folks who need to hear Taps and help find Heath. What I'd like to do is freeze his accounts, then shut down—" She shook her head. "No, no time for that."

But I already had a plan forming, if she could find me Heath . . . "How are you with a rifle?"

"Better than most. Probably not as good as you."

"No problem. You just need to be able to hit the side of a moving barn."

※

WE MET RODRIGUEZ at a rest stop. She looked haggard, and her limp was worse than usual, but then, she might have been up even longer than we had, trying to figure out which way to jump when she learned we were all going to be "downsized."

She slid the newspaper with the memory stick hidden inside over to Raven. "You know what to do now, right?"

Raven nodded.

Rodriguez's gaze flicked between Raven and me, calculating.

"You're helping us save a lot of lives," Raven said. "Thank you."

"Yes," I said, trying to find my character; I had no precedent for this. "Lives of our . . . friends." I stammered a little over the word, but Rodriguez just took it as emotion.

"Well, some of us know the meaning of loyalty, even if others don't. Heath's got a meeting at the house in Reston today. I'd use that to finish the job." Without another word, she picked up her cane and left.

I WAITED FOR Heath's car by the side of the road. It was the most deserted stretch on the route he had to take, with the best cover.

"Stand by," Raven said into my earpiece.

I saw the headlights of the Audi come over the slight rise, and tensed, feeling the familiar, welcome rush of adrenaline.

"Confirmed. It's Heath."

Boom.

The driver lost control of the big black sedan and it spun, once, twice, three times, even more beautiful for the scary physical forces at play. If I wasn't careful, I'd be crushed. I had to judge the distance with caution. The car didn't flip over— thanks to Heath's skill—but was now facing the wrong way down the road, only twenty meters from me.

"Nice placement," I said.

"Get going," she replied.

Heath was conscious but dazed and didn't even notice me appear at the door. I took out a little emergency hammer and broke through the window glass, spraying Heath with perfectly square fragments.

"Jayne," he said, hurt and confusion in his eyes.

As soon as I looked at his face, I knew I was wrong. I was about to commit a terrible mistake, killing a good man, a dedicated patriot. Raven had lied to me. I felt my stomach fall away, and a terrible nausea welled up in me. What had I done? Why had I believed her?

Then his eyes cleared, and filled with recognition, fear, and then confidence. "Jayne," he said again, more surely, with a deep breath.

It was the start of a lie. I'd let the last dregs of sentiment cloud my judgment. Doubt fled. "This is for the Department."

He opened his mouth again and I shot him, two taps, in the head.

He slumped and the light left his eyes. The blood began to pool around him.

I watched and thought about what he'd meant to me. I fired two more shots, right in the heart, just to make sure.

I dropped the gun, rifled his wallet, then dropped that. As I worked, it came to me: loyalty was not just found in adhering to a hierarchy or playing by rules. It had to be demonstrated. Apart from hiring me, Heath had never had to show he had my best interests at heart. I'd worked, and ate, and lived with Raven, even if it was only for a few months. She'd come to me when we were all in danger, instead of vanishing. That was loyalty. As grateful as I was to Heath for a job that suited me so well, I'd fallen prey to his praise.

That stung, but it felt right. I owned it. Lesson learned.

I realized that more than traitors, I hated loose ends. And there were still a couple left.

RAVEN AND I drove back to her place, discussing what had to happen next. In the kitchen, there was a little bit of awkwardness, as we both went for the gunslinger seat at the same time, but eventually, I just moved the table to suit both of us. We looked at each other, and our smiles died away. All that was left was to deploy the program to warn and scatter the other operatives.

She set up her gear with the same kind of reverence that I took care of my weapons: earbuds, memory stick, Stapleton's phone, her notebook computer, a glass of wine she took forever to select. At last, she took a sip of the wine, and inserted the earbuds.

She must have seen my disapproval because she rolled her eyes. "Oh, don't be such an ass-aching puritan. We all have our work rituals."

"Fine, whatever." I began to dismantle my secondary weapon to clean it. I put my primary on the table, casually, as if it were next. I'm no fool. "Are you really sure it's safe for you to . . . ?"

She put her pistol on the table, too. Also within easy reach, I noticed, with approval. "If I'm smart enough to know about this, and I'm smart enough to find it, doesn't it follow that I'm smart enough to do it safely?"

I shrugged. She was right, but to me, the depths at which she worked was like dabbling with the dark arts. Moving through the information, leaving no trace, changing people's lives without ever seeing them? Something about it suggested magic.

She saw my discomfort and smirked. "Look, there are kids in Malaysian slums who can do this stuff."

"Yeah? How do you know that?"

"Because as far as everyone else at this level of expertise is concerned, I'm one of them right now. Now . . . I need to work."

She'd opened a playlist—I heard a bouncy K-pop tune—and her eyes unfocused before she'd finished the sentence.

While she was busy, tap, tap, tapping away, I concentrated on my SIG. But the pleasant necessity of cleaning it didn't bring any comfort today.

After a few moments, my spidey sense started tingling. I saw Raven's eyes come back into focus—she kept working but was now aware of the world around her. Seeing me go on alert, she paused, then sighed, heavily, as if frustrated. There was no noise, just . . . something that said it would all happen now.

Her eyes went to the window.

The shot missed both of us—and the computer, thank god—but knocked her piece off the table. We both reached for my pistol at the same time. She was faster, but smart, and, sure, I'll say it: She was polite. She let me grab it, and I shot at the window. She, closer to the back door, all but evaporated to the alleyway, pulling her knife from its sheath. Her earbuds pulled out, but not before she inadvertently dragged the computer off the table and onto the bench behind her.

My angle was off, but it would have taken a miracle to make the shot. I was close enough, though and hit the frame, splintering the wood and shattering the glass.

No—the glass was shattered by the two shots that came my way at almost the same time. For a moment, I couldn't tell if I was hit—there was glass and blood everywhere—but I heard a muffled curse and movement outside. I grabbed for the computer, steadying it on the bench.

The program hadn't finished loading. I glanced at the prompt, watching the timer count down before the authentication codes changed and we were unable to launch the program.

Another suppressed shot. Then another, and then quiet.

I grabbed Stapleton's phone and managed to touch the screen before it locked up again. I found the code and punched it in.

It was still counting down.

I hit "Enter."

The little countdown icons went blank and then disappeared. Nothing happened.

After an eternity, I saw the message "Upload Complete."

I wanted to collapse in relief, but I needed to find out what that silence after those shots meant. So far, there were no sirens, but was either Raven or Hsu still alive?

I found her at the mouth of the alley, dragging Hsu's body behind her. She looked up, and I nodded: All was well. She sighed with relief and I grabbed Hsu's legs and quickly got him out of sight. We bundled him into a tarp and then into the trunk of her car in complete privacy.

The alley really was perfect.

"That was risky," she grumbled.

I nodded. "But like I said, it was possible that Hsu would come looking for us. He'd seen you when we were at the coffee shop, after all."

I'd gotten my wind back and was feeling chipper. Beat up, but good, like after you've done a brutal workout and found a little extra, even though it felt like you'd had all the stupid beat out of you. Or paid your taxes or crossed something nasty off your to-do list.

I *loved* crossing things off my to-do list.

After we shut the trunk, Raven leaned back with a heavy sigh, collecting herself. "One more reason I'd rather not work in meatspace."

"Meat's only a problem if you're not careful." Then I caught myself falling into old patterns. "You did well back there. You committed to getting him because you were closer to the door. If you hadn't, we would have lost him."

"I figured you could enter the authentication code. Nice work yourself."

We dumped the body in a location that she picked, claiming she was the only one who knew about it. She wasn't, but it was a very good spot, and if we'd both made mistakes on this job, it was nice to let her feel like she'd fixed hers.

The way home was quiet, both of us realizing that there was one question left. Back at her place, we mopped up the blood and picked the glass out of our wounds, making a stitch here and there. Finally, there was nothing left to do but face the last issue head on.

She took it on herself to start the conversation. She went back to her wine cabinet and poured herself another glass. Then she pulled out a lowball, pouring a scant quarter inch of a very nice bourbon into it. She held it out to me, nothing showing behind her eyes.

I nodded, accepting the glass. "Everyone we just saved—everyone who knew us—assumes we're dead or scattered, just like they are. You did all the right things, as far as I'm concerned. You'll never see me again."

She took a moment to look me up and down, deciding. Finally, she nodded. "Yes. We're good."

We surprised each other by showing relief, clinked glasses, and drank.

Still, for some reason, I was loath to leave it there. "I don't expect I'll see you, either."

"Probably not. But . . . if you should need me, you can reach me under the name of 'Alexandra Poe.' I'll keep an eye out."

I grinned, acknowledging her joke. But still, I said nothing, chewing my lip.

She watched me, and sighed. "There is no shame in admitting that it's nice to work with someone who knows her stuff," she said. It was the rebuke of an older, wiser sister. "We are an endangered species, you know. Only about fifty of us in the world can do what we can do, and it's not as if we can discuss it with anyone else. It's lonely, our work."

I was still unwilling to admit I'd miss the Department, as relieved as I was that it was gone for good, its operatives saved, its traitors punished. No more attachments to trip me up again. A clean start. But Raven had had my back, when it mattered, and she'd saved our people, risking herself. That mattered. That was loyalty. Maybe some attachments were okay.

"I suppose. If you need me, I'm sure you can find me. But you'll have better luck if you address the correspondence to Meghan Leakey."

She raised an eyebrow again, surprised.

"Hey, I don't intend to be ignorant all my life." I grinned ferally. "When you started calling me 'Cave Girl' and 'paranthropus' and all that shit, I thought I should find out if that was as bad as you meant."

"Turns out it isn't," she said.

Nasty

Toni L.P. Kelner

Nobody made me take on the role of official black sheep in the family, but sometimes I wonder if things might have been different if I'd had a different name. You see, my name is Natasha—Tasha to my friends—but my sister Hailey was only six when I was born, and according to family legend, she started calling me "Nasty" because she couldn't pronounce my name correctly. Funny thing is, she didn't seem to have any trouble pronouncing anybody else's name. And she never did stop calling me Nasty.

I spent a lot of years trying to live up to that name, or maybe down to it. Lousy grades, toking behind the bleachers at football games, drinking at parties with black sheep from other families. My parents would probably have been happier if they hadn't known what I was up to, but my snitch of a sister made sure they heard about every class I skipped, every visit to the principal's office, every boy I made out with, and every lipstick I shoplifted from the drug store.

Hailey's biggest score was when she somehow found out that I was flunking out at Catawba Valley Community College. I'd been on my way back to Rocky Shoals to break the news myself, but Hailey got to the house first, so by the time I got home, they'd had an hour to get riled up. Mama cried, Daddy thundered at me, and though Hailey didn't say anything, when she was sure nobody else but me was looking, she smirked.

I know from therapy sessions I took much later that I shouldn't blame anybody else for my behavior getting even worse after that, but I've got to tell you, my sister's smirk got under my skin nearly as much as her continuing to call me Nasty.

After half an hour of the crying and yelling—and of course the smirking—I'd had it. I flipped them all off, packed up as much of my stuff as I could fit into a duffle bag, and called my best friend Addalyn to give me a ride. I didn't even care where I was going, but it turned out to be Asheville, a couple of hours away from Rocky Shoals. For the next few years, I alternated between couch-surfing and renting cheap apartments while working junk jobs. I also started taking drugs.

Hailey told people in Rocky Shoals that I'd become estranged from the family. I guess she thought that sounded better than advertising the fact that nobody in the family wanted anything to do with me. For a long time, I didn't want anything to do with them, either. Even after I finally got my head out of my butt and quit the drugs, I stayed away.

My wakeup call was when I found out Mama had died. I hadn't even known she was sick—no one bothered to tell me. Daddy said I didn't have to come to the funeral if I didn't want to, and when I showed up, he barely spoke to me other than to make it plain that I wasn't welcome at the house. He wouldn't believe that I'd been off the drugs for years. Mostly, anyway. I was still smoking pot. It wasn't legal in North Carolina yet, but everybody knew it was just a matter of time, and I had a tiny patch behind my house in Asheville to grow my own.

I'd never gotten into twelve-step programs, but I knew about making amends. After Mama died, I started doing just that. Maybe Daddy and Hailey weren't interested, but I did reconnect with some of my old friends. If I hadn't, I'd probably never have known when Daddy got cancer a few years later.

It hit him bad, and I suspect that him wondering how much time he had left made him decide to give me a chance. When I showed up at his door unexpectedly one day, he actually let me in and we really talked. It wasn't easy—there had been a lot of hard words between us over the years—but it was a good visit. He even asked me to come back. After that, I came every chance I got.

I cooked for him a few times, but the doctors were giving him chemo and it made him so sick he couldn't eat. I'd heard that weed would help with nausea, so I brought him some and got him to try a joint, and he said it did settle his stomach. He even got the munchies afterward.

Knowing that the arthritis in his hands would make it hard for him to roll his own joints, I made up a bunch for him and filled the cigarette dispenser on the coffee table.

The dispenser had been his mother's, and I'd always loved that thing. It was made of wood, and the front looked like a tiny bookcase. When you wound it up and pushed the button on top, a song played and a dog's head popped out of the top with a cigarette in its mouth. Daddy never smoked, but he'd kept it filled with candy cigarettes for years, and every kid who came into the house had played with it.

Daddy wasn't entirely happy with the idea. He said he didn't know that he wanted to keep illegal drugs in his house, but when I came the next week, he asked if I had any more.

He and I would smoke and talk for hours during those visits. He confessed that he'd thought I'd done a lot worse things than I actually had. That was Hailey's doing. She'd made up all kinds of tales. Sure, I'd taken drugs, but I'd never dealt coke or cooked meth the way she said I had.

The only times I'd been in trouble with the cops was minor stuff from when I was running around with my fellow black sheep. Most of those kids had grown up to be solid citizens, no matter what Hailey claimed: Gail was a lawyer, Randi had her own hair salon, and Addalyn was a cop in Rocky Shoals. I was only a woodworker, but I had my own business designing and installing custom cabinets, with a waiting list of potential clients. One day Daddy told me he was proud of me. We both cried.

I started coming more often to give him rides to the doctor. Hailey lived less than a mile away, but when Daddy called her, she was always busy with work or church or something. He swore that she did come sometimes, but she never showed up when I was there. Though he never said so directly, I was pretty sure she was trying to get him to shut me out of his life again.

Not long before he died, Daddy told me wanted to change his will. He'd left everything to Hailey because she'd convinced him that I'd take my share of the estate to buy drugs and I'd either end up in jail or dead from an overdose. Now he'd decided that he wanted to give me half of everything.

I thanked him but told him not to. I had a house and money in the bank, so I didn't need anything. Besides, I didn't want Hailey claiming that I'd bullied him or forged his signature after he was gone. The only thing I wanted was that cigarette dispenser.

Daddy got worked up over that. He said that wasn't fair because the dispenser wasn't even worth anything. Back when he'd been able to hit the local flea markets, he'd seen the same thing selling for fifty bucks at most, and ours was likely worth less because we'd played with it so much. But I insisted that the dispenser was what I wanted, so he finally relented and promised that it would be mine.

We had a year and a half to make up for lost time before the cancer took him. I was there at the hospital with him at the end and saw Hailey for the first time in years. We hugged for his sake, but I don't imagine that she meant it any more than I did.

My sister hadn't changed a bit. Maybe she was older and had a husband and grown kids, but she still hated me as much as ever. When Daddy told her he hadn't changed the will, so she could have everything except the cigarette dispenser, she demonstrated that she could still smirk like a boss.

I spent the night before the funeral in Daddy's house so I wouldn't have to drive from Asheville so early in the morning. Besides, I knew it would be my last chance. Hailey would have kicked me out before we finished picking out the coffin if she hadn't known how it would look to everybody in town, but I knew that as soon as he was buried, she'd make sure I never set one foot inside that door again.

The funeral was small, but some of those old friends Hailey still sneered at came to pay their respects. Addalyn even arranged a police escort. She and I spent a few minutes talking over old times after the burial, which meant Hailey got back to Daddy's house before I did.

She was smirking big-time when I came in the front door. I would have thought she was just rubbing it in that she was going to inherit the house if the cigarette dispenser hadn't been missing from its usual spot on the coffee table.

I asked Hailey where it was, and at least her husband Joe looked embarrassed when she pretended she didn't know what I was talking about and then asked if I was sure it had been on the table. When I reminded her that Daddy always kept it there, she just shrugged and said she'd look for it and let me know if she found it. When I offered to help her look, she turned me down flat. After all, even if she did find the dispenser, the will said that the house and all its contents were hers and hers alone. As for Daddy's last words, she said that there was nothing in writing, so she didn't have to pay any mind to anything a dying man might have said. That's when she brought out the smirk again.

In years past, I'd have been tempted to wipe that expression right off her face, but I didn't want my last memory of my childhood home to be of me beating the crap out of my big sister. So I just left, and didn't even respond when she called me Nasty one last time.

I didn't go straight back to Asheville, though. Instead I found a place where I could park and watch the house while I used my cell phone to call my cop friend Addalyn and have a little conversation with her. When Hailey and Joe left the house, I dialed Addalyn again to let her know, then followed them back to their own home and parked in a shady spot where they wouldn't notice me.

Addalyn drove up just as Hailey and Joe pulled into their driveway, and she climbed out of her patrol car to tell them that the department had received a reliable tip about the presence of something illegal in their car. Hailey sputtered and fumed, but Joe saw the neighbors were watching and told her to be quiet and let Addalyn look.

It only took Addalyn a couple of minutes to find the cigarette dispenser— Hailey hadn't bothered to hide it. She also hadn't taken time to open it, so it wasn't until Addalyn pushed the button and the doggie's head popped out with a joint in its mouth that Hailey realized she'd laid claim to a hefty stash of weed.

I hadn't asked Addalyn to arrest Hailey, just to scare her good, but my sister got angry. When she tried to grab the dispenser out of Addalyn's hand, and then pushed her away, Addalyn got mad, too. That's when she pulled out her hand-cuffs. I left then because I was laughing so hard I thought sure Hailey would hear me. I kept grinning for most of the drive back to Asheville.

Addalyn called me a day or two later and asked if I wanted her to "lose" the dispenser out of the evidence locker so she could send it to me, but I told her she didn't have to. What I didn't tell her was that the one at the police station wasn't Daddy's dispenser anyway.

I'd had a hunch Hailey would pull something, so before Daddy passed away,

I'd gone on eBay and bought one just like his. The night before the funeral, I hid the real one in my car, and left the replacement on the table for Hailey to find. And of course I'd filled it up with a fresh batch of weed, just for her.

It was kind of a nasty thing to do, but sometimes you've just got to live up to your name.

Mother Church

Joshua Corin

An upright piano occupies a moonlit corner of the music room at St. Theresa's Academy for Young Women. The piano is in a timeout. Ribbons of duct tape stretch along its wooden back like lashes.

"It's not that a wire broke," says Sister Agnes. "It's that two wires broke at the same time. We must have installed them at the same time. We've replaced so many parts on that old piano, it's no longer that old piano."

Mother Millicent casts a glance toward the moonlit corner. "The spirit of a thing never wavers."

"Okay, well, the spirit of the thing needs two new wires. Fortunately, they're not expensive. You must have enough left over in petty cash to cover two piano wires."

"I remember when we got the piano. Years ago. It was a donation from another school, an elementary school, over on Quincy, down where the mall is now. They were upgrading their equipment."

"There's an elementary school on Quincy?" asks Sister Agnes.

"Oh, it's not there anymore. Now it's part of the property of the mall. And to answer your question: No, we don't have enough left over in petty cash to cover two piano wires. But it's not a problem. I'll simply fill out a budgetary request and submit it to Father Rook."

"Dear Lord."

"Come now, Sister Agnes—where is your faith?"

⁂

MOTHER MILLICENT IS alone in the chapel, save God. She peers up at Him, stares Him square in His pinewood eyes. He's a bit blurry around the edges, reminding Mother Millicent to make an appointment with her optician. As she tidies up her whispered prayers, Father Rook pokes his long neck out from his rectory. "Ah! I thought I heard someone," he says, and then sneezes twice in quick succession.

Mother Millicent genuflects toward her Lord, rises, and follows Father Rook into his office.

"Can't seem to shake these dear allergies." He takes out a nasal spray and shakes it like a bag of cat treats. "The doctor prescribed me this. You ever tried nasal spray? You shake it like so, squirt it up one nostril, and the dear stuff leaks right back down. Whose fault is that? The doctor's? The nasal spray's? Gravity's? I want to know who to blame."

"Have you tried one of those sinus pots? You know, with the spout? You fill it with water and . . . well, it does wonders for the sinuses. My grandmother swore by it. She'd rinse out her sinuses every morning before brushing her teeth. Maybe it could help you. You know, for your allergies."

Father Rook pouts in consideration. "Fair enough. So, Mother Mary Millicent, you didn't loiter behind after mass to discuss my allergies. What's on your mind?"

"It's our piano."

"Really? I just had it tuned."

"The school piano. The one downstairs. It's seen better days."

"Haven't we all?" he sniffles.

"Of course. But yesterday, two of the wires in the piano broke and—"

"Who broke them?"

"This wasn't the result of some prank, Father, although I can understand why you might assume that. Like I said, the piano is old. Now I've investigated the costs and—"

"We don't have any spare wire in the supply closet?"

"Why would we have any spare wire in the supply closet?"

"Because your piano has, and I quote, 'seen better days,'" he replies. "And now you're going to ask me to approve a request to purchase new wire, which you know I can't do because you've already submitted your budget."

"Actually—"

"I'm sympathetic to your plight. I am. But I've only been here three months. You've been here thirty-seven years. Surely you know better than to be unprepared for emergencies. Now if you'll excuse me, I think my nose is bleeding."

He tilts back his head, stretching his long neck, and stuffs halves of Kleenex up his nostrils. The tissues blossom into a pair of roses.

IN ANY GIVEN year, St. Theresa's has eighty students, quartered off by grade. At first glance, these eighty students appear nondescript, costumed in the good Catholic schoolgirl ensemble of white blouse, pleated skirt, and flat black shoes. At second glance, maybe while riding behind a group of them on a city bus, one starts to notice peculiarities. Why has one dyed the tips of her hair purple? Why has *another* shaved off all her hair? Is *that* one's earring chained to her nose ring? Does one girl really have barbed wire tattooed around her neck? And the one with the cigarette burns on the backs of her hands—what is up with *that*? These are supposed to be good Catholic schoolgirls.

They are not good Catholic schoolgirls.

By and large, the students who attend St. Theresa's do so because they have been expelled from everywhere else. Their specific acts of disobedience are as varied as they are irrelevant. When your English teacher implies that you will never make anything of yourself and you punch her in the left tit, does it matter that the reason you keep failing her tests is because of your undiagnosed dyslexia?

The dyed hair and neck tattoos are tolerated by the holy sisters at St. Theresa's because, after years on the job, they can identify the difference between nonthreatening and threatening disruptions. And there have been threatening disruptions. The sisters have confiscated butcher knives, kitchen knives, sewing needles, pipe bombs, knuckle-dusters, safety razors, and enough dime bags and joints to outweigh a melon. Were they not all immediately turned over to the police, the sisters could have raised all their funds and then some from raffling them off.

Most of the girls learn to adjust. Most of the girls want to adjust. Most is not all. Several years ago, one clever scamp exasperated her classmates and faculty with such ferocious success that Mother Millicent nicknamed her the Antichrist.

TO STEADY HER mind after such an unsatisfactory conversation with Father Rook, Mother Millicent heads that evening to Silvio's Gym. Were she younger, were the temperature warmer, she would have walked the eight blocks west.

However.

She removes her veil, tucks away her cross, and dons a pair of prescription sunglasses. She could be Greta Garbo. She boards the crosstown bus.

Experience will cure Father Rook of his naivete. Experience will teach him that a budget which could not be stretched for repairs to the ceiling tiles, which are crumbling, or the toilet in the faculty bathroom, which is cracked, or the blackboard in the tenth-grade classroom, which is missing, or the language arts textbooks, which are crumbling, or the science textbooks, which are crumbling, or the math textbooks, which are crumbling, or the history textbooks, which are crumbling, could not contain a line item to anticipate a snapped piano wire. Father Rook's predecessors had been older when they had arrived at St. Theresa's and already understood the value of flexibility. Father Rook will learn too. Mother Millicent will teach him.

But not tonight. Tonight belongs to Silvio's. Mother Millicent has been coming to Silvio's for years, ever since the very same crosstown bus she is on now broke down in a blizzard and she was forced to find shelter in the nearest well-lit room, in this case a sweat-choked gym, and became instantly enthralled. She had stumbled upon their Thursday Night Fights; on Thursdays nights, the pugilists are women.

Mother Millicent pays her $10 entry fee and a few bucks more for a cup of ice cubes and beer, and she takes her seat. She used to sit in the back row, but over the years, her near-sightedness has forced her closer and closer to the front. Tonight, she's in the second row.

First to fight are the up-and-comers. The bell tolls and the women emerge from their corners. Their gloves match their sports bras. The ref reminds the women what not to do and then sidesteps away. The bell tolls again, and the women go at each other like storm clouds.

Mother Millicent has never hit anyone, not once. She has *been* hit, and repeatedly so. Over the years, students have slapped her across the cheek, across the jaw, over the ear. Punched her in the lips, in the nose, in the collarbone. But she never took the prescribed painkillers, not once, *gloriamur in tribulationibus*, amen.

None of the fighters on tonight's card are former students, but every so often, Mother Millicent recognizes a name and face. It's more common for her to spot a former student among the crowd. Not once in her many years of attendance has any of them seen through her disguise.

If that ever happened, how would she react? What would she say? That this moist, malodorous gym and these bloody bouts are her sanctuary from her sanctuary? That she is here to hide from the burdensome stare of God?

"YES, BUT IN the words of St. Paul," says Father Rook, "suffering produces perseverance; perseverance, character; and character; hope."

The chapel's ceiling has a dead light bulb, directly above the port side of the third pew, so he is five rungs up a forty-eight-foot ladder and steadily climbing, although his legs have begun to wobble like worms.

Mother Millicent stands below, gripping the ladder base. "Hope doesn't fix pianos or seal the cracks in the faculty toilet or cure mold."

"Mold?"

"Half the desks have mold growing underneath them. It's all in the assessment I gave you last month."

Father Rook is halfway to his destination. His eyes are shut. His legs continue to wobble, and now so does the ladder.

"I can do that if you want," Mother Millicent reminds him. "I must've replaced all these bulbs countless times."

"No, thank you. I've almost got it."

He doesn't move.

So Mother Millicent carries on: "I was thinking we maybe have a fundraiser. Like a bake sale or a raffle. Or a talent show. Sister Agnes says that some of the girls have some real singing ability. We can charge something reasonable. $10 a ticket. A few bucks more for refreshments."

"And what am I to say to the parent who calls me up, rightfully upset, and asks me why we need to raise funds on top of the thousands of dollars that he has already given to this school? For many of these people, those thousands of dollars represent a great sum. Yes, it's an investment in their child's academic education and spiritual salvation, but they need to trust us, Mother Mary Millicent, and nobody trusts a man who mismanages money."

They hear a distant hiss and a squeak. The school bus has returned the girls from phys pd. Father Rook pushes past his fear and climbs some more, eyes still shut, climbs, climbs, until the fingertips of his right hand graze the chapel's rough stucco ceiling and set upon the smooth glass curve of the dead light bulb.

The girls rush in. They scamper herd-like down the stairs to the classrooms. A few of them call out their hellos to Father Rook and Mother Millicent. Only when the final sounds of their footfalls have faded does the good father speak: "Mother Millicent, I seem to have left the new bulb on my desk. Be a dear and fetch it for me, please."

TONIGHT'S CARD HAS Letty Wallis scheduled for the third fight, but that can't be right. Or at the very least, that can't be the same Letty Wallis who spent four years at St. Theresa's. That Letty Wallis was a black-haired hummingbird who flitted about the halls and the dilapidated classrooms, chirping nonstop, her hands and wrists tucked into oversized sleeves. When Mother Millicent had learned Letty sold her Ritalin for clothes and makeup and a half-decent breakfast, she let it slide. The black-haired hummingbird was a classmate of the Antichrist. Some sins are relative.

There was one girl, for example, not too long ago, that Sister Claire caught in the middle stall of the lav with the wire hanger.

But points of no return are unchristian, even if the door to the tenth-grade classroom has come off its hinges and the upright piano is still missing two wires and now Sister Agnes is missing the smartphone she was using to play an accompaniment for her voice classes.

The Scriptures do not mention critical mass, not once.

But Father Rook will come around. She simply hasn't given him the correct argument yet. Everyone can be persuaded, especially those with an open heart, and what is the Church but a heart cleft wide open to welcome all of humankind.

With a rattle of a bell, the fighters for the third bout enter the ring. The woman in yellow is St. Theresa's Letty Wallis. Her black hair flows out from her headgear like decorative ribbons. Her arms are thin and bare, but her gloves are stretched tight to hide her wrists. She is barely taller than the post in her corner of the ring.

Her opponent, in pink and mauve, is a grizzly.

When the bell rattles again to sound the start of the fight, Mother Millicent winces. She dares not watch and dares not look away. Letty flies toward the muscle mass of her foe's torso and unleashes a barrage of stings with her yellow fists. She targets each of the hulking woman's ribs like a madcap xylophonist. Her arms swing with such alacrity that they become yellow blurs, they become comets, crashing against kidneys and breasts and lungs.

Mother Millicent shakes her fists in triumph and inspiration.

Then the monster in the pink top and mauve trousers swipes her right paw at Letty, and it's enough to knock the bite-sized St. Theresa's alumna three feet across the mat and into the ropes. The ropes closest to Mother Millicent.

She has the best seat in the house for what happens next.

"ARE YOU A RELATIVE?" the EMT asks.

"What? No. I . . . I was at the fight and . . . please, can I ride with her? I used to be her teacher."

The EMT shrugs and then helps Mother Millicent into the back of the ambulance. He and his partner don't appear too concerned even though their battered patient remains unconscious during the entire twelve-minute ride to the hospital. But they don't know Letty Wallis. They don't know that this current stillness is so unlike her.

Her face is a rocky terrain of bruises, a purple mountain majesty of bruises. Her jaw is so off-center that her chin is more aligned with her left ear than her nose. Her black hair is stringy with perspiration and pus and blood.

Mother Millicent unhides her necklace, switches out her glasses, redons her veil, and prays for her former pupil. She entreaties the Virgin Mary. She entreaties Jesus Christ. She is halfway through a missive to St. Jude, her favorite of the saints, when the ambulance parks alongside the ER.

Mother Mary Millicent is asleep by the time the pugilist's swollen, purpling eyelids finally flutter open. Her pupils inflate to accommodate the light of her curtained-off room and then fix their focus on the old woman in the chair and her veil and her dangling cross . . .

"Fuck," says Letty, "am I dying?"

However, because of the injury to her jaw, Letty can only open her mouth wide enough to part her misshapen lips and so, with her restricted enunciation, her inquiry is more tone than word.

But it's enough to stir Mother Millicent awake. She catches Letty's gaze of horror and leans toward her with a soft smile.

"It's okay," Mother Millicent rubs the back of Letty's right hand. She traces the girl's fingers. "You're going to be okay."

Letty attempts again to speak.

Mother Millicent pats the girl's hand. "Shh. I know. I know."

A tear slides down from the torn corner of Letty's right eye.

"Is there anyone I should contact? Here, let me give you my phone so you can write down their name. Let me just open the Notes app. All right. Here you go. All done? Now let's see what you typed. Oh. You want to know why I'm here. Oh. Well, I'm here because, well, nobody should have to suffer alone. And anyway, you were my student. You will always be my student. I remember the first time you were called to my office. You . . . what's that? Sure, here you go. They keep it a bit chilly in here, don't they? Do you want me to get you another blanket? I can ask the . . . Okay, thank you. Let's see. Oh. Well, I knew you would be here because . . . well . . . actually . . ."

"THERE HAS TO be a list," says Mother Millicent. "Nobody keeps lists like the Catholic Church."

"And you'd prefer not to ask Father Rook for the list."

Mother Millicent shrugs. The two of them are eating ham sandwiches in the cafeteria. "He'll find out either way, Sister Agnes, and that's fine. That's as it should be. This isn't meant to be some kind of subterfuge. But this is a test of our ingenuity."

"With all due respect, schools hit up their alumnae for contributions all the time. It's not that ingenious. I'm just surprised we've never done it before."

"We are not beggars."

"The world is full of beggars. It's foolish to pretend otherwise."

"This has always meant to be a place of empowerment."

"I can make some inquiries at the diocese."

"That was what I was thinking, Sister Agnes. You *are* friendly with what's-his-name."

"Yes. I am friendly with what's-his-name. Consider it done."

THE LIST IS COLOR-CODED.

Mother Mary Millicent studies it for a long while, and then she enlists aid from Sister Georgina, the school's math teacher. Together they pore over the twenty-seven-page spreadsheet as the amber glow of Mother Millicent's office lamp buzzes along.

"Are you sure there wasn't a top sheet explaining what each color meant? Usually there's a top sheet."

"This is all there is."

After fifth period is over, Sister Agnes joins in.

"I can call and ask," she says. "It would take two seconds."

"We are educated women! We can figure it out."

The three of them puzzle over the spreadsheet.

"Pink at least makes sense," says Sister Georgina.

"It does?"

Sister Georgina points out the shared last known address of the pink-colored names. It is a familiar address. All three of them have, at one time or another, taught at the local prison.

There are 54 pink names. 54 out of a total of 2391.

Mother Millicent treats herself to a banana from the cafeteria. By the time she returns, Sister Georgina and Sister Agnes have cracked the code on the yellow names. They are all deceased.

"But why yellow?"

"Why not yellow?"

After that, the rest of the code falls into place.

The blue names, for example, belong to the alumnae with a reported annual income over $500,000.

"Why blue? Why not green?"

"Maybe the person who made the spreadsheet is colorblind."

It is, the women decide, as good an explanation as any.

THE PLAN IS to divide the blue alumna among the faculty, whereupon they each will embark on personal visits. It's harder to say no face-to-face.

"I remember some of these girls," Sister James opines. "The only word in their vocabulary is no."

"They're obviously different now."

"Because they're older or because they're rich?"

"Speaking of, did you see whose name is near the top of the list?"

"Why are you surprised? Evil is always ambitious. And she was evil."

"Maybe she's different now too."

"Oh, are you volunteering to ring her doorbell?"

The sisters disperse to perform their task. Some carpool, some take public transportation. They each select a pair of current students to accompany them. Sister Agnes, having drawn the short straw, visits the Antichrist in her penthouse, unaccompanied, but no one answers the door, not even a maid.

By the end of the month, and with half of the blue girls solicited, the women of St. Theresa's have amassed a total of $3975 in personal checks.

But how much do they need? Mother Millicent takes it upon herself to tally the damages. Nobody knows the school better than she. She works slowly, going room to room. She takes copious notes. She interviews all of St. Theresa's instructors and some of St. Theresa's better students to augment her conclusions with what they believe the school must have.

She then visits several hardware stores and thrift stores and online retailers to match her list with hard numbers.

She finalizes her calculations. She reaches a sum.

Thank Christ it is Thursday night.

THERE IS A goldfish bowl by the refreshment stand. It is a collection pot for Letty's recovery. It is half full of cash. Mother Millicent adds her own tithe and takes a seat near the front.

She did visit Letty one more time in the hospital, just after the surgery to reset her jaw. The expansive window along the western wall of her room offered abundant sunlight, which made the thin metal rails affixed to the bottom of her face glow as if blessed. Mother Millicent sat beside Letty, with her back to the light, and stayed an hour.

The names on the title card are, fortunately, all unfamiliar. Her cross, tucked inside her blouse, is cold against her breastbone, cold to the marrow. She lays her cup of icy beer on the floor and hugs herself for warmth. The bouts will begin soon enough.

A tall, slender woman sits beside her. She smells like fresh cherries. Her hair is shorter than it used to be, but otherwise . . .

"You can't blame me," says the Antichrist. "I had to see for myself. And you can't blame Letty. She always was a talker."

"You look well," Mother Millicent replies.

"Do I? I married up. But then again, so did you. Although I hear St. T's not doing so well."

"It perseveres."

"That would tick me off. Knowing the Church has all this money and they're letting your school, a place that does real good, rot away like an old and lonely woman. Tell me, Mother Millicent, is that why you come here? To learn how to fight back?"

"The Church didn't deface the school's map of the Holy Land with pornographic sketches."

"Oh, I'd forgotten about that! But that wasn't me. I can't draw to save my life. That was Hannah Barr."

"Whom you encouraged."

"Since when was conversation a sin?"

"What do you want?" Mother Millicent turns and asks her.

"I told you: I had to see for myself. And here you are. Her Holiness Mother Mary Millicent attending the Thursday night fights. So just how bad are things at St. T? Is the roof ready to cave in?"

"We're taking care of it."

"Shaking down your former students is nice, but why not have a real community fundraiser? Put on one of those Christian haunted houses. The school's already got the cobwebs and the stench. Or set up a carnival. Sell some cookies door to door."

"I'll take your suggestions under advisement."

The pugilists for the first bout are announced. They saunter in from the locker room. The crowd cheers them on.

"You know what I've wondered," says the Antichrist, "all this time?"

"Which poison is the most undetectable?"

She chuckles. "You're the one who taught me that a nun, when she takes her vows, changes her name. She becomes Sister Mary Something, and the Something is the name of a saint. But there is no Saint Millicent."

"I said that a nun often takes the name of a saint. There are historical exceptions."

"I see. You hoped to become historical."

"I hoped to honor a saintly woman. Someone from my childhood."

"Oh my. More secrets. Who knew Mother Mary Millicent was so mysterious? Coming here for years, incognito. Has anyone ever asked your name here? What do you tell them? I know what name you all used to call me. Behind my back. You'd gather together after school, all you beatific brides of Christ, and gossip like magpies. And you point the finger at me for a little conversation? No wonder you're so full of shame."

The pugilists climb into the ring. The cheering fades.

"I know my sins," says Mother Millicent, "but my name is not one of them. I chose it to honor my grandmother. She was the one light in a childhood that was so full of darkness. And yes, when I told the officiates what name I chose, there was resistance. They implored me to change my mind. To conform. They had no idea why I fought so hard, why I was so stubborn. They mistook my conviction for pride. 'And pride is a mortal sin, Annie Parr!' I can still hear their voices. As clearly as I can hear yours. And they couldn't have been more wrong. If this was going to be my last choice as Annie Parr, it was going to be a virtuous one."

Mother Millicent, feeling much warmer now, picks up her beer and takes a sip. Shortly thereafter, the bell rings and the first bout commences. The Antichrist does not say another word.

HAVING ACCUMULATED NEARLY $4000 in donations, Mother Millicent now has to do the inevitable. Come Monday morning, she knocks on the door to Father Rook's rectory.

He looks up from his desk. His handkerchief is stuffed up his nostrils, leaving a ratty piece of white linen to droop in front of his lips like a secondhand veil.

"Bloody nose," he tells her.

She sits across from him. Her notebook is in her hands.

"So," the priest says nasally, "how can I help?"

Mother Millicent opens her notebook. Between its cover and its first page is the stack of checks. She hands the checks to Father Rook. She explains their origin.

He reviews them. Occasionally, he mutters a comment, his mouth still hidden behind his handkerchief veil. Finally, he looks up at her.

"I seem to have misplaced my calculator. What's the total sum?"

She tells him.

He nods in agreement. "That seems right. Hrm. So. What we have here, it appears to me, is that you decided it was more prudent to ask for forgiveness than permission."

"Actually—"

"No, no. It's okay. It's commendable, in its way. And the evidence speaks for itself. You have been industrious."

"It wasn't just me. Everyone pitched in. Including many of our students."

"I assume none of them handled the checks."

"Actually—"

"No matter. You can rest assured, Mother Millicent, that this adventure of yours has received my full support, even if it's after the fact. Consider these checks deposited. Next, we should come up with a list of capital improvements, ordered by priority, and assign the funds accordingly."

And there it is. Mother Millicent buries her impulse to break out a prideful grin. The test has been passed. "Actually, I've already—"

"But that, if you don't mind, will have to wait. Believe it or not, I can still feel the blood sliding down my nose. I think I may need to go to the emergency room."

AS A MATTER of tradition, Mother Millicent offers extra credit to any student willing to serve that week as school secretary. On the week after Father Rook's trip to the emergency room, the school secretary is Bev Chan, a likeable junior with a fondness for reciting poetry, protecting freshmen, and huffing cleaning supplies.

So it is Bev Chan who greets the postman when he arrives. She wishes him a lovely day, sneaks into the supply closet to spend a few minutes with an open bottle of antiseptic, and then skips down the hall to Mother Millicent's office to hand-deliver the mail. Then she sits, because standing is no longer an option.

Mother Millicent notes the oscillations of Bev's pupils. The girl really has promise, especially in language arts, but she needs to cut it out with the huffing. Part of the problem is her parents. Part of the problem is always the parents. Bev's parents, for example, are—

"Who's Annie Parr?"

Mother Millicent frowns. What did this addled girl just say?

"It's one of the letters? In the mail? It's, like, addressed to Annie Parr? Is she, you know, a former student or something?"

Mother Millicent rifles through the day's mail. Sure enough, there's a letter addressed in careful script to Ms. Annie Parr c/o St. Theresa's Academy. Even as she opens it, she knows who it's from.

Except there isn't a letter inside. There is a sheet of paper, folded like a letter, but that's only to conceal a bank check, which slides out and falls like a feather into Mother Millicent's lap.

THEY ARE IN the music room, taking a break from installing the new piano wires that Father Rook bought, when Mother Millicent shows Sister Agnes the check.

It takes a moment for Sister Agnes to register what she's holding. Then she holds it up to the light, as if she could ascertain the qualities of a counterfeit.

"It's real," says Mother Millicent. "I even called the bank."

"I don't think I've ever held this much money. Ever."

"Sister Agnes, I would assume most people haven't."

They both sit in silence, save for the clarion call of seven figures on a piece of paper. Sister Agnes then speaks:

"And all because you randomly ran into her on the street?"

"We didn't talk for long."

"It must have been long enough. Long enough, at least, for you to confide in her. Share your original name. With the Antichrist."

"But don't you see? That's what did it. I opened up to her and she felt . . . I don't know . . . moved by the Holy Spirit."

"So moved that she decided to trap you with a big fat check."

"If this is a trap, let me be trapped! Let us all be trapped! This isn't some kind of devilish temptation. There are no strings. With this money, we will finally, *finally* be able to transform St. Theresa's into the school it has always been meant to be. No more close calls with building inspectors or health inspectors."

"Mother Millicent . . ."

"There are those who believed—and you know this is true—there are those who believed that the sorry state of our school was appropriate. That it was the perfect environment for girls like ours. But what will they say now? What will they say when they see the same girls, our girls, standing in front of whitewashed walls, and holding brand-new textbooks? This slip of paper isn't a trap. It's our girls' salvation."

"And you trust the Church is going to just give it all back to us? All this money? To do as we see fit?"

"Yes. They will do what's right. Granted, it will take a little footwork to get the bank to allow me to even cash this check. I've got my original Social Security card tucked in a drawer somewhere. And granted, whatever's mine becomes the property of the Church as per canon law—you're absolutely right about that—but when I turn over this sum, they will see it for what it means to this school. Otherwise, why keep us open at all? In fact, as we speak, Father Rook is at the diocese discussing the alumni donations on our behalf. Cheer up, Sister Agnes. Our long fight is nearly over. By the way, did you ever find your missing phone?"

THEY FIRST SEE it the following morning when they file in for morning mass. The students, of course, react the strongest: some gasp, some giggle, some make jokes. The sisters are less vocal but no less shocked.

Father Rook watches it all from his pulpit. His lips slice his face from ear to ear. If the man were any happier, he would die of a burst heart.

"I want to tell you," he says, "the story behind our new addition. Maybe you've heard about our recent alumni fundraiser. Women, just like all of you, now successful, thriving, by the will of God and by transformative education—they donated almost five thousand dollars to our betterment. They gave back to a place that gave them so much. And so the question became how does one honor such generosity, such charity? Christ is clear on this. One honors charity with good works. Which begs a second question. What good works can we do that best honor Christ? Well, I am sure you're in agreement that our new addition honors Christ in a way that befits His Majesty."

As per custom, Mother Millicent is at the rear of the chapel. Even with her glasses on, Father Rook is little more than a black-clad blur, but she can see the gargantuan new crucifix behind him with flawless clarity. She shuts her eyes and can still see it. It too is flawless. She can touch her arm and feel the smooth cedar of its muscles. She can close her hands and feel its perfectly carved nails push through the soft flesh of her palms.

LATER, IN HIS rectory, Father Rook greets her with a wide-armed embrace.

"You'll never believe what happened," he tells her.

She doesn't reply. Her notebook is clutched in both hands. The check lies pressed within it like a leaf.

"Last night, I'm in the drugstore, looking to get some new nasal spray. And I'm there in the aisle and what do I see? Tell me. What do I see?"

She doesn't reply. She doesn't sit.

"A neti pot! And I figure why not? What do I have to lose?"

"What do you have to lose?"

"Exactly. And I buy it. And a bottle of water because it says not to use tap water. And I get home and I follow the instructions. I fill up the pot. Have you seen one? It kind of looks like an elephant, don't you think? I add salt to the water. And I tip back my head and I tip the spout . . . the elephant's trunk . . . I tip it into my nose and let the water pour in. Oh, it felt strange. I mean, I could feel the salt water coursing through my sinuses! And then it drained out the other nostril, all full of . . . well, you don't need to hear the details. Let's just say it made a mess. But I followed the instructions. I did it again. The other nostril this time. And I went to bed. And a miracle occurred!"

"How nice."

"No, you don't understand. I can breathe freely." He demonstrates, inhaling and exhaling. "I haven't been able to breathe like this in, I don't know, *years*. It's as if God has rolled a boulder off my face. Oh my. Now. I bet you're here about our crucifix. Well. It was the bishop's idea, really. He reminded me that what this parish has lacked more than new windows or a few piano strings is aspiration. Our students need to come to mass and feel inspired. I'm sure you'd agree that the presence of Christ in their hearts and minds is more valuable than a refreshed textbook or fancy desk. The girls come here because they're mischief-makers. They need a role model, and the sight of Our Lord on that cross, every day, will affect them."

Mother Millicent waits until he is finished. Then she nods. Then she opens her notebook and takes out the check. "We've had one final donation from an alumna."

"Oh?"

She shows him the amount.

He gasps. He sits.

"If your eye offends, you pluck it out . . . but who actually does that?" she asks him. "I certainly couldn't. Could you, Father Rook? If I told you the author of this check were spiteful and that this check is her effort to shame me, force me into the role of the sacrificial lamb, would it change your mind about accepting it?"

"I don't understand . . ."

"I was never tempted. I want you to know that, Father. Not once did I even consider leaving this vocation. Sure, it would have allowed me to wrest control of this windfall out of your grip, but the cost would have been my soul and that choice never even crossed my mind. But that doesn't mean I have to be complicit. There is a third option, though I doubt it ever occurred to this check's author. Or to you."

"What do you mean?"

She responds with a smile, and continues to smile as she rips the check up into a million little pieces, smiles still as Father Rook shouts at her to stop, begs her to explain herself, demands she come back and explain herself, but she's left his room, gone, far from even the cloying tenor of his voice.

My Favorite Nasty Woman

Charlaine Harris

When my friend Toni Kelner (aka Leigh Perry) asked me to write about a Nasty Woman I admired, I was very happy to discover I had many to choose from: Jane Austen, who surely led an extraordinary secret life for a parson's daughter; Joan of Arc, manipulated and used by everyone around her, who yet managed to stay on her course; Cleopatra, who did her best to keep her country intact and to protect her family's ownership of the throne of Egypt; Ruth Bader Ginsberg, who remains a monument of intelligence and integrity.

But in the end, I choose Sara Paretsky. Sara is an extraordinarily skilled and well-informed writer. Her protagonist, private eye V.I. Warshawski, is the least girly, most determined, and most intelligent woman in crime-writing fiction. Aside from these admirable qualities, V.I.—very much like Sara herself—is not afraid to speak her mind and take action . . . and be prepared for the consequences. These are character traits I find admirable.

Women on Fire

Jacqueline Winspear

I f there's one phrase I loved when I first heard it upon coming to live in America, it was "skin in the game." It seemed to really hit the spot in describing the connection between an event and the personal impact it might have on an individual. I loved it because it's a reminder of an investment—be it the strength in our knees if we take up running, or the importance of our vote in an election. If the outcome affects us, then we've got skin in the game. And if you live in the Western states or any other region impacted by wildfire, and the talking heads are all opining on what could or should have been done [to avoid a conflagration], and whose head should be rolling—then you have skin in the game.

What that means is that if we could lose our lives, homes, and means of making a living in a finger snap when warm winds blow the wrong way at the wrong time, we should be able to see the wood for the trees. We have a responsibility to ourselves to become more educated about wildfire—not only so that we have a greater awareness of the misinformation and outright lies surrounding the politics of fire, but to find our voices when our elected leaders both locally and on the national stage start making decisions that impact our personal safety, our way of life, our environment, and our individual and collective future. But be aware—there are a lot of gray areas when it comes to wildfire—and sadly, the all-important gray areas where truth resides are often completely smoke-shrouded in the fire and fury of burning homes and political rhetoric.

Wildfire is a naturally occurring phenomenon—sparks from automobile exhausts or overhead power lines notwithstanding. In indigenous societies throughout the Americas, protecting communities from wildfire was "managed" by women, so I turned to women working with fire as I sought to begin my own education into the dynamics, economics, and politics of wildfire.

I first interviewed Amanda Stamper, Nature Conservancy fire manager for the states of Oregon and Washington, and also chair of the Oregon Prescribed Fire Council, in August 2018. I had been commissioned by *Womankind* magazine to write a piece focusing on women who had experienced the sharp end of the four elements—Stamper was my "fire" subject. It was during our initial conversation, as I learned more about her work and her passion for protecting land and communities while revitalizing the environment through the "laying down of fire," that I realized how woefully underinformed I was—and that in living cheek by jowl with tinder-dry California scrubland and forest, and on a property within the wildland-urban interface, I had some serious skin in the game. I decided I'd better get myself some knowledge—and that's not such an easy thing to do. Says Stamper, "Politicians can't see the whole situation, and there's so much confusion [about the nature, cause, and control of wildfire] being generated."

Maybe we should start with a little history—a few insights into how we've come to a place today where different constituencies are at loggerheads.

First of all: *Fire.* We are a civilization burnished and branded by fire. Our very existence is dependent upon a great ball of fire in the sky. It nudges us awake in the morning and signals a time of rest in the evening—even if our "fake fire" inventions, from the candle to the Light Emitting Diode, keep us awake into the small hours. When our ancestors rubbed a couple of dry sticks together and created fire, they opened the door to progress—and that progress has taken us all the way from cooked meat to the industrial revolution and beyond. Fire shipped us across oceans and upward to the moon. But with advancement came detachment. Healthy respect became man vs. nature. And along the way, privilege, discrimination, and intellectual domination led us to ignore the innate knowledge of fire held by indigenous communities. Something dangerous attended our ability to bend fire to our will—and that was a diminishing respect for the raw power of wildfire and the wisdom to defer to those whose understanding came from centuries of fire tending.

Women had an innate understanding of nature's healing power held in grasses, plants, shrubs, and forest because they used those resources in creating tinctures, balms, and beverages to cure all manner of ills. That knowledge extended to the behavior of the plant world and foliage in fire, so women led the laying down of fire—the regular ritual burning of dead and dangerous brush to prevent conflagration on a broader scale. What we call the "prescriptive" or "controlled" burn today not only allowed those native American communities to protect their homes, but they were able to clear land for the growing of crops, to hunt, and to play. And if wildfire came, it was left to burn, for they knew the field and forest needed fire to release new life and regenerate.

So far, so good. To a great extent, prior to the twentieth century, landowners followed the prescriptive burn protocol, and they also understood that some fires are best left to just burn out—you can't chase every small fire. And people used fire every single day, so there was a sense of living cheek by jowl with flame. I grew up in rural England, and even as a toddler I remember living in a cottage at the edge of a significant conifer forest where we had no electricity, so our light was via oil lamps and my parents cooked on an old cast iron wood stove. Fire drove the steam-hauled trains that connected us to the wider world, and as I grew up I worked on the farm—and I remember as a child making bonfires of the old, dry hop bines from the season just passed. Fire was an element that defined our lives.

In the United States—and other countries—the early 1900s saw the beginning of men fighting fire in a systematic way. Following on from Federal sequestration of significant tracts of land in the late 1800s, Teddy Roosevelt gave America the gift of her wildlands and wide-open spaces when he created the National Parks. Huge tracts of forest came under federal ownership, and Roosevelt's right-hand man in this endeavor—Gifford Pinchot, a wealthy intellectual and lover of the American west—became the first head of the fledgling Forest Service. Again, so far, so good.

But they would not tolerate fire.

Young men fresh out of Yale Forest School* with a love of the land became the first rangers and were sent into the forests of Oregon, Washington, Idaho, and California. They had explicit instructions to stop any fire, any time. Fire

---

* The Yale Forest School is now the Yale School of Forestry & Environmental Studies.

suppression, as opposed to fire management, took the upper hand. But as we know, fire is a naturally occurring phenomenon. Lightning plays a part—there are tens of thousands of lightning strikes throughout the west every year—and so does climate. Certain trees need fire every ten to fifteen years to regenerate—and if they don't burn, the raw material for fire builds up, thus the kindling is laid and waiting.

We'll get to the nature of trees, fuel, and the forest soon enough, but let's stick with Teddy and Gifford—the latter a very handsome man, by all accounts—for a while. As Stamper notes, "1910 changed the game. We had started to put out fires, and we began to treat fire as the enemy, not as a tool." She adds that the frame of reference for the Pinchot school of thinking about fire was the European forests—which are not as fire adaptive.

Stamper points out that during this period, "climate oscillation" helped, giving the area a cool wet period. Then it changed again. It was this same period that inspired the building of the great river dams in the West—the planners thought those rivers would run at the same strength forever, little knowing the weather pattern was an anomaly. And that's why the water wars are upon us today, and man-made lakes created by damming rivers are running dry. Commenting on the effects of climate oscillation, Stamper adds, "Fires are not bigger than they used to be—they're just bigger than the last hundred years." And of course, that's when most development has taken place.

Now back to the Teddy and Gifford show—I know you're wondering what happened in 1910. When it came to creating public lands as a legacy for the American public, needless to say there was a fair amount of pushback from certain members of Congress—men who believed in the private ownership of land, and that the land was a resource for people to do what they wanted. Logging and development come to mind. And as experience will often inform us, when big money men are talking, the word "plunder" can hang in the air, unspoken. But Teddy and Gifford were giving the American people their temples. The ancient forests would be theirs forever, a gift of wildness in an increasingly industrial America.

So Teddy and Gifford persevered, with Gifford writing many of Teddy's more crowd-pleasing speeches. Yet as Timothy Egan explains in *The Big Burn*, "Pinchot the missionary now professed that wildfire was akin to slavery—a blight on the young country, but something that could be wiped out by man. While nature could never be conquered, it could be tamed, tailored, customized." And that's when nature showed just how much skin *she* had in the game.

The constant fighting of every small wildfire and a move away from the pre-scriptive burn—what we would call "fire suppression" as opposed to "fire preven-tion"—led to what was arguably the worst wildfire in western history, when in 1910 the drought-stricken national forests of Washington, Idaho, and Montana were hit by monster winds that whipped smaller wildfires into an inferno that crossed the border into British Columbia. It was fought by some 10,000 men, many of whom were burned to death in the conflagration.

Though we have to thank Teddy and Gifford for the gift of our national parks, those great swathes of land were set aside for the people at the same time fire suppression had come of age, and there would be no going back for decades. It's important to add that fire prevention through prescriptive burning continued in regions such as the Southeast, but in the West, man would still be on fighting terms with nature. Enter the roads—and stay with me here. A little more history, and then we'll get right back to those women tending fire.

Stephen J. Pyne's *Fire In America* remains one of the perennial texts for would-be fire ecologists, and for me—fast becoming a fire bore at the dinner table—it was enlightening. In the 1997 edition, Pyne notes that the, "postwar [WWII] era was a dazzling period of [fire] equipment development, most spectacularly with aerial firefighting, and most effectively with ground-based vehicles." The "major orgy of road building" in the 1940s, together with established and new logging roads, meant that there was greater access for fighting fires. And according to Pyne, along with that access came "a decline in controlled burning as a tool of fire suppression. More and more Americans elected to attack fire directly rather than backfire against it, so that even in fire control, America substituted the py-rotechnologies of internal combustion for those of open flame."

It's time to start thinking about all that equipment—the aircraft, the tenders, backhoes, the oxygen equipment required for men going deeper into the forest to fight and suppress fire—and as fast as new gear was developed, so it was utilized. *Ker-ching, ker-ching.* America had become obsessed with fighting fire rather than fire tending to prevent fire. And we were becoming detached from the possible outcomes of those developments—until the flames licked at our feet.

Let's move on. Let's look at the trees, then back at the wood.

In terms of fire, broadly speaking trees fall into two categories: trees that suppress fire and trees that accelerate fire. Here are some things to know about trees—and don't worry if you don't have green fingers, this is pretty easy. And remember this is a "broad brush" outline, so bear in mind there are some gray areas.

- The timber industry likes certain kinds of wood. Redwood comes to mind—it's sought after in construction as it's impervious to various pests. It also provides a perfect example of the misinformation perpetrated by politicians who want to "Log, baby, log." Redwood is a natural fire suppressant. Those old trees with the crowns so high you think they will touch the clouds—they can slow and even halt a fire. The lesson here is that timber worth something to the industry is also worth keeping in the forest.

- The wood that is least valuable to the timber industry is generally fire accelerant. That means it's fuel. Really powerful fuel. The timber industry doesn't want it, so they leave it in the forest. It costs money to move timber and they don't move what they can't sell.

- Young trees are fire accelerants because their crowns are still low—"young" can be 20–30 years old for a redwood.

- Wildfires often start not in the forest, but in the scrubby land adjacent, and if a forest area has previously been clear cut and then replanted, that fire starting in the grass will whip through the adjacent young woodland like . . . well, like wildfire. Think of young trees as if they were a bunch of teenagers partying—then lightning strikes. There is some suggestion that the recent devastating Paradise fire really went out of control when it hit an area of clear-cut forest now full of young trees.

- Then there's something called "slash." When logging companies go in to clear cut, they only want wood that is a certain diameter, so they cut away the lesser branches and leave it where it lands, and it becomes—yes, kindling, though it's called "slash" in the timber industry. Teen trees and dead wood—a recipe for disaster. Oh, and clear cutting is when the timber company goes to the forest and takes everything in a given area. In the earlier days of the timber industry, there was more of a connection to the community, and arguably a paternalistic approach to forestry. Selective cut was the norm—only taking certain trees, leaving the elders, and at the same time they removed slash and those worthless trees that become fire accelerants. Not so anymore.

So, despite what you may have read, according to Amanda Stamper, "We can't log our way out of wildfire risk." And raking leaves doesn't help either, Mr. President.

Back to today.

In late September 2018, I spoke with Katie Sauerbrey, preserve manager and burn boss at the Nature Conservancy Sycan Marsh Preserve in Oregon. Sauerbrey manages 30,000 acres of restored marsh and mixed pine forest and oversees all fire restoration efforts. "Prescribed fire is a big part of my job," says Sauerbrey. "Ponderosa pine, especially, has a burn life of eleven to fourteen years—this is a normal process we have reconstructed using fire scars and other methods. Prescriptive burn keeps the forest resilient, and we are burning 1000–1500 acres per burn job." As a neophyte, I needed a description of "burn life" so Sauerbrey explained, "If a forest has a burn cycle [the natural cycle of burning to regenerate and clear the forest floor] of ten years, and it hasn't burned in a hundred years, that means it's holding ten times the fire risk, ten times the fire load than it should—and that's an enormous risk." And that was all I needed to know about that to scare me.

Perhaps this is where we zero in on exactly what prescriptive burn entails. I had not heard that particular term when I first interviewed Stamper, but she explained that I was probably more familiar with "controlled burn." Oh yes, I thought, I know what that is—a bunch of guys in a dry meadow burning up the grass and keeping an eye on it. Let's just say I had the sense to inquire about prescriptive burn instead of embarrassing myself with my assumptions, because a straw poll of various friends has revealed that most people think it's just a bunch of guys in a field burning up the grass and then walking off and leaving it.

The crucial element is that *prescriptive burn can prevent 40% of wildfires, yet it is impacted by politics, economics, climate change, and misinformation.* I italicized to get your attention. Let's put that under the microscope, because if you've read this far, you have skin in the game, and a 40% reduction in risk of wildfire eating up your home, livelihood, and perhaps your life is something you want to know about.

Before an at-risk area can be subject to prescriptive burn, certain elements have to be in place. A burn permit must be obtained from the jurisdiction—from whoever is responsible for the land and the neighboring community. As Stamper says, "I have to liaise with a lot of organizations—and [for example] Sycan Marsh will be different from Eugene. All regulating agencies have to be on board, from the Department of Forestry to the fire departments, air protection agencies, regulating agencies—and there's often pushback from fire departments—but we meet and talk them through the burn plan." Issues of liability come into play, along with smoke management and meeting all regulations.

Then there's the weather.

A prescribed burn can only be carried out if certain temperature, humidity, and wind conditions are present, so there's a narrow window of time to—ultimately—prevent wildfire using prescriptive burn. And climate change has narrowed that window, according to Katie Sauerbrey. "We usually work with fire in fall," says Sauerbrey, "but now we're down to a two-week window [due to climate change] to use fire as a beneficial tool. We have to adjust how we use fire and the needs of the ecosystem as we support forest resiliency in the face of climate change." Sauerbrey went on to say, "If we're going to get ahead [of the wildfire risk], prescriptive burn is an important tool."

And the irony in all of this, says Stamper, is that, "We'll get to burn day, with all the work and permits in place, yet a farmer will go ahead with his own burn." Yes, the private landowner can just do what he or she likes before anyone knows what they're doing, but if fire management professionals want to decrease risk of wildfire by 40%, they are hampered by costly and time-consuming administration.

Lenya Quinn-Davidson summed up the power of the prescribed burn: "The simplest way to think about fire management is as a version of treatment in an area vulnerable to fire. Other versions include grazing, logging, mastication (grinding) of fuel. Of all those, the only completely effective process is fire, because it consumes all the fuel; it doesn't leave any behind." And as Katie Sauerbrey said, "Fire is an essential part of forest health. Fire is medicine."

Budgets are an incendiary topic in fire management and firefighting and given the number of gray areas in the whole question of wildfire management, it's important to look at how the impact of increased fire risk on available funds may well bring different constituencies together as time goes on. Says Amanda Stamper—who began her career as a member of a hot shot team fighting forest fires while she was a student at the University of Oregon studying for her BA in Philosophy (which she followed with a Master's Degree in Natural Resources, Fire Ecology and Management at the University of Idaho): "If I am fighting fire, everything is at my disposal. I have unlimited funds—which is as it should be. But if I am preventing fire—managing risk with prescriptive burn—then I have to watch every cent."

I asked Stamper if fighting fire was a bit like war—there are people who make a lot of money in a time of conflict, and they make a lot less during peacetime. I wondered if the "business" of fire had any similarity—and as I asked the question, I was thinking of the Boeing 747 I had seen dumping fire retardant over the hills near my home one wildfire season. I thought about the helicopters flying overhead and I considered the industrial nature of fire, from trucks to gear, and right down to Band-Aids.

"We should be fiscally responsible fighting fire," said Stamper, adding, "There's a disturbing culture that doesn't hold anyone responsible. Aircraft cover, as an example, has questionable effectiveness. And a large fire management team costs five dollars per acre to be effective, whereas fighting fire costs upwards of one thousand dollars per acre. Firefighting is incredibly expensive—and the private contractors would rather bid for wildfire fighting, not prevention, because it looks better on paper for them." She goes on to explain, "Fire is an industrial complex. It's a money-making venture, and I have a beef with that. There are companies making a ton of money from the problem—they've got contracts for food, showers, water tenders (vehicular water tankers), etc. And if you want to retire from the fire service, you can buy a tender, have someone drive it, and you can make money. Fighting fire has an open checkbook, even with a Finance Unit Leader to control costs."

Ultimately, though, it's the human cost of wildfire that disturbs Stamper. "Fighting fire is hard on people," she says. "My whole job [as a fire fighter] was to take down trees and burned houses. And you can't keep putting people in front of fire risking their lives."

Going forward, as the landscape of fire management and firefighting is challenged by greater risk of wildfire due to climate change, drought, and suburban development encroaching upon wild lands, it's clear that collaboration is key—between federal agencies, the timber industry, and us, the general public with skin in the game. Sometimes, though, the necessary collaboration can be an uphill climb, as underlined in a July 2018 paper, "Co-Managing Wildfire: Conversations You Need to Have Right Now," by Drs. Branda Nowell, Anne-Lise Velez, and Toddi Steelman. The authors describe a "don't worry, we've got this" culture across jurisdictions that continues to pervade incident command.

But at the same time, there are stories of individual innovators breaking through bureaucratic, institutional, and cultural barriers. Stamper, Sauerbrey, and Quinn-Davidson are evidence of individual innovation and a passion to address increased wildfire risk through collaboration, enabling them to protect communities while tending the land and supporting the natural process of restoration and rejuvenation of our wildlands and forests.

Says Quinn-Davidson, who works with the Northern California Prescribed Fire Council on a regional and state level and the Humboldt County Prescribed Burn Association on a local level [see www.facebook.com/hcpba], "My work at the local level is about building relationships. It seems to me that we've dehumanized our relationships in this country, and I'm inspired by seeing people on the ground level caring about their communities and coming together to work—it's a buffer between the rhetoric and the local community."

Quinn-Davidson also liaises with the US Forest and Park Service, and comments that, "We are seeing a change, especially in California with Cal Fire (www. fire.ca.gov)—we're moving in a new direction. The more we have wildfires—and we will, due to climate change—we will see more prioritization of fire management projects. The attitude toward prescribed fire has changed radically, with Cal

Fire supporting a lot of controlled fire. We have to be more strategic together, because everything is becoming more extreme."

Amanda Stamper reiterates that there is much to be learned from the traditional culture of burning, and now works alongside tribal members "fire tending"—laying down fire to regenerate and support the natural world while protecting humans from the ravages of wildfire. "Part of the problem," says Stamper, "is the result of the man versus nature approach—it's very masculine. If you talk to women in tribal communities, they have a more holistic approach. Women tend and relate to the landscape—their relationship is not about ego. With the masculine approach, fire is the enemy. But fire has many faces."

"For the most part, people want to do the right thing," says Quinn-Davidson. "Both the Carr fire and the Delta fire took with them a lot of industrial timber lands, so the companies have a lot at stake—now is the time for us to look at compromises. Fire can bring people together to talk about all the things we care about. Creating this kind of [local] venue is important. Ranchers form the main demographic, but it's really great to see timber companies sitting down with Save the Redwoods."

Stamper adds, "We want to work with the fire departments. We're sharing. We're professional and we follow the same rules with the same training." But she adds, "To be clear—a lot of companies are team players. Logging is not a thorn in my side. I'm against polarization in the conversation—pointing a finger at environmentalists who point a finger back. But we're entering an era when everything is changing."

So what about the rest of us? Perhaps it's time to become more involved in issues connected not only with wildfire, but with the extreme elements that threaten our lives and homes. I recently wrote a blog post about wildfire, and among the many responses were a surprising number from current or former real estate agents. To a person they had a story that went along these lines: In their time they had seen land that was previously out of bounds to development due to its location in a fire or flood risk zone, suddenly being opened up to construction. One commented, "Where there was once hillside, there are now monster homes—and I've watched them burn twice in the past few years." Another described seeing new housing swallowed up by flood in an area known to be at risk.

Ker-ching, ker-ching. Someone, somewhere made money from those areas being released for development.

If you live in an area at risk from fire or flood, you have skin in this game. Only it's not a game. It's a real looming threat. Yes, you may have your go-kit ready for evacuation (do you?), but what about using your voice? Increasingly fire management agencies and fire departments are leading local meetings. Do you attend? If not, then go. Ask questions. Inquire if a program of prescribed burn—cheaper than fighting fire—is appropriate for your area, and if it's in the plans. Ask now. You, too, can become a fire bore. That new housing development might not be on your doorstep, but if its up close to wild land or forest, and it's hit by fire—that fire will spread faster, so it's not a crime to find out why it was permitted in the first place, or to speak up it if it impacts neighborhood safety.

If we want to play a part in protecting our lives, homes, and communities from fire, it would serve us to educate ourselves. I'm only just starting to learn the language, but I believe I have a responsibility to be part of the conversation. If you have skin in the game, just raking leaves is not enough in this new world of wildfire.

Sources and Acknowledgements

Interview with Lenya Quinn-Davidson [Northern California Prescribed Fire Council, Humboldt County Prescribed Burn Association], in discussion with the author, November 2018.

Interview with Katie Sauerbrey [preserve manager and burn boss, Nature Conservancy Sycan Marsh Preserve], in discussion with the author, October 2018.

Interview with Amanda Stamper [fire manager for Oregon and Washington, Nature Conservancy; chair, Oregon Prescribed Fire Council], in discussion with the author, September 2018.

Egan, Timothy. The Big Burn: Teddy Roosevelt and the Fire that Saved America. Boston: Mariner Books, 2009.

Pyne, Stephen J. Fire in America: A Cultural History of Wildland and Rural Fire. Seattle: University of Washington Press, 1997.

Carle, David. *Burning Questions: America's Fight with Nature's Fire.* Westport: Praeger, 2002.

Nowell, Branda, PhD; Anne-Lise Velez, PhD; and Toddi Steelman, PhD. "Co-Managing Wildfire: Conversations You Need to Have Right Now." Fire Adapted Communities Learning Network [2018], https://fireadaptednetwork.org/co-managing-wildfire-conversations-you-need-to-have-right-now/.

Afterword

Women on Fire was written in October 2018, long before publication—it can take a lot of time to bring a book to fruition—so a few more words on the subject of fire are warranted. Since I interviewed the three extraordinary women working at the scalding end of fire management, wildfire risk has become even more of a constant in the minds of people living in areas vulnerable to fire and not only due not only to the risks posed by climate change, but power outages, local and regional evacuation drills and a certain siege mentality. When I was working in London in the late 1970s and 80s, we had that same level of pit-of-the-stomach preparedness, always on the lookout, but in that case it was due to the IRA bombings. Now, according to a November 2019 op-ed in *The Guardian*, we are living in "The Age of Fire."

I've heard many people talking about leaving the western USA, and articles have been written with titles such as "Is California Finished?" or "Is The Dream Over?" And in the midst of the rhetoric, developers continue to build homes in fire-risk areas and people are paying good money to live in canyons with breathtaking views—canyons that would be blocked by traffic in seconds should an evacuation order be given. On the flip side, thousands of goats have been deployed on hillsides, chomping back tinder-dry brush to limit the risk of wildfire—because most fires do not start in a forest, they start in brushland—and we're seeing more fire management, the laying down of fire to prevent fire. Local communities are creating armies of volunteers to go door-to-door advising on the clearance of fire-accelerant shrubs and trees, and on the importance of having a personal evacuation plan. This is the new normal.

In October 2019, my local community was without power for four days during a period of high winds: Such was the risk of fire should downed power lines cause sparks and flames. And lest we think we are being picked on, at the same time Sydney, Australia was enveloped in smoke from the devastating Queensland fires. Floods have swamped the UK, Kenya, and parts of the USA, and the list goes on.

The closing paragraph of *Women on Fire* speaks to the importance of personal responsibility. Nature is in the process of batting last, having her say about humanity's treatment of the natural world. As the writer of this essay, the crucial piece I came away with is the responsibility and necessity of direct involvement when wildfire—or for that matter any natural disaster—threatens our way of life. For some of us that means big changes, for others just small efforts. It might mean using our voices when really we're not used to rocking the boat. It might mean playing a bigger part in community efforts to keep everyone safe. As I watch teams of firefighters heading toward another wildfire, I have Amanda Stamper's words echoing in my mind: *You can't keep putting people in front of fire risking their lives.* The solution has to be in not waiting for someone else to save us, but doing our best to save ourselves by working together, becoming fire-wise, looking out for our neighbors, and assuming all the elements of personal and collective responsibility that in the past have brought us through the very worst of times. May that ethos do so again.

The War Never Ends

Kate Thornton

I wasn't going to tell this story again, ever.

It was always going to be a secret, one of those big, awful things that you put away in the back of your mind and only remember in the night when you can't sleep and all the mistakes and embarrassments of a lifetime come creeping out to keep you awake.

I never imagined I would ever need to tell it. I guess I was waiting for someone special.

It was just luck, me finding you like that. If I hadn't looked up at just the right time, I might have missed it all. That alley was pretty dark.

Before I tell you about it, though, why don't you get comfortable? As comfortable as being tied to a shabby office chair with a gag in your mouth will allow. It's good quality duct tape and you aren't going anywhere soon, so settle in. Who knows? By the time I tell you what happened, maybe you'll understand. Or maybe I will.

Like most women, I've been to hell. As a woman in the Army, I was lucky enough to get a round-trip ticket when a lot of brave soldiers got the one-way special. But the Army wasn't my only hell, and looking back, I know there was nothing I could have done. No amount of confidence or preparation could have changed what happened, and the fact that I no longer carried a weapon made not one damned bit of difference. Keep that in mind. A gun can't always help.

There's no way to describe that unique bond among vets that means you don't have to say anything, relive anything, unless you need to. And it's why, when we tell all the funny jokes, sing the ridiculous songs, recount the pranks, and in general celebrate our time together, we refer to it as Telling War Stories. We don't tell the real ones. Recollections of the unthinkable are best left for therapy sessions and nightmares.

Chief Warrant Officer Artie Gibson and Sergeant First Class Joe Escobar were my buddies. That meant we watched out for each other and respected the boundaries that our lives back home gave us. That's a fancy way of saying we didn't sleep with each other. Hey, those guys were attractive, but they were spoken for, and I had to walk that line between being friendly and being professional. But I'm not exaggerating when I say the bonds between us were stronger than common friendship.

Artie was tall, a good thing since his weight eventually got the better of him, with red hair that turned white one year. He had once been a cop and still radiated that confidence and dark humor. Joe was slightly built, with honeyed skin, black hair, and soft brown eyes. He'd done a stint with a three-letter agency and had a couple of degrees, but he enlisted in the Army instead of opting for Officer Candidate School.

We met in Intel Training and got sent to language school together. Then we got sent to some very bad places together. Artie and I got to go home after a year, but Joe didn't make it out for another eighteen months. We were stationed stateside after that, teaching students who got younger every year.

My retirement party was a blowout bash at Fort Mason. I bought a nice house in the suburbs, lined up a job with a local defense contractor—my security clearance was worth good money—and bought a new working wardrobe.

There was a Starbucks on every corner, so I wasn't going to go without my morning coffee, but there was no Artie, no Joe. Artie Gibson and Joe Escobar retired shortly after I did and went to work for a different defense contractor, some hush-hush security outfit. They were both still local, but once you're out, you lose touch.

My job was reliable, lucrative, and comfortably boring right up until that day.

It was about six o'clock in the evening, still warm and light out. My car was parked at the back of the outdoor lot because I had come in too late to get a good spot up close, and in the morning, when I was energetic and even perky, that didn't matter. But at the close of a long day, it was a trudge in heels out to the back forty.

I'd like to say that the parking lot was secure—a chain-link perimeter fence with razor wire, video surveillance, and a handy guard—and that was true except they were reconfiguring the lot and a whole huge piece of the fencing was down, cameras obstructed by heavy equipment and construction stuff. Okay, the guard shack was there, but it was far from my parking place, out of shouting distance.

Not that it mattered. I never saw him until he hit me.

Stunned by a sharp blow to the center of my back, I went sprawling down next to my car, unsure of what had happened. I thought maybe I'd been hit by a piece of stray equipment or debris. My second thought, the one I truly believed, was that I had been shot.

I rolled over to see what had happened and he kicked me hard in the side. I lost my breath and was unable to scream, but I got a very quick look at him. He wasn't watching my face, though, and didn't see my eyes widen in the half-second before a stinking rag was shoved over my mouth and nose and I went out like a cracked bulb.

I'm not saying I've never awakened naked in a strange place with a pounding headache before. But all my former experiences had been strictly voluntary, and the mornings after were just the awkward sort.

This was nowhere near that. For one thing, the headache was intense and was coupled with the feeling I had been run over by a truck. I was so sore I could hardly move, but I wanted to know where I was, so I tried to sit up and look around. I was in the backseat of my own car, a late-model four-door sedan. I was partially clothed—I still had my blouse and jacket on, and my skirt was hiked up around my waist, but still there. My shoes, pantyhose, and panties were missing.

The dried blood, bruises, and intense pain confirmed I had been raped.

I unlatched the door, leaned out, and vomited.

The sky was lightening with the approaching dawn. It was about five in the morning, which meant I had been unconscious for nearly twelve hours. Pretty soon the early birds would be arriving for work and I didn't want to be found by them.

I slowly sat up, steadied myself and took deep breaths, grateful to be alive, trying not to cry. Then the rage took over. My anger gave me the strength to move, pull my skirt down, and get out of the car without collapsing on the pavement.

My handbag was under the car, where it had rolled. I dragged it out and managed to get back in the car, this time in the front seat. My hands shook as I called 911. The dispatcher patched me through to the local cops and I told them what had happened. An ambulance showed up a bit later and a police officer met me at the hospital. By then I was crying and unable to stop, oblivious to the exam, the lights, the noise, and the headache from hell.

The officer took my statement and assured me they'd do what they could. The doctor gave me a sedative and I went to sleep. I won't say what I dreamed—it's better no one else lives with that particular nightmare, not even you.

But nightmares you have at night are a lot different from the ones you have during the day. I thought I was okay. I mean, I knew I was physically banged up some, although repeated tests assured me my attacker hadn't left me with any grisly diseases. But I thought I was strong mentally, strong enough to deal with this.

I wasn't.

I started to spin right out of control. The company was scared spitless that I would sue them or something, so the Human Resources folks sent me to therapy and gave me a couple of weeks off.

I spent one afternoon at the police station, looking through pictures of degenerates. I didn't recognize any of them, though a few bore a resemblance to platoon sergeants I had crossed swords with in the past. I even sat with a sketch artist but had to reluctantly admit the rapist was ordinary-looking. I guess monsters do not always look the part. And that split-second glimpse just wasn't enough. There was no DNA but my own in the rape kit—the bastard had been careful, something that was a relief from the disease point of view, but a disappointment in the conviction department. The cops were sympathetic, but overworked, and I knew this degenerate scum would only be caught if he got careless in attacking other women.

At work, I couldn't concentrate. I felt an overwhelming shame and anger. Everything made me either jump or burst into tears. There were times when the rage I felt was strong enough to keep me from breathing, much less from doing a decent job at work. The turning point came when I stood shaking in the break room and screamed when my boss lightly touched my shoulder. He sighed, sent me home, and told me to see a doctor.

"And take all the time you need," he said. "We'll get someone in to cover for you." I felt my job slipping away.

That evening I called Artie and told him everything. I was still holding the phone and crying when the doorbell rang and I panicked. Me, who had faced the noise of bombs and the horrors of war. I looked out the peephole and saw not only Artie, but Joe, too.

Joe closed the door, made sure the lock was turned, and took the phone out of my hand. Artie was already in the kitchen, poking through cupboards, making coffee and looking for cookies.

Artie returned from the kitchen to inform me that the milk in the fridge was now cheese, so coffee would have to be taken black.

We all sat at my little coffee table, drinking strong black coffee and eating stale cookies in silence.

Finally, I spoke. "Thanks for coming over. I guess I don't really know what to do, and I know you're busy . . ." The tears started up again.

"We want to help," Artie said. "No, we are going to help. Joe and I talked about it on the way over. We're going to help you." Artie sounded so confident. "I think if we get this scumbag, you'll feel better."

I laughed out loud, the first laugh I'd had in days. "Aw, thanks, but if the police can't find him, what makes you think you can?"

"Well, for one thing, we're not the police," Artie said. "We don't have to be too concerned with lawyers and our pensions." Artie had been a cop and knew the limitations of the job.

"Yeah," Joe agreed, his smile widening. "And we have access to a lot of, uh, equipment and resources they don't have. I bet we can give this a pretty good shot."

"Equipment and resources? I thought you guys worked for some little security outfit."

They looked at each other, then back at me. "Uh, it's a pretty sophisticated little security outfit," Joe said.

"Yeah," Artie agreed. "Sophisticated. So, are you in?"

"I don't know." I was intrigued by the idea.

"There's a lot we can do. We can go over the scene, do some research, maybe find other victims of this dude. Jerks like this, it's never a one shot. They keep on until they're stopped. But once we find him, you'll have the final decision."

"What do you mean?" I knew what I wanted to do, first with a rusty knife, then with some barbed wire and pair of pliers.

"Revenge doesn't always work, but it will be your decision."

"I don't have a problem with that," I said.

"Okay, hon, we'll get started right away. Joe is going to work his magic with the computer while I go out pounding the pavement. You just sit tight and try to feel better. We'll come back tomorrow with a friend and secure your premises. When we get closer to this jerk, we want to make sure he can't bother you here."

For someone who had just heard about what had happened to me, Artie sounded like he had already been on the job for a while.

The next day Artie showed up with a person in overalls. "This is Buzz," Artie said. Buzz had wiry black hair, glasses, and an impressive toolbox.

Buzz grinned. Buzz was a woman.

"Buzz is going fix it so you don't have to worry about anyone breaking in here."

Buzz went to work, and soon I had a fancy electronic lock and gizmos on the windows, too. She set up an unobtrusive little thingy on the outside of the door. It looked like a piece of plastic, maybe an address holder. "You just put your finger right there," she said, positioning my hand over the small device, "and it knows it's you. No one else can activate it and if anyone disables it, we'll know immediately." Buzz also installed a camera on the door which I could access from my phone.

Later, Artie took me back over the incident, gently pulling out details I was too upset to have thought about in my statement to the police. Too old-school to use a recorder, he took copious notes. He already had a copy of the police report and the sketch, both of which he was careful to keep in a file folder so I wouldn't see them and get distracted.

I relived it for him as calmly as I could, remembering odd things like the color of the sky, the angle of the broken fence, what other cars were around and what I could see underneath them. When he took me through the quick glimpse of the rapist's face, I remembered even more—the mouth open in a snarl, the smell of the pavement, the chemical rag. The eyebrows, too perfect.

The worst part was recounting how I'd called the cops. "Okay, hon," Artie said, "that's enough. Let's stop here." By then he had dozens of sheets of yellow legal paper covered with his scribbles.

"Joe and I are going to cross-reference everything you've told us and start narrowing it down. We've already pulled up all the similar attacks—you know, lone woman, parking lot, drugged and assaulted in her own car—as well as a bunch of others. Joe's going to expand the referencing nationwide. You know how he is with a project like this."

I knew he was smart and computer-literate. Heck, in the Army he had done everything, including drive my Humvee. I also knew he was like a dog with a bone when he got interested in something.

"Once we get a few suspects, we'll have you take a look at some pictures, then we'll see what we can do."

"I don't understand, Artie. Why can't the cops do all this?"

"Hon, we've got more time and resources than they do. And besides, even if they found him, there's no guarantee there'd be enough evidence for a conviction. These slimeballs walk free all the time."

"But what about your boss? Will they just let you, you know, do stuff on your own?" I knew my boss—if I still even had my job—wouldn't let me just run off and help someone else on the company dime.

Artie and Joe exchanged glances again. "Uh, yeah, hon," Artie said. "We get to do our own stuff all the time."

"It sounds like a job I'd like to have," I said wistfully. I might get cleared to go back to work, but I wasn't sure I ever wanted to go back. I didn't know if I could ever park in that lot again, ever feel safe again.

"I think we can work something out," Joe said. "I mean, if you're interested after we get this thing settled."

At the time, I didn't know exactly what they did, but I did know that they

worked fast. A few days after our interview Artie came by with a plain-looking
file folder full of pictures.

"These might be a little disturbing," he said, "but see if you can't take a look
and maybe something or someone will look familiar."

I started flipping through the pictures. They were all men, some shot from a
distance and grainy, others looking like publicity shots. A couple looked like they
were mug shots and at least one looked post-mortem. I picked out four pictures.

"These look familiar," I said. "I mean, maybe not him but you know, familiar
somehow."

Artie nodded. "Yeah, you know these two men," he pointed to two of the pictures, "and I was hoping there'd be at least one more that would jog your memory
a bit."

Artie was right. Two of the pictures were of soldiers we had served with, men
in our unit whose faces were ordinary enough for me to not place them right off.
Guys out of uniform and out of context.

But the other two shots were of some man in a suit in a corporate lobby and
another photographed from a distance standing next to a pickup truck. Corporate guy had a briefcase and a determined look about him, his head down and not
much of his face visible. I couldn't say what it was about him that I recognized.
The other picture, the one with the pickup truck, showed a guy in jeans and a
tee shirt. His face was turned toward the camera and he was just about to put on
sunglasses. The eyebrows, I thought.

"I think that's him," I said. "It's the eyebrows . . . too perfect."

My stomach started to turn, and I turned the photo face down.

Artie nodded. "Yeah, that's what we thought, too. He's the same one, hon. The
other picture is him, too. When he puts on a suit and pays a visit to companies
like yours, that's what he looks like. He gets to travel quite a bit, but he has a nasty habit that seems to follow him from defense contractor to defense contractor."

I forced myself to look at the picture of the man in the suit. I wasn't sure I'd
seen him at work. There were a lot of guys in suits, lots of the government inspectors, security teams, sub-contractors, you name it. But the other picture—Pickup
Truck Man—I was pretty sure about him.

"He's pretty careful," Artie said. "Always targets in a parking lot with no surveillance, always drugs the victims once they're knocked down from behind, and up until you, never lets any of the women get a look at him. That nasty stuff he drugged you with is called A.C.E.—it's an alcohol, chloroform, and ether combination."

"There are . . . others?"

"At least four that we've found," Artie said, "maybe more. Not everyone reports this kind of rape."

"So, what do we do now?" I asked.

"That's up to you, hon. I doubt that we could make a charge really stick without some hard evidence."

"We can't just let him walk," I said indignantly. "He'll keep on doing it. And what if he kills someone? He's got to be stopped; he's got to pay for what he's done." The rage and pain burst through my calm and the tears stung my eyes.

"We won't let him walk."

His name was Lonnie Carter and he was an inspector from DCMA, the Defense Contracts Management Agency. He was assigned to my company, but he had worked at several other defense contractor locations in the past few years.

Artie and Joe had a pretty complete file on the bastard, and he sure looked like my attacker, but there was no way to prove it. I knew nothing we had would stand up in court.

"He keeps souvenirs," I said, remembering my missing shoes, panties, and pantyhose. "Maybe we could find out where he keeps them."

"It's a good idea," Joe said, "but even with them, it might be a stretch in court. Still, if we could find your stuff, we could be absolutely sure he's the right one."

In the end, we decided that the direct approach would be best. The thought of actually talking to him made me physically ill, but there was no way around it. I would confront him, and we would get a confession. We rehearsed what I would say and do. Each time we went over it, it got easier.

Joe and Buzz staked out Carter's temporary office, a modular office trailer in the same parking lot where he had assaulted me. Artie rode with me in my car and I braced myself as we parked in my old spot, about thirty feet from the brown painted trailer. I hadn't really noticed it before. I must have thought it belonged to the construction company that was doing work there.

I shook as I walked to the trailer. I knew Artie had my back and I knew Joe and Buzz were watching from a van on the other side of the road. But I still felt sick.

I walked in without knocking. He was sitting at his computer and looked up as the door closed. I knew it was him as the color drained from his face and he recognized me.

I aimed a pistol at his face. "It was you, wasn't it? You raped me in the parking lot."

"N-no! I—I don't know what you're . . ." He started to get up from his chair.

"Sit down." He sat. "You see, the problem is that shits like you brutalize women and then get away with it. I don't think that's right."

He scowled at me. "You can't prove anything. My lawyer will chew you up and spit you out. Or did you come looking for seconds?" He smiled a nasty smile.

You know what? I still have those dreams, those nightmares, even today, after everything, where I shot him in his ugly face, spattering blood and brains all over his whiteboard and the back of his expensive leather chair. But they are just dreams.

What really happened then was that Artie took him into custody, Joe and Buzz provided evidence for a search warrant, and there was enough in Lonnie's souvenir trunk at his mother's house to connect him to six other attacks.

He was convicted on five counts—they couldn't ID two of the victims—and he got the maximum, which in this state is eight years on each count. We did the right thing, everything by the book. He's still in prison.

Oh, and I got that job with Artie and Joe. You'll never guess where they worked. Let's just say that it was a dream job and I loved it.

All of that was a long time ago. I'm retired now, and Artie and Joe are both gone.

I thought that seeing justice done would help me deal with the whole experience, and to be fair, it has. After all, revenge doesn't always do what you want, no matter how good you think it might feel for a short time.

I still carry the little Beretta, though it couldn't help me then. I guess it came in handy tonight, though. The look on your face was certainly worth it.

Remember back when I said I never wanted to tell this story again? I never did, but seeing you there in that dark place, hearing that girl's whimpers as you brutalized her, the whole thing came roaring back like it happened yesterday. The rage, the anger, the frustration, all of it. As fresh as the night it happened. I know you aren't the same monster who raped me, but that doesn't matter now. I have you tied up and gagged and once again, I have the power, not you. I can dial the cops or pull the slide.

That girl is going to have to go through the same hell I did. I want to help her. I think I did the right thing once, but I'm not sure what that means anymore. I wish my friends were here.

The Lesson

Allison A. Davis

Rookie Jacinta Morales relaxed her grip on the steering wheel and reached for her Philz coffee cup. Philz was where cops went, and she wanted to be a cop. Now lukewarm, the bitterness coated her mouth as she drank.

"Let's go down Mission Street, take a right." Sergeant Petersen, her field-training officer—FTO—like the army, everything was acronyms—with nearly 15 years on the job, white, straight with a rulebook focus, was searching for another street lesson for her.

She turned the Crown Vic down Mission and adjusted herself where her vest itched.

"You okay, Morales? Uniform bothering you?"

The guy missed nothing. Ugh. "Fine. I'm used to uniforms." Truth was it itched like crazy and rode up around her neck. She needed a better fit or to learn to live with it. She had learned to love her ACU, her army combat uniform, not only because it saved her life, but also because its pockets contained all her comforts: MREs, lip balm, water, and a knife she favored for hand to hand. Maybe when her vest stopped a bullet, she'd like it better.

Her street action was more important than her desk work to move from probationary to cop, and the observant eye of her FTO was like a knife against her back, waiting for her to move wrong and make a mistake. At least his comments kept her focused and gave her a heads-up so she could adjust her actions, if necessary. Petersen was a *guero*, but an okay guy, even if he didn't understand why a Latina wanted to be a cop. Especially a Latina who had been to war and had a hard time coming home.

His voice interrupted her thoughts. "Let's focus on the homeless today, something we face every day we're out on the street."

As Jacinta had learned at the academy, homelessness caused a spike in petty crime in affected areas, so police presence helped. She knew that from personal experience, too. Her parents owned a restaurant in the Mission—low-margin, backbreaking work—and the homeless added to a business's burden with their trash and human excrement, and by blocking access to their stores. Cops cleared one tent area only to have another spring up.

"There." He pointed and Jacinta saw a blur of dirty gray whiskers against a pink building.

She slowly drove by to give the guy a chance to notice them and hopefully get up and go somewhere else.

"You do well at this, you can join the department's Homeless Outreach Unit."

She hoped Petersen was jibing her. "Thanks, but I want to be a cop, not a social worker."

"Then think twice about being a police officer. The sidewalks are your territory as much as any part of the City, and get used to this, as more and more social work falls to cops." He switched from lecture to lesson, turning to her. "Remember, you're not here to arrest him, but you want him off the street."

"I know." She pulled over and opened the car door.

"Call it in first."

Shit, she was already missing steps. "Right." She sat back in the seat, took a breath to relieve the weight in her stomach, and made the call. "Homeless guy, doing a welfare check."

"Copy, thanks. 10–4."

"Let's see how you do with him." Petersen nodded at her as they got out of the car, meaning she was to go it alone. As training dictated, he stood watch between her and the car in case something happened.

Jacinta was aware of Petersen's intense scrutiny, which was part of his reputation. An average guy in height, weight, and intellect, word was Petersen had achieved his career peak as an officer. He wasn't going to get smarter or stronger, or any higher in rank, so he embraced his instruction of new cops as his holy duty, making him a tough grader.

As Jacinta approached the homeless man, she studied him as if he were an enemy noncombatant in country. A white guy who appeared older than he probably was—late twenties or early thirties probably. He couldn't have been on the street too long, judging by the absence of lines in his face and the taut muscles in his neck. His hands, in spite of black nails and scraped knuckles, still looked strong. Shoes but no socks. Shaking her head to ward off the smell of his soiled clothes, she nudged the man with her steel-toed boot.

"What are you doing out here? Come on man, let's sit up."

She heard Petersen behind her. "Keep a tactical edge." She had gotten too close and was already making mistakes.

She backed off a few steps. "How do I know he's breathing?" she said over her shoulder, trying to cover her error. Turning back, she looked at the homeless man more closely. His collapsed body dressed in familiar combat fatigues triggered a vivid memory of another man in fatigues, or pieces of him, near a crumpled armored personnel carrier in dust and desert heat. She felt her peripheral vision go, street noises fading as she froze for a moment, the image so graphic she swallowed and tasted metal.

"Ask him his name. Come on, Morales, this is basic."

She watched a *paletero* man selling ice cream, Cheetos, and *chicharrones* as he pushed his cart past them without looking, ringing his bell.

"You okay, Morales?" She saw Petersen's eyes fall to the fatigues and then back up to her. "Or do you want an ice cream?"

She didn't want her FTO thinking she was affected by her war experience, that she couldn't handle this. She made herself smile at Petersen's near-joke. "No ice cream. I'm okay." Inside her head, she was hearing the reassuring voice of her commanding officer, telling her to stay focused on the minute, and the hour will take care of itself.

Do the job.

She exhaled, unclenched her hands, and this time she just saw a homeless man who needed to cleaned and fed.

"Hey, sir, I need you to respond."

The man grunted but didn't open his eyes. She was glad he was conscious, anyway.

"I'm going to approach." She'd need to get closer to figure out if he was injured or sick.

"Watch yourself."

Petersen's warning stung her a little—this was nothing compared to Iraq. She wasn't afraid of this guy.

She prodded the man's leg with her boot again. "You need to sit up, sir, and tell me your name."

"Yeah, what of it?" The guy's arm came up to shield his eyes and he squinted. She removed her cap, ran her hand through her hair, put the cap back on, determined to stay in the game and get this done. Get this man off the street.

She nudged the man harder. "Let's get up. Can we . . . ?"

"You can't do shit." The man slumped back against the building.

A drunk in fatigues—a disgrace to the uniform. She wanted him up. "Come on. You can't stay here. Where's home?"

"I ain't going anywhere. Here's just fine." The man patted the sidewalk, eyes unfocused.

"You want me to cover over there, Morales?"

She needed to make the man move so Petersen wouldn't take over, wouldn't think she couldn't handle this. She had pegged the homeless man as ex-military, and she'd seen freak-outs in Iraq, where taking them back to their training sometimes snapped them out of it. Maybe she could reach this guy. She wanted to try.

"Name and rank, soldier."

"Fuck you." The man pulled his arms off the sidewalk and into his lap.

"Name and rank, now." She tried again, with a firmer voice.

"Name's Washburn. Private First Class Washburn to you." His laugh caught in a phlegmy cough, his chest heaving. He leaned back against the building, eyes shut.

Jacinta exchanged glances with Petersen and claimed a small victory for herself. Her lesson had turned into something else.

"You need to stand up, Private First Class Washburn. Can you do that?" She got in his face with her best command voice.

Washburn's eyes suddenly opened wider. Using the wall, he stood and aligned his feet as if standing at attention. "Yes, sir."

Maybe this was working. She hovered over him, nearly willing him to come back to the present, like she had.

Washburn, a tall, rangy man, steadied himself on the wall as he stood. His eyes were open but squinty, and Jacinta could not get him to look at her. As he stood, the inside of his pants was exposed and wet, the smell powerful. Jacinta saw the man he must have been—a fighting machine, solid and strong—now transformed into this pathetic shell, a soldier who'd given up. She wanted him to care again—to want to live again.

Petersen moved closer to her. "Now that you have him up, Morales, what's next?"

Jacinta ignored him and faced Washburn. "Okay, Private, we're going to take you somewhere to get cleaned up."

"That ain't it." Petersen gave her a "thumbs down" and shook his head, then did the thumb and little finger gesture for making a call.

Damn, her third error. She was supposed to call in the EMTs. She clicked into dispatch, eyes focused on Washburn, who was still standing, if unsteadily. "White male, late twenties or early thirties, about six-one, one hundred seventy, in distress, name is Washburn, appears in need of Homeless Connect services."

"Emergency?"

"No." Jacinta looked him over. "Maybe a 5150." She'd get him picked up on a harm to himself or others—he clearly couldn't take care of himself.

"Roger, you want a pickup?"

"Yeah, he needs a checkout—maybe a social worker."

"Copy, we'll get you a van. 10–4."

She glanced at Petersen, wondering how to keep Washburn upright while they waited.

"You could just leave him be," said Petersen. "If he offends your sense of pride?"

What did that mean? Was he jabbing at her vet status?

"I'm going to help him out." She made the decision as she spoke, meeting Petersen's eyes. "I thought you wanted me to deal with this."

"Each situation is different. Your job is deciding what to do."

"He's a vet."

"Don't play favorites, Morales."

Jacinta couldn't read Petersen's face to see if she was screwing up, if he was coaching her, or if this really was her call.

She'd already made her decision.

She turned to the homeless man. "We're going to get you some help, Washburn."

"With all due respect, sir, I don't want to go anywhere. I'm just fine right here."

Even as he played along, she heard the slurred hopelessness.

"I don't think so, soldier. You aren't assigned to these quarters."

Washburn opened his eyes wide and his arms went rigid. Jacinta tensed.

"I'm not a fucking soldier anymore, and I don't have to do a fucking thing you say, not one fucking thing." He staggered. "Don't you get it? He's dead, they're all fucking dead."

A woman pushing a stroller moved quickly past, and a man stood in the doorway of a *taquería* staring at them. Washburn was scaring people, and she needed to calm him down before Petersen took over.

"Morales!"

Damn it. "It's okay, Petersen. He's having a flashback. I know what to do." She steadied her breathing, trying to catch Washburn's eye.

"Hush now. Be careful." Jacinta put her arm out as the ex-soldier wobbled. He looked her dead in the face and then took a swing. She ducked to the right. He staggered, tried again, and stumbled forward, yelling, "Incoming, incoming!"

Petersen spoke into his radio. Jacinta threw out an arm to Petersen to get him to give her more time—to tell him it was okay. Washburn swung at her again and Petersen drew his gun.

"Petersen, I got this!"

While Washburn towered over her by at least four inches, he was off balance. His knees were buckling, his breath was shallow, and sweat poured down his face. This was a human being consumed by fear and despair, not someone bent on harming someone else.

She stepped into him before he could swing again and put him in a restraint hold before Petersen could call her off. Hand to hand she could do, learned to do, to make up for her small size. As she spun him, pushed him up against the wall and cuffed him, something fell from his pocket with a clink. Sweat matted her shirt to her chest underneath her vest, dripping down her sides. She spoke into Washburn's back.

"Don't play games with me, Private First Class Washburn. I got you up against the wall. Now I get to tell you what to do." She had half an eye on Petersen, willing him to put his gun away.

"Fuck you. Like you know what the fuck is going on. Spic!" Spitting that last word at her, he twisted, his shirtsleeve moving up his arm to reveal the edge of a tattoo. Ignoring his slur, she pushed up the sleeve to see the full tat. Boots, an M4, and a helmet balanced on top. Fallen soldier.

"Hey!" Washburn twisted again, eyes large.

"It's okay, Washburn. It's OK." The tattoo told her what she needed to know.

"He's subdued. Not a threat," she said for Petersen's benefit. Petersen nodded at her and holstered his gun before speaking into his radio again. She stayed focused on Washburn.

She should have put on latex gloves before she'd started to interact with him, especially with Petersen taking notes. Washburn was gritty and sticky and had rubbed on her uniform as he struggled. The smell of him was in her throat.

Now he bounced against the wall, speaking into his chest. "Dead dog, pow, wow, it's a bomb, oh God . . ."

Jacinta held onto his arms, still cuffed, as his knees gave out and he slumped onto the ground. He swayed back and forth, whispering, "Oh God, Oh God," under his breath.

Where the hell was that van? Jacinta scanned the sidewalk to find what fell from his pocket. With one hand on his arm to keep him under her control, she reached for it. A glint made her think maybe it was money. She picked it up and ran her thumb over it.

Shit. A Silver Star. You didn't get one of these if you froze in combat or weren't anywhere near it. You got it because you saved someone's life or went *guano loco* pulling someone to safety.

Her lieutenant had recommended that she get a Silver Star for killing a potential suicide bomber. Desert glare, a black burqa, exploding red. She only had one shot before the woman reached the convoy and blew them all up. But at that time, while they awarded silver stars to brave women medics, they did not give them to women with combat kills. Back then, women weren't supposed to be in combat—weren't supposed to be killers.

She waved the medal. Petersen scrunched his brow and shrugged.

"What is it?"

Jacinta still had her hands on the cuffs, keeping Washburn calm. "It means he's definitely a veteran," she said to Petersen. "Maybe one of those new VA programs could help him."

"Give it to the social worker," Petersen said.

"Yeah, where the hell are they?" She flicked her wrist with her watch on it at him.

Petersen laughed. "Get used to it."

It took nearly twenty minutes from the time they called before a white van with Homeless Connect across the side pulled up on the curb and two guys got out.

"Okay, let's go." Jacinta lifted Washburn by the handcuffs, holding him firmly as he tried to twist free.

"Hey, what the fuck?"

The EMT, Wilson on his name badge, said, "We don't transport people that have been arrested." Jacinta noted he wore latex gloves.

"He's not under arrest. I just subdued him until someone can throw him in a shower." Jacinta patted Washburn on the shoulder. "Behave yourself."

She removed the cuffs and hoped Washburn wouldn't freak out again. "He was having a flashback, but he's okay now. He's a vet, so I suggest that a social worker set up something with the VA to get this guy some help. He's not so far gone, but there's probably some mental trauma and substance abuse, and he won't be good for anything if he keeps this up." The EMT ignored her and instead opened up the back of the van. Jacinta was dismayed to see metal seats and restraints.

The second young guy, who didn't have a name tag on, looked her up and down, and then back at Petersen. "She new?"

Petersen nodded.

"I'm a social worker, Bill Schotz." He also wore latex gloves and shook hands with Jacinta. "No gloves?"

She reddened, knowing she should have had gloves on. Petersen cleared his throat.

Schotz leaned on the van and crossed his arms. "Ma'am. We know Washburn; this isn't his first time. It's maybe his twentieth time." He pointed at her hands. "And next time, you might want to use gloves."

What the hell? Was this guy judging her? He glanced at her hands. One still held the medal. "So, you've cleaned him up, got him help, and he still ends up on the street like this?"

"Yep."

"This man served his country, won this medal, and this is his life?" She was holding the medal up now, wanting to shove it in Schotz's face.

Schotz chucked her on the shoulder. "We're here, right? And we keep doing this over and over again. We'll get him cleaned up . . . again."

"But he's a vet. The VA should help him." If Petersen weren't taking notes on her performance, she'd tell this guy to go fuck himself. He didn't care if Washburn lived or died . . . didn't think it mattered.

"Yeah, tell Congress. Not in this century," he said. "He's on the list. What they tell all of them."

"But damn it, that's why we served! The country is supposed to have our back."

"Wait. You're a vet?"

"Yeah."

"And now a new cop?"

"Yeah . . . ?"

Schotz eyed her, a smirk on his thin face. "Don't learn, do you?" He turned to get Washburn.

Petersen's voice interrupted before she could respond. "She's a good cop." He stepped toward her.

Jacinta nodded at Petersen, surprised and grateful, and turned to Schotz. She wasn't done.

"Do you know what this is?" She held the Silver Star in his face.

"Hey," Washburn swayed, reaching for his medal, nearly hitting the social worker.

Schotz threw his hands up in mock surrender. "Hey, I'm here to help him. Don't yell at me."

"Twenty times? You call that help? Do you know what the guy had to do to get this? He risked his life—in the middle of combat."

Jacinta glanced at Petersen, who had his hands on his belt, relaxed.

She turned to Washburn. "What'd' you do to get this?"

"Nothing. I stole it."

"Bullshit, Washburn. You're fucked up because of something that happened out there. What happened?" She held up the medal again but he didn't lunge for it. Instead he slumped back down again, his face collapsing, then his shoulders, and before the EMT could reach him, he had curled up in a ball on the sidewalk.

Petersen was standing next to her now.

"No one asked him? No one saw this medal in his pocket? Twenty times in and out, and what the fuck?" Her hand holding the medal shook.

Schotz's eyes moved from the man on the sidewalk to Jacinta to Petersen. "I didn't know what that was, thought it was just a drunk's trinket."

"It's his souvenir from hell." She squatted down, next to Washburn. "Where? Where did you serve, Washburn?" She gripped his shoulder, ignoring the smell, pulling him to face her.

He uncurled a bit, his eyes red, his face wet.

"Where?"

"Fallujah."

She shut her eyes, and then opened them. She knew the answer but asked anyway. "When?"

He sniffled, wiped his nose on his arm, and sat up. Jacinta sensed Petersen, Schotz and the EMT around them, but only as background. She was locked in. "When?"

"2004."

"Ah, fuck." Her hand now rested gently on his shoulder. She looked him in the eye and felt his pain.

For the first time, Washburn smiled. "Yeah."

"You lived. You got both legs, that's something." She peered at his dirty face, really wanting him to know she understood.

"The stuff they took, you can't replace, you can't fix." He focused on the sidewalk while he spoke.

"Who were you with?"

"2nd Brigade Combat Team, 2nd Infantry Division." His speech wasn't slurred now.

"In the heart of it."

"Yeah." Washburn stared at his feet. Shoes, no socks.

Jacinta squeezed his shoulder and stood up, facing the other men. "This guy was in one of the hardest-fought, bloodiest battles—the first battle against insurgents. Not Saddam's forces."

She turned back and squatted down next to Washburn. "I was in Fallujah just a few years after that."

Washburn nodded.

"You need something to do."

"I need to die," he replied. His rheumy eyes held so much sadness. "I shouldn't be here."

"Not up to you." Jacinta yanked him up from under his arm. This time he wasn't dead weight, and he leaned on her. "You lived. You lived for a reason. You owe it to the others to stay alive and figure out what that reason is."

Washburn stared at Jacinta and shook his head. He wasn't so drunk that he couldn't understand. His jaw tightened even as he swayed.

The EMT, Schotz, and Petersen backed away when Jacinta gently persuaded Washburn to go to the van. "Go. Get cleaned up, and then figure out what your orders are. This ain't it."

The EMT then moved behind them. "Come on, Washburn, you know the drill. Like the little lady said . . ."

Washburn turned and stood tall in the face of the EMT. Petersen tensed, his hand on his gun. Jacinta moved closer to Washburn, to shield him if necessary.

Washburn wiped his face with his hand and spoke. "Show respect. She's a soldier and a cop. And she's seen some shit, too. Y'all spend time wiping the asses of us drunks, but you never had to run your hands through what's left of your best friend after an IED shredded him. Gone door to door with snipers aiming for you, cleaned out a house and it's a kid that has the gun? And for what?" When he finished, he climbed into the van on his own.

Jacinta pulled open his hand and put the medal in it. "Keep this to remind yourself: You got things to do."

Washburn nodded.

Schotz shook his head. "He never, ever spoke of the war before."

"You ever ask him? There's a person under that piss and dirt, a person with a history." She tried not to shake, sweating heavily under her vest. "Listen to him and folks like him. Don't write him off. Why did you do take this job if you don't give a shit?"

"Morales. Don't hit him." Petersen was only half joking.

"I'm fine," she said, staring Schotz down. He needed to know what he was doing wasn't right.

She got in the driver's seat and waited for Petersen to get in. She felt pounding in her head and tried to get her breathing under control.

"Maybe you got a little personally involved there?" Petersen said, always bringing it back to the training.

"Yeah, next time I wear gloves." She wiped her hands on her pants and pulled the car away from the street. The smell stayed with her the rest of the day.

Harpy

Catriona McPherson

I f this were a college town, these would be frat houses now. Red cups like tulip heads all over the lawns and tennis shoes heaped like stove lengths on the porches. If it were a commuter town, they would be family homes. Vans in the drives, hoops by the curb. But this town being *this* town, they were facilities. Nursing homes, senior centers, residential care. They went by many names.

Such big old houses, with such spacious rooms and such wide pocket door-ways—going cheap for the square footage too—it was inevitable. *Facilities* didn't need garage space or swimming pools. They didn't need eat-in kitchens, great rooms, or master suites with walk-through closets. They were ideal.

The street had five of them in a row from the stop sign to the dead end. Happy Glade, Sunset View, Sweet Meadows, Golden Acres, and the harpist's destination: Bella Vie. She passed through the gate and up the walk, ascended the steps, crossed the porch and rang the bell.

A buzzer sounded, and the lace curtain hanging in the door's half-window was swiped aside to reveal a frowning face above pink scrubs. The harpist smiled. The frown deepened. But the door opened anyway.

"Help you?" The aide had a face made for smiling, broad and flat with creases bracketing a wide mouth. Solemnity sat awkward on it.

"I'm sorry I'm late."

The aide looked over her shoulder at the empty hallway behind her. "Late?" she said. "Is someone expecting you?"

"I'm the harpist." A flare in the aide's eyes. "The end-of-life harpist. I have a booking here today."

"Ohhhh." The aide drew out the sound, like a musical note. "That's *your* harp? Someone delivered a harp. We didn't know what to make of it."

"And I apologise. I meant to be here before it. But here I am." The harpist spread her arms, her wide sleeves forming an arc that the morning sun shone through. "End-of-life harpist," she said again.

"You . . . what? You play while . . . ?"

"I do."

"And who did you say ordered you?" They were inside now, with the door closed up again. The harp sat in the curve at the bottom of the staircase, framed by the flourish of the banister. It looked as though it belonged there but, on its wheeled base, it was ready to go.

"The voicemail message was indistinct," the harpist said. "Weeping, you know. Only to be expected. But . . . don't *you* know? Don't *you* know which one of your residents needs me?"

The aide put her hand to her waist, a quick gesture, and another frown to match. Diverticulitis? Acute appendicitis? A stitch from rushing to answer the door?

"My beeper," she said, plucking it from her belt and hitting a button. "Excuse me."

Left alone, the harpist kicked the brake on the wheeled base, regretting as ever that it looked like a delivery dolly. The harp itself was so beautiful and that pressed-board square with the casters below such a false note. She had considered some kind of skirt; a pelmet to skim the ground and hide the workings, but the image had fixed itself in her head of an over-groomed little terrier, prancing around the ring at a dog show, silky coat rippling. And the phrase she had heard to match it was "dust ruffle."

The unlovely casters ran smoothly over the polished boards of the hall as she guided the harp, feeling it thrum under her fingers. In the passageway, on the carpet, smoother still. There were bound to be residents' bedrooms here on the first floor. She would find someone.

DEEDEE WAS NAPPING, as he always did in the afternoons these days. These weren't the siestas of his youth, when lunch was three hot courses and a bottle of Montepulciano, when not even two cups of bitter espresso knocked back like shots of hooch could keep him up, when the sound of a girl's quiet breathing at his side was like a lullaby. These naps were sideswipes of his drug regimen, the cost of another day above ground. His blood pressure was in range, thanks to that fistful of pills he gobbled every morning; his ankles fit in his shoes; his bladder let him sleep for two, three hours at a stretch; the pain in his knees was mild enough for a walk each evening, keeping his lungs clear. He had seen it happen plenty in his years at Bella Vie. A fall, a broken hip, bed rest, pneumonia, box. Like clockwork. Well, not for DeeDee, he'd go out on his ninety-ninth birthday, with a girl on each arm and a fat cigar. Drowsy afternoons were worth it.

He heard the door open, through the light drifting fog of his dream. Housekeeping, his brain mumbled. Or what did they call them? An *aide*. Collecting laundry, dispensing toilet rolls, maybe bringing letters. He felt himself begin to fall deeper again, no reason not to.

Then came a sound he couldn't place. His brows twitched. Real or dreaming?

"Mr D'Angelo? Donnie?"

DeeDee opened one eye and turned his head. His curtains were drawn and the room was dim, but there was someone there. He wasn't dreaming. There was a stranger standing in the middle of his carpet, holding . . . something. DeeDee opened his other eye. It was as tall as a man and it glinted gold in the chinks of light from the gap in his curtain.

"Who are you?" he said. His voice was a toad's croak.

"Do you know who sent me?"

"Sent you?" DeeDee struggled up against his pillows. "Someone sent you? What *is* that thing?" It was bigger than an Uzi. Wrong color too. It was bigger than Thor's hammer, bigger than a piledriver. Could there be a crossbow that size?

"*Maybe* someone sent me. To play you out."

He had heard it called many things, but that was new. "Play me out," he echoed, mouthing the words to himself. His morning pills were working: therapeutic blood thinner, low-dose beta-blocker, regulatory diuretic, anti-inflammatory painkiller, and a prophylactic antibiotic. DeeDee's blood didn't clot, his kidneys didn't fail, his knees didn't seize up, and no infection invaded him nor stroke befell him. But as he cast his mind back to those days—the business he took care of before the three-course lunch, the business he took care of when he got out of his bed after each siesta, knotting his tie and kissing the girl—he felt a twinge in his chest. As he listed the people who might have sent someone to "play him out" after all these years, he felt the two girls and the fat cigar and the ninety-ninth birthday fade like a dream on waking, as a strong hand reached under his ribs and gripped him hard. He heard the first ripple of her fingers over the strings and had time to wonder again if it was real before his heart swelled to match the chord and flowered in him and stopped forever.

MRS. CRAVEN WAS bent over her sewing. She had embroidered her own wedding veil, exquisite tiny stitches in a cloud of lace. She had embroidered her babies' clothes, their names bright on white cotton and rings of trucks or ducklings round the hems. She had embroidered twelve dining-room-chair covers, with flowers of the month in worsted silks on a stiff satin ground. And now she gripped a needle as thick as her worn wedding band in fingers pulled to claws, all nail and knuckle. She pushed it through cheesecloth, drawing a fat worm of wool. Like a child.

And she smiled like a child as the door opened, turning to see who was coming to visit with her today. She liked them all—doctors to floor sweepers—but, if she was honest, the stranger's face was a feast to her eyes. A new face, with a new voice to match, someone to hear her stories for the first time, ask her children's names and tell her they were pretty. She beamed, then her face grew solemn with wonder as she saw what the stranger was wheeling into the room.

"Lana?"

"Who are you?" Even her piping voice was that of a child.

"I'm the . . . harpist. Someone sent me."

"What was the thing you didn't say?" Lana Craven's forty years at the front of a classroom had tuned her antennae.

"End of life. I'm the end-of-life harpist. Forgive me."

"Play, play," Lana said. And, as the chords soared, she raised her voice to a reedy peep and asked: "Who sent you? My darling Steven? Is he waiting? Or is it my boy? Did he find his way from that jungle? My friend? She didn't turn to me for help, but did *she* send you?"

"Oh," said the harpist. "No. You misunderstand me."

But Lana Craven shook her head and opened her arms. Steven was there, tall and straight. Strong again, clear-eyed and steady, wearing the suit he had bought for their wedding day. And Stevie was there, too young for war, in his cotton romper with his name and the ducklings. And Laine was there, the salt to her pepper pot, the cheese to her cracker, best friends once more. Lana walked towards them all, still smiling.

ONE MORE AND quits, the harpist told herself, pushing open the door at the end of the hallway, where Gillette Bander sat in her electric wheelchair, her neck braced, her wrists strapped, her feet in fixed boots on the footrest. Gillette met the harpist's eye and nodded stiffly, dragging against her restraints.

These cases, the harpist always thought, were worth an extra effort. She cast her mind out like a fishing net and snagged Carole King, Fleetwood Mac, Janis Ian, and The Doors. She smiled and let her fingers fall gentle as a snowflake on the strings.

Gillette's jaw softened first, and her head sank back into the cushion behind her. Her arms dropped slack on the rests of her chair, away from the straps' chafing. Her thighs flattened onto the hammock of the seat underneath. Her knees flopped outwards.

The harpist played on, louder now, tapping her foot and nodding her head as Gillette's eyes ceased their flutter.

Then the door blatted open and, white coat sailing out behind, a doctor strode in. The aide in the pink scrubs hovered behind him, round face still frowning.

"What do you think you're doing?" the doctor said.

"Nothing," said the harpist. It was true. Gillette Bander's jaw was rigid again, her teeth clenched and her neck tendons ropey. Her arms strained upwards against the wristbands and her knees jounced. "Nothing at all."

"Who are you?" the doctor said. "On what authority are you here?"

"No one," said the harpist. "None." It was easier that way. "I'm leaving."

"What about *this*?" the doctor called along the hallway after her. The harp strings protested but whether at being roughly touched or being left behind was hard to say.

"Don't worry," the harpist called back, over her shoulder.

"Hey!" She heard it faintly through Gillette Bander's closing door. "What the—Where did it go?"

Either Happy Glades, Sunset View, Sweet Meadows, or Golden Acres, the harpist thought. Until she was out from inside these walls she wouldn't know.

She stepped onto the porch and let the door of Bella Vie close behind her. There it was! Two doors down, at Sweet Meadows. The delivery driver was wheeling it carefully up the pathway to the ramp and already she could feel the strings—from the breeze, from the friction of the brick path under the dolly, from the habit of years—start to sing.

WWGHD:
What Would Grace Hopper Do?
Making art in "interesting times"

Robin C. Stuart

This period in history is overwhelming. Internment camps at the United States border. Civilians gunned down in our streets, malls, movie theaters, schools. Our country turning a blind eye to dictators while attacking our allies. I sometimes feel guilty about prioritizing a frivolous activity like writing.

I fight crime for a living. For fun, I write crime fiction where heroes and villains are in plain view. Good triumphs over evil. But it sometimes feels wrong. Like I should be doing something "more important." Then I sit down at my keyboard. I ask myself, "What would Grace Hopper do?"

Who is Grace Hopper? Rear Admiral Grace Murray Hopper earned a PhD in mathematics from Yale in 1934, one of only four women to do so at that time. She became an associate professor at Vassar College until 1943, when World War II inspired her to join the United States Naval Reserve. She was assigned to the Bureau of Ordnance Computation Project at Harvard University where she was the third-ever person to work on and with the Mark I computer at Cruft Laboratory, used to calculate precise construction and targeting for the Manhattan Project. Admiral Hopper literally wrote the book on computing as the author of "A Manual of Operation for the Automatic Sequence Controlled Calculator" for the Mark I. In 1949, she worked on the first large-scale digital computer intended for business use, the UNIVAC I. She went on to lead the team that wrote the first compiler that translated human-written instructions into machine-readable code, and then wrote the first business-oriented computer programming language. Because of Admiral Hopper's vision, leadership, and perseverance, today we have digital equipment that is easy to build, easy to use, and can do more than one thing at a time.

Why do I look to this particular hero? There are obvious cultural parallels between World War II and today. History is repeating, sadly. But it's not that. Admiral Hopper didn't just go to work and do her job. She reveled in it. She created something out of nothing, over and over. Sometimes because she was ordered to do so. More often, by all reports and her own admission in later interviews, she forged ahead on passion projects based on her own initiative. One does not rise to the level of excellence demonstrated by Admiral Hopper's life work and multiple awards, including the Presidential Medal of Honor bestowed on her posthumously by President Obama, simply because she "had" to. What comes through loud and clear to me is her enthusiasm. She never stopped. Even after retiring from the Navy in 1976 at age 79, she went to work in the private sector at Digital Equipment Corporation where she stayed well into her eighties. That shows love, and love shows faith in the future.

And so, I write. Because I can. Because I have stories to tell. Because I love it. As Grace Hopper showed us, love multiplies through our creations. Add in the community of artists and that multiplier increases exponentially. The x factor is the support creators give each other and the world we inhabit. We share our words, voices, visual and structural creations, movements, sounds. Our creations may provide escape or inspire others to create. Some of those creations may take the form of solutions to challenges no one has even thought of yet. Creation is where we find our solace and our power.

Admiral Hopper could define the mathematical value of x, the "proof." I'm not a mathematician, so instead I heed my own call. By writing, I express my gratitude to my fellow creators, including you. As you're reading this, your imagination is engaged. Run with it. Build on it. Pass it on. The world needs you. And at those times you feel overwhelmed, outraged, frustrated or powerless, ask yourself . . . what would Grace Hopper do?

WILD Womb

Sandi Ault

*For
Indigenous Women
Everywhere*

1: Woman Standing Alone

IT WAS LUCK that I found her in time. In the middle of a warm April afternoon, the winds suddenly shifted to the east and began to blow with increasing ferocity. Clouds rolled in, blanketing the peaks to the west with shadow, and the sky darkened even though it was hours before dusk. I had been patrolling the area to the north of Tanoah Pueblo since early that morning, but the quick change in the weather meant a snowstorm was coming, and it could trap me in the high country. So I took a shortcut down to the new route that skirted the northwestern edge of the pueblo. Though this road was only a few weeks old, big trucks had already carved deep ruts in the dirt and gravel surface as they rumbled back and forth to the site where a mining company would soon commence forcefully removing resources from beneath the ground. My Jeep bounced along the now-empty track as I wrestled the wheel to maneuver in and out of the grooves. In the distance, I saw a figure, standing alone in the middle of the trail.

As I drew closer, the woman did not move. Her face was streaked with blood, her bruised eyes swollen nearly shut. Her left arm hung at an odd angle. I pulled to a stop, scrambled out, and hurried up to her. Sidewinding missiles of icy sleet began to pummel us—one by one at first—rapidly increasing in frequency and impact, splatting on my jacket, striking the woman's head and face, and drumming steadily on the hood of my rig. "What's happened to you? Come on, get in the car. Are you able to walk? Let me help you."

She turned her head to look at me, staring through the mere slit of one ravaged eye as she began to shuffle toward the passenger door of the Jeep. I helped her into the seat, and she cried out with pain, grabbing her broken arm with the opposite hand. As I fidgeted with the seat buckle, I noted how tiny this woman was; she couldn't have weighed much more than a hundred pounds. There were bruises on her forearms, and her lower lip was cracked, oozing a thick stripe of coagulating blood.

Back in the driver's seat, I said, "I'm out of range, no comms until I get up to the junction, so I can't call an ambulance. Do you want to go to the Indian health clinic on the pueblo?"

"No!" She cleared her throat several times, then said, "Could you take me to my grandmother's?"

"You need to go to a hospital. I'll take you to the one in Taos."

"No, please," she croaked. "My grandmother will take care of me."

"That arm is badly broken. Unless your grandmother is a doctor, she can't take care of that. You need to either go to the clinic or the hospital in Taos."

"They'll call the police. And if I talk to the cops again, he's gonna kill me."

"Who's going to kill you?"

She leaned her head to one side. "Never mind," she said. "I'm a dead woman anyway."

I sped on, more worried now than before. "What's your name?"

"Valentina Blackbear."

"I'm Jamaica Wild. I work for the BLM. I'm also a liaison with the tribe, I can act as an intermediary with the police. But we have to get you some medical attention first."

More and more sleet globs splatted against the roof, creating a constant clatter. Near the junction of the mine road and the county highway, a mob of protesters lined the road, holding signs like the ones that were pasted all over in town: *No violen el vientre de la tierra* (*Don't violate the womb of the Earth*). When a full-page ad bearing that slogan had published in the local paper this week, declaring that Taos Valley was the womb of the Earth and must not be defiled, the citizens began to mobilize against the environmental threat that had descended upon them. I slowed, then stopped as a handful of demonstrators moved to block my way. Menacing faces sneered through the windshield as they leaned over the front of my Jeep. Several with soaked hair and bitter expressions banged their fists on the hood of the car—mistakenly thinking that the BLM emblem on the doors identified me as one with the enemy who had come to fracture their land, poison their water, and steal their resources.

A woman hurled a handful of wet red mud at the windshield, shrieking through the storm: "Evil! You're evil! Shame!"

Suddenly, the sleet turned to hail and the sound of it pelting the roof of my rig was as loud as a Gatling gun. As the storm pummeled them with icy marbles, the protesters pulled their jackets over their heads and broke for cover in their cars on the side of the county road.

I pulled the mic from the dash clip and thumbed the switch. "Dispatch!" I yelled to make myself heard over the pounding hail: "This is BLM, Agent Wild."

"Go ahead, Wild," the dispatcher's voice crackled, confirming that I was now in radio range.

"I am transporting an injured adult female to Holy Cross Emergency. Request triage team for multiple fractures, contusions, and abrasions. ETA thirty minutes."

"Ten-four, Agent Wild. Will advise medics."

I turned to console my passenger, who was now slumped into the door, head pressed against the window, eyes shut. I saw a dark wet stain on the seat between her legs.

I reached out and gently touched her shoulder. "Valentina, are you pregnant?"

She managed to right herself in the seat again, looking down as she did so. "Not anymore," she muttered. And then she passed out.

2: Body of Evidence

DINI BLACKBEAR, AN elder in the Tanoah tribe, could not go anywhere off the reservation on her own. For one thing, she didn't have a driver's license, and she likely didn't have a birth certificate either, because eighty years ago, they didn't issue them to Indians born at the pueblo. In addition to this, Dini couldn't drive because she was blind. All the same, this did little to limit her activities and abilities. She was, in fact, among the tribe's most revered healers, a past member (and one of only a few women) who had served on the War Council, and an esteemed storyteller and keeper of the tribal memory.

I first met Dini several years before at a *bake*, when we worked together with dozens of other women who—in a single day—made hundreds of loaves of bread for a feast, baking them by the dozens over wood fires in outdoor adobe ovens called *hornos*. I always saw Dini at ceremonies and dances at Tanoah Pueblo, and she—like the other women of the tribe—referred to me teasingly as *White Girl*, while I respectfully called her *Grandmother*, as was the custom. Now, she bustled toward me down the corridor of the hospital wrapped in her Pendleton blanket, with a young girl two steps behind her hurrying to keep up.

The youth tapped Blackbear on the shoulder as they approached, and said in a loud whisper, "White Girl." The old woman raised her chin, sniffed, and came to an abrupt stop in front of me. "Where my granddaughter?"

"She's in here, Grandmother. She's sleeping."

"You come me," she pressed a finger into my chest, then turned and held up a hand to halt her companion, who turned and went to join other members of the tribe who were settling into the chairs at the end of the corridor.

I followed Blackbear into the room and closed the door. The lights were off; the windows offered only dim grey light due to the storm, now producing snow. The grandmother bent over to examine Valentina's face with her fingertips. An IV drip containing pain medicine had already taken effect, so the young woman did not rouse. The healer continued her tactile examination of her patient, running her hands across the shoulders, down the arms, and under the covers across her chest and abdomen and along both legs. Dini started, raised up, and straightened the sheets. She whispered in a coarse voice. "No more baby."

"It's possible that she lost the baby," I said, "from the trauma to her body."

She shook her head from side to side. "Valentina cry to me next other time, say she wish she not have this baby, her husband be angry, not want it, he not provide for no more baby, not even the ones already here. We pray. We sing, grind corn, burn cedar. Then we make herb. She drink that tea right away, but no. Her moon not come. Still got baby, and it grow. Herb did not take it. So she know baby must come." She stood as still as a statue for several minutes. Then she let out a long sigh. "But now I not find baby there."

I wanted to ask a question, but in the Tiwa language, there is no way to say *no* to a request. They have no word for such a refusal. As a result, it is considered rude to ask questions. Over time, I had learned a few ways to get around this. "I'm thinking that you know who beat her like this."

Dini Blackbear snorted. "That one she marry, Rudy, he many time beat her. My Valentina just nineteen, already got two little one. Rudy drink, take drug, he beat her. He make trouble her work, come there mad, want money all time, Valentina lose her job. She tell me she cannot make enough money, feed more babies. Now this baby gone."

I felt my face growing hot with anger. "I want to make sure Valentina's two children are safe."

"They safe now. She teach them: They father get mad—*run*. He start trouble, they run, many time. They go over maize field, Liz Yellow Tallow house. Liz got them this time so I can come here."

"I need to know for sure that it was Rudy who did this to her."

Dini Blackbear nodded. "Everybody know Rudy. He beat her many time."

"Valentina told me that she's called the police before."

"They come, make him go 'way, tell him come back when he not drunk. Tribal Police say they not get in family business, they do nothing. When Valentina tell priest she not want baby, he say that a sin—tribe will shame her, make her not welcome. She have no choice."

"I need to find out where Rudy is now. And I need to know his last name."

"Cardenas. Might be casino. Idelle García—she work there—he in bed with that one."

"The Tribal Police are sending an officer to take a report," I said. "Someone should be here any time now. I told Valentina I would talk to them, and I'd try to keep them from talking to her until she's ready."

"They not do nothing," Dini Blackbear said. "No difference who talk them. Nothing change."

IT WAS NOT a Tribal Police officer, but rather FBI agent Diane Langstrom, who knocked at the door, then stuck her head in. She gave the elder a nod of respect, then turned to me. "Could I speak with you a moment?"

I stepped out into the hall and looked at my friend Diane, trying to figure out why she was there. She spoke before I could. "I came here to talk to Valentina Blackbear."

"She's asleep; they sedated her to set her broken arm."

"They told me at the nurse's station. We got a call from Tribal Police, a code black."

"No, it's not a code black. She was badly beaten, but she's alive . . ."

"Not her. Her husband, Rudy Cardenas. He's dead."

"What?"

"A friend of his found him at home, face down in a bowl of elk posole."

This explained Diane's presence. The FBI was always called in for suspicious deaths on Indian lands. "Natural causes?"

"Looks like a homicide. We're running tests on that posole. The Field Medical Investigator thinks some kind of poison caused massive internal hemorrhaging."

"Valentina isn't going to be able to talk for a while. I'm guessing Tribal Police told you that she called the cops on him several times for domestic violence."

"Yeah, they said they threw him in a cell a few times to sober up; one time she filed a restraining order, then let him come back home."

"I think the beating she got might have caused her to miscarry."

"I hate this case already, and I'm just getting started. I'm going to need your help with the Indians; you know they won't talk to me. We'll do a joint investigation—BLM, Tribal Police, and the agency."

"She told me if she talked to the police again about him that he would kill her."

"Maybe she took matters in her own hands. If that's the case, a jury might see it as justifiable homicide."

"I don't think that's what happened. Right before she passed out, she said she was a dead woman already."

"Could have been a confession."

"No. I'm pretty sure it wasn't. I took it that she was afraid that *he* was going to kill *her* if we involved the police."

Right then, Dini Blackbear stuck her face out the door of the hospital room and made a low warbling whistle. The young woman who had accompanied her came running at top speed. The elder whispered in her ear, and the girl spun and hurried away down the hall, past the Indians holding vigil in the chairs near the nursing station and disappeared in the direction of the front entry. Diane and I looked at one another, then turned to look at the old blind woman. She seemed to know our gaze was upon her. She pulled her head back into the now-dark room and softly closed the door.

3: The Stew

ELK POSOLE WAS a prized delicacy at Tanoah Pueblo. The best cooks in the tribe soaked dried hominy kernels until they were plump but still chewy, then blackened whole red chilies over a wood fire—peeling and seeding them and then pulverizing them in a *molcajete* to make the smoky red saucy gravy in which they cooked the chunks of elk. I did not know a Pueblo man who could resist the dish, so if you wanted to poison one of them, elk posole would be the perfect delivery system.

While Diane left to speak with hospital personnel, I stepped back into Valentina's room and addressed Dini Blackbear. "I imagine your granddaughter knows how to make elk posole."

"Good as me!"

"I wonder if you have made any elk posole recently."

"Men hunt, meat maybe last through winter. This time it spring, I have no elk left."

"But some people freeze some to make it last through the year."

She cocked her head to one side, considering this. "Rudy got lot of hunting buddy, maybe they freeze some. Valentina never enough food for the little ones. But if somebody give her some meat, she can make it last long time in that stew, add plenty dry corn, make a good gravy. Get some bread for soak up that gravy."

"I wonder if she made posole this week."

"If she got meat, she make posole."

"The girl who brought you here—you whispered something and she ran off."

"I tell her go tell Liz keep little ones safe from bad news."

"You heard what we were talking about in the hall? I'm sorry, we tried to keep our voices down."

"No. I feel. Like with baby. Baby gone. Now him—that one beat her—gone too."

It was traditional not to speak the name of the dead, so I, too, found a way to refer to Rudy Cardenas without saying his name aloud: "Yes, the children's father has died."

"*Unh!*" She grunted. Tanoan elders, especially the women, often made this guttural sound to release something that they perceived toxic.

AS WE HEADED for the parking lot, I told Diane I wanted to view the crime scene. We drove separately to the Blackbear/Cardenas home at the pueblo. Inside the otherwise neat and tidy dwelling, the kitchen walls and cabinets were splattered with blood, everything in the room out of place—dishes tossed and broken on the counter and floor, a calendar ripped from the wall, three wooden chairs smashed, splintered, and missing legs. Just one chair stood upright, its back support cracked across the top and one of the spindles missing near the center. The table was deeply gouged, a corner dinged so that shards of splintered wood protruded from the edge on one side.

Diane said, "We read it like this: He tore the place apart, beat the crap out of his wife, then set the table back in place, picked up that chair, and sat down to eat a bowl of posole as if nothing had happened."

"How could anyone eat . . . ?" I couldn't even finish the thought. I turned away and studied the short length of countertop and the stove.

A cabinet door bore a trail which looked like four bloody fingers dragged from top to bottom, suggesting that Valentina had perhaps tried to grasp it to hold herself up, but instead sunk to the floor. A smaller cabinet door above the stove dangled open, off-kilter, torn from its upper hinges. A red stain made a corona around the largest burner on the stove "That where you found the posole pot?" I asked.

Diane nodded. "We fingerprinted the pot handle, but the dipper had gravy all over it, so they couldn't get anything off of that. I sent a sample of the posole along with the pot prints by courier to the lab in Albuquerque. We should get results back any time now."

THE SNOW CONTINUED as I drove out to the small casino at the entrance to the pueblo, but the ground was too warm for it to accumulate. In spite of the weather, every slot machine was occupied, the entranced gamblers hypnotized by lights that pulsed, flashed, and whirled enough to induce a seizure. Speakers blasted high-decibel whoops, sirens, dings, and gongs so that I couldn't hear myself when I asked for Idelle García. The bouncer pointed at a pretty dark-haired woman who was standing at one of the card tables. As I walked toward her, she smiled.

"Idelle García?" I said, holding out my BLM agent badge. "I'd like to talk to you about Rudy Cardenas."

"You catch him trying to fence my stuff?"

"I'm not here about stolen property. You're involved romantically with him, I understand."

"Make that *was* involved with him. I sent him packing a few weeks ago. Did you find my flat-screen?"

"When was the last time you saw him or spoke to him?"

She frowned. "Wait. If this isn't about the stuff he took, then what's it about?"

Although I had every right to investigate any incident on BLM lands, I truly had no law enforcement authority on the Tanoah reservation, joint investigation or not. I was a resource protection agent, and I worked as a liaison to the tribe because the lands I protected abutted pueblo lands. Because I had cultivated re-lationships with the tribe over the years, I was often turned to when law enforce-ment or other non-Indian matters arose that required getting information from the Tanoans. I tried some deliberately vague official-speak: "I'm investigating an incident that took place near where the new mine is going in. Rudy has been working on the mine site prep."

She wagged her index finger in the air. "Let me guess: He's in trouble with his job. Listen, that guy is bad news, and I'm well rid of him. He didn't tell me he was married. I only found out when one of the guests here told me."

"You're not Tanoan, then?" I had suspected as much once I had gotten close enough to see her features better.

"No. I just work here. I live in town. Anyway, when I found out Rudy had a wife, I was gonna throw him out. But he promised he would leave her as soon as he had the money to get his own place. That lasted about two weeks until I real-ized there was never going to be enough money. He started going in my purse, swiping cash. About the third time it happened, I confronted him. We had a big fight and the next day while I was at work, he used the key and went in my house and took my flat-screen and some other things. So I changed the locks and told him to take a hike."

"And when was that?"

"I can tell you exactly, because he tried to make a lame joke about it. He said he had only taken the stuff as an April Fool's Day joke. But the sonofabitch never brought it back, so not very funny."

"What was he doing with the money he made working for the mining company?"

"He drank, he did drugs. He would bring his check in on payday and buy rounds and gamble the whole thing away in one night. He was always asking the floor managers here for credit, getting into trouble with the other guests. I wouldn't let him come to my place anymore, once I caught on to him. I think he wore out his welcome with everyone."

4: The Abomination

THE NEW WAR COUNCIL at Tanoah Pueblo had made a deal with the devil.
A primary source of molybdenite—used in the production of stainless and structural steel—had been identified on the border of the reservation the previous
year. This discovery was mentioned in an annual report by my own agency, the
Bureau of Land Management. Condelsus, a multinational mining conglomerate
and subsidiary of ChinaMines, quickly sent lobbyists to Washington to persuade
the BLM to lease the mineral rights on the public lands. But the operations
would encroach on Tanoan tribal lands, so they also needed to make a deal with
the tribe.

Condelsus sent an acquisitions team to northern New Mexico to entice the
impoverished Tanoah Pueblo to allow them to desecrate their beautiful boundary
lands in order to further enrich Chinese billionaires. The previous War Council
had already permitted magnates from Las Vegas to establish the small casino near
the entrance to the pueblo, a move that had introduced deepening debt, increased
alcoholism, and an uptick in divorces among the Tanoah, who found themselves
lost between their rich but economically unsustainable cultural heritage and the
false promises of outsiders with designs for using tribal lands for profit.

Instead of waiting to see whether the casino would ultimately benefit the
tribe or have an adverse overall affect, when the new War Council was empowered in January, they ignored the outcries from wise elders and better-educated
youth and permitted Condelsus to come wining and dining. The corporation
started with swanky, all-expense-paid trips to Belize for the council members.
But the Indians had learned from the casino deal to take as much swag as they
could get before putting pen to paper. Next, Condelsus offered a grant to the buf-
falo keepers that would create dividends for annual veterinary care and feed for
the herd. They followed on with an unconditional donation of a hundred grand
to the health clinic, just to show that Condelsus had a heart. The War Council
thanked them profusely but stipulated that what the tribe needed was jobs, so the
mining company agreed to a policy of preferred hiring of Tanoah Tribe members

and signing bonuses for those who were also military veterans. The War Council still didn't lift their pens. The grabber was the offer of a fleet of new tricked-out trucks for the tribe: one for each council member, custom-built and detailed with the tribal seal. Condelsus got a temporary right to proceed with the infrastructure only, the War Council members would soon get new rides, and the final deal to begin blasting and digging was set to be signed when the new pickups arrived. Then the mining operations could begin.

DIANE HAD GIVEN me the details on the Tanoah man who had reported Cardenas's death. Jesús Alveda, a longtime friend of Rudy's, grew up with him at the pueblo and they had both joined the Army after high school. The two had taken advantage of the signing bonuses and gotten jobs with Condelsus. For three weeks, they had earned overtime pay as well as their normal hourly rate due to the rush to complete the new infrastructure before the custom trucks for the tribe arrived.

Jesús told the Tribal Police that he had gone by Rudy's house after work to warn him that if he didn't show up at the job the next day, he would be fired. The door to the house was standing open, so Jesus went inside. That's when he found Cardenas face-down in the bowl of posole.

THE POSOLE WAS what interested me; if the Medical Investigator was right and the poison was in the stew, I was determined to find out how it got there. I drove to the home of my medicine teacher, Momma Anna. She welcomed me inside, but as soon as I told her Valentina had been beaten and was in the hospital, she hastily grabbed her blanket and put it around her shoulders. Before I could say more, she interrupted. "You take me Dini Blackbear." And on the half-hour drive to the hospital in Taos, she never said another word.

5: *Remedio*

MY CELL PHONE rang as I stood in the corridor of the hospital, a few yards from where Momma Anna, Dini Blackbear, and a host of other Puebloan aunties conversed with one another in Tiwa. I stepped into the lobby to take the call.

Diane's voice sounded flat: "There was only one set of prints on the pot handles, and we haven't found a match. Valentina Blackbear is not in the system, so I need to fingerprint her. I just talked to the nurse's station and evidently they're still keeping her sedated. I'm sending Tim Rainwater from the Tribal Police to stand by and let me know when Blackbear is awake. But the lab has identified the toxins that caused the internal hemorrhaging."

"Toxins? More than one?"

"Yep. Let's see, there's *Daucus carota,* or Queen Anne's lace. And blue cohosh. And wild pennyroyal. They said the pennyroyal was probably the killer, but evidently all of these induce bleeding."

I knew that wild carrot—or Queen Anne's lace—was used by many of the Puebloan women as a form of natural birth control. Centuries ago, the Indian tribes in New Mexico had been forcibly baptized in the Catholic Church, initially as slaves of the Spanish settlers, and continuing through the generations. Over time, the traditions of the Church had blended with those of the tribes until they were almost inseparable. Though any form of prescription birth control violated the dictates of the Church, the Tanoan women still quietly practiced the ancient herbal methods for planning births in their families to coincide with good years when there was plenty to hunt and harvest to support new lives.

Since Dini Blackbear had told me that they had tried giving Valentina an herbal tea to induce menstruation in the early weeks of her pregnancy, this news about the type of poison that killed Cardenas wasn't looking good for the women of the Blackbear family.

I approached the group gathered near Valentina's room. "Grandmother," I said to Dini Blackbear, "I need to speak with you."

She raised her face, but she did not move.

"I would like for us to talk alone for a minute or two," I said.

"We talk this way," she said, spreading her arm as if to include all the other women.

"I think it should be just the two of us."

"You speak here."

"I want to know about the herbs."

The women gave a collective gasp. My medicine teacher spoke, "You not sing this time, grind corn, you not speak that."

I knew something of the reverence the Tanoah showed to plants. Once, Momma Anna had told me to give money to the peyote plant in her kitchen window and to speak to "him" with a request. Now, I surmised that I wasn't supposed to talk about the miraculous herbs that had helped women manage their reproductive cycles for centuries, because I had not done the proper ceremony beforehand. I thought about this for a moment, then answered Anna directly: "I feel sure that you have done the ceremonies recently. Maybe you could help me understand about the herbs."

The grandmothers turned to Momma Anna to see what she would do. She reached over and whispered directly into Dini Blackbear's ear. Dini nodded and spoke: "I am keeper the herbs. I am the one, not my granddaughter. You take me. I make the posole."

I looked at Momma Anna. "How did you know about the posole?"

My medicine teacher frowned at my question, but she did not scold me. Instead, she answered, "Everyone at village know. Jesús tell one, they tell next one, then next. We all know."

Blackbear spoke again, more emphatically. "I make posole. I am the one."

I lowered my head in frustration. "That's not what you said before. I'm trying to get to the truth here, and this is not helping. I'm going to pretend like we never had this conversation. I have to go someplace, but I'll talk with you again in the morning."

When I stepped outside the hospital door, soft, fat flakes of snow were falling, and now a blanket of white covered the ground.

6: The Womb

AS I DROVE the same road where I had found Valentina Blackbear just hours before, the snowfall diminished and the cloud deck above me began to break up, allowing patches of blue-black sky and a few tiny stars to show. The new site built by Condelsus crouched against the base of the mountains, looking like an alien with an exoskeleton of formidable fencing, its torso a tight row of prefab buildings on an angular paved pad surrounded by tall aluminum poles like feelers irradiating the entire area with severe white light. I could barely make out the snow-covered peaks behind the site—the beautiful, soft, and sacred mountains that a Chinese-owned greed-siege machine would soon scar forever, blasting a deep extraction pit and gouging ugly terraces of laid-bare dirt and rock around it, riddling it with roads to cart out the wealth they craved so much that they would desecrate the earth to have it.

Though it was now nearly nine in the evening, I knew that a crew stayed on site to protect the equipment and facilities from vandals and thieves. I approached the gate and held up my badge for the guard to see. "BLM agent. I'd like to talk to whoever is in charge here."

"The superintendent is here. Let me get him. I'll open the gate and you park right there." He pointed.

I parked my Jeep where he'd indicated, got out, and leaned against the door, looking at the sky as more and more stars made themselves visible against the ink-black blanket of night. The guard returned with another man, pointed at me, and then went back to close the gate while the superintendent gave me a sober look. "What can I do for you, Agent?"

"I need to know what you can tell me about a couple of your employees, Jesús Alveda and Rudy Cardenas."

"Why? They get drunk and get thrown in the pokey?"

"Just tell me what you can, please."

"Night and day, those two. Alveda comes to work every day, gets here early, takes care of his tools, cleans up after himself, one of the last guys to leave. Cardenas is always late, always some excuse, does as little as possible, too many absences. And we paid him a vet bonus when we hired him. His pink slip is sitting on my desk with his final paycheck, which isn't much because he only worked an hour or so before he took off at coffee break and didn't come back today."

"Anything of note happen before he left?"

"Same as usual. He showed up late, hung over, and wasn't getting anything done. I gave him a warning. He's got a temper, that one. Just got in his truck and drove away."

"Did Alveda witness the warning? Did he know you were going to fire Rudy?"

"Everybody witnessed it. And everybody with a brain in their head around here knew how this would end. This wasn't the first time I've warned him, but it will be the last."

I HAD JUST gotten back to the county highway when my cell phone rang. Diane said, "Tim Rainwater with the Tribal Police got to the hospital about fifteen minutes ago. They've taken Valentina Blackbear and gone."

"Who took Valentina?"

"The night nurse said a whole group of Indians were out in the hall when she went to help another patient with the bedpan, and when she came back out, they were gone. She didn't think much about it and was preparing the tray of evening medications when Officer Rainwater got there and went to check on Blackbear. She wasn't in her room."

"But she was sedated!"

"They must have taken her back to the pueblo. Rainwater and I will meet you at the main entrance."

7: *Santuario*

FACING EAST, THE centuries-old, three-story adobe structure that endured as the iconic and picturesque symbol of Tanoah Pueblo spanned the west side of the dirt plaza. The Indigo River lined the east. At the foot of Sacred Mountain, the north side of the plaza housed the kivas where the men in the tribe practiced rituals that had been handed down from one generation to another since before the time of Christ. On the southern edge of the plaza stood a sixteenth-century adobe church, *Nuestra Señora de la Purísima Concepción*. The churchyard was surrounded by a low adobe wall, and the roof of the tiny sanctuary was graced with a bell tower, complete with a bronze bell that had been cast by Spanish friars who had followed the conquistadors here in the late 1500s. This remote pueblo had no priest, other than occasional visits from the one in Santa Fe. The *Santuario* was overseen by Sister Florinda Maez, who lived in a small room at the rear and saw to the needs of the faithful.

When we arrived at the entrance to the pueblo, Officer Rainwater advised

Diane and me that Sister Florinda wanted to speak with us. He walked us from the gate beside the gravel parking lot to the plaza, where it was forbidden to drive motorized vehicles.

The nun waited at the archway in the church wall. "Oh, Jamaica, I'm so glad you're here. We have a situation. I need to talk to my superiors, but there is nothing I can do until morning. I could not resist—I had to give them sanctuary."

"The aunties? Did they bring Valentina here?"

Sister Florinda nodded her head vigorously. "Yes. Seven aunties are saying they all helped to poison Rudy Cardenas after he beat Valentina again. I don't believe them but I told them to come in, what else could I do? Until I can talk with the bishop in Santa Fe, I am offering sanctuary to all of them."

Diane raised her eyebrows. Tim Rainwater put a hand to his chin, then said, "I can't go in there if Sister Florinda has offered sanctuary."

"Well, someone needs to go in there," Diane said, "to try to talk some sense into those old ladies."

I asked Sister Florinda, "Okay if I come in and talk to the aunties and see how Valentina is?"

"Certainly," she said. "Valentina is fine. We folded up some blankets and put her on the altar. She's resting comfortably. The nurse came over from the Indian health clinic and is going to care for her here. It turns out they are sisters."

At this, Diane spoke up, "I didn't know she had a sister . . ."

"Not sisters by birth," I interrupted. "Clan sisters. Everyone here has dozens of sisters and brothers in their clan, and the relationship is just as binding as if they'd been born to the same parents."

NO ELECTRICITY OR running water were allowed in the old part of the pueblo, where many still lived in the old ways. Because of this, the only light inside the *Santuario* came from thick beeswax candles mounted in sconces along the sidewall of the chapel, while a flickering red glow emanated from the jar candles that were lit before the altar. The aunties lined up facing me, as if to protect the young woman who lay on the long slab.

"No more," Momma Anna said to me as I approached, and the others echoed her: "No more."

"No more men tell women, what they do their body. No more hurt them, force them give children when the men they not love and care for those children, not love and care for those women. No more harm women, scar women, no more. They do this, maybe they get what Rudy got."

"I'm here to help," I said.

DIANE WAS WARMING herself with the heater, idling the car's engine in the lot near the entrance to the pueblo. I climbed in the front passenger seat. "I want to look at that kitchen one more time," I said.

"I was just thinking the same thing." She put the car in drive.

THE BLOOD-SPATTERED WALLS and broken dishes and furniture painted an even more gruesome picture with the dark of night outside the windows. We searched the whole house, though it didn't take long—for the family had few possessions. "The herbs had to have been in some kind of a container," I said, rummaging through the only drawer in the kitchen while Diane went through the pockets of the coats hanging from hooks on the wall.

"Right. They had to have been carried in here in something, they had to have been dumped into the stew from something . . . even a cloth or a napkin. Forensics bagged the trash; we didn't see anything there."

I raised up in frustration and took a long glance around, settling my gaze on the small cabinet door which dangled cockeyed from one hinge over the stove. I got up on the chair Rudy had spent his last moments on and peered deep into the cupboard. Nothing inside. "You said you sent a sample of the posole to the lab in Albuquerque."

"Yeah, that's how they . . ."

"Where's the rest of it?"

"In the freezer at the office. Why?"

"I have an idea," I said.

AT THE FBI field office in Taos, Diane pulled a hefty vacuum-sealed pouch from the freezer. It made a loud *thunk* when she laid it on the desk. "It's hard as a rock."

"It won't hurt anything to put it in some warm water, will it?"

"I doubt it. The posole had been heated on the stove. Besides, the poison has already been identified from the sample."

Fifteen minutes later, we fished the pouch out of the sink and started to squeeze it with our hands. The frozen chunks began to come apart as we kneaded the bag and examined the loosened contents through the plastic. We did this over and over, breaking up icy clusters of hominy and elk meat. Once it was all fairly fluid, we held the bag up in front of a desk lamp and began to massage the pouch of posole in a grid-like pattern. I squeezed what I thought was a hunk of elk meat and said, "Wait! What's this?"

We isolated the dark lump by working it up toward the top of the pouch and allowing gravity to pull the rest of the posole to the bottom. "That looks like meat," Diane said.

"But it doesn't feel like meat," I said. "Here, squeeze it."

Instead of coming apart like the other chunks of elk had with pressure, this held its form, no matter how much we pressed and prodded. A thin tendril of something came away from the mass and dangled from one edge.

"That's a tiny leather pouch," I said. "It's a medicine bag."

8: *El Vientre de La Tierra*

BEFORE DAWN, DIANE started preparing her report. We were lacking confirmation of one fact. I headed back to Tanoah Pueblo to talk to the women. Tim Rainwater was still standing guard outside the church wall and bid me good morning.

I stepped inside the *Santuario* to find the klatch of aunties and grandmothers cooing excitedly around the altar. Sister Florinda was waving her hands and beaming. I walked down the aisle to the front and saw Valentina sitting upright, the nurse bracing her so she could sip some water.

The wounded woman on the altar looked at me, her eyes less swollen, but still bruised, some of the color back in her cheeks.

"Good morning," I said.

She spoke with a gravelly voice: "You saved me. Thank you."

"If I'm really going to save you, I have to ask you something and I need you to answer truthfully. Where are the herbs your grandmother gave you to make your moon come?"

She looked at Dini Blackbear. Dini nodded, and Valentina looked back at me. "They are in a little leather pouch in the cupboard over the stove. I didn't want the children to get them."

I smiled. "That's all I needed to know."

I made my way back toward the entry, with most of the aunties on my heels, only a pair of them staying behind with their patient. As I reached for the door handle, Momma Anna spoke in a harsh whisper: "You not arrest her. We all did it."

I replied in a hushed voice: "Before I say anything, I need to know if you have told Valentina about her husband."

Momma Anna shook her head no. "She only wake up now."

Speaking softly so that my voice would not carry, I told the women that the case would be closed, and that no charges would be filed. Valentina had just confirmed what had made sense to us: That with small children in the house, she had stored the medicine bag in that high cupboard so that the young ones could not get into it. Rudy Cardenas was almost certainly responsible for his own death. In the brawl he conducted in the kitchen, we concluded that he had slammed Valentina against the cupboards so hard that it not only detached the cabinet door above the stove, but also likely knocked the tiny pouch of herbs into the stew. When he sat down to enjoy the dish, Cardenas had literally poisoned himself.

The other aunties joined the group as I was speaking, and Sister Florinda hurried up last, blurting out what had transpired overnight in the *Santuario*. "We made a decision . . . or rather, the women here made a decision . . ." As she spoke, I noticed that dawn had arrived outside and a soft yellow light glowed through the two stained-glass windows. "The women are going to the War Council to stop the violation at *El Vientre de La Tierra!*" I smiled to hear this joy at rebellion from a Catholic nun.

But the aunties looked a little confused.

"The womb of the Earth," I translated. "You're going to cancel the mining contract?"

Momma Anna spoke as the others nodded their heads enthusiastically. "*Unh!* That the same as Valentina. No more. No more that—forcing women, make them give what is not safe, what make pain. This Earth our mother. No men come here, tear apart our mother, take what they want. Them men on that War Council, they listen us, or maybe they not like what we do."

The aunties all laughed.

Then Dini Blackbear said, "We go now, get everyone in village up, stop that mine. Then we bake bread, have feast tonight. We honor our mother, every mother, every one that give life."

An Insurrection

Bette Golden Lamb

S puttering static from the communications module alerted the android pilot that not all was well. The search craft dipped into a dangerous dive to within a hundred feet of the planet's surface . . . and shook violently.

The unit commander's voice blared, cutting through the groans of disintegrating metal. "Don't tell me you lost another useless Egger and its defective chick."

An immediate reply was mandatory.

"The winds are distorting the sensor receptors," the pilot said, watching a spectrum of red, green, and purple flashing lights bounce and reflect on the steering yoke.

"Are the piezoelectric crystals still functioning?" boomed the squawking connect to Command Central.

"There are distortions. The ion activity is very high."

Lightning continued to jolt the single-seater, and the Zuban android turned from the computer monitors to visually scan the ground surface. In the distance a dark network of lava tubes was now almost obscured by a frenzy of dust whipping through the atmosphere.

The garbled voice continued, "Do you have a fix on them?"

"No, but there's a rebound ping," the pilot said. "The two of them are out there. Somewhere."

The communication system was barely viable; static distorted almost every other word.

"What a useless piece of junk you've turned out to be, 403," said the commander. "Useless."

"Yes, sir," said the android.

"WAIT FOR ME, Momma!" The child tried to run in the footsteps of her grumbling mother.

"An incubator. Just an incubator!" Iella shouted into the wind. Her long legs continued to outstride the ten-year-old, widening the distance between them.

"Wait!" cried the breathless girl. "Momma, please!"

The tall woman stopped, pressed a fist against her pregnant belly and yanked the child protectively to her side. The girl's violet eyes spilled hot tears over her blistered cheeks.

They kept trying to outrun the silica storm that tore at their skin as they headed toward a far-off, dormant volcano that covered the horizon of the vast treeless landscape.

Iella's massive thighs and Zuban legs stretched and strained as she raced across the scorching sands, half-lifting her daughter off the ground with every step. She dared only a glance over her shoulder at the threatening swirl that nipped at their tracks. The orange sky and midday sun were almost lost, hidden behind peaks of rising dust clouds.

Iella winced, swallowed hard to clear the clogging silt in her throat and nostrils.

"The bastards have won; we'll die out here anyway."

"Momma! Where are we?"

The woman stopped abruptly, turned, knelt, and grabbed up the child.

"Quiet, Opal. You hear me?"

The girl flung her arms around her mother's neck. "I'm afraid, Momma."

Iella's knees buckled. They both collapsed to the ground.

"I'm sorry, baby," the woman cried. "I'm so sorry."

"COME IN, 403! Have you located them yet? Damn it! Where the hell are you? Your signal's fading again."

Android 403 switched to manual control and tightened its seat harness.

The craft shuddered violently.

"Hey, you worthless electronic piece of shit, answer me! Those assholes in that fancy tech lab really had a warped sense of humor when they—"

The pilot crushed the craft's squawk box with two fingers before it clicked off the communication's system with the flip of a tiny switch in its neck. It returned both hands to the bucking steering mechanism as the storm continued to pummel the search craft.

The android turned from the computer complex to again visually scan the planet's surface, now buried in the swirling dust. The vessel twisted into a slow spin, picking up speed until the winding momentum tightened and large chunks of its metallic skin ripped away.

IELLA AND OPAL crawled out of the pulsating wind and into the mouth of a black lava tube. The woman held a map up to the dim light at the entry, studied the coordinates, and nodded to herself.

"This has to be the way."

Iella squeezed her daughter's hand as they inched along the wall of the cave. When the light was gone, they dropped onto a mound of soft white silica, rested until their panting breaths slowed to inaudible sighs.

"I can't let them find us, Opal."

"Would they kill us, Momma?"

"Yes."

"Does it hurt to die?"

She gathered Opal into her arms and rocked her gently, soothed the matted white hair away from the child's face and sang silly songs, struggling to still the pangs of fear that festered within both of them.

Opal's skin was blistered, burned a bright red, adding more damage to that caused by previous exposure to the sun's lethal rays. How much longer could she have lasted out there?

"We won't die. Not if we can find the colony."

"What colony, Momma?" Opal's lashes fluttered, her lids drifting down toward sleep. "What colony?" she repeated, now jolted awake as Iella's body stiffened.

A figure limped toward them. The woman held her breath; her eyes glinted with fear and hatred.

"Get out of here!" she ordered, standing. Her silver Zynec suit accented her ripe, pregnant belly and the bunched muscles of her arms. Her fists opened and closed, ready to strike out at the Zuban android pilot.

"Your face is burned," it said, offering her packets of healing, revitalizing medications. "Use it. Put it on the child."

"You don't care whether we're burned or not," Iella said. She snatched the packets from its hand. "You're going to send us back to them, aren't you?"

It removed a phaser from its holster, pressed a finger to the side of its neck, and listened to the built-in central communication network. Iella tensed, her eyes wide. She studied the weapon.

"Communication is distorted, almost completely lost until the storm is over." It fired the weapon at the closest rocks; the blast lit up the area.

The android looked superficially like all Zubans—tall with heavily muscled arms and legs. Even its jade-colored eyes had the same intensity as all humanoid male creatures. Yet, its appearance would deceive no one—its skin had a slight metallic sheen that gleamed in the artificial light. It had been badly damaged— exposed wires hung from the folds of its neck, hip, and a leg that had been partially crushed. It hobbled to a large rock and stood for a moment, finally dropping onto a pile of sand.

"What are you doing here?" Iella asked, focusing on the android's damaged leg.

"You are to come back with me. The Corporation does not allow its property to go unaccounted for."

"I'm a Zuban woman," she said, raising a fist. "I belong to no one."

"An erroneous perception." It meticulously fingered the exposed tentacles of wires at its hip joint. "You must deal with reality. You are only a female clone. A female cloned to breed. The Corporation and The Deciders gave you life for that function. You have adhered to The Directive in the past. If you want to survive, you will continue to follow The Directive."

"Stop it!"

The android looked at her, then turned away and again methodically attempted to realign the wires on the flattened hip, probably damaged when its craft crashed. As the 403 worked to articulate the leg to its torso, Iella moved to its side, squatted down. The android's jade crystalline eyes focused on her, glowing eerily in the dim light.

"Can't you understand?" she said, touching its shoulder. "I know what will happen to me. This is my last child. There will be no more cycles. I'll be terminated. But I can't let The Deciders destroy Opal."

"Termination is a part of every process. With every beginning there must be an end. The Deciders have deemed she does not meet Zuban standards. She is not perfectly energized. She must be terminated. That is The Directive."

"Why can't they leave us alone? Why can't you let me keep her?"

The android turned from Iella and again attempted to reconnect its synaptic linkages. "It is not my function to answer your questions. We are all the property of The Corporation. You must follow The Directive. I must follow The Directive."

Iella nodded, but tears welled in her violet eyes and trailed down her cheeks. "I'm ready to die, but I can't let them kill my Opal just because someone's decided she isn't a perfect Zuban." Her voice grew ragged. "I let them take all my babies. They had no right to take them as if they meant nothing to me. Take them as though *I* was nothing."

"They belonged to The Corporation. You do. I do." The android's voice sputtered, then continued. "Your children are better off without you. They are now altered, genetically enhanced, conditioned to better suit the harsh environment of Zuba."

"But they were *my* babies. Mine!"

The android shook its head. "You are merely a female clone, created to reproduce selectively. You must follow The Directive. You *will* follow The Directive."

"But what does that mean? Can't you see that I feel? I hurt inside?" She clutched the 403's arm, held onto its uniform until the material bunched up between her grasping fingers. "Don't you see . . . I'm . . . I'm a being, no matter why I was created. I'm now something . . . something more."

The android shrugged off her hand, turned back to its damaged leg and tried to tuck in the loose connectors. It labored, twisted, and turned, but the wires kept protruding, their frayed ends poking out in an asymmetrical clutter.

Finally, the 403 yanked the limb off and threw it at the cavern wall. The sound echoed again and again within the multiple tubular passages.

THE LIGHT HAD almost faded to blackness; he knew the woman and child could barely see. The 403 studied them.

The woman was as tall as him, obviously near her birthing time. Her yellow, burned skin was heavily wrinkled; thirty years on Zuba had drained any rejuvenating moisture. Yes, she would be terminated soon.

It turned its attention to the girl. She, like her mother, already showed a deepening network of skin etchings. Her face was badly blistered and swollen, and there was a slight irregularity in the jawline—The Deciders would never accept that deformity. The 403 watched as the woman moved to the daughter's side and wrapped an arm around her. They smiled at each other.

The android turned away. It shifted its focus, pulled and tucked carefully at the exposed wires around its neck. It raised its phaser and fired continuously into the porous rock of the ceiling.

The walls around them sprang to life with radiant, dazzling colors. The android scanned the area intently as the woman and child shielded their eyes from the penetrating brilliance.

"These paintings are very old." The android pointed a probe at each of the surrounding surfaces. "Laso-tech dates them at 2555." Its jade eyes studied the wild array of abstract symbols.

The woman and child squinted past the pain of the blinding light.

"Momma! Look at the pretty colors!" The girl pulled at her mother's hand.

Outside, the storm had blown itself out, leaving in its wake mounds and mounds of silica that now covered the entrance to the lava tube. The three of them sat and studied the ancient, pitted walls.

Wild shades of red streaked across yellows and purples. The ancient artist had splashed the paint, then created dazzling swirls and patterns, figures that seemed to dance off into space. At first the eye was confused by the onslaught of vibrant stimulation, but soon, it focused on explicit symbols that led the viewer through the intricate maze of color.

"What does it mean, Momma?" Opal stretched on tiptoe to run her fingers across the painting's surface.

"I think—"

"It describes the fourth planet of Unis, in the Virgo Supercluster," the android interrupted. "It is the story of the children of Zuba."

"Yes," Iella said.

"Tell it to me," Opal begged, her violet eyes shining.

Iella spoke softly: "Our ancestors colonized Zuba, arriving from distant reaches of the galaxy." She turned to smile at her daughter before returning her gaze to the painted wall. "But they couldn't have babies fast enough to make up for the numbers of dying people." She turned and spoke directly to the android. "So the doomed colony created cloning farms where intensified techniques of artificial insemination assured continuous reproduction. In time, an acceptable cloning growth and population pattern evolved.

"It was the clones that created the children of Zuba. *We* are the ones who saved Zuba. Yet—"

"Momma! Don't stop! I want to know more!" She danced around Iella. "Please!"

"We are citizens," Iella said, covering her face, "but they only want our wombs. Now we are forced to live in total isolation from the rest of Zuba. Our only companions are the robots that feed and clothe us."

Opal's glowing eyes dimmed in disappointment.

"We were never free. Never free to choose. Our destiny was to reproduce. That was The Directive."

"That *is* The Directive," the 403 said.

"I won't go back," Iella screamed, her words echoing throughout the lava tubes. She ran toward the android, snatched up its discarded leg, and held it over the 403 like a club.

The android aimed the phaser at her. "Put that down!"

Opal ran and stood between the android and her mother. "Don't hurt my Momma."

The 403 hesitated; its green eyes studied the pregnant woman and her child, its weapon at the ready. It pressed a finger to its neck—electronic signals spilled through its circuitry. It pressed the volume control.

"Where are you, you useless piece of junk? Damn it, isn't it about time we terminated the 403s? Report! Report!"

The android paused again, inspected the woman, then the girl. The two females stood defiant, side-by-side, fists clenched.

"You did not tell the whole story," the 403 said. "The painting also tells about the free colony, the underground city of Zuba."

"I know," Iella responded softly. She lay the android's leg down, and carefully lowered herself to the ground with a grunt, rubbing her hand back and forth across her huge belly. "That's the way," she whispered, pointing to one of the passageways down the lava tube.

The Android held its weapon steady, swinging the muzzle back and forth between Iella and Opal.

"403! Where the hell are you? Report, damn it!"

"Opal and I must go, but we can't leave you behind to tell them. The colony must survive," Iella said, tightening her grip around a jagged lava rock.

"Report! Do you hear me? Report!"

The phaser's green ready signal glinted; the android's weapon was now aimed between Iella's eyes.

"Where are you, 403? Stupid machine! The Directive! Follow The Directive! Report!"

The android's jade eyes sparkled like jewels as it holstered the weapon. "I will go with you."

"No!" Iella shouted.

"Momma, let it come. We can help it, fix it."

"But it's not a person. Just an android!"

"You're not a person," the android shot back. "Just a clone!"

"Come in, 403!" the commander screamed again. "Come in!"

The pilot slowly removed the communicator chip from its neck and crushed it. The clone and the android scrutinized each other.

"And The Directive?" Iella challenged.

"The Directive has expired."

The following story is loosely based on the molestation charges by former Minnesota Congressman Jim Knoblach reported by his daughter Laura.

Daddy's Girls

Libby Fischer Hellmann

The scent of smoke woke Jamie. At first she thought it was a neighbor's fireplace—they'd been going through a cold snap. But the smell continued to seep into her bedroom, bringing with it an acrid, sour odor.

She knew what to do. She grabbed a towel from the bathroom, soaked it in running water, and raced into the hall. The smell was more intense there, snaking up from downstairs. Her pulse sped up, throat tight. An intense wave of heat rolled over her, burning through the layers of her skin. She rushed downstairs as orange-yellow flames started to lick the walls, arcing higher with each burst. Throwing the towel over her head, she ran toward the front door, but just then a tree crashed in front of her, across her path, its branches still ablaze. She started to hyperventilate, the smoke closing in, the flames even more intense. Frantic to escape, she had no time to wonder how a tree had fallen inside the house. No time to think. She had to get away. She climbed over the tree, the flames scorching her legs, and reached the front door. It was locked. She would be burned alive.

Flames licked her feet, teasing up her legs. She was choking, her skin on fire, clothes alight. She tried to force the door open but it wouldn't budge. She whipped around. The fire surrounded her. She tried to scream, but nothing came out.

Jamie woke in a sweat, gasping for breath. She glanced around the room. Dark but cool. The windows, as usual, were open, as they always were, even in winter. She switched on the bedside lamp and took a few deep breaths. On the other side of the bed, her husband Steve was lightly snoring. She got out of bed to check on Kenny, their four-year-old. Peacefully asleep. She was safe. They were okay. Weren't they?

Twenty-five Years Earlier

CLUTCHING HER BARBIE doll, eight-year-old Jamie ran downstairs after her bath. Mama was giving her little sister Lisa a bath now, but Jamie got to go first, because she was four years older. She felt clean and cozy, ready to bid good-bye to the day. Her father was watching the news in his La-Z-Boy chair.

"Do you want to see my dolly?" she asked.

"Sure, honey."

"I fixed her hair." Jamie brandished the doll like an award, holding it up straight so her father could see how she'd combed Barbie's straw-like hair. "Like Mommy does for me."

"She looks beautiful. Just like you," he added. "Come on up here." Jamie stretched her arms up, and her father swept her into his lap. "There you go. Now, show me how you fixed her hair."

Jamie smoothed her fingers over the doll's head, tamping down stray hairs.

"Like this?" Her father raised his hand and smoothed down Jamie's hair.

Jamie nodded appreciatively.

"What about her back? Did you ever think she might want her back tickled?" Her father's hands, which had been smoothing Jamie's hair moved lower, lightly caressing her neck and shoulders. "You are such a tiny person." He laughed.

"I grew half an inch, Mrs. Fullerton said."

"The school nurse?"

Jamie nodded again. She was deep in his lap when he started to move around a little. Not with his entire body. Just below the waist. Making slow, wide circles. At the same time, he clasped Jamie closer and bent his head toward her neck.

"Daddy, that doesn't feel good."

"Mmm . . ." he whispered. "But it can. Just relax, baby." His lips nibbled her neck.

Jamie squirmed and tried to free herself. "Stop. I have to go to bed."

He didn't move for a few seconds. "You're right. Give Daddy a kiss."

Jamie pecked him on the cheek.

He scrunched his face into a frown. "No. A real kiss." He showered her neck with kisses, then moved to her cheek and lips. Jamie turned her face away.

The Present

AFTER THEIR FLIGHT from Seattle, Jamie and Steve rented a car at O'Hare and drove to Jamie's family home on the North Shore of Chicago. Her parents had never moved, perhaps assuming they'd play Grandma and Grandpa, babysitting the kids so Jamie and her younger sister, Lisa, would have "private" time with their spouses.

Lisa was still living in Chicago, so their parents still had one daughter nearby to take care of them as they aged. Until her death a day earlier, her mother always begged Jamie to visit. Jamie never did.

Jamie hadn't seen her father in fifteen years, but as they drove up the expressway, her hands began to shake. She tried to muster up the grief that any child has for the passing of a mother, but it wouldn't come. She knew why. Her mother had been in denial. And Lisa was too young, at least at first, to understand what was going on. Jamie had faced her father alone.

Aside from her therapist, Steve was the only person she trusted without reservation. Now, he covered her hand with his.

"What if I'm wrong? What if everything's okay?"

"Then you can let it all go. Permanently."

He made it sound so simple.

When they arrived, three other cars were parked on the driveway. She took her time retrieving her suitcase and trudged to the door, skirting the puddles from the melting snow. She no longer had a key. She didn't want one. She rang the bell.

Her sister, Lisa, opened the door. She gave Steve a perfunctory kiss on the cheek, then turned to Jamie. Jamie tried to give her a hug, but Lisa took a step back to avoid it. "We weren't sure you would actually show up."

Twenty Years Earlier

AT FOURTEEN, JAMIE was in that awkward stage between child and woman. She'd just started her period, which should have made her feel special and womanly. But she still wore a training bra, unlike Laurie Sturgiss, whose early development had boys falling all over her. Laurie made the most of it, wearing blouses that showed off her cleavage, and short skirts that revealed coltish legs. Jamie knew she was supposed to long for the time that she would look like Laurie Sturgiss, but deep down she was terrified. She didn't want to grow up. She wanted to remain a prepubescent girl with a training bra. That would break the spell, wouldn't it?

Last week her father had cornered her in the kitchen. Jamie had just come home—she'd made sure she had extracurricular activities at school that kept her away until dinnertime, but today was Institute Day for teachers. She'd spent as much time as she could at her best friend Kathy's, but Kathy's family was going out for dinner, and Kathy had to get ready.

So Jamie walked home. When she saw her father's car in the driveway, she almost ran back to Kathy's to beg them to take her along to the restaurant. Instead she slipped inside and went into the kitchen. No one was there. Her mother had made chocolate pudding last night, and there were a few extra cups. She opened the fridge and leaned in to get one. As she did, she felt a slight breeze which meant the kitchen door had swung open. A presence loomed at her back.

"Hello, honey. Where have you been? I've been waiting for you." Her father threw his arms against the fridge door, trapping her between the closed door and his body.

Jamie froze. She wanted to throw up.

"You want to see my dolly?" Over the years those whispered words had become his secret code. He pressed himself against her and started grinding his hips. She was old enough now to know what the hard lump against her butt was.

"Where's Mom?" she choked out.

He covered her mouth with his hand. "Upstairs taking a nap. Don't wake her," he whispered into her ear. "Just go with me. Swivel those hips. Show me how much you missed me."

"Stop!" she shrieked through his hand. But it came out as a squeak, not a scream.

"You don't mean that, baby girl." He dropped kisses on the back of her neck. Jamie squirmed, trying to free herself, but he was stronger. She gave up. All she could do was wait for him to finish.

Eventually his moan of satisfaction told her it was over, and he loosened his hold. Jamie spun around, ready to bolt, when she saw a crack between the swinging kitchen door and the wall. Lisa swiftly withdrew from the opening.

The Present

"WHERE IS HE?" Jamie asked.

Lisa pointed with her chin toward the living room. "He's in there."

"How are you managing?" Jamie said awkwardly. "Is there—is there something I can do to help?"

"You want to help?" Jamie wasn't sure, but she thought Lisa's eyes narrowed. Then, as if her sister suddenly changed her mind, she shrugged. "After we put Mom in hospice, there wasn't much to do but wait."

"Why didn't you call me? We would have come to, to—well, at least to wait with you." Jamie smiled wistfully. "At least we could have played cards." Jamie had taught Lisa how to play War, Fish, and Crazy Eights when they were younger, and Lisa had picked them up quickly. Within weeks, she was beating Jamie regularly. Jamie didn't mind. Playing with her sister was the only activity she liked to do at home.

"We didn't need you here," Lisa replied, her voice frosty. This time there was no denying the anger in her voice.

Steve jumped in. "Why don't I take our stuff upstairs?"

"I'll come too," Jamie replied hurriedly. She turned to Lisa. "My old room?"

"Whatever."

Jamie's room hadn't changed since she was a teenager. A princess canopy bed, luxurious for one, crowded for two. A white bureau and rug. Red Hot Chili Peppers posters on the wall. Jamie swallowed. "I don't know if I can—"

"You can," Steve said.

"But Lisa was so hostile. Where is that coming from? I hoped we'd be more—well—bonded. Understanding one another."

"Give her a break. It's been tough on her. You left, but she's been here taking care of your parents. She probably feels you abandoned her."

"But I didn't—you know that. I didn't abandon anyone. I had to escape." Jamie frowned. "How she could have stayed here all those years—with them—is beyond me."

Seventeen Years Earlier

BY THE TIME Jamie turned sixteen, her father would come into her room at night, reeking of Old Spice and sweat. The scent still made her retch. He would squeeze into the canopy bed beside her and whisper that she was his angel, his princess, his true love. Everything they shared together was in the name of love. He even brought God into it—the Holy Father had sanctioned their union, because He wanted more love in the world. Jamie knew he was full of shit, but he was a lawyer; he had words on his side.

Sometimes she wished she really was a princess who could wave a magic wand and make him disappear. Other times she thought about screaming at the top of her lungs. But that would wake everyone else. Did she really want her mother and Lisa to know? To share her guilt and shame? Yes, Lisa had seen them through the kitchen door two years earlier. But Lisa was only ten then. Did she really know what she was seeing?

By the time Jamie turned seventeen, she was depressed all the time, and she harbored fantasies of killing him and then committing suicide. At the same time, though, she discovered a seed of rebellion had sprouted. What if she didn't have to put up with him? What if she shared what was going on with someone? Technically still a child, she had no power. But adults did. And some of them had words as powerful as her father's. Could they make him stop?

Her mother had been talking about more mother-daughter time together, so Jamie invited her out for coffee. At a comfortable, well-scrubbed coffee shop, she spent some of her babysitting money on lattes, then haltingly said, "There's something I need to tell you, Mom."

"Sure, sweetheart." Her mother sipped her drink. "These are so good, aren't they? Thanks for coming up with the idea."

"Mom, this is going to be hard for you to believe. But it's true."

"What is it?" Concern washed over her mother's face. "You know you can tell me anything."

"Okay." Jamie took a breath. "Did you know that Dad has been acting—behaving—well, inappropriately with me?"

Her mother startled. "What?"

"Mom, he comes in my room several times a week. After everyone—well, you and Lisa—are still asleep. And—well—he touches me. And more. In places I don't want him to."

Her mother broke eye contact with her and stirred her latte. "What are you talking about, Jamie?"

"Mom, I can't believe you don't know. Or at least suspect *something*. It's been going on for years. You had to have some inkling bad things were happening."

The coffee cup clinked as her mother set it down a little too hard. "Jamie, are you . . . no, I can't believe this. You're making it up. Your father would never do anything to hurt you."

"I'm sure he thinks he isn't. He tells me how much he loves me. That I am his angel, and we're doing it in love. But, Mom, I can't take it any more. It has to stop. I want to kill myself."

Jamie's mother turned her face away from Jamie's and shook her head. "You brought me to this place just to lie to me about your father? You are an evil child."

"Mother, he's been molesting me since I was eight years old."

"Why are you telling such lies about your father?"

"They're not lies. I need you to make him stop. You should have stopped him nine years ago."

"I can't believe you're accusing your father of this. What's wrong with you?"

Jamie fought to control her breath. "I—I can't believe this. You're actually blaming me. He's a pedophile! He abuses me—has abused me almost my entire life! What about all those nights he left you alone in your bedroom? Where do you think he went?"

"He was sleeping on the couch. Because he snores."

Jamie stared at her, eyes wide. "You can't be serious."

Her mother continued to stir her latte with the little wooden stick. "Your father loves you, Jamie. Unconditionally. Like a father. Not a—a predator. He's a very affectionate man. You're misinterpreting things."

She was pleading now. "Mom, when you're not home, he makes me watch him take a shower. He's been doing that for years. He used to make me play with his 'dolly.' Now he just . . ." Jamie's voice broke.

"Stop, Jamie. I don't know where—What are you trying to prove?"

"Mom, I'm begging you. Please talk to him."

"I most certainly will not. You're imagining it. He's only trying to love his girls. And you are an ungrateful spoiled teenager."

DEVASTATED BY HER mother's betrayal, Jamie held on by turning to the people she was supposed to trust. The next day she made an appointment with the high school social worker. The woman took a lot of notes, looked worried, and said she'd get back to her, but nothing happened and two weeks later, the counselor was gone. No one in the school office would tell her why, but Jamie figured her parents had had the woman fired. Her father was an important man, after all, and donated to the school's football team.

Her mother was calm when Jamie accused her of arranging Ms. Turner's dismissal.

"This has gone too far, Jamie. You need to stop spreading these horrible, disgusting lies."

"You know they're not lies, Mother."

Her mother looked up, eyes cold. "If you persist, we will be forced to send you away."

"Send me away? Where?"

"To a mental hospital. There's something wrong with you, Jamie, and I don't know what else we can do. Neither does your father."

Jamie tried one last time with their parish priest. He reddened and coughed and said he'd look into it. He never got back to her.

Jamie finally surrendered. If her father continued to sexually abuse her, and no one believed her when she told them, then nothing mattered. She didn't matter.

She became a wild child, drinking, drugging, hanging out in cars. Letting boys screw her at will. One or five at a time, what did it matter? The world was full of predators. She may as well let them prey. She developed a reputation as the class slut. She didn't care. High school became a blur of boys, beer, and her father. It wouldn't last. She planned to kill herself the day after graduation.

The Present

JAMIE TOOK A shower, changed her clothes, and walked down the same staircase to the same living room. Her father, in an identical La-Z-Boy chair, looked as if he hadn't moved in sixteen years. His eyes were closed. "Hi Dad," she said quietly.

His eyes flew open. He seemed to have trouble focusing and ran his tongue around his lips. "Is that you? Jamie?"

"Yes, Dad."

"You came home." His voice was full of wonder.

"To help you bury Mom."

He pulled the handle of the chair until he was upright. Finger-combed his hair. "How long are you staying?"

"Until the funeral's over."

Steve walked into the room. "You remember my husband, Steve."

"Of course." He shot Steve an appraising glance. "Hello, Steve. You taking care of my little girl?"

Fifteen Years Earlier

JAMIE DIDN'T KILL herself after graduation. The same instinct for survival that fueled her to tell her mother, the social worker, and the parish priest kept her from slitting her wrists. Eventually, she scraped together enough money for a plane ticket and fled as far away as she could. Once in Seattle she cobbled together three jobs: one as a waitress, one as a nanny, and one as a receptionist in a psychiatric clinic, where the key benefit was free therapy. She started community college at night. Three years later, she transferred to the University of Washington.

She broke all contact with her family until her therapist suggested that she tell them where she was in case of an emergency. Rather than call, Jamie wrote them a letter.

In time the high-school slut became an OB-GYN. She joined a practice, started her professional life, and met Steve, a professor at U-Wash. A year later, Kenny was born. The only reminder of her childhood was a recurring dream in which she was consumed by fire.

After five years of therapy she was ready to go public with her story. She discussed it with Steve, analyzing the potential effects on them, the family back home, even on baby Kenny. She maintained the climate for women had changed. She expected to be believed. Retribution wasn't her goal. Life was too short. She just wanted the truth to come out.

On a balmy spring day in April, Jamie called the Northfield Police Department in Illinois and filed a criminal charge of sexual assault against her father. A year-long investigation ensued. She was deposed twice; so was her father. Her mother, Lisa, Steve, and some of her high school friends were also interviewed. Although the investigation wasn't public, enough people knew about it, she discovered, that her father was asked to "retire" from the law firm at which he'd been a thirty-year partner. Her mother, a mean bridge player and a community volunteer, quit her game and isolated herself at home.

The conclusion of the investigation was abrupt. The police recommended charges against her father be dropped. There was not enough evidence to proceed, and events were nearing the statute of limitations. It was a "he said, she said" situation, which, unfortunately, would never be resolved through the judicial system.

Jamie's lawyer had prepared her for the outcome. But there was a sense of relief as well. She wouldn't have to testify in court. She wouldn't be a party to the public destruction of her family. She wouldn't be the object of scorn and derision, or, worse, pity. She went back to her medical practice. Perhaps the new souls she helped usher into the world would find it a kinder, more joyous place than she did.

The Present

AFTER HER MOTHER'S funeral and after everyone had gone home, Jamie headed into the kitchen to store the leftover food. Her father and Lisa would be eating it for weeks. But that was the point, wasn't it? Jamie made sandwiches for everyone, then wrapped the cold cuts. She was returning them to the refrigerator when she felt the breeze of the swinging kitchen floor. She turned around. It was her father, his head tipped to the side, smiling the way he did when she was a little girl.

Startled, Jamie backed into the refrigerator door. "What are you doing?"

"I want my little girl to see her dolly."

Jamie sucked in a breath. "If you take one more step, I'll call 911."

"But you are my angel. My princess. I've missed you so much."

A wave of energy swept over her, filling her with an uncontrollable rage. "Don't you realize what you did to me? Do you really have no idea how thoroughly you destroyed my life?"

"What I did to you? Me? *You* broke my heart when you ran away." He kept coming toward her.

She grabbed a knife off the kitchen counter. "I'm warning you. Stay back. You're a fucking monster!"

"All I wanted to do was love you. You were—you are special. My girl."

"Steve!" Jamie shouted. "Steve, I need you!"

Her father ignored Jamie's cries. "No one was like you. Not your mother. Not even Lisa."

"You are a—what did you say?"

"You heard me. You are special." He smiled, almost tenderly.

The memory of her sister's face peeking through the crack surfaced. "Lisa, too . . ." Jamie glanced at the swinging kitchen door. "Monster doesn't begin to describe what you are."

The door opened again. Lisa's cheeks were flushed, her eyes wide, her body language rigid, even more so because of the revolver in her hands. She faced their father.

"You lied!" she thundered. "You didn't love me like you said. It was always *her*, wasn't it?" She waved the gun at Jamie. "It was always what *she* did to you. How *she* betrayed *you*. But now—now—after all these years, you *still* want her." She shook her head furiously. "What a fucking sorry excuse for a father you are." She aimed the gun at his chest.

Her father opened his mouth, but nothing came out.

Lisa pivoted toward Jamie. "It doesn't matter. It was your fault anyway."

Jamie felt strangely calm. "I understand, Lisa. That's why I came back."

"What the hell are you talking about?"

Jamie carefully replaced the kitchen knife on the counter. "Please, put the gun down, Lisa. We can help each other. I know what you're going through. Let's deal with it together. We're sisters."

"You? The town slut? You loved it! He gave you a taste of it, and you proceeded to fuck everyone in town. At least I had the decency not to embarrass the family." She took a step backward, sobs wracking her body.

Jamie's hand closed into a fist, and she raised it to her mouth. "Oh my God. He told you I was the bad child and you were the good one, didn't he? And you believed him. It's not true, Lisa. Please. I love you, and I want to reconnect. You're my only sister. My only family."

Lisa blinked, eyes wide and unseeing. "A little late for that, isn't it?" Lisa wheeled around to her father. "Want to see my dolly, daddy?"

Her father shrank against the wall.

"Drop the gun, Lisa," Jamie said quietly. "It won't solve anything. Let the police sort this out."

"A lot of good that did when you tried," Lisa said. "No. It ends now." Lisa aimed the revolver at her father.

The kitchen door flew open, and Steve rushed in. He hurried toward Jamie, but she motioned to Lisa. Steve whirled around, saw Lisa with the gun aimed at her father.

"Lisa," Jamie called out. "Give the gun to Steve, okay? We can work this out. Nobody needs to get hurt."

Steve started to close in on Lisa. Her eyes narrowed and she swung the gun to him. "Don't come any closer, Steve, or I swear I'll kill you too."

Panic washed over Jamie. Her sister's eyes were wild, darting from Jamie to Steve to their father. Anything could happen. Why hadn't *she* called the police? She slid her hand into her pocket and fished for her cell. It wasn't there. It was in her purse. In the living room.

Suddenly her father lunged at Lisa and tried to grab the revolver. But Lisa, stronger and faster, sidestepped away from him. She raised the gun with both hands.

"Lisa, DON'T!" Jamie screamed.

A shot rang out.

Their father staggered back against the wall and seemed to withdraw into himself. He tottered, twisted, and slid down the wall toward the floor. A whoosh of breath—or was it a sigh—escaped. Then he collapsed, a Rorschach blot of blood expanding across his shirt.

Lisa cried out, an inhuman scream of pain and release. She stared at her father, her face blank. The gun fell from her hands and skittered across the floor. The smell of gunpowder lingered in the air.

Jamie picked up the gun and yelled to Steve. "Call 9-1-1." She slipped her arm around Lisa's shoulders. "Listen carefully." She lowered her voice. "This is what we're going to do."

A month later

THE LOCAL POLICE were unexpectedly considerate when Jamie told them Lisa shot her father in self-defense. Was it a lie? Perhaps some would call it that, but when taken in the context of what her father had done to his girls, Jamie decided it was justified. Apparently, the cops did too, because a few days later someone somewhere convinced the State's Attorney not to file charges. Jamie wondered if that was officialdom's way of balancing the scales after so many years of shame and despair. She cremated her father's body and prayed for his soul.

She prayed for Lisa as well. It quickly became apparent that something had snapped in her sister. After firing the gun, she'd slipped into a semi-catatonic state. She could not—or would not—speak a word or make eye contact with anyone. Jamie wasn't altogether surprised. It would take another lifetime to untangle the decades of sexual abuse, lies, deceit, and denial. But Jamie had survived with the support of people who cared. She would do the same for her sister.

So she placed Lisa in a psychiatric clinic and visited her every day. She brought books and music, but spent most of her time talking softly, reassuring Lisa that she was okay, and that Jamie would never leave her. She told her about Seattle, how mild it was compared to Chicago, how cosmopolitan, how health and fitness were part of the culture. Except for See's chocolates, of course. She was sure Lisa would love the West Coast.

She also brought a deck of cards, and every day suggested they play one of the games they'd enjoyed as kids. But Lisa wouldn't. In fact, Lisa ignored her sister, slipped on her earbuds, and fiddled with her iPod. After two months, Jamie was close to despair. While the doctors were cautiously optimistic Lisa would recover, they wouldn't commit to a timetable. They told Jamie to keep on trying; It was the right thing to do.

The first daffodils of spring were poking out of the earth when Jamie arrived at the hospital three weeks later. Lisa was in the common room, staring at the TV. Jamie went to her and gave her a kiss on her head. Lisa turned to her sister and eyed her. That was more of a response than Jamie had seen since the funeral. Could she dare to hope?

"Want to play some cards?" Jamie asked.

Lisa raised her eyebrows. Another response.

"War? I have another deck." She started to bend over her bag to pull it out.

Lisa shook her head.

"Crazy Eights?"

Again, Lisa shook her head.

"Fish?"

Lisa's eyes brightened. Jamie thought she was trying to smile. Her lips parted. And then, miracle of miracles, Lisa nodded. "Fish," she croaked.

It was the first word she'd said in almost three months. But to Jamie it was the most important word she'd ever said. Jamie let out a breath, grinned, and dealt the cards.

Interview with Senator Barbara Boxer

Kelli Stanley

Former Senator Barbara Boxer (D-California) is a legendary public servant; venerated for her uncompromising fight for civil rights, the working class, and the environment, she served the people in California and the United States as a member of the House of Representatives for a decade (1983–1993) before spending the next twenty-four years in the Senate (1993–2017).

Tenacity, courage, compassion, and resolve—these were the qualities that characterized Senator Boxer's career as a politician. Indeed, her recent bestselling memoir, *The Art of Tough*, is aptly named. She is a fierce and unapologetic progressive, and an inspiration to not only Californians, but to people around the globe who are resisting the rise of fascism.

She has been one of my heroes since I first saw her speak in 1985.

KELLI: In the US, the #MeToo movement has helped strengthen women's sense of self and empowerment, while globally, women are striving for greater representation and political participation. At the same time, forward progress is being brutally opposed—in India, for example, as women gain a greater voice politically and socially, incidents of physical attacks against them have increased. Here in the US, even while Dr. Blasey Ford bravely spoke against confirming a sexual predator to the highest court in the country, she received (and is still receiving) death threats. Senator Boxer, can you comment on where we find ourselves today as women and describe what you think might come next? How do we weather the backlash, continue our progress, and stay strong?

SENATOR BOXER: The answer to our staying strong in the face of hate and fear and prejudice is to stick together and broaden our base. That means making sure we include women of all ages and ethnicities and men of good will. I lived through the civil rights movement where the danger was out there every minute of every day. There were horrible slayings and intimidation of all kinds. The answer: Win people over with your dignity and strength and spirit. Clearly, we haven't yet reached that new era of racial equality, but our national institutions have changed dramatically as the fight goes on.

KELLI: Senator, your career in public service has been legendary—you exemplify not only whip-smart political acumen and leadership, but strength, resolve, and an adamantine toughness when defending and championing civil rights, the environment, and other progressive causes. Today, partly in reaction to the unprecedented governmental crisis in which we are enmeshed, we are witnessing a surge of Democratic female candidates.

Senator, what is your advice to Democrats—particularly women—running for office at this juncture? How can we defeat the forces arrayed against us and restore this nation?

SENATOR BOXER: My strong advice to women candidates for office is this: First and foremost be yourself . . . be authentic. Voters smell a phony from miles away. Think about what you want to *do*, not what you want to *be*. Walk in the voter's shoes. The election is not about you, but about them.

Know your stuff. Keep your cool. In short, I believe there is only one reason to run for public office: to make life better for people.

KELLI: Our own efforts with Nasty Woman Press are multifold: to raise money for organizations like Planned Parenthood and to inspire Resistance through the sheer act of reading. The epithet of "nasty woman" has become a badge of honor, and many of us draw inspiration from the "nasty women" of literature and history.

Senator Boxer, can you share with us one of your own favorite fictional or historical "nasty women" and explain why you admire her?

SENATOR BOXER: My favorite "nasty" woman in modern history is Rosa Parks. After being forced to sit in the back of the bus because of her skin color, this working woman showed her courage, her bravery, and her sense of self-esteem by doing a very simple but criminal act: She sat in the front of the bus. I cannot tell you how moved I have been my entire adult life by Rosa Parks's activism. She was arrested because of this stupid, despicable law and the whole country saw segregation for what it was.

One of the highlights of my career was being present when President Bill Clinton gave her the Presidential Medal of Freedom.

The Cycle

Travis Richardson

Rose slammed into the floor, her head bouncing off the threadbare carpet. She curled into a tight ball before Curt's boots made contact. He kicked her several times, swearing at her in a drunken drawl. The intense pain caused Rose to wonder if this was it. Her last breath. She bore down. No, she would not black out. This human turd would not kill her. She held on, and then it was over. Curt ambled out of the trailer, breathing hard and mumbling. Most of his remarks were incoherent, but he spat out the words "stupid bitch" very clearly.

It took Rose several minutes to stand. Her back, arms, legs, head, everything ached. She had to be strong. Had to make it through. She stumbled into the kitchen, opened a can of Red Bull, and swallowed a handful of generic ibuprofen. She dabbed her lips with a paper towel. Blood seeped through the white fibers in bright crimson. She ran her tongue over her teeth. None looser than before. She did a quick spot check of her body. Nothing broken. Good. She avoided doctors whenever possible.

Opening up the freezer, she took out a couple bags of frozen peas. She didn't eat peas, but always bought bags for days like this. She walked into the bathroom and looked into the mirror. Yep. Her left eye would swell shut soon enough. The freezing touch of the bag to her skin brought her to full consciousness, wiping away the lingering brain fog.

Time to move on. She grabbed her suitcase from the closet. The one her mother had used back when she was a girl and they moved from house to house to house. A rueful smile crossed her lips. This blue synthetic case was the most consistent thing in her world. No human or animal could match its unwavering loyalty. Always there for her when she needed it. When she had to go.

She packed her things. Took some of Curt's too, including the roll of cash he kept hidden in a coffee can. Stupid moron didn't even own a coffee maker. Less than an hour after Curt stumbled out of the trailer, en route to a bar, she took off in her puttering Chevy Aveo with one hand on the wheel and the other pressing peas to her face.

She left Gainesville and made it up to Tallahassee in two hours. With Curt's cash, she paid a week's rent for a motel room. A few days after the swelling went down, she covered her bruises with makeup and searched for a job at several hair salons. She got a chair after her third day trying. A few nights later, she went out for drinks with a couple of fellow stylists.

Entering a trendy bar, several sets of eyes focused on Rose. Some were shy, others alpha aggressive, but none felt right. She sipped her overpriced drink while electronic dance music thumped.

"Damn, girl," Clarissa said. "I've been coming here a couple of years, and I've never got as much attention as you're gettin' now. What's your secret?"

"Don't have one," Rose shouted over the music. "It just happens. Been a problem for me."

"Wish I had your problems," Jessica said.

Drinks came their way, compliments of men who sauntered over, trying to be suave. The white-collar dudes with open dress shirts and perfect white teeth were cute at best, trying hard to capture Rose's attention. She wondered how they would take seeing yellow bruises peppered across her nude body. Would they still try to fuck her? Maybe turn out the light and forget what they saw? Horny men will make exceptions for almost anything in the moment.

By the time Rose left the bar, Clarissa and Jessica had hooked up with men for the night. Good for them. She drove to her motel but could not muster the will to go inside the dilapidated room. She'd seen a dive bar down the road with Harleys and jacked-up 4x4s in the parking lot. Her kind of place.

Rose walked the half block, receiving a cacophony of whistles and car honks. Inside, she heard the familiar chords of Skynyrd's "Simple Man." Rebel flags hung on the walls, and testosterone permeated the air. She'd have her pick for sure.

Then she spotted him. The one.

He wore a muscle shirt with tattoos running all the way up his bulging arms. His shaved head glistened under the pool table light. He lined up a shot with a hard scowl that looked permanent.

"Excuse me, Miss." A drunken man with desperate eyes blocked her view. "I see you come in here, and I knew—"

"Excuse you." Rose stepped around the man, sashaying to the pool table.

The man, still concentrating, looked up to see Rose. She gave him a flirty, yet timid smile. He glared and returned to his shot. His cue ball knocked the orange striped thirteen away from the pocket and scratched.

"Goddammit!" He gripped the cue stick like a bat, looking like he might smash it against the wall.

His friend, a wiry suck-up, shouted, "Oh, man!" He fished out the cue ball. "I so thought you had that, man."

"I did. But then I got distracted." He glared at Rose.

She flushed. This was the man, indeed.

THEY FUCKED HARD that night. Bill had tats on his back, stomach, and legs. Even his hairless pubic area read "The Beast" in Old English font. Her bruises didn't faze him at all.

She was up before dawn. Navigating through Bill's dilapidated house, she found the kitchen. Unwashed dishes piled high in the sink. She made eggs and coffee.

He lumbered into the kitchen thirty minutes later in his boxers, rubbing his bleary eyes. She remained nude.

"Made you some breakfast."

She cleared papers and empty beer bottles off the counter and placed a plate in front of him.

He looked at the eggs and then her. Studying her face before analyzing her body, he spent less time on her breasts and more on the bruises. He showed no emotion, only concentration.

"Don't like your eggs scrambled?"

He looked down at the eggs. Smirked. "Prefer over easy. Runny."

"I can make you another—"

"No. This'll do." He took a bite. Chewed slowly and grimaced. "This shit's dry. Remember over easy and runny. Got it?"

She nodded.

"What's your name again?"

"Donna."

"Donna what?"

"Donna Love."

"Sounds like a porn name." Bill shoveled eggs into his mouth.

Rose shrugged. "You go with what you're given."

"Tell me more about yourself. Last night's a bit fuzzy."

"I just moved here this week. Don't have any friends yet."

A cruel smile crossed Bill's lips, exposing yellow egg in his teeth.

ROSE MOVED IN the next day. Sex that night turned to mild abuse with slaps and light choking. When she made eggs in the morning, over easy and runny, he said they were undercooked. Too runny.

The next night, she cleaned the kitchen before he got home from his demolition job. He balled his fist and asked why she didn't clean the rest of the house. He didn't hit her then. That happened a week later. And then two days after that. She couldn't go to work after the second beating. Her co-workers would've called the police when they saw her. In the morning, after Bill left, she packed her things in the trusted suitcase, taking a roll of money she'd found squirreled inside a hole in the bottom of a mattress. She left a note behind on the living room coffee table.

Once she traveled a few miles out of town, Rose pulled into a rest stop and placed a call from a public phone. Curt answered. As soon as he heard her voice, he screamed, calling her a slew of names and threatening to kill her. She laughed with a confidence she had never shown him before and gave him her message.

SHE MOVED TO Mobile, Alabama next and found work at a beauty parlor immediately. A week later she met Ben at a bar and moved in. He waited almost two months before hitting her.

Next was Birmingham. Tony didn't wait so long. Only four days after she moved in. She grabbed her things, left a note, and made a call from the road.

Two stops in Mississippi, and then she met Jimmy Tremble in Shreveport. He was the right one, but wrong because he was a cop. Smart enough not to bruise her face, he still did damage. When Rose left, she thought he might have cracked a rib or two. He also hid more money that the rest. Not her usual $500-to-$3000 grab. She took, as far as she could tell, around twenty grand from a safe in the floor. The combination was his own birthday. It had to be since there was nobody else important in his world.

All of the men from Rose's life—all those still alive—wanted to kill her, but Jimmy had the resources to find her. She cut her hair and dyed it black. Abandoning the Aveo, she bought a used Honda Civic for cash. While it would have been better to leave the state right away, she couldn't. Not yet. Because of her rule: She lived in two cities per state before moving on. It had to be done this way. If not, her world might spin into chaos.

In New Orleans, she met Antoine. His enormous torso, wrapped in a tight T-shirt with the word "Security" across it, looked tense and ready to burst with unchecked destruction. He rebuffed her advances, but by the end of the night he'd given in. She'd drank so much she couldn't walk. He carried her to her car. Later, when he lay her on his bed half-conscious, she expected to be stripped and savaged. But Antoine tucked her under the sheets and wished her a good night. Before she fell asleep, she thought, *What's this bullshit all about?*

ROSE WOKE UP to the smell of bacon and coffee. She was surprised to find her clothes on. Confused, she stumbled to the kitchen and found Antoine hulking over a small stove with bacon sizzling in one pan and scrambled eggs in another. He turned and smiled. She almost fell backwards. Her brain swam in confusion. His eyes, his teeth . . . were different. What was it? Genuine sincerity? No hidden agenda behind a false smile? No, dudes like him weren't that way.

"How you doin' today, sweet miss?"

"I . . . uh . . ." She let her mouth slack wide.

"Oh, you don't remember how you got here, and now you're wondering what you're doing in this huge black man's house."

"No, I remember you. The bouncer. You took me here last night."

"You were in no condition to drive."

She thought about her car and the $12,000 stuffed in the trunk under the spare tire. She wheeled around, getting her bearings.

"My car. What did you do with my car?"

"Don't worry, it's out there in the driveway."

Rose followed his finger and ran to the living room. Through the window she saw her Honda. It looked the same as it did yesterday, but he could've taken everything out of the trunk. She rushed into the bedroom and found her purse, but not the keys. She marched back to the kitchen.

"Where the fuck are my keys?"

Antoine pointed over her shoulder. "On the table."

She saw them. Holy shit, he probably went through her car last night after she passed out. No wonder he was eager to tuck her into bed instead of humping.

She swiped the keys and headed for the door.

"I made a mess of bacon and eggs for you," he shouted as she tore down the porch steps.

If he took her money, she was going to kill him. No, she was going to cut his balls off and feed them to him along with his bacon and eggs. Then she'd kill him.

She popped open the trunk. It was stuffed tight with all of her earthly belongings. They were packed in exactly the same order as the other day. Either Antoine didn't touch anything, or he was the most cautious man she'd ever crossed. He probably didn't go through her shit, but she couldn't be sure.

She heard voices. Turning, she saw boys throwing a football on the street. She needed to get gone, find a secluded place, and then count her money.

"Hey." Antoine stood at the door holding a plate with food on it.

Rose slammed the trunk shut. Shit, did she just show him her hand?

"What?"

"I just thought you might want breakfast. I know I'm big, but I made quite a lot and shouldn't eat it all by myself."

She squinted at him. Was this guy for real? Probably not. Had to be a ploy to get her back inside his house. A slow smile crept across her face. She understood that.

"Yo, Mister Antoine, you gettin' yourself some white tail?" one of the boys with a football shouted. His partners laughed.

"Shut your mouth, Trey, or I'll knock your teeth inside your empty head."

Fierce rage tightened Antoine's face. Rose strode to him, like a moth to a bonfire.

SEATED, ANTOINE APOLOGIZED for the boy's remark. "They're just dumbass kids."

"It's okay." She took a bite of eggs. Her eyes widened. The spicy, cheesy scramble did jumping jacks on her tongue. "Yummy. This is super delicious."

His eyes averted from hers, apparently shy about his cooking talent. "Thank you. Grandma's recipe. May she rest in peace."

She glanced around the house, noticing how clean he kept the place. A funny relief calmed her nerves. "You're a gay bouncer, right?"

Antoine's eyebrows contracted. "The hell you talking about?"

"It's okay. I don't judge."

"Lady, I'm a living, breathing heterosexual male."

"Really?" She arched her eyebrows and searched for any sign of a lie.

He brought his fist down, causing the plates to clatter. "Did I stutter?"

Rose shook her head, feeling a flash of fear mixed with security.

"Think you know me, huh?" Antoine said. "Let me tell you who I think you are."

"Be my guest."

"I think you're a woman used to being abused. A woman who don't know no better. You drag your sorry ass from one closed fist to the next."

A rage welled up. "You don't know me."

"No, I don't. But I saw your bruises."

"What? You took my clothes off?" Multiple confused emotions ricocheted inside her head.

"No, ma'am. I saw the bruises on your arms. When I carried you, you squeaked. Said your ribs were smashed up."

"Yeah. So. I fell down some stairs. Doesn't mean I've been beaten."

He threw his hands in the air. "Whatever you say."

"It's the truth."

"Uh huh."

She took a sip of coffee. It was good but had a weird aftertaste.

"What did you put in this coffee?"

"Chicory. I mean it's chicory coffee."

Rose nodded. She'd heard of that. Different, but good.

Antoine leaned forward. "Listen, I know you're probably in a tight spot. I've seen it before."

She watched him carefully. What was he getting at? Men usually didn't say that until after she moved in and they thought she was powerless. His big brown eyes looked sincere and sad.

"And New Orleans ain't no place for the vulnerable. Not one bit. People here can sniff that miles away and will eat you alive. Understand me?"

Rose nodded. She felt odd. Touched.

"Why are you being so kind? When I saw you at the bar you looked so mean, angry."

Antoine let out a deep bass laugh. "I know. That's the way I gotta be for the job. Certain people see kindness as a weakness. I'm liable to get attacked. I don't like it, but it's what I gotta do."

"Do you like being a bouncer?"

His eyes watered for an instant, and then he shook his head and shrugged. "It's a job. A big mofo like me, what else can I do?"

They ate in silence.

ROSE THOUGHT SHE'D leave after breakfast, but somehow she couldn't. Something powerful like a magnet kept her inside the house. She insisted on cleaning his dishes. It was the least she could do. Then the bedsheets she'd soiled with her dirty clothes.

She found out that Antoine had inherited the house from his grandmother. He made it a goal to keep the place as neat as she had. He wanted to be a chef, but his bulk made it hard for him to get a gig even as a busboy or a dishwasher.

"Folks take one look at me, and all they see is security. That's it."

By late afternoon, she planned to hit the road and find a new boyfriend at a New Orleans bar if luck might swing her way.

"Thanks again." She had her hand on the door.

"Wait." Antoine moved his body from the kitchen to the front door. For a big man he was quick. "I, uh, do you know where you're stayin' tonight?"

Rose shrugged. "I . . . I don't know. Figured I'd get a motel or something."

"Why waste money when you don't got to?"

"Are you offering for me to stay here?" Rose's jumbled emotions searched for solid ground. He wasn't her type by a long shot, but he had something she couldn't resist. What was it?

"If you want to, that's fine with me. Just offerin' until you get your feet planted."

He grinned a sweet, kind smile. She let her hand drop from the doorknob.

"Okay, just for a few days."

ROSE WASN'T SURE how it happened, but a couple days turned into a couple of weeks. Antoine made no demands on her. He cooked breakfast before noon and 5:00 p.m. lunch/dinner before heading to work, and she consumed. Half-heartedly, she looked for work, but she still had Jimmy's ill-gotten money to live off of for quite a while. She slept in his guest bed, and he never made a move on her. So fucking strange.

He would leave around seven in the evening and not return until after three or sometimes as late as five in the morning, depending on the business volume that night. Rose watched TV and searched the internet. She cooked him meals after his exhausting nights at the club, and damn if the man wasn't appreciative. It was even crazier because all of the other shitheels she cooked for couldn't figure out how to boil water, yet they insulted her meals. Antoine could cook circles around her, but he said thank you and meant it. She wondered when the other shoe would drop.

Searching online, she found that Jimmy, the Shreveport cop, had put an APB out for her. Fortunately the bulletin wanted Darlene Little, her Shreveport alias. Unfortunately, she'd told Antoine that was her name. Dammit. If only Antoine were different. She'd put things in motion, and this would be all over. She could move on. Head to Texas or Arkansas next.

Yet she could not will herself to leave Antoine. Something about him made her solid, filling a void she didn't know she had. They hadn't even had sex yet. She was dying for it, but she waited for Antoine to make the first move. She would have thought he rejected her, but his kind warmth told her he was undeniably attracted to her.

One night he came home with a knife wound. He refused to go to the doctor. His grandmother had gone to the hospital for a broken foot and ended up dying of pneumonia.

"Hospitals are death traps."

Rose studied the wound, a clean stab on his left flank. "You need some stitches."

"It'll heal."

She shook her head. Stubborn man. "Look, I can sew this up." She had learned to stitch wounds on her mother, then later on herself, sometimes one-handed.

That night she slept in his bed. No sexual contact, just comfort and care for a kind, beaten man. Three nights later, they made love. Slow, sensual, and wonderful, Rose had never experienced anything like it before.

In the morning, she woke in a panic. Anxiety coursed through her veins. What the hell was she doing? She did not want this. She was deviating from her life plan. Her promise.

"You okay, baby?" Antoine mumbled with his eyes closed. His giant warm hand touched her back.

"Yeah, fine. Just . . ."

He opened his eyes, concern brimmed throughout them.

"What?"

"I'm not good at relationship shit."

"You used to having a man beat you? Like the only way you deserve love is through violence."

Rose's body tensed. "No." She said it too quickly. Might as well have said yes. "It's more complicated than that."

"Life is. For sure."

Antoine kissed the top of her head and lumbered out of bed. Hardened scars mapped across his naked body, not unlike hers. Rose smiled. Had she found her soulmate? What the hell? She had believed the concept of soulmates was bullshit created for the weak and sentimental. Who knew, maybe they actually existed.

She landed a job at a salon the next week. She kept her hair shorn close and dyed black. She worked for cash, so there was no record of her. She had her state-issued beauty certificate from Iowa under her legal name if she was questioned. She preferred not be registered with the state, the same way she did with all of her other gigs. As an extra precaution, she changed her name to Darla Lowe, instead of Darlene Little as Antoine knew her. Damn that cop.

For the first time in her life, Rose felt like she might settle down. Such a strange, foreign idea. Since she was a child, life with her mother had meant one man after another. Sometimes moving in the middle of the night with all of their belongings stuffed into a trunk and hitting the road before Mommy's passed-out boyfriend woke up. Almost every move happened after some asshole gave her mother a beating.

The chaos and uncertainty had a consistency Rose expected, along with her mother's sad smile as she tried to put sparkles on their shitty life. Days after Rose turned fifteen, her mother was no more. Murdered by abusive stepfather number four. He slammed her head against the corner of a kitchen counter that had no give. A year and a half with foster molesters, and she took off on her own, flocking to the same breed of men who abused her mother. It was part inescapable attraction, part revenge. No man received the latter if he never raised a hand to her. Until Antoine, every man had. Worthless bastards.

The problem with Antoine, besides her own self-acknowledged, scrambled-up brain, was her unfinished business in Louisiana. Unlike her other exes, Jimmy Tremble was a loose end. The Shreveport cop intertwined misogyny and psychopathic anger with the power of his gleaming I-have-a-tiny-dick badge. A homicidal time bomb. The money she stole from him came from prostitutes, dealers, and other people he had an edge over and would shake down. She felt certain he had murdered a prostitute or two already. He practically admitted it to her when he tried to scare the bejesus out of her. If she stayed hidden long enough, Jimmy would do something stupid enough that even the Shreveport police force, as blue-line blind as they were, could not ignore it. Until then, he'd always be a threat.

SHE HAD JUST returned from a lunch break when Glenda, the salon owner, pulled her into the supply closet. The cramped space also served as the stylists' break room. The intense look in Glenda's eyes and trembling of her hands let Rose know that something serious had happened.

"While you went out, this mean-looking dude came in here looking for you."

Rose relaxed. Everybody who saw Antoine for the first time had the same reaction.

"It's okay. He's just my boyfriend."

"Your boyfriend?" Glenda's eyes bulged.

Not everybody in the south accepted interracial relationships. She had thought Glenda had an open mind, but apparently not. But then she remembered she'd told Antoine never to show up at work. Doing that, especially after she said no, was a sign of possessiveness. Was he turning on her? Revealing his true self?

"Does your boyfriend go around offerin' two-thousand-dollar rewards for findin' your skinny ass?"

Rose froze. "What?"

Glenda reached into her back pocket and unfolded a black-and-white flyer with her picture in it. It was from several months ago, which now seemed like an eternity, when she'd had the blonde perm. Rose took a few dry breaths, steadying herself. A funny thought crossed her mind. He's only offering ten percent of what was stolen. Cheap bastard.

"Look, I know the type, honey. An abusive lawman. Cops are the worst. They can slap you seven ways silly, and there ain't a damn thing you can do about it. Am I right? Nobody would listen to you if you try to call it in."

Rose balled her fists and nodded, willing herself to keep tears out of her eyes. Glenda put a soft hand on her shoulder and squeezed. Rose knew when she first met Glenda that she had led a hard life, and no doubt she saw her reflection in Rose.

"You don't need to worry about me." Glenda gave her a look of solidarity.

"Who else did he talk to?"

"Mindy and Etta. Don't worry about Mindy. She's had her trouble with cops and don't trust them none."

"And Etta?"

"Etta's so dense, she didn't even know that it was you in the pictures since you were all blonde in them."

They shared a sly smile.

"But I'd watch your back. If he's goin' around town with this flyer, there are people would sell you out for two dollars. No telling what they'd do for two thousand."

Rose nodded. Shit, shit, shit. Where else would Jimmy go? No doubt he was hitting salons in the state. Would he try bars too? Would Antoine recognize her in those photos? Glenda turned to the door.

"Wait. Did he say what crimes I committed? This flyer just says crimes."

"I asked. He said you were a prostitute and a thief. Well, he didn't use the word prostitute."

She gave a sideways smile and walked out the door. Rose counted to ten and exited. She felt bad about leaving this job, but Glenda would understand.

OVER FOUR NIGHTS, she worked up her nerve to tell Antoine she had to leave. She met him at an after hours bar that some of the bouncers went to at night, far away from the Quarter. When he saw her enter the bar, the scowl melted away from his face, and a huge, beautiful grin emerged. She felt like the lowest form of human waste. She didn't get a word in before Antoine walked up to her, dropped on a knee and proposed.

Flabbergasted was not a strong enough emotion. In her fast twenty-seven years she had had multiple proposals. Often last-ditch efforts by abusers to sink their predatory talons into her. She'd take the ring because she knew she'd pawn it later, and saying no might lead to immediate, deadly violence. When Antoine held up the ring, Rose wanted to shout, "Don't you know who I am? You deserve better!" Instead she teared up and ran as fast as she could to her car.

SHE DROVE BY Jimmy Tremble's house several times in three days. Never stopping or hesitating, but moving past at normal speed like the other cars in the neighborhood. He worked the night shift and had another woman. Blonde like Rose had been when she scrubbed and cooked in that house of humiliation and violence. Her replacement wore sunglasses even when it was cloudy and moved slowly, like a woman in pain.

Fucking bastard.

While Rose considered herself an expert on setting up murders, she didn't know how to do it directly and get away with it. A cop would be especially tricky. She never owned a gun, and if she had one, it was an ex's she took on the way out the door along with a few other prized possessions to sell.

With the eight thousand she had left, could she find somebody to do a hit job? While murders might be cheap in Louisiana, cop murders wouldn't be. And then getting away with it . . . was it possible? No, she wouldn't hire out, and she wouldn't get Antoine involved. This was her issue alone.

She hated what she'd done to Antoine. He texted and called several times a day with some of the kindest, most heartbreaking words. He didn't know what he had done wrong. Rose wanted to tell him, wanted to shout while rending her clothes and hair, "You did nothing wrong. You did things right. Everything right . . . and that's the problem!" Instead she texted: *Need time. Pls be patient with me. Sorry.*

ON SUNDAY MORNING, Jimmy climbed into his yellow F-150 plastered with Trump and NRA bumper stickers and backed out of the drive. Even though he didn't tow his boat, she hoped he was going fishing. But she knew where he was heading when he took I-49 South.

Five hours later, he parked his massive truck in a French Quarter parking garage. Rose zoomed ahead, parking in a nearby hotel. They charged a fortune, eight bucks for every fifteen minutes. She didn't want to lose him, but she wasn't going to find herself trapped with him inside a garage either. A minute later she found him. In an area packed full of cocky assholes, she could pick Jimmy out from the rest. The big man on the street with an air of invincibility that people noticed from blocks away.

Rose was glad she was wearing a Saint's ball cap, big sunglasses, and an unflattering oversized T-shirt. No one would look twice at her compared to all the carnal distractions. He walked into Acme Oyster House. She did not. Instead she went across the street to the 21st Amendment Bar. While the Penthouse

Club would give her better a view, she didn't want to have to endure horny men on their way in or out of the strip club. She ordered bourbon on the rocks and swiveled her chair to watch Acme. She saw why he'd come back to New Orleans as Etta waddled into the door. Idiot bubblehead. She'd be lucky to get half the money Jimmy promised.

Rose's big concern was how much Etta knew about her. She seemed dense as a bucket of used motor oil and so full of herself that she didn't pay attention to anybody else. But she had asked about her man and where she lived. Rose remembered Etta's shocked expression when she casually mentioned she was living in the Holy Cross neighborhood of the Ninth ward.

"That's not safe for a white girl to live."

Yet it had been, until her white ex-boyfriend came looking for her. Sure, she heard the popping of gunfire any given night, somewhere in the vicinity. But Antoine's street seemed different than those around it. She knew all of Antoine's neighbors. The boys on the street were good kids, even if she could see Trey, the loudest in the group, going astray in a year or two. The houses were filled with hardworking families, trying to pay their bills and make sure their kids did their homework. She had related none of this to Etta. Fuck her.

Rose glanced up at the rifles bolted to the wall over the bar. If only they were loaded. Then a horrible, sickening thought vibrated through her head. What if Antoine had gone into the salon looking for her to beg forgiveness and had given Etta his phone number or, even worse, his address? Holy fuck.

Etta left thirty minutes later and didn't look thrilled. Jimmy had stiffed her, and Rose wondered by how much. He came out a few minutes later, heading for Bourbon Street with a cell phone in hand. Rose paid her bill and hit the street, mixing in with the human debris. He walked up to the club where Antoine bounced. A line stretched out the door. Good. Jimmy walked past, eyeing Antoine hard. Rose looked at the time. Dammit, Antoine must be pulling a double shift. Her heart ached looking at him.

Rose walked across the street and waited. Jimmy would come back. She sensed it somehow. But what would he do? He wouldn't engage Antoine in hand-to-hand combat. Cowards don't play fair. Hopefully he didn't go back to his truck for a gun. Please Lord, no. If he did, she'd rush him. She swore to God and all the angels.

A long twenty minutes later, obviously having steeled himself up with liquid courage, Jimmy finally walked up to Antoine. He had nothing in his hands, just balled fists. She exhaled air she didn't know she'd held.

"Hey Antoine. Yo, Antoine," Jimmy shouted at her man.

Antoine looked up, his face a snarl. "Who the fuck are you?"

Jimmy glared back, flushing red. Rose suddenly realized one of the reasons she'd subconsciously chosen Antoine that first time in the bar. Jimmy was a fucking racist.

Holy crap. No telling what crazy shit he'd pull. The two men kept their eyes locked until Jimmy broke the trance, shaking his head and walking away with long, hurried strides. Confusion clouded Antoine's features as he watched the mustached man's back.

Rose followed her ex, who had pulled out his phone again while dodging people. He walked up the steps of the parking garage. Rose lingered, listening to his boots on the stairs and then dashing up a flight when she was certain he cleared a level. Although Jimmy held the phone to his ear, he didn't speak much. She only heard him say, "Can you wait and give it to me again in a sec? I'm almost to my truck."

When Rose heard the familiar deep rumble of his Ford, goosebumps rose on her arms. Running back to her car, she knew where Jimmy was heading. Fucking cops need just a name or some nugget of information and they can find people faster than any civilian could.

SHE PARKED THREE houses away from Antoine's place. Jimmy pulled up minutes later. Rose squeezed the steering wheel, racking her brain, thinking what she should do. Calling the cops wouldn't work. He hadn't done anything. Yet. Jimmy opened his truck door and strode across the street to the house.

Standing outside the door, he rang the bell. Jimmy obviously knew Antoine was bouncing. Must be double-checking to see if anybody else was inside. Perhaps somebody like herself. He stepped off the porch and looked around. Rose remembered he had once said that cars were more effective for taking criminals

down than bullets. Perhaps if he walked back to the truck, she'd take the opportunity. But he didn't. Pulling on a pair of gloves, Jimmy snuck back behind the
house instead.

A pang of panic hit Rose. Her fears were confirmed when she saw a flashlight
beam shining through the windows of the darkened house. She waited for him
to come out again, confirming that she and Antoine lived together. Or was he
planting bullshit evidence against Antoine? Her rage boiled up. Nobody should
ever set up someone like Antoine.

After an hour, she knew Jimmy's plan. No, it wasn't a setup. It was even
worse—an ambush. Should she call the police now? Breaking and entering was
a full-on felony. But if he didn't shoot the cops first, he'd probably explain his
way out of the situation. Even if they did take him in, he'd probably leave un-
scathed, as NOPD had their hands full. Worse, Jimmy would know beyond a
doubt where Antoine lived, and he'd inevitably come back. No. She had to stop
him now. Tonight. Not for her safety, but for Antoine's. It was up to her to complete the cycle herself.

She focused hard, thinking of ways she could extract Jimmy out of the house
before Antoine lumbered back, exhausted after a hard night's work. Then she
saw Trey ambling down the street, smoking a cigarette. Rose rolled down her
window.

"Hey, Trey."

He did a quick double take. "Yo, Darlene." He only knew her by the name
Antoine knew her by. "I thought you ran out on my man Antoine. That was cold,
yo. My man's hurtin' real hard."

Rose winced. "Trey, can you do me a favor? See that yellow truck there?"

"Yeah, that's an ugly white man's truck. Friend of yours?"

"No. But he broke into Antoine's house, and I think he means to kill him."

Trey's eyes grew hard. "Why'd he do that?"

Rose returned the hard look. Trey shook his head.

"I get it. White woman problems. Who is he?"

"Ex-boyfriend. Cop from Shreveport."

"Oh shit, you in trouble big time."

"Yeah, I can handle that if it's on me. But I can't have Antoine in this danger. Can you do me a favor?"

Trey puts his hands in the air. "I don't want no trouble with cops."

"He's out of his jurisdiction. Besides . . ." She pulled two hundred dollars from her purse. "I'll pay you some money."

Trey's eyes lit up, but he took a step back. "I don't wanna die for chump change."

"No. I don't want you to die either. So you gotta be quick. I'll pay you more after this is all over. A lot more."

Trey clenched his jaw and looked away. She knew he would do it.

ROSE STARTED HER car and put it in drive but kept her foot off the brake. Once it rolled a few feet, she pulled the emergency brake. She watched Trey walk down the street with a brick in his hand. He looked back and forth for witnesses. He stopped by Jimmy's truck and turned to Rose's car. She nodded, even though she doubted he could see her in the dark. He stepped up on the truck's running board and with two hard swings, he shattered the driver's side window. The F-150's alarm howled as the headlights and brake lights flashed.

"Run, Trey, run," Rose shouted inside the car.

He did. Seconds later, a tall figure with a ski mask bounded out of Antoine's door. Rose dropped the parking brake. Jimmy shouted "Get back here, shithead," as she pushed on the accelerator. He stood in the middle of the street and pulled out his pistol. He widened his stance and lined up a shot on Trey sprinting down the road, his young body highlighted by pale moonlight. Rose plowed into Jimmy as he squeezed the trigger. The shot rang out and followed by the loud thumps of his body hitting the hood and then smashing the windshield. She stomped on the brakes. Jimmy rolled off the car into the street. She thought he might be dead until he moved an arm. Rose slammed on the gas, aiming her driver's-side tire for his masked face.

TREY HELPED ROSE load Jimmy's corpse into the truck bed. It was an awful mess. She thought Trey might vomit. He hyperventilated but didn't puke.

"This is fucked-up shit."

She nodded, horror and triumph swirling in her head.

Fortunately none of the neighbors looked out the windows. Gunshots were common enough, and nobody wanted to be a witness. Still didn't mean they could stand around with a dead cop in a truck bed.

She drove the truck wearing gloves she used for dye jobs. Trey followed. Although he was only fourteen, he insisted he could drive. One headlight on her Honda was askew. While that put Trey at risk for the highway patrol or some local lawman to pull him over, her risk was greater with the body. She didn't know exactly where she was going, just south to the swamps. She wasn't shocked to find that Jimmy's truck had a shovel inside along with rope and waders. Too bad he hadn't brought his boat.

She drove west on US 90 and then south on LA 24. She continued on smaller roads and then a dirt road. Trey diligently kept behind her. They were far enough in the boonies that if some crazy Cajun jumped them, they'd be screwed. She had Jimmy's pistol next to her, but she didn't think she could win a gunfight against locals.

Finally, she found a spot that looked isolated enough. They pulled Jimmy's corpse out of the truck bed and dragged it to the edge of a marsh. She threw the pistol into the water. Trey sighed.

"I could've used that."

"That gun was probably hot," Rose said as she stepped into the hip waders. "You don't want to be anywhere near that thing."

She snapped one bracelet of Jimmy's handcuffs to his wrist, the other to a heavy tool kit taken from the backseat. After dragging the body to shore, she heaved her ex's body into the swampy muck and let go under the beam of the flashlight that Trey held. The body sank. She hoped some local alligators would help finish the job. Her corrected mistake. An end to the cycle.

They drove ten miles further to another remote location. There she grabbed a heavy log, put the truck in gear, and let the decaying wood fall on the gas pedal. She jumped from the truck and listened to it rumble into the darkness, as it slowly sank into the bayou. Trey waited for her by the Honda.

"Damn, that's a fine truck."

"Too bad you've never seen it."

Trey looked confused and then smiled. "Ah, like I didn't see you run over that po-po's head."

"Exactly."

When they got back to the neighborhood, she paid Trey two thousand bucks. She knew that amount of money might lead to trouble. She hoped not, but damn if the kid didn't deserve it. Besides, as Antoine proved, people can be surprisingly different than one's narrow expectations.

She hosed down the street where Jimmy's blood and brains had puddled. Then she washed off the blood on her car. She'd attribute the car damage to a suicidal deer. Although something like that would never happen in New Orleans, it was a common occurrence elsewhere in Louisiana. Spent, she staggered to the front porch steps and waited.

The blackness of the night seeped into a dull gray coming from the east. The sun would rise soon, and Antoine would come home. If he'd let her, she'd beg for forgiveness on her knees and explain herself. Her real name, all her deeds. No lies.

She'd tell him how she went from one abuser, stealing his sentimental shit and money, and go to the next one. Same state, but different city with some distance between the last. When she'd leave the second abuser, she'd leave a note letting him know that she was heading back to her old boyfriend. Address included. Once on the road, she'd call the older ex and tell him that he had a small dick and she loved her life with the latest flame. She'd add that he was going to kick his ass. Get the bastard all riled up and then hang up, leaving him apoplectic.

Inevitably, like following directions from a script, every single latest boyfriend would attack her former abuser. Guns always came into play. Usually both had firepower. In every single instance, one ended up dead. The other ended up sentenced to prison for life, which was almost as good as dead to Rose. In what she could find on the internet, the defendants would mention her, using one of her fictitious names, but the police didn't care seem to care. They had a killer.

All of this Rose did in honor of her mother. Eleven states starting in Missouri and working her way east and then south. Twenty-one boyfriends taken down, Antoine being the only exception. The one who threw her well-oiled machine out of whack.

Headlights came down the street. Antoine in his grandmother's old Chevy Caprice. She swallowed and whispered "I can do this. I can do this."

At no point in her life, even with a knife pushed against her throat or staring down the barrel of a gun, had Rose felt more afraid.

Learning to Fly

Alison Gaylin

The envelope was pink, with a faint jasmine scent. Monique Von Tremper's name and address were written on the cover in red ink—a careful, girlish script that reminded her, briefly, of her own handwriting when she was young, the fan letters that she would send to the boys in *Tiger Beat*, those kissable photos, such a sweet, innocent time. She turned the envelope over. Held it close to her face and inhaled the jasmine, nearly as strong as it had been when it had first arrived in the mail. Interesting how tenacious a fragrance could be. The letter was, after all, 30 years old.

Monique could still remember the day she'd received it. She'd been married to Johnny for a year, and he'd been on tour for most of it. Here she was, the wife of a famous musician—one of her two life goals achieved at the age of 18 (the other had been learning to fly)—and yet she had felt so lonely, rattling around in this Bel Air castle of his, his servants fetching things for her with secret sneers on their faces.

Flora, the housekeeper, had brought Monique the letter with her morning tea and the newspaper and the rest of the mail. At the time, Monique was on a liquids-only diet, because she was flying out to Barcelona to meet Johnny the following day. He was taking her to Ibiza, and she'd wanted to look good in a bikini.

Anyway, the diet made her cranky and dull and kind of hopeless-feeling, the way most things did back then once the novelty wore off. She picked up the pink envelope, choking on its flowery scent. Barely even looked at it. "This isn't for me," she'd said to Flora. "It's a fan letter."

"No, Ma'am. It has your name on it. See?"

That girlish script. *Mrs. Johnny Von Tremper*, it read, that perfectly formed *Mrs.* glaring out at her, the way it still did now. She turned it over, looked at the return address: Linda Lee. Oh, how she'd scowled at the name back then.

Linda Lee was a super-groupie, rejected by Johnny and deeply jealous of Monique. She was a bitter woman who at 30 seemed ancient back then, all frosted hair and sinew, with frown lines between her brows that looked as though they'd been chiseled in granite. For a time, Linda Lee had stalked Monique, turning up at every store she shopped at, an uninvited guest at every party she went to on her own. Linda Lee, with her cobalt eyes and her cigarette breath and her warnings: *He's not who you think he is. He's not a good person. He's trouble.* A litany of them, over the phone and in person, each one crazier, more hysterical. *I'm telling you for your own good. I know things about him. Bad things.* Linda Lee, stinking of smoke and lies.

Monique began hanging up on her, and, after a while, the calls became less frequent. More time passed, and she could shop and go to parties without fear of confrontation. Linda had moved on, to new musicians, new obsessions. Or so Monique had thought. And then the letter arrived.

After Flora left her bedroom on that long-ago morning, Monique held Linda's letter up to the light, squinting and straining to make out at least one word until finally, she'd been able to read two: *your husband.*

"You don't give up, do you?" She said it out loud. And then she saw another word: *Proof.*

There are some moments in life that are like doors cracking open. You stand there, peering at the sliver of light on the other side, and you make a choice. You open the door wide and risk burning your eyes. Or you close it gently and live in the calm, cool dark.

That morning, Monique had placed Linda Lee's letter, unopened, at the bottom of her underwear drawer. She'd reasoned that she was starving from her diet, that she was too lightheaded to focus on whatever nonsense was written inside. *I will read it,* Monique told herself back then. I *will read the letter as soon as I'm in the right headspace.*

Everything sped up from there, a dizzying, dreamy blur. There was the Ibiza trip, then trips to Morocco and Florence and London and Tokyo, a safari in

Namibia, many weeks spent cruising the Mediterranean in Johnny's superyacht. There were three failed pregnancies and a short-lived diet pill addiction followed by a rehab stint and longer and longer absences on the part of her husband, to the point of her acceptance and ultimate apathy. There had been groups of new friends and hours-long brunches at the Sunset Marquis and two yappy little poodles named Gin and Tonic that Johnny refused to be in the same room with, those rare times when he was home. There had been private concerts for congressmen and sheiks and Russian billionaires, their wives and girlfriends glittering at their sides and smiling blankly at Monique when she tried to make conversation. Gin passed away, then Tonic. And then a star for Johnny on the Hollywood Walk of Fame, a profile of the two of them in *Los Angeles Magazine* titled, "After 25 Years, the King of Easy Listening Still Loves His Queen." Before Monique knew it, she was middle-aged, with frown lines of her own that she regularly erased with Botox and a vague uneasiness and dissatisfaction that she regularly erased with Xanax and weed. She signed up for flying lessons. Chickened out.

Monique's friends marveled at the length of her marriage. "What's your secret?" they would ask. And Monique would pull out her practiced, wry smile. "It's simple really," she would reply. "Don't get divorced." As though life was some terrific joke, and she was in on it.

Through it all, Linda Lee's letter had remained at the bottom of Monique Von Tremper's underwear drawer—as much a constant in this sprawling Bel Air mansion as Johnny's white baby grand piano and the spicy scent of Monique's favorite incense, that letter all but forgotten . . . until now.

Monique's throat tensed. Her lip began to tremble. She craved her vape, but it was too early in the day for that and besides, Johnny was receiving an honor tonight—a Lifetime Achievement Grammy, which would be the first Grammy he'd ever received in his 50-year career. If she smoked weed now, Monique would be passed out by the time her stylist, Caitlyn, arrived.

Don't open the letter now. Wait until after the ceremony.

"Are you all right, Mrs. Von Tremper?" said Flora, who always moved about the house in soft sneakers, quiet as a ghost. Never once had Monique felt Flora's presence in a room before hearing her voice, and it was the same now. "I'm fine."

She turned to Flora, whose eyes were aimed not at her face but at the article on the kitchen table—the op ed in today's *L.A. Times* titled "The King of Easy Listening and a Lifetime of Lies: A #MeToo Story . . ." by Linda Lee.

Monique gave Flora a long, intent look. "She's just looking for publicity, you know."

"Of course, Ma'am."

"She knows he's getting the Lifetime Achievement Grammy tonight. She's trying to piggyback on that. She even put it in the title."

"Yes."

"She never got over her obsession with Johnny. All these years later, she's still taking swipes at him."

Flora nodded slowly. Monique was aware of the tone in her own voice, the defensiveness in it, the way it kept pitching up and up and up. Her cheeks reddened, her gaze stuck on the last paragraph: *It wasn't just me. There were many more women who had similar experiences. I've heard stories. I've seen pictures. And I have no doubt it continues, to this day.*

"It's shameless," Monique said quietly. Though that word tripped her up: Pictures. The specificity of it.

"Yes, ma'am. Shameless."

"I mean . . . She barely even knew him . . ." Monique's voice trailed off. She heard the efficient tap-tap of her husband's hard-soled shoes on the marble staircase, so light and vigorous for a man his age. Johnny had never fallen prey to the excesses common to musicians. A vegan before it was trendy, he never drank, didn't touch drugs or even smoke cigarettes.

He frowned on Monique's pot use, and once told her that he considered the body to be not so much a temple as a crystal palace, wondrous yet breakable. He'd said it early in their marriage, after she'd had too much to drink at a party. When she'd woken up the following morning, her whole body aching along with her throbbing head, she found him standing over her with a glass of orange juice, solicitous yet scolding. *The thing about crystal palaces, Babe. They only stay beautiful if you keep them pristine.*

It was one reason why Monique knew Linda's op-ed was a lie. Linda claimed that after one of his concerts, Johnny had invited her to his hotel room, where he'd drugged and raped her. Now, Monique wasn't naïve enough to believe that

The King of Easy Listening was a virgin when they'd met, or that he hadn't indulged in a consensual road dalliance here and there. But he'd never drug any-one—he had too much respect for the human body. And of course he wasn't a rapist. That was just absurd.

"Hey, Babe," Johnny said.

Monique looked up at him, resplendent in a velvet tux, a blue silk ascot that matched his eyes. Her breath caught a little, as it always did when her gaze met his, a feeling that wasn't altogether pleasant. Should she still feel starstruck around Johnny, after all these years? Shouldn't she know him better than that? She dropped the letter into the pocket of her silk robe. "Excited?" she said.

"For what?"

"For tonight, of course. The Grammy."

"I hate making speeches. I'd rather just do my music."

"Well, I'm happy they're finally recognizing you."

He smiled. It felt like a reward. "Caitlyn is here. She said to meet her at the cabana." Monique stood up, and as she did, she saw his smile drop away, those blue eyes of his fixed on the newspaper, the op ed piece, his tanned face filling with something dark and cold.

"Oh," Monique said, the letter pressing into her side. "Johnny, listen. I—"

"You read that. That . . . thing she wrote. That crazy woman. You read it."

"I don't believe a word of it. I bet nobody else does either. Honestly, the idea that she could use a worthy and important feminist movement to spread lies. It's just disgusting, really. And let me tell you, it says a lot more about her than it does about you."

Johnny stared at Monique for a long time without speaking, her words hang-ing in the air between them. Seconds passed, maybe a full minute, the coldness in him building to a point where Monique could actually feel it on her skin. And then finally, he spoke. "You're incredible, Babe."

"Huh?"

"You're probably the only person on the planet who still reads newspapers."

Monique plastered on a smile, made herself laugh. "Better go meet Caitlyn." She walked across the cool Mexican tile floor, through the marble kitchen and out the glass doors, into the bright sun without turning around to look at him. But all the while, she could feel him, watching her.

The patio bricks were warm against the soles of Monique's feet, and a gentle breeze rustled her hair as she headed past the row of gardenias, their sweet, buttery scent. Her favorite flower. Planted for her at Johnny's request by Raoul, the gardener. As she moved toward the infinity pool where she swam laps every morning in an effort to keep her crystal palace as pristine as possible, Monique found herself thinking about Flora—how she'd left the room just before Johnny had entered it, how in all the years she'd known her, Flora never seemed to be around when Johnny was.

Caitlyn was standing just outside the cabana in a crop top and yoga pants, waving a manicured hand at Monique as she approached. "Hello, gorgeous! You're gonna love the looks I brought for you."

"I can't wait."

Caitlyn skipped up to her. "Don't tell Johnny," she said in a stage whisper, "but I brought us some champagne."

Monique padded over to the cabana. Swallowed champagne and made conversation as Caitlyn threw one gown on her, then another, and finally the third and final gown, made of heavy satin, which she deemed "perfection."

Monique felt like a doll, Caitlyn an overzealous child, sweeping her hair off her face, pinning it to her scalp with sapphire-encrusted barrettes, clipping diamonds on her ears, and rouging her cheeks and painting her lips in a color she proudly announced was called Iconic Red, oohing and aahing the whole time. Finally, when Caitlyn was done, she turned the full-length mirror to Monique, her face flushed with the thrill of it all. "Voila!" She practically screamed the word.

Monique stared at her own reflection. The gown was blue, to match Johnny's eyes.

"What did I tell you?" Caitlyn said. "What did I say about this look?"

Monique drained the rest of her champagne glass. "Perfection," she said.

Once Caitlyn was gone, Monique stumbled across the cabana in her weighty gown and strappy heels, determined not to trip on the hem. She was so unaccustomed to drinking that just one glass had made her tipsy, and so she went to the coffee table, pulled her spare vape out of the drawer and took a long drag from it, just to take the edge off the champagne. Johnny disapproved of her smoking weed because she tended to overeat when she did, and he hated it when she gained weight. But he'd never know. She'd only taken one drag after all, and the ceremony wasn't for a few hours. She'd have it together by then.

"Ma'am?"

Flora was in the doorway, shifting from foot to foot. Monique had no idea how long she'd been standing there. "Don't tell Johnny."

"Pardon?"

"About the vape. Please. It was just one puff."

"Of course not, Ma'am." She gave her a reassuring smile. "Shall I take your robe?"

"My robe?"

Flora nodded at the silky thing, hanging on a hook at the far end of the cabana.

"Oh. Sure." As she said it, Monique remembered the letter in the pocket. "Just a minute," she said, and plucked it out, just as Flora was taking it off the hook.

"That's a beautiful dress, Ma'am," Flora said. "I'm sure he will be proud of you."

"Thank you." The tension eased out of her shoulders, and Monique sat down on a wicker chair, grateful for the weed, the gown's skirt fanning prettily around her.

FLORA LEFT. MONIQUE started after her but sat down again. The letter felt thick in her hand. She had to open it, if only to prove once and for all that Linda Lee was a liar, obsessed with Johnny, wrong about everything she'd written in that op ed piece.

All right, Linda. Let's finally see what you had to tell me.

As she opened the envelope, Monique didn't feel nervous. It may have been the pot, but she found herself remembering a dream she had once, in which she was flying over the ocean, strong and free, and with Johnny hanging on to the hem of her skirt, screaming for dear life.

Maybe she would take flying lessons, at long last. Maybe this was the time.

Dear Monique,

 I've tried to warn you about your husband. You won't listen, and I can't say that I blame you. He cleans up well. He's a star. And as far as you're concerned, I'm someone who can't be trusted. I get all that. But I can't let you go on living the way you are, without knowing who your husband really is. These pictures were given to me by someone who cares about you and who didn't know where to turn. I can't tell you who. I promised I wouldn't.

 I didn't want to have to show them to you—they aren't pretty. But the truth rarely is when it comes to Johnny Von Tremper. You don't believe me when I tell you that he's capable of evil. So here it is. Proof. Let the truth set you free—I truly hope it will.

Yours,
Linda

"Dramatic, aren't we?" Monique whispered.

In the envelope, along with the letter, Linda had placed a series of Polaroids. Monique slipped them out, holding her breath. Then turned them over, one by one: Claude, Johnny's drummer; Leon, his bassist; Ricky, his guitarist. And finally, Johnny himself. Each was grinning at the camera, each taking his turn with the same poor woman—naked, unconscious. It took her a few moments to recognize the woman as herself.

Monique's dress felt tight. Her heartbeat thrummed in her ears, and her whole body shook, black creeping into her field of vision, one word running over and over in her mind. *No, no, no, no* . . . . She thought back to that morning, waking up hung over and Johnny standing over her with a glass of orange juice, his face impossible to read. *No, no, no, no* . . . .

Young. Newly married. Believing she was safe.

"My God." She'd meant to whisper it, but it came out a scream. Flora was in the room instantly, rushing to catch her as she fell from the chair and talking to her, talking and talking, an urgent, desperate whisper. "I found them in his drawer. I gave them to Miss Linda. I didn't know what else to do . . . I was scared. Scared for you. Why, Mrs. Von Tremper? *Why did it take you so long to open that letter?*"

"I'm weak," Monique said as she lost consciousness. "I'm so, so weak."

MONIQUE DROVE JOHNNY to the Grammys in their Escalade, his greatest hits blasting over the speaker system as he rehearsed his speech. When they arrived at the Shrine, she let the valet take their car and posed with her husband of thirty years on the red carpet, his hand at her waist, her dress picking up the blue of his eyes. When he gave his speech, thanking his "sweet angel Monique" for all she'd brought to his life, she smiled glowingly from her front row seat. Once he was through, she led the audience in a standing ovation. At the afterparty, she sipped a glass of seltzer water and posed for pictures with Johnny and his bandmates—Claude, Leon, Ricky.

She chatted with their wives, the three of them cracking jokes, thanking Johnny for paying for their kids' educations, their face lifts, the mortgages on their homes. "We have to have you guys over for a barbecue," Claude said at one point. And Monique smiled hard at him, trying to read his eyes. This went on and on, Monique moving through the night as though she were moving through a dream, for that's what it was, really. This evening. Her life. Every minute of it, for the past thirty years. A dream.

And now, at last, she was waking up.

Just around midnight, Johnny said, "You ready to go, Babe?"

"Am I ever," she said. "Am I ever ready to go."

THERE ARE SOME moments in life that are like doors cracking open. You stand there, peering at the sliver of light on the other side . . . But here's something you might not know: The longer you spend in the dark, the more that light burns you when you finally walk through.

"Are you stoned, Babe?" Johnny asked.

They were on the Pacific Coast Highway now, blackness all around them and Monique's window open, the breeze ruffling her hair. "No. Why?"

"You usually aren't this quiet unless you've been hitting that vape."

Monique swallowed. She stared out the windshield "How many of us?"

"What?"

"How many girls did you drug and pass around?"

"Ah. You are stoned." He chuckled.

Monique said nothing.

"Monique. Babe. Why would you even ask me that?"

She looked at him. His face was utterly sincere. A tear trickled down her cheek. She brushed it away. "I just wanted to see," she said, "how easily you could lie to me."

He frowned at her. "Is it that stupid newspaper article? Is that what's gotten you like this?"

"No, Johnny. It wasn't the newspaper article."

"Menopause? Aren't you taking pills for—"

"It was pictures. I saw Polaroids. Of you. And your bandmates. And me."

"What do you—"

"*You raped me.*"

"Where did you find those pictures?"

She gripped the wheel. There it was. The truth. "How many more were there?" she said. "How many more girls?"

He exhaled.

"How could you do that to me, Johnny? You swore to love and protect . . ."

The words died in her throat. She could feel him shaking next to her. The whole seat vibrating. She thought he might cry, that he might put his arms around her and beg for forgiveness and swear he'd make it up to her, to all the women, whoever they might be. She thought he might say that he had problems, that he needed help, or that he was young and cruel back then but her love had changed him. *I'm sorry, Babe. I'm so, so sorry.*

Johnny said, "There's a nondisclosure agreement in your prenup. You say a fuckin' word, I'll make sure you're broke and in jail."

"What?"

"You heard me."

"Yeah," she said. "I did."

Monique jammed her foot on the accelerator.

"What are you doing?" he said.

"Original plan."

Monique spun the steering wheel. The Escalade veered across the empty highway. It sailed through the barrier and over the edge, the bumper crunching. The smell of burnt rubber was all she could breathe. It was a dream, not a nightmare but a dream, never-ending and pure. The whole world arced and spun, stars racing past the windshield, through the driver's side window and then behind her, bright blurs in the night sky.

Johnny's scream filled the car, as high and pointless as the scream of an animal, or a child. And for that one moment, just before they hit the rocks, Monique knew, at last, what flying felt like.

The Gifts

Heather Graham

Life is a strange and wonderful journey, with every individual experiencing it differently. Through our years, from the very first, we learn and grow, experience more, and learn and grow some more. Eventually we hope the journey leads to wisdom—a wisdom that often leads us to realize and appreciate the gifts we've received from our family.

My own journey started off well: I had two loving parents, and even as a child, I considered myself a lucky human being.

And I was. After all, I was the daughter of immigrants who believed in America and in many ways defined what was best about their new home.

My mother came from Ireland. They were a "mixed" family at a time when two religious factions were busy hating—and killing—one another over which church to pray in. Her belief in America was amazing, passionate, and whole-hearted. She saw it as a place for everyone, where the color of skin meant nothing; where faith was great, but all faiths were respected; and where people were welcome to think, feel, and practice what they believed. Women had rights—with more rights to come—and who you loved was your business and your pride, not a shame or a stigma.

Mom was so determined to be American and speak "American" English perfectly that she could be a grammar-dictator, quick to correct me—and my friends—on any misuse of the language! And education—well, she was the original Google. And how she prized learning! Whenever I or my sister—and then our children—asked a question she couldn't answer, she would say, "I don't know. Let's look it up." And so we learned both the value of research and self-reliance at the same time. Mom worked for an ad agency for years, allowing me to head for casting calls for several commercials, where fantasy first gave me a call . . . she was as instrumental *in* my life as she'd been instrumental *to* it. Yes, I was lucky, lucky to start my journey this way . . .

My father's family had immigrated from Scotland—my grandfather had been offered a great job in northern Wisconsin as the manager of a logging camp. Dad was a big man, tall and broad-shouldered, good "Highlander" stock, I was told. He looked like "Mr. Clean," and, in fact, all the neighborhood children called him by that name. He didn't care; I think he rather liked it.

I lost him when I was far too young, not a child, but just the tender age of twenty. But he has been with me in my heart every day of my life, and I am grateful. My father, too, gave me many gifts.

Once, I was playing at the park with a school group, waiting to be picked up by my dad. At that time, he worked nights and my mom worked days. I was very young, maybe five, and I was thirsty and went to the drinking fountain. While I was there, an old white woman came up and yelled at me and scared me to death. She said, "Wait until your father gets here and I tell him what you did."

I was shaking with shock and fear, wondering what I had done. Neither of our parents ever struck us, but I was very afraid of disappointing my dad.

He came and listened to the woman. Then he just frowned and shook his head and told her, "Water has no color."

He took my hand and led me away. I wasn't in any trouble, had done nothing wrong. I later learned that I had taken a drink out of the "wrong" fountain before desegregation.

My father's words stayed with me. I later realized how beautiful they were. Difference wasn't *wrong*—it was *normal*. The color of someone's skin was something to be celebrated, not evaluated, just like a choice (or not) of religion, or if a person were gay or straight or bi or transgender. *Diversity* was good; diversity and the acceptance and celebration of it was profoundly, profoundly *American*.

My dad never preached or tried to pound any beliefs or ethics or morality into us; he simply taught us by being himself. He embodied the gift of what made—and makes—America great.

This is not to say that people are perfect or that they should be on pedestals.

My family has suffered through fierce battles with addiction, and my parents weren't perfect. I loved them, of course—they were my parents. My dad had belonged to Alcoholics Anonymous since World War II, and his drinking had done a lot of damage to relationships in his early years. My mother could be a closet drinker. They were far from rich, but they worked hard, and my sister and I were always provided with what we needed, and *sometimes* provided with what we wanted.

But the really important things they gave us were free—those were the gifts that really mattered.

Love. Acceptance. Empathy. Respect. A strong work ethic. Patriotism.

I wish I had a chance to tell them, "Thank you." They gave me the wonder of *people,* friends from everywhere with every shade of skin, of every religion, every gender identity, and of every sexual preference.

They gave me America. A country as imperfect as all else—but one in which we have laws that protect us, and one in which we have the right to speak and act daily in a manner to make her a better place, a wondrous true melting pot, a land in which equality for all is both real and a dream we can keeping striving to achieve in every fashion.

Contributing Authors

MARIA ALEXANDER is a multiple award-winning author of horror and mystery fiction. Since 1999, her short fiction has appeared in critically acclaimed publications and anthologies. She also writes humorous mystery fiction under the pen name Quentin Banks. *No Rhyme Goes Unpunished* is her debut thriller satire. *Death on the Argyle* is due out Summer 2020. For more information, visit her website at www.mariaalexander.net.

SANDI AULT is the author of the *WILD Mystery* Series, as well as other works of fiction and nonfiction. Ault has won the Mary Higgins Clark Award, the WILLA Award for Contemporary Fiction, two Spur Finalist Awards, as well as numerous other awards. She is a frequent contributor to periodicals regarding western and Native American life, art, ruins, petroglyphs, and wildlife, and is a sought-after speaker on topics related to the vanishing West and its indigenous beings. www.sandiault.com

ERIC BEETNER is that writer you've heard about but never read. When you finally do you wonder why you waited so long. There are more than 20 books like *Rumrunners, All the Way Down,* and *The Devil Doesn't Want Me,* so you'd better get started. He also hosts the podcast Writer Types and the Noir at the Bar reading series in L.A.. He's been described as "The 21st Century's answer to Jim Thompson" (*LitReactor*), has been nominated for three Anthonys, an ITW award, Shamus, Derringer and five Emmys. Seriously, what are you waiting for? www.ericbeetner.com

CARA BLACK is the *New York Times* bestselling author of eighteen, soon to be nineteen, of the Aimée Leduc investigations set in Paris. *Murder in Bel-Air* will be published by Soho Press in June 2019. The Wall Street Journal said of her *Murder on the Left Bank,* "Even after 17 books, Ms. Black has intriguing corners of Paris to reveal—from an enclave of ateliers once home to the likes of Gauguin and Rodin to a crime-ridden neighborhood where 'no one wanted to be witnessed witnessing'." She has received multiple nominations for the Anthony and Macavity awards. In Paris she was awarded the Médaille de la Ville de Paris in recognition of her contributions to French culture. Cara gets to Paris whenever she can for research. She lives in San Francisco with her husband and dog. carablack. com

SENATOR BARBARA BOXER served for more than thirty years in Congress, representing the people of California. A devoted and passionate liberal, she championed civil rights, care for the environment, and health care. In 2016, she published a bestselling memoir, *The Art of Tough: Fearlessly Facing Politics and Life.*

DANA CAMERON writes across many genres, but especially in crime and speculative fiction. Her work, inspired by her career in archaeology, has won multiple Anthony, Agatha, and Macavity Awards, and was nominated for the Edgar Award. Three of Dana's Emma Fielding archaeology mysteries were made into movies for the Hallmark Movie & Mystery Channel. www. danacameron.com/

JOE CLIFFORD is the author of several books, including *Skunk Train, The One That Got Away, Junkie Love,* and the Jay Porter thriller series, as well as editor of the anthologies *Trouble in the Heartland: Crime Fiction Inspired by the Songs of Bruce Springsteen; Just to Watch Them Die: Crime Fiction Inspired by the Songs of Johnny Cash;* and *Hard Sentences,* which he co-edited. Joe's writing can be found at www.joeclifford.com.

ANGEL LUIS COLÓN is the Derringer and Anthony Award–nominated writer of five books, including his latest novel *Hell Chose Me.* In his down time, he edits anthologies and produces "The Bastard Title," a podcast featuring interviews with writers. Keep up with him on Twitter via @GoshDarnMyLife. angelluiscolon.com

JOSHUA CORIN has written novels for Random House, comics for Marvel, videos for Cracked, essays for Medium, and now this short story for Nasty Woman Press.

ALLISON A. DAVIS writes poetry (most recently in Three Rooms Press Annual Dada Magazine, *Maintenant 12 and 13*), short stories, and is currently shopping her novel, *But Not For Me.* With a background in journalism and art criticism, her day job is a senior partner at Davis Wright Tremaine LLP, a national law firm.

HALLIE EPHRON is the *New York Times* bestselling author of eleven suspense novels reviewers call "deliciously creepy." Her newest, *Careful What You Wish For*, is about a professional organizer married to a man who can't pass a yard sale without stopping. In a starred review, *Publisher's Weekly* called it "outstanding." Five-time finalist for the Mary Higgins Clark Award, Edgar, and Anthony awards finalist, she blogs on Jungle Red Writers (www.jungleredwriters.com).

DANNY GARDNER is a multiple award–nominated author of genre fiction, including *A Negro and an Ofay*, his debut mystery novel. In another world, he is a stand-up comedian and screenwriter, and also the founder of Bronzeville Books. Born and raised in the Chi, he lives and works in Los Angeles. www.bronzevillebooks.com

ALISON GAYLIN, a *USA Today* and international bestselling author, won the 2019 Edgar Award for Best Paperback Original. Her work has been published in the US, UK, France, Belgium, the Netherlands, Japan, Germany, Romania and Denmark, and she has won and been nominated for numerous awards, including the Shamus, Macavity, Anthony, ITW Thriller, and Strand Book Award. In addition to her novels, she has published numerous short stories and collaborated with Megan Abbott on the graphic novel *Normandy Gold* (Titan/Hard Case Crime, 2018). She is currently at work on her 12th book.

HEATHER GRAHAM is a legendary *New York Times* and *USA Today* bestselling author of more than two hundred novels and novellas, published in twenty-five languages. She has been honored with awards from booksellers and writers' organizations, including the prestigious Silver Bullet and Thriller Master awards from the International Thriller Writers and the Lifetime Achievement Award from Romance Writers of America. Heather's books have been selected for the Doubleday Book Club and the Literary Guild, and she has been quoted, interviewed, or featured in such publications as *The Nation*, *Redbook*, *People*, and *USA Today* and has

appeared on many newscasts including *Today* and *Entertainment Tonight*.
www.theoriginalheathergraham.com

RACHEL HOWZELL HALL, author of the bestseller *They All Fall Down*
(Forge), writes the acclaimed Lou Norton series. She is also co-author of
The Good Sister with James Patterson, which was included in the *New York
Times* bestseller *The Family Lawyer*. She is on the board of directors for
the Southern California chapter of Mystery Writers of America, and lives
in Los Angeles. Her next novel, *And Now She's Gone*, will be published
September 2020. www.rachelhowzell.com

CHARLAINE HARRIS is a true daughter of the South. Born in Mississippi,
she has lived in Tennessee, South Carolina, Arkansas, and Texas. Her career
as a novelist began in 1981 with her first book, a conventional mystery.
Since then, she's written urban fantasy, science fiction, and horror. In
addition to over thirty full-length books, she has written numerous short
stories and three graphic novels in collaboration with Christopher Golden.
She has featured on bestseller lists many times, and her works have been
adapted for three (soon to be five) television shows. Charlaine now lives at
the top of a cliff on the Brazos River with her husband and two rescue dogs.
She has three children and two grandchildren.

TONI L.P. KELNER is actually two authors in one. As Toni, she's written
eleven mystery novels and co-edited seven anthologies with Charlaine
Harris. She won the Agatha for Best Short Story, and has been nominated
for the Anthony, the Macavity, and the Derringer. As Leigh Perry, she
writes the Family Skeleton mysteries featuring adjunct professor Georgia
Thackery and her pal Sid, an ambulatory family skeleton. *The Skeleton Stuffs
a Stocking* is the most recent.

ELLEN KIRSCHMAN, PhD is an award-winning public safety psychologist
and author of *I Love a Cop: What Police Families Need to Know; I Love a
Firefighter: What the Family Needs to Know*; lead author of *Counseling Cops:
What Clinicians Need to Know*; and three mysteries, *Burying Ben, The Right
Wrong Thing*, and *The Fifth Reflection*, all told from the perspective of police
psychologist Dr. Dot Meyerhoff. She blogs with *Psychology Today* and is a

member of Sisters in Crime, Mystery Writers of America and the Public Safety Writers Association. She publishes an occasional newsletter. Sign up on her website at www.ellenkirschman.com.

BETTE GOLDEN LAMB was the author of ten crime novels with her husband J.J. Lamb, including the Gina Mazzio medical thriller series. Bette was also a Registered Nurse and a professional ceramicist and artist whose work was featured in juried exhibitions throughout the country. She also wrote *The Russian Girl*, an acclaimed historical novel based on her own family history. Bette passed away in 2019.

JAMES L'ETOILE uses his twenty-nine years behind bars as an influence in his novels, short stories, and screenplays. He is a former associate warden in a maximum-security prison, a hostage negotiator, facility captain, and director of California's state parole system. He is a nationally recognized expert witness on prison and jail operations. He has been nominated for the Silver Falchion for Best Procedural Mystery and The Bill Crider Award for short fiction. His published novels include: *At What Cost, Bury the Past*, and *Little River—The Other Side of Paradise*.

JESSICA LOUREY writes about secrets. She is the bestselling Agatha, Anthony, and Lefty-nominated author of mysteries, nonfiction, YA adventure, magical realism, and feminist thrillers. She is a tenured professor of creative writing and sociology, a recipient of The Loft's Excellence in Teaching fellowship, a *Psychology Today* blogger, and presenter of the "Use Fiction to Rewrite Your Life" TEDx Talk. You can find out more at www.jessicalourey.com.

SEANAN MCGUIRE is an award-winning author of books, comics, and a horrifying number of short stories. Most of her work is either urban fantasy or biomedical science fiction (often published under the name Mira Grant). Seanan lives and works in the Pacific Northwest, where she shares a large, somewhat ramshackle farmhouse with an assortment of creepy dolls, vintage My Little Ponies, and outrageously oversized fluffy cats. When not writing, Seanan can usually be found in the nearest cornfield, continuing her campaign to bring the Great Pumpkin to her home.

CATRIONA MCPHERSON is the national best-selling and multiple award–winning author of the Dandy Gilver series of preposterous detective stories, set in her native Scotland in the 1930s. She also writes darker contemporary standalone suspense and has recently begun the *Last Ditch* trilogy, loosely based on her immigrant experience in a northern California college town. Catriona is a proud lifetime member and former national president of Sisters in Crime, committed to advancing equity and inclusion for women, writers of color, LGBTQ+ writers and writers with disability in the mystery community.

VALERIE PLAME worked to protect America's national security and prevent the proliferation of nuclear weapons and other weapons of mass destruction as a former career covert CIA operations officer. She has written for many national publications, including *Time, Newsweek, CNN, The Daily Beast*, and *The Huffington Post*, and is the author of *The New York Times* best-selling memoir *Fair Game: My Life as a Spy, My Betrayal by the White House*, which was released as a major motion picture of the same name starring Sean Penn and Naomi Watts. Along with Sarah Lovett, she published the well-received fictional spy thrillers *Blowback* and *Burned*. Valerie lives in Santa Fe, New Mexico, where she is running for Congress in New Mexico's 3rd Congressional District in 2020.

TRAVIS RICHARDSON is originally from Oklahoma and lives in Los Angeles with his wife and daughter. He has been a finalist and nominee for the Macavity, Anthony, and Derringer short story awards. He has two novellas and his short story collection, *Bloodshot and Bruised*, came out in late 2018. Find out more at www.tsrichardson.com

KAIRA ROUDA is an award-winning journalist and marketing executive best known for creating the first women consumer-focused real estate brand, "Real Living." Her first book, *Real You Incorporated: 8 Essentials for Women Entrepreneurs* encourages women to put their passions into action and create the life of their dreams. She took her own advice, began writing novels, and is now an international bestseller. She lives in Southern California with her family. Her latest book is *The Favorite Daughter*. Visit KairaRouda.com for more.

SJ ROZAN is the bestselling author of 16 novels and over 70 short stories. Her work has won the Edgar, Anthony, Shamus, Nero, and Macavity Awards, the Japanese Maltese Falcon, and the PWA Life Achievement Award. She lives in NYC. www.sjrozan.net

CLEA SIMON is a former journalist and the *Boston Globe*-bestselling author of three nonfiction books and more than two dozen mysteries. While most of these (like her most recent, *An Incantation of Cats*) are amateur sleuth mysteries, she also writes darker crime fiction, like the rock-and-roll suspense novel *World Enough*, which was named a "must read" by the Massachusetts Book Awards. Her upcoming psychological suspense *Hold Me Down* returns to the music world, focusing on sexual abuse and recovery, as well as love in all its forms. She can be reached at www.cleasimon.com

ALEXANDRA SOKOLOFF is the Thriller Award-winning, Bram Stoker and Anthony Award-nominated author of thirteen bestselling supernatural and crime thrillers. The *New York Times* has called her "a daughter of Mary Shelley" and her books "Some of the most original and freshly unnerving work in the genre." As a screenwriter she has sold original scripts and written novel adaptations for numerous Hollywood studios. She is also the author/presenter of the internationally acclaimed Screenwriting Tricks for Authors workbooks, workshops and blog. Her Thriller Award-nominated Huntress Moon series follows a haunted FBI agent on the hunt for a female serial killer, smashing genre clichés and combatting the rise of violence against women on the page, screen, and life. alexandrasokoloff.com

JOSH STALLINGS was born in Los Angeles and now lives and types in the San Jacinto mountains. Surrounded by cedar, pine, and oak forests, he spends his days dreaming up nefarious plots, evil crimes, and redemptive tales. His novel *Young Americans* was nominated for both a 2016 Lefty Award and an Anthony Award. His hard-boiled Moses McGuire trilogy (*Beautiful, Naked & Dead*; *Out There Bad*; *One More Body*) found itself on over fourteen best of the year lists. His short fiction appears all over the damn place. www.joshstallings.com

KELLI STANLEY is the critically acclaimed and multiple award–winning author of the Miranda Corbie noir series set in 1940 San Francisco, including *City of Dragons*, *City of Secrets*, *City of Ghosts*, and *City of Sharks*. Other works include historical mysteries set in Roman Britain and numerous short stories and essays. A *Los Angeles Times* Book Prize Finalist, her proudest achievements have been her inclusion as a literary heir of Dashiell Hammett by his granddaughter in *Publisher's Weekly* and her founding of Nasty Woman Press on November 9th, 2016. Her next novel is set in 1985 in Humboldt County, California. kellistanley.com

WENDY CORSI STAUB is the *New York Times* and *USA Today* bestselling author of more than 90 novels over a 27-year career. Her latest psychological suspense novels, *Little Girl Lost* and *Dead Silence*, (William Morrow), launched a psychological suspense trilogy that concludes with *The Butcher's Daughter* (September 2020). A three-time finalist for the Simon and Schuster Mary Higgins Clark Award, she's won an RWA Rita Award, an RT Award for Career Achievement in Suspense, and the RWA-NYC Lifetime Achievement Golden Apple, and been honored five times with the WLA Washington Irving Prize for Fiction. She lives in New York. wendycorsistaub.com

ROBIN C. STUART is a veteran cybercrime investigator and contributing author to the short story anthology, *Fault Lines: Stories by Northern California Crime Writers*. She consults on all things cyber security for Fortune 100 companies, authors, screenwriters, and media outlets including BBC and NowThis News. Robin is also a significant contributor to the Tech Interactive (formerly known as The Tech Museum of Innovation) acclaimed Cyber Detectives, one of the museum's most popular permanent exhibits, which earned praise from the Obama Administration.

KATE THORNTON is a retired US Army officer with over 100 short stories in print and has edited several anthologies. She lives in Tucson, Arizona, where she is active in both Sisters in Crime and Arizona Mystery Writers. She is also active in several veterans groups, encouraging women veterans to pursue recognition and benefits. www.katethornton.net

JACQUELINE WINSPEAR is the creator of the *New York Times* and National Bestselling series featuring psychologist and investigator Maisie Dobbs. Her first novel—*Maisie Dobbs*—received numerous award nominations, including the Edgar Award for Best Novel and the Agatha Award for Best First Novel. It was a *New York Times Notable Book* and a *Publisher's Weekly Top Ten Pick*. Her standalone novel, *The Care and Management of Lies,* was a finalist for the Dayton Literary Peace Prize in 2015. In 2019 Jacqueline published her 16th novel, *The American Agent,* and a nonfiction book, *What would Maisie Do?* a journal featuring excerpts from the Maisie Dobbs series. jacquelinewinspear.com

About Nasty Woman Press

We are a 501 (c)(4) nonprofit publisher pledged to fight fascism, racism, misogyny, anti-Semitism, homophobia, Islamophobia, transphobia, and bigotry while promoting human rights and civil rights in the United States and around the globe.

As writers, readers, editors, artists, librarians, designers, publishing professionals, and creative, principled human beings, we cherish the planet and our fragile environment, support science and education, and value health and social services. We believe in taking care of each other. We believe in a better, kinder world.

Every Nasty Woman Press anthology is created around a theme; that theme is linked to the nonprofit to whom profits from the sale of that book will be donated.

Shattering Glass is the first of our anthologies. Profits from this book will be donated to Planned Parenthood. For more information or to become a member, please visit nastywomanpress.com.

ADMINISTRATION/DESIGN

Erin Mitchell
DIRECTOR OF OPERATIONS
hewpr.com/

Sherryl O'Neil
BOOKKEEPER

IKAM Creative
WEBSITE
www.ikamcreative.com

Kris Lacore Toscanini
LOGO DESIGN
www.kriscribbles.com

FOUNDERS GOLD CIRCLE

Toni McGee Causey
Allison Davis
Davis Wright Tremaine LLC
Elyse Dinh-McCrillis
Ken Isaacson
C.J. Lyons
Roger and Maki Morris
Linda L. Richards
Kris Toscanini
Pamela Vaughn

RESISTANCE GOLD CIRCLE

Deborah Coonts
Margery Flax
Helen Goldsmith

SHATTERING GLASS PRODUCTION

Archie Ferguson
COVER DESIGN
www.archiefergusondesign.com

EDITORIAL COMMITTEE
Heather Graham
Andrew Grant
Toni L.P. Kelner
Kelli Stanley

COPYEDITORS
Laura Blackwell (Head)
Helen Goldsmith
Aubrey Hamilton
Beth Renaldi

PRODUCTION & LAYOUT EDITORS
Laura K. Curtis
www.laurakcurtis.com
Jaye Manus
jwmanus.wordpress.com

SPECIAL THANKS
Kimberley Cameron
www.kimberleycameron.com

CPSIA information can be obtained
at www.ICGtesting.com
Printed in the USA
LVHW101326280620
659164LV00024B/1075